FICTION GALLERY

Also available:

Gotham Writers' Workshop
WRITING FICTION
The Practical Guide from New York's Acclaimed Creative Writing School

Gotham Writers' Workshop®

FICTION GALLERY
EXCEPTIONAL SHORT STORIES SELECTED BY NEW YORK'S ACCLAIMED CREATIVE WRITING SCHOOL

EDITED BY ALEXANDER STEELE AND THOM DIDATO

BLOOMSBURY

Published by Bloomsbury, New York and London
Distributed to the trade by Holtzbrinck Publishers

All papers used by Bloomsbury are natural, recyclable products made from wood grown in well-managed forests. The manufacturing processes conform to the environmental regulations of the country of origin.

Library of Congress Cataloging-in-Publication Data

Gotham Writers' Workshop fiction gallery : exceptional short stories selected by New York's acclaimed creative writing school / edited by Thom Didato and Alexander Steele.—1st U.S. ed.
    p. cm.
Includes bibliographical references and index.
ISBN 1-58234-462-0 (pbk.)
1. Short stories. 2. Short stories, American. I. Steele, Alexander. II. Didato, Thom. III. Gotham Writers' Workshop.

PN6120.2.G68 2004
813'.0108—dc22

2004005432

First U.S. Edition 2004

1 3 5 7 9 10 8 6 4 2

Interior and cover design by 2x4, New York City
Typeset by Palimpsest Book Production Limited,
Polmont, Stirlingshire, Scotland
Printed in the United States of America by Quebecor World Fairfield

CONTENTS

INTRODUCTION

They say that Alexander the Great wept when he realized there were no more lands left for him to conquer. The lover of short-story anthologies will never have a similar reason to weep. Multitudes of such anthologies populate the shelves of libraries and bookstores—ranging from the annual Best of the Year roundups to comprehensive classroom-ready texts to those anthologies organized around every conceivable niche (Latin America, Jewish, Christmas, tennis, cats, breaking up, ghosts, amnesia, etc.)—and new ones keep emerging all the time.

What might cause one to weep, especially if you're a writer of short fiction, is that only a sliver of the general public today reads short stories at all. Some will say the short story is a casualty in the ongoing war for grabbing the consumer's entertainment dollar, losing out to such brash challengers as movies, TV, music, and electronic games, not to mention bestselling books. Others will say it's the fault of the writers themselves because nowadays their short stories are so subtle or "artistic" that no one much wants to read them except other like-minded writers. Perhaps one is the result of the other.

And thus, let *Fiction Gallery* enter the fray. If this book has a reason to exist in the geography of short-fiction anthologies, it is this: We've taken pains to select stories that the general public will find gripping and entertaining. By that we mean these short stories will grab you in the opening paragraphs, keep you turning pages all the way through, and linger afterward in a way that makes you wish you had someone to discuss them with at the dinner table or office water cooler.

To assist with our selection process, we pictured a hypothetical reader. This person is spending a few days at a friend's beach house, and though she reads now and then, she is not a reader of so-called literary fiction and probably hasn't read a short story since high school. One night a slashing rain prevents a stroll on the beach and there is, surprisingly, no TV on the premises, so she prowls around the house searching for a source of amusement. She finds a few assorted books on the bookshelf in the hallway. Normally this person might grab one of the popular suspense novels she sees there, but alas, she's read every one of them. It comes down to a choice between *The Homeowner's Plumbing Manual* and *Fiction Gallery*. She picks up the latter, stretches out in that comfortable chair by the bay window, and, to the accompaniment of rain, finds herself loving story after story. Hours later, almost halfway through the book, she retires to bed, secretly hoping the rain will continue throughout the following day.

Does this mean we've chosen stories for the lowest common denominator? Oh, no. We've selected only stories of the highest literary quality. Many of the acknowledged masters of short fiction are included here; many of these stories are winners of prestigious fiction prizes. And every single story demonstrates a writer in full command of the art and craft of creating exquisite short fiction. In fact, if our beach house were to be visited the following week by a literary snob who never read anything without disassembling it to find its faults, he too would be highly impressed with the stories herein. This is good stuff, in every sense of the word.

You may be wondering about our title. After some rumination on this point, we settled on *Fiction Gallery*. We found the title intriguing, blending as it does a sense of the written word with the visual sense of paintings and sculptures looming throughout an art gallery or museum.

As in an art gallery, you may wander at will, reading the stories in any order you desire. Or you may place your faith in the curators, reading the stories in the order presented. Our gallery is divided into sections that deal with various aspects of life—youth, romance, family, work, strange circumstances, life's end—allowing the stories to reflect off each other, making the sum of each section even more illuminating than its individual parts. And if you choose to read the entire book in order, you'll find that the stories have been arranged with an eye toward progression, the cumulative effect resembling the satisfying dramatic arc of a novel.

Some other things about the term *gallery* seemed appropriate. *Gallery* refers to the upper tier or "cheap seats" of a theater, and the phrase "play to the gallery" means to appeal to the masses, which is not far removed from our vision of enticing the general public. Not only have we chosen stories with wide appeal but, as in the days of ancient Greek drama, we've made sure that the bill included enough comedy to temper the tragedy. Our title may also make one think of a shooting gallery, and if this book conjures a whiff of carnival atmosphere, all the better.

Indeed, *gallery* manages to imply both the high art of a revered museum and some outright whizbang entertainment value. Not bad for a single word. Not bad for a book, either.

A few other things about the stories we've chosen.

Seeing as how Gotham Writers' Workshop is a writing school, some readers may expect to find teaching about the craft of writing inside these pages. Those readers will not be disappointed. Here, however, you will find no lectures or exercises or discussion questions. For those you can look to our classes or our previous book, *Writing Fiction*. But, as practically any accomplished writer will tell you, the best way to learn the craft of writing is to read and absorb and study the work of great writers, and you'll find plenty of opportunity to do that with these stories, each one a virtual textbook on the art of fiction.

Close inspection of the stories will also reveal that the stories have been chosen to demonstrate a myriad of approaches to handling all the major elements of fiction craft. For example, most of the various techniques for point of view—first person, first person unreliable, first person peripheral, second person, third person single vision, omniscient, objective—are illustrated in these stories. As a further bonus, you'll find interviews with three of the authors whose work is included in this book—T. C. Boyle, Jhumpa Lahiri, and Hannah Tinti. The interviews provide insight on how these writers go about the craft of cobbling their stories together, and you'll also get some of their philosophical thoughts on the art of fiction. In short, we hope students and teachers of writing will find this book a valuable, perhaps treasured, resource.[*] And if you're just bumming around our beach house, don't let any of this get in the way of your sheer reading pleasure.

---

[*]Teachers and students will find useful craft analysis of the stories in this book by visiting Gotham Writers' Workshop online: *www.WritingClasses.com*. Go to the home page of the Web site, click on "Writers' Toolbox," then click on the link to "Fiction Gallery."

Most of the stories here are contemporary works by American authors, but you'll find exceptions in both categories. We've decided to stick with stories that fall under the rubric of literary fiction, even though many excellent stories exist in such genres as mystery, suspense, science fiction, and horror, and, indeed, some of our stories carry overtones from these genres. We've also avoided, for the most part, those stories that have become "regulars" on the anthology circuit. And, yes, we know that we've failed to include some of the major players in the short-story game, such as Poe, Hemingway, and O'Connor (Flannery; we've got Frank), but we wanted to give some other writers a chance to play.

Finally, let us point out with pride that we have included three stories by writers who have taught fiction writing at Gotham Writers' Workshop. This is something we wanted to do but only if we could find stories by teachers that matched the caliber of the other works. Turns out, this wasn't a problem. We read many first-rate stories by Gotham Writers' Workshop teachers, all of whom are accomplished writers, before settling on stories by Peter Markus, Jess Row, and Hannah Tinti, whose work can easily lie alongside the likes of Dorothy Parker and Raymond Carver.

And that's the rundown of what we've got. If you're now eager to read, we set you free to stroll through our gallery. For those of you who will feel better armed for your journey with a little information about the art form you're about to encounter, let us humbly offer . . .

A SHORT OVERVIEW OF THE SHORT STORY

Like jazz and baseball, the short story can be claimed as an American invention, and a relatively new one at that. Though we might consider folk and fairy tales as a kind of precursor, the short story's real debut was in the early nineteenth century, the time marked most notably by Nathaniel Hawthorne's collection *Twice-told Tales*, which first appeared in 1837. The first novel, by contrast, is often considered to be Murasaki Shikibu's *The Tale of Genji*, written in eleventh-century Japan, and Western literature's first novel is often considered to be Miguel de Cervantes's *Don Quixote*, which arrived in 1604.

Edgar Allan Poe wrote a favorable review of Hawthorne's collection, in which he attempted to state the principles of a short story (which he then called the "prose tale"). Most fundamentally, Poe opined that the short story should have a more unified effect than a novel, an effect enhanced by the fact that the short story could be read in a single session. Poe wisely stated, "During the hour of perusal the soul of the reader is at the writer's control."

The soul of the reader is at the writer's control.

This, in essence, is the beauty of a short story. The short story is brief enough so that the reader may be lured into the world of the story and not be released into the daylight of reality until the writer has told his tale. The reading experience becomes akin to the total immersion of watching a play or movie in a darkened theater, and yet the experience allows the magical interplay of language and imagination that only prose offers. No other art form provides quite this mixture of bewitchment.

Thus, the only comprehensive definition one can make of a short story is that it be a work of prose fiction brief enough and unified enough so that it can and should be read in one continuous reading. As for captivating the reader's soul, well, that depends upon the writer's talent.

Further guidelines for the short story have been attempted. The story should: revolve around a single incident, contain few characters, utilize only one character's point of view, not cover too long a time span, culminate in a surprising or revealing moment. These are useful guidelines, often employed, but many great short stories have broken them without losing their grip on the reader's soul, and so let's not consider any of these rules inviolable. As long as it's short and unified, there are no boundaries on the writer's creativity in telling the tale. In fact, the brevity allows writers even more latitude than a novel to tell their stories in a wildly innovative way. One of the odder stories in our book is Daniel Orozco's "Orientation," where the writer uses a stunt that might not work for three hundred pages, but in short form it succeeds deliciously.

So if brevity is the main mark, how short should a short story be? Most short stories run from ten to twenty-five pages, when placed in a book, but really they can run anywhere from one to fifty pages.

One page may seem too brief for a story to establish much emotional traction, but it can be done, and recently very short stories, often known as flash fiction, have become something of a trend. The story doesn't even have to take a whole page. Accepting a barroom bet, Ernest Hemingway wrote a short story in a mere six words. Here's the entire thing:

For Sale, Baby Shoes, Never Worn.

This is the typically spare Hemingway at his most spare, but damn if this isn't a compelling story. Can you easily forget it? The shortest story in this book runs only two pages and a number of them run under ten pages, each providing the impact of a complete tale, the words achieving the perfect economy of a Yeats poem or a Chopin nocturne.

Once a story approaches fifty pages it's a toss-up whether to call it a short story or a novella. The label doesn't really make much difference, but if a choice must be made, perhaps it comes down to whether the story does or doesn't seek the concentrated effect of which Poe spoke. The longest story in our gallery, Ethan Canin's "The Palace Thief," pushes the limit of short-story length, and yet it rushes forward with a sprinter's momentum, making it almost impossible to stop anywhere before the finish line. And so it *feels* like a short story.

Not only did Poe define the short story in his review of Hawthorne, he took up the mantle himself (a very black mantle in his case) and penned a catalog of short stories that brilliantly exemplify what he was talking about. Think back to the first time you experienced the thrillingly awful shock of "The Tell-Tale Heart" or "The Cask of Amontillado" or "The Masque of the Red Death." Has your soul ever been so completely at the mercy of a writer's control? Other writers, such as Washington Irving and Mark Twain, were also pioneering the world of short fiction around this time. These early stories were frequently of a mysterious or macabre or whimsical nature, which makes sense because such extremes of imagination lend themselves especially well to the concentrated intensity of a short story.

As the twentieth century neared, however, a new slant on the short story emerged, more tuned to the subtle nuances of everyday life. The leader of this movement is generally thought to be the Russian writer Anton Chekhov, who published over two hundred short stories, the first appearing in 1882. (Around this time, Guy de Maupassant and Kate Chopin were also writing in a similar vein.) The likes of Hawthorne's haunted happenings and Twain's far-jumping frogs were replaced by more mundane events that seemed to mirror the lives of the readers, and breathless plotting was replaced with a more lifelike unfolding of incident. The short story proved an adept form for capturing these realistic glimpses of human existence. Not only did Chekhov control the reader's soul, he made the reader give it a good search.

All kinds of other short-story fads and fashions have come and gone since, each leaving memorable stories in their wake—pulp, sentimentalism, realism, postrealism, modernism, postmodernism, the *New Yorker* style, minimalism, metafiction, experimentalism, etc. However, in the broadest sense, most stories can trace their origin to either Hawthorne or Chekhov. Short stories that embrace page-turning plots, most notably those that fall into one of the genre camps—mystery, suspense, science fiction, horror, and let's include magic realism—can be thought of as descendants of Hawthorne. Stories more inclined to caress characters drifting through everyday reality, which includes the bulk of literary fiction, are closer descendants of Chekhov.

Noted author Michael Chabon recently accused the contemporary literary short story (his own included) of having lost its "sense of mystery and ancestral tale." He was saying that literary fiction has become too introspective, too uneventful, too Chekhovian for its own good. As a response, he edited a short-story anthology containing new stories that harkened back to the outright thrills and chills of Hawthorne, Poe, and company. Though we certainly don't want to throw out Chekhov's baby with the bathwater, Chabon makes a good point. Perhaps much of contemporary fiction could benefit from more reliance on good old-fashioned storytelling.

Indeed, most of the stories we've chosen for this book could trace their lineage to both Hawthorne and Chekhov, synthesizing the strength of the two schools into stories that are both page-turning and relevant to our lives. Though we haven't veered too far into the experimental camp, we also have one or two stories that might leave both Nathaniel and Anton a bit puzzled, but probably in a good way. And, in a nod to history, we've bookended our gallery with actual stories by Chekhov and Hawthorne. If you find these old-timers a slight challenge to read, please give your soul a little room to adjust and you'll soon understand their timelessness.

If you're not a frequent reader of short fiction and this book turns you on to the wonders of the short story (our great desire), where do you turn for more? Well, it's a bit harder for the general public to stumble upon short stories than it once was. In the first half of the twentieth century, short stories were everywhere, included in nearly every major magazine, as talked about as today's popular TV shows. Before he went to Hollywood, F. Scott Fitzgerald earned the bulk of his income penning short fiction, a luxury sadly denied our current crop of writers. Nowadays, a few major magazines, such as the *New Yorker, Harper's,* the *Atlantic, Esquire,* even

Playboy (which we buy solely for the fiction), bravely carry on the tradition, including at least one short story in most issues. But the vast majority of short stories make their appearance in another type of publication, the literary magazine.

Most people are unaware of literary magazines, but there are hundreds of them. These magazines are dedicated to the proliferation of good literature. Like resistance fighters, they operate largely underground, fighting the good fight to champion Art over Commerce, which explains why they're not so well known. Literary magazines are where most short fiction is first published these days, along with poetry and, in some magazines, creative nonfiction. Some of these magazines exist only in print, others only online, and others still put forth material in both media. Larger bookstores and libraries carry the more prominent literary magazines, and, aside from the ones offered free online, these magazines can be obtained through subscription. An easy way to infiltrate the world of literary magazines is to visit the Web site of *Poets & Writers* magazine (www.pw.org) and go to the links page, where you'll find links to the Web sites of many of these magazines. (Also, in the Credits section of this book, you'll find in which magazines the stories in this book were first published.)

As for books, many writers have published collections of short stories, so if you find a writer you particularly admire, seek out his or her work this way. But nowadays publishers are reluctant to award writers the plum of a collection unless the writer is famous or perceived to have a shot at fame, probably through a forthcoming novel, which makes the need for the literary magazine all the stronger. And then, of course, there is the endless supply of short-story anthologies, which will never leave the zealous Alexanders of short fiction without volumes of stories to conquer.

Yes, if you seek to find a short story these days, they exist aplenty. However, the larger challenge is for the short stories to find the plentitude of readers that they fervently deserve. If you are holding this book, then an assortment of exceptional short stories have indeed found *you*. And be warned: they will grab you from the start and not lessen their grip until their story is told. Even then, they will attempt to keep following you, perhaps a few of them lingering inside your soul for good.

So . . . enter our Fiction Gallery.

Alexander Steele

STARTING OUT

We all start off the same way, as a kid—a rookie to the world who has to look up to everyone, at least literally, and learn everything for the first time. Childhood is quite the seesaw, the highs higher than a ball bouncing over the clouds, the lows lower than a detention hall a hundred feet underground. And then there's the breakneck speed of it all, going from mewling baby to rebellious teen in a mere sixteen years or so. Once grown up, most of us miss it like heck but wouldn't go back there for all the allowance money in the world.

Anton Chekhov's "A Trifle from Life" portrays one of those tiny moments that have such earthshaking impact on a child. The young boy in this story lives in a broken home (easily recognizable even though these are wealthy folk in nineteenth-century Russia). The current man of the house has no idea what kind of shocking life lesson he happens to give the boy.

Religion can be intimidating to kids, and, for Catholic children, few things are as terrifying as that first visit to the confessional. That's what the Irish lad in Frank O'Connor's "First Confession" faces. Not only must he wrestle with the concept of hell and the logistics of the confession box, but, to make things really trying on his soul, he has a big sin to confess— thoughts of murder.

In ZZ Packer's "Brownies," we meet a colorful troop of black Brownies who are determined to get their vengeance on a troop of white Brownies, one of whom is suspected of using a very bad word. An ambush attack is strategically mapped out. But battles seldom go according to plan, and camp life is seldom as idyllic as advertised. The nature that gets most explored at Camp Crescendo is that of the human kind.

Regardless of where kids grow up, that place is their home. The brothers in Peter Markus's "What the River Told Us to Do" are as much a part of their home as the mud in the earth. And they will move from this home no more willingly.

For better or worse, children are usually influenced by the grown-ups around them. The adolescent girl in Myla Goldberg's "Going for the Orange Julius" listens to her grandmother, a jazzy lady who teaches an advanced course in femininity. This tale is like a new take on Little Red Riding Hood, where a mall substitutes for the woods, Grandma is scarier than the wolf, and the path leads toward the land of adulthood.

A TRIFLE FROM LIFE

ANTON CHEKHOV

A well-fed, red-cheeked young man called Nikolay Ilyitch Belyaev, of thirty-two, who was an owner of house property in Petersburg, and a devotee of the race-course, went one evening to see Olga Ivanovna Irnin, with whom he was living, or, to use his own expression, was dragging out a long, wearisome romance. And, indeed, the first interesting and enthusiastic pages of this romance had long been perused; now the pages dragged on, and still dragged on, without presenting anything new or of interest.

Not finding Olga Ivanovna at home, Belyaev lay down on the lounge chair and proceeded to wait for her in the drawing-room.

"Good-evening, Nikolay Ilyitch!" he heard a child's voice. "Mother will be here directly. She has gone with Sonia to the dressmaker's."

Olga Ivanovna's son, Alyosha—a boy of eight who looked graceful and very well cared for, who was dressed like a picture, in a black velvet jacket and long black stockings—was lying on the sofa in the same room. He was lying on a satin cushion and, evidently imitating an acrobat he had lately seen at the circus, stuck up in the air first one leg and then the other. When his elegant legs were exhausted, he brought his arms into play or jumped up impulsively and went on all fours, trying to stand with his legs in the air. All this he was doing with the utmost gravity, gasping and groaning painfully as though he regretted that God had given him such a restless body.

"Ah, good-evening, my boy," said Belyaev. "It's you! I did not notice you. Is your mother well?"

Alyosha, taking hold of the tip of his left toe with his right hand and falling into the most unnatural attitude, turned over, jumped up, and peeped at Belyaev from behind the big fluffy lampshade.

"What shall I say?" he said, shrugging his shoulders. "In reality mother's never well. You see, she is a woman, and women, Nikolay Ilyitch, have always something the matter with them."

Belyaev, having nothing better to do, began watching Alyosha's face. He had never before during the whole of his intimacy with Olga Ivanovna paid any attention to the boy, and had completely ignored his existence; the boy had been before his eyes, but he had not cared to think why he was there and what part he was playing.

In the twilight of the evening, Alyosha's face, with his white forehead and black, unblinking eyes, unexpectedly reminded Belyaev of Olga Ivanovna as she had been during the first pages of their romance. And he felt disposed to be friendly to the boy.

"Come here, insect," he said; "let me have a closer look at you."

The boy jumped off the sofa and skipped up to Belyaev.

"Well," began Belyaev, putting a hand on the boy's thin shoulder. "How are you getting on?"

"How shall I say! We used to get on a great deal better."

"Why?"

"It's very simple. Sonia and I used only to learn music and reading, and now they give us French poetry to learn. Have you been shaved lately?"

"Yes."

"Yes, I see you have. Your beard is shorter. Let me touch it. . . . Does that hurt?"

"No."

"Why is it that if you pull one hair it hurts, but if you pull a lot at once it doesn't hurt a bit? Ha, ha! And, you know, it's a pity you don't have whiskers. Here ought to be shaved . . . but here at the sides the hair ought to be left. . . ."

The boy nestled up to Belyaev and began playing with his watch-chain.

"When I go to the high-school," he said, "mother is going to buy me a watch. I shall ask her to buy me a watch-chain like this. . . . Wh—at a loc—ket! Father's got a locket like that, only yours has little bars on it and his has letters. . . . There's mother's portrait in the middle of his. Father has a different sort of chain now, not made with rings, but like ribbon. . . ."

"How do you know? Do you see your father?"

"I? M'm . . . no. . . . I . . ."

Alyosha blushed, and in great confusion, feeling caught in a lie, began zealously scratching the locket with his nail. . . . Belyaev looked steadily into his face and asked:

"Do you see your father?"

"N-no!"

"Come, speak frankly, on your honour. . . . I see from your face you are telling a fib. Once you've let a thing slip out it's no good wriggling about it. Tell me, do you see him? Come, as a friend."

Alyosha hesitated.

"You won't tell mother?" he said.

"As though I should!"

"On your honour?"

"On my honour."

"Do you swear?"

"Ah, you provoking boy! What do you take me for?"

Alyosha looked round him, then with wide-open eyes, whispered to him:

"Only, for goodness' sake, don't tell mother. . . . Don't tell any one at all, for it is a secret. I hope to goodness mother won't find out, or we should all catch it—Sonia, and I, and Pelagea. . . . Well, listen. . . . Sonia and I see father every Tuesday and Friday. When Pelagea takes us for a walk before dinner we go to the Apfel Restaurant, and there is father waiting for us. . . . He is always sitting in a room apart, where you know there's a marble table and an ash-tray in the shape of a goose without a back. . . ."

"What do you do there?"

"Nothing! First we say how-do-you-do, then we all sit round the table, and father treats us with coffee and pies. You know Sonia eats the meat-pies, but I can't endure meat-pies! I like the pies made of cabbage and eggs. We eat such a lot that we have to try hard to eat as much as we can at dinner, for fear mother should notice."

"What do you talk about?"

"With father? About anything. He kisses us, he hugs us, tells us all sorts of amusing jokes. Do you know, he says when we are grown up he is going to take us to live with him. Sonia does not want to go, but I agree. Of course, I should miss mother; but, then, I should write her letters! It's a queer idea, but we could come and visit her on holidays—couldn't we?

Father says, too, that he will buy me a horse. He's an awfully kind man! I can't understand why mother does not ask him to come and live with us, and why she forbids us to see him. You know he loves mother very much. He is always asking us how she is and what she is doing. When she was ill he clutched his head like this, and . . . and kept running about. He always tells us to be obedient and respectful to her. Listen. Is it true that we are unfortunate?"

"H'm! . . . Why?"

"That's what father says. 'You are unhappy children,' he says. It's strange to hear him, really. 'You are unhappy,' he says, 'I am unhappy, and mother's unhappy. You must pray to God,' he says; 'for yourselves and for her.'"

Alyosha let his eyes rest on a stuffed bird and sank into thought.

"So . . ." growled Belyaev. "So that's how you are going on. You arrange meetings at restaurants. And mother does not know?"

"No-o. . . . How should she know? Pelagea would not tell her for anything, you know. The day before yesterday he gave us some pears. As sweet as jam! I ate two."

"H'm! . . . Well, and I say . . . Listen. Did father say anything about me?"

"About you? What shall I say?"

Alyosha looked searchingly into Belyaev's face and shrugged his shoulders.

"He didn't say anything particular."

"For instance, what did he say?"

"You won't be offended?"

"What next? Why, does he abuse me?"

"He doesn't abuse you, but you know he is angry with you. He says mother's unhappy owing to you . . . and that you have ruined mother. You know he is so queer! I explain to him that you are kind, that you never scold mother; but he only shakes his head."

"So he says I have ruined her?"

"Yes; you mustn't be offended, Nikolay Ilyitch."

Belyaev got up, stood still a moment, and walked up and down the drawing-room.

"That's strange and . . . ridiculous!" he muttered, shrugging his shoulders and smiling sarcastically. "He's entirely to blame, and I have ruined her, eh? An innocent lamb, I must say. So he told you I ruined your mother?"

"Yes, but . . . you said you would not be offended, you know."

"I am not offended, and . . . and it's not your business. Why, it's . . . why, it's positively ridiculous! I have been thrust into it like a chicken in the broth, and now it seems I'm to blame!"

A ring was heard. The boy sprang up from his place and ran out. A minute later a lady came into the room with a little girl; this was Olga Ivanovna, Alyosha's mother. Alyosha followed them in, skipping and jumping, humming aloud and waving his hands. Belyaev nodded, and went on walking up and down.

"Of course, whose fault is it if not mine?" he muttered with a snort. "He is right! He is an injured husband."

"What are you talking about?" asked Olga Ivanovna.

"What about? . . . Why, just listen to the tales your lawful spouse is spreading now! It appears that I am a scoundrel and a villain, that I have ruined you and the children. All of you are unhappy, and I am the only happy one! Wonderfully, wonderfully happy!"

"I don't understand, Nikolay. What's the matter?"

"Why, listen to this young gentleman!" said Belyaev, pointing to Alyosha.

Alyosha flushed crimson, then turned pale, and his whole face began working with terror.

"Nikolay Ilyitch," he said in a loud whisper. "Sh-sh!"

Olga Ivanovna looked in surprise at Alyosha, then at Belyaev, then at Alyosha again.

"Just ask him," Belyaev went on. "Your Pelagea, like a regular fool, takes them about to restaurants and arranges meetings with their papa. But that's not the point: the point is that their dear papa is a victim, while I'm a wretch who has broken up both your lives. . . ."

"Nikolay Ilyitch," moaned Alyosha. "Why, you promised on your word of honour!"

"Oh, get away!" said Belyaev, waving him off. "This is more important than any word of honour. It's the hypocrisy revolts me, the lying! . . ."

"I don't understand it," said Olga Ivanovna, and tears glistened in her eyes. "Tell me, Alyosha," she turned to her son. "Do you see your father?"

Alyosha did not hear her; he was looking with horror at Belyaev.

"It's impossible," said his mother; "I will go and question Pelagea."

Olga Ivanovna went out.

"I say, you promised on your word of honour!" said Alyosha, trembling all over.

Belyaev dismissed him with a wave of his hand, and went on walking up and down. He was absorbed in his grievance and was oblivious of the boy's presence, as he always had been. He, a grown-up, serious person, had no thought to spare for boys. And Alyosha sat down in the corner and told Sonia with horror how he had been deceived. He was trembling, stammering, and crying. It was the first time in his life that he had been brought into such coarse contact with lying; till then he had not known that there are in the world, besides sweet pears, pies, and expensive watches, a great many things for which the language of children has no expression.

FIRST CONFESSION

FRANK O'CONNOR

All the trouble began when my grandfather died and my grandmother—
my father's mother—came to live with us. Relations in the one house are
a strain at the best of times, but, to make matters worse, my grandmother
was a real old country woman and quite unsuited to the life in town. She
had a fat, wrinkled old face, and, to Mother's great indignation, went round
the house in bare feet—the boots had her crippled, she said. For dinner
she had a jug of porter and a pot of potatoes with—sometimes—a bit of
salt fish, and she poured out the potatoes on the table and ate them slowly,
with great relish, using her fingers by way of a fork.

Now, girls are supposed to be fastidious, but I was the one who suffered
most from this. Nora, my sister, just sucked up to the old woman for the
penny she got every Friday out of the old-age pension, a thing I could not
do. I was too honest, that was my trouble; and when I was playing with
Bill Connell, the sergeant-major's son, and saw my grandmother steering
up the path with the jug of porter sticking out from beneath her shawl I
was mortified. I made excuses not to let him come into the house, because
I could never be sure what she would be up to when we went in.

When Mother was at work and my grandmother made the dinner I
wouldn't touch it. Nora once tried to make me, but I hid under the table
from her and took the bread-knife with me for protection. Nora let on to
be very indignant (she wasn't, of course, but she knew Mother saw through
her, so she sided with Gran) and came after me. I lashed out at her with
the bread-knife, and after that she left me alone. I stayed there till Mother

came in from work and made my dinner, but when Father came in later Nora said in a shocked voice: "Oh, Dadda, do you know what Jackie did at dinnertime?" Then, of course, it all came out; Father gave me a flaking; Mother interfered, and for days after that he didn't speak to me and Mother barely spoke to Nora. And all because of that old woman! God knows, I was heart-scalded.

Then, to crown my misfortunes, I had to make my first confession and Communion. It was an old woman called Ryan who prepared us for these. She was about the one age with Gran; she was well-to-do, lived in a big house on Montenotte, wore a black cloak and bonnet, and came every day to school at three o'clock when we should have been going home, and talked to us of Hell. She may have mentioned the other place as well, but that could only have been by accident, for Hell had the first place in her heart.

She lit a candle, took out a new half-crown, and offered it to the first boy who would hold one finger—only one finger!—in the flame for five minutes by the school clock. Being always very ambitious I was tempted to volunteer, but I thought it might look greedy. Then she asked were we afraid of holding one finger—only one finger!—in a little candle flame for five minutes and not afraid of burning all over in roasting hot furnaces for all eternity. "All eternity! Just think of that! A whole lifetime goes by and it's nothing, not even a drop in the ocean of your sufferings." The woman was really interesting about Hell, but my attention was all fixed on the half-crown. At the end of the lesson she put it back in her purse. It was a great disappointment; a religious woman like that, you wouldn't think she'd bother about a thing like a half-crown.

Another day she said she knew a priest who woke one night to find a fellow he didn't recognize leaning over the end of his bed. The priest was a bit frightened—naturally enough—but he asked the fellow what he wanted, and the fellow said in a deep, husky voice that he wanted to go to Confession. The priest said it was an awkward time and wouldn't it do in the morning, but the fellow said that last time he went to Confession, there was one sin he kept back, being ashamed to mention it, and now it was always on his mind. Then the priest knew it was a bad case, because the fellow was after making a bad confession and committing a mortal sin. He got up to dress, and just then the cock crew in the yard outside, and—lo and behold!—when the priest looked round there was no sign of the fellow, only a smell of burning timber, and when the priest looked at his bed didn't he see the print of two hands burned in it? That was because the fellow had made a bad confession. This story made a shocking impression on me.

But the worst of all was when she showed us how to examine our conscience. Did we take the name of the Lord, our God, in vain? Did we honor our father and our mother? (I asked her did this include grand-mothers and she said it did.) Did we love our neighbor as ourselves? Did we covet our neighbor's goods? (I thought of the way I felt about the penny that Nora got every Friday.) I decided that, between one thing and another, I must have broken the whole ten commandments, all on account of that old woman, and so far as I could see, so long as she remained in the house I had no hope of ever doing anything else.

I was scared to death of Confession. The day the whole class went I let on to have a toothache, hoping my absence wouldn't be noticed; but at three o'clock, just as I was feeling safe, along comes a chap with a message from Mrs. Ryan that I was to go to Confession myself on Saturday and be at the chapel for Communion with the rest. To make it worse, Mother couldn't come with me and sent Nora instead.

Now, that girl had ways of tormenting me that Mother never knew of. She held my hand as we went down the hill, smiling sadly and saying how sorry she was for me, as if she were bringing me to the hospital for an operation.

"Oh, God help us!" she moaned. "Isn't it a terrible pity you weren't a good boy? Oh, Jackie, my heart bleeds for you! How will you ever think of all your sins? Don't forget you have to tell him about the time you kicked Gran on the shin."

"Lemme go!" I said, trying to drag myself free of her. "I don't want to go to Confession at all."

"But sure, you'll have to go to Confession, Jackie," she replied in the same regretful tone. "Sure, if you didn't, the parish priest would be up to the house, looking for you. 'Tisn't, God knows, that I'm not sorry for you. Do you remember the time you tried to kill me with the bread-knife under the table? And the language you used to me? I don't know what he'll do with you at all, Jackie. He might have to send you up to the Bishop."

I remember thinking bitterly that she didn't know the half of what I had to tell—if I told it. I knew I couldn't tell it, and understood perfectly why the fellow in Mrs. Ryan's story made a bad confession; it seemed to me a great shame that people wouldn't stop criticizing him. I remember that steep hill down to the church, and the sunlit hillsides beyond the valley of the river, which I saw in the gaps between the houses like Adam's last glimpse of Paradise.

Then, when she had manoeuvred me down the long flight of steps to the chapel yard, Nora suddenly changed her tone. She became the raging malicious devil she really was.

"There you are!" she said with a yelp of triumph, hurling me through the church door. "And I hope he'll give you the penitential psalms, you dirty little caffler."

I knew then I was lost, given up to eternal justice. The door with the colored-glass panels swung shut behind me, the sunlight went out and gave place to deep shadow, and the wind whistled outside so that the silence within seemed to crackle like ice under my feet. Nora sat in front of me by the confession box. There were a couple of old women ahead of her, and then a miserable-looking poor devil came and wedged me in at the other side, so that I couldn't escape even if I had the courage. He joined his hands and rolled his eyes in the direction of the roof, muttering aspirations in an anguished tone, and I wondered had he a grandmother too. Only a grand-mother could account for a fellow behaving in that heartbroken way, but he was better off than I, for he at least could go and confess his sins; while I would make a bad confession and then die in the night and be continually coming back and burning people's furniture.

Nora's turn came, and I heard the sound of something slamming, and then her voice as if butter wouldn't melt in her mouth, and then another slam, and out she came. God, the hypocrisy of women! Her eyes were lowered, her head was bowed, and her hands were joined very low down on her stomach, and she walked up the aisle to the side altar looking like a saint. You never saw such an exhibition of devotion; and I remembered the devilish malice with which she had tormented me all the way from our door, and wondered were all religious people like that, really. It was my turn now. With the fear of damnation in my soul I went in, and the confes-sional door closed of itself behind me.

It was pitch-dark and I couldn't see priest or anything else. Then I really began to be frightened. In the darkness it was a matter between God and me, and He had all the odds. He knew what my intentions were before I even started; I had no chance. All I had ever been told about Confession got mixed up in my mind, and I knelt to one wall and said:

"Bless me, father, for I have sinned; this is my first confession." I waited for a few minutes, but nothing happened, so I tried it on the other wall. Nothing happened there either. He had me spotted all right.

It must have been then that I noticed the shelf at about one height with my head. It was really a place for grown-up people to rest their elbows, but in my distracted state I thought it was probably the place you were supposed to kneel. Of course, it was on the high side and not very deep, but I was always good at climbing and managed to get up all right. Staying up was the trouble. There was room only for my knees, and nothing you could get a grip on but a sort of wooden molding a bit above it. I held on to the molding and repeated the words a little louder, and this time something happened all right. A slide was slammed back; a little light entered the box, and a man's voice said: "Who's there?"

"'Tis me, father," I said for fear he mightn't see me and go away again. I couldn't see him at all. The place the voice came from was under the molding, about level with my knees, so I took a good grip of the molding and swung myself down till I saw the astonished face of a young priest looking up at me. He had to put his head on one side to see me, and I had to put mine on one side to see him, so we were more or less talking to one another, upside-down. It struck me as a queer way of hearing confessions, but I didn't feel it my place to criticize.

"Bless me, father, for I have sinned; this is my first confession," I rattled off all in one breath, and swung myself down the least shade more to make it easier for him.

"What are you doing up there?" he shouted in an angry voice, and the strain the politeness was putting on my hold of the molding, and the shock of being addressed in such an uncivil tone, were too much for me. I lost my grip, tumbled, and hit the door an unmerciful wallop before I found myself flat on my back in the middle of the aisle. The people who had been waiting stood up with their mouths open. The priest opened the door of the middle box and came out, pushing his biretta back from his forehead; he looked something terrible. Then Nora came scampering down the aisle.

"Oh, you dirty little caffler!" she said. "I might have known you'd do it. I might have known you'd disgrace me. I can't leave you out of my sight for one minute."

Before I could even get to my feet to defend myself she bent down and gave me a clip across the ear. This reminded me that I was so stunned I had even forgotten to cry, so that people might think I wasn't hurt at all, when in fact I was probably maimed for life. I gave a roar out of me.

"What's all this about?" the priest hissed, getting angrier than ever and pushing Nora off me. "How dare you hit the child like that, you little vixen?"

"But I can't do my penance with him, father," Nora cried, cocking an outraged eye up at him.

"Well, go and do it, or I'll give you some more to do," he said, giving me a hand up. "Was it coming to Confession you were, my poor man?" he asked me.

"'Twas, father," said I with a sob.

"Oh," he said respectfully, "a big hefty fellow like you must have terrible sins. Is this your first?"

"'Tis, father," said I.

"Worse and worse," he said gloomily. "The crimes of a lifetime. I don't know will I get rid of you at all today. You'd better wait now till I'm finished with these old ones. You can see by the looks of them they haven't much to tell."

"I will, father," I said with something approaching joy.

The relief of it was really enormous. Nora stuck out her tongue at me from behind his back, but I couldn't even be bothered retorting. I knew from the very moment that man opened his mouth that he was intelligent above the ordinary. When I had time to think, I saw how right I was. It only stood to reason that a fellow confessing after seven years would have more to tell than people that went every week. The crimes of a lifetime, exactly as he said. It was only what he expected, and the rest was the cackle of old women and girls with their talk of Hell, the Bishop, and the penitential psalms. That was all they knew. I started to make my examination of conscience, and barring the one bad business of my grandmother it didn't seem so bad.

The next time, the priest steered me into the confession box himself and left the shutter back the way I could see him get in and sit down at the further side of the grille from me.

"Well, now," he said, "what do they call you?"

"Jackie, father," said I.

"And what's a-trouble to you, Jackie?"

"Father," I said, feeling I might as well get it over while I had him in good humor, "I had it all arranged to kill my grandmother."

He seemed a bit shaken by that, all right, because he said nothing for quite a while.

"My goodness," he said at last, "that'd be a shocking thing to do. What put that into your head?"

"Father," I said, feeling very sorry for myself, "she's an awful woman."

"Is she?" he asked. "What way is she awful?"

"She takes porter, father," I said, knowing well from the way Mother talked of it that this was a mortal sin, and hoping it would make the priest take a more favorable view of my case.

"Oh, my!" he said, and I could see he was impressed.

"And snuff, father," said I.

"That's a bad case, sure enough, Jackie," he said.

"And she goes round in her bare feet, father," I went on in a rush of self-pity, "and she knows I don't like her, and she gives pennies to Nora and none to me, and my da sides with her and flakes me, and one night I was so heart-scalded I made up my mind I'd have to kill her."

"And what would you do with the body?" he asked with great interest.

"I was thinking I could chop that up and carry it away in a barrow I have," I said.

"Begor, Jackie," he said, "do you know you're a terrible child?"

"I know, father," I said, for I was just thinking the same thing myself. "I tried to kill Nora too with a bread-knife under the table, only I missed her."

"Is that the little girl that was beating you just now?" he asked.

"'Tis, father."

"Someone will go for her with a bread-knife one day, and he won't miss her," he said rather cryptically. "You must have great courage. Between ourselves, there's a lot of people I'd like to do the same to but I'd never have the nerve. Hanging is an awful death."

"Is it, father?" I asked with the deepest interest—I was always very keen on hanging. "Did you ever see a fellow hanged?"

"Dozens of them," he said solemnly. "And they all died roaring."

"Jay!" I said.

"Oh, a horrible death!" he said with great satisfaction. "Lots of the fellows I saw killed their grandmothers too, but they all said 'twas never worth it."

He had me there for a full ten minutes talking, and then walked out the chapel yard with me. I was genuinely sorry to part with him, because he was the most entertaining character I'd ever met in the religious line. Outside, after the shadow of the church, the sunlight was like the roaring of waves on a beach; it dazzled me; and when the frozen silence melted and I heard the screech of trams on the road my heart soared. I knew now I wouldn't die in the night and come back, leaving marks on my mother's furniture. It would be a great worry to her, and the poor soul had enough.

Nora was sitting on the railing, waiting for me, and she put on a very sour puss when she saw the priest with me. She was mad jealous because a priest had never come out of the church with her.

"Well," she asked coldly, after he left me, "what did he give you?"

"Three Hail Marys," I said.

"Three Hail Marys," she repeated incredulously. "You mustn't have told him anything."

"I told him everything," I said confidently.

"About Gran and all?"

"About Gran and all."

(All she wanted was to be able to go home and say I'd made a bad confession.)

"Did you tell him you went for me with the bread-knife?" she asked with a frown.

"I did to be sure."

"And he only gave you three Hail Marys?"

"That's all."

She slowly got down from the railing with a baffled air. Clearly, this was beyond her. As we mounted the steps back to the main road she looked at me suspiciously.

"What are you sucking?" she asked.

"Bullseyes."

"Was it the priest gave them to you?"

"'Twas."

"Lord God," she wailed bitterly, "some people have all the luck! 'Tis no advantage to anybody trying to be good. I might just as well be a sinner like you."

BROWNIES

ZZ PACKER

By our second day at Camp Crescendo, the girls in my Brownie troop had decided to kick the asses of each and every girl in Brownie Troop 909. Troop 909 was doomed from the first day of camp; they were white girls, their complexions a blend of ice cream: strawberry, vanilla. They turtled out from their bus in pairs, their rolled-up sleeping bags chromatized with Disney characters: Sleeping Beauty, Snow White, Mickey Mouse; or the generic ones cheap parents bought: washed-out rainbows, unicorns, curly-eyelashed frogs. Some clutched Igloo coolers and still others held on to stuffed toys like pacifiers, looking all around them like tourists determined to be dazzled.

Our troop was wending its way past their bus, past the ranger station, past the colorful trail guide drawn like a treasure map, locked behind glass.

"Man, did you smell them?" Arnetta said, giving the girls a slow once-over, "They smell like Chihuahuas. *Wet* Chihuahuas." Their troop was still at the entrance, and though we had passed them by yards, Arnetta raised her nose in the air and grimaced.

Arnetta said this from the very rear of the line, far away from Mrs. Margolin, who always strung our troop behind her like a brood of obedient ducklings. Mrs. Margolin even looked like a mother duck—she had hair cropped close to a small ball of a head, almost no neck, and huge, miraculous breasts. She wore enormous belts that looked like the kind that weightlifters wear, except hers would be cheap metallic gold or rabbit fur or covered with gigantic fake sunflowers, and often these belts would become nature lessons in and of themselves. "See," Mrs. Margolin once said to us, pointing to her belt, "this one's made entirely from the feathers of baby pigeons."

The belt layered with feathers was uncanny enough, but I was more disturbed by the realization that I had never actually *seen* a baby pigeon. I searched weeks for one, in vain—scampering after pigeons whenever I was downtown with my father.

But nature lessons were not Mrs. Margolin's top priority. She saw the position of troop leader as an evangelical post. Back at the A.M.E. church where our Brownie meetings were held, Mrs. Margolin was especially fond of imparting religious aphorisms by means of acrostics—"Satan" was the "Serpent Always Tempting and Noisome"; she'd refer to the "Bible" as "Basic Instructions Before Leaving Earth." Whenever she quizzed us on these, expecting to hear the acrostics parroted back to her, only Arnetta's correct replies soared over our vague mumblings. "Jesus?" Mrs. Margolin might ask expectantly, and Arnetta alone would dutifully answer, "Jehovah's Example, Saving Us Sinners."

Arnetta always made a point of listening to Mrs. Margolin's religious talk and giving her what she wanted to hear. Because of this, Arnetta could have blared through a megaphone that the white girls of Troop 909 were "wet Chihuahuas" without so much as a blink from Mrs. Margolin. Once, Arnetta killed the troop goldfish by feeding it a french fry covered in ketchup, and when Mrs. Margolin demanded that she explain what had happened, claimed the goldfish had been eyeing her meal for *hours*, then the fish—giving in to temptation—had leapt up and snatched a whole golden fry from her fingertips.

"*Serious* Chihuahua," Octavia added, and though neither Arnetta nor Octavia could *spell* "Chihuahua," had ever *seen* a Chihuahua, trisyllabic words had gained a sort of exoticism within our fourth-grade set at Woodrow Wilson Elementary. Arnetta and Octavia would flip through the dictionary, determined to work the vulgar-sounding ones like "Djibouti" and "asinine" into conversation.

"*Caucasian* Chihuahuas," Arnetta said.

That did it. The girls in my troop turned elastic: Drema and Elise doubled up on one another like inextricably entwined kites; Octavia slapped her belly; Janice jumped straight up in the air, then did it again, as if to slam-dunk her own head. They could not stop laughing. No one had laughed so hard since a boy named Martez had stuck a pencil in the electric socket and spent the whole day with a strange grin on his face.

"Girls, girls," said our parent helper, Mrs. Hedy. Mrs. Hedy was Octavia's mother, and she wagged her index finger perfunctorily, like a windshield wiper. "Stop it, now. Be good." She said this loud enough to be heard, but lazily, bereft of any feeling or indication that she meant to be obeyed, as though she could say these words again at the exact same pitch if a button somewhere on her were pressed.

But the rest of the girls didn't stop; they only laughed louder. It was the word "Caucasian" that got them all going. One day at school, about a month before the Brownie camping trip, Arnetta turned to a boy wearing impossibly high-ankled floodwater jeans and said, "What are you? *Caucasian?*" The word took off from there, and soon everything was Caucasian. If you ate too fast you ate like a Caucasian, if you ate too slow you ate like a Caucasian. The biggest feat anyone at Woodrow Wilson could do was to jump off the swing in midair, at the highest point in its arc, and if you fell (as I had, more than once) instead of landing on your feet, knees bent Olympic gymnast-style, Arnetta and Octavia were prepared to comment. They'd look at each other with the silence of passengers who'd narrowly escaped an accident, then nod their heads, whispering with solemn horror, *"Caucasian."*

Even the only white kid in our school, Dennis, got in on the Caucasian act. That time when Martez stuck a pencil in the socket, Dennis had pointed and yelled, "That was *so* Caucasian!"

When you lived in the south suburbs of Atlanta, it was easy to forget about whites. Whites were like those baby pigeons: real and existing, but rarely seen or thought about. Everyone had been to Rich's to go clothes shopping, everyone had seen white girls and their mothers coo-cooing over dresses; everyone had gone to the downtown library and seen white businessmen swish by importantly, wrists flexed in front of them to check the time as though they would change from Clark Kent into Superman at any second. But those images were as fleeting as cards shuffled in a deck, whereas the ten white girls behind us—*invaders,* Arnetta would later call them—were instantly real and memorable, with their long, shampoo-commercial hair, straight as spaghetti from the box. This alone was reason for envy and hatred. The only black girl most of us had ever seen with hair that long was Octavia, whose hair hung past her butt like a Hawaiian hula dancer's. The sight of Octavia's mane prompted other girls to listen to her reverentially, as though whatever she had to say would somehow activate their own follicles. For example, when, on the first day of camp, Octavia made as if to speak, and everyone fell silent. "Nobody," Octavia said, "calls us niggers."

At the end of that first day, when half of our troop made their way back to the cabin after tag-team restroom visits, Arnetta said she'd heard one of the Troop 909 girls call Daphne a nigger. The other half of the girls and I were helping Mrs. Margolin clean up the pots and pans from the campfire ravioli dinner. When we made our way to the restrooms to wash up and brush our teeth, we met up with Arnetta midway.

"Man, I completely heard the girl," Arnetta reported. "Right, Daphne?"

Daphne hardly ever spoke, but when she did, her voice was petite and tinkly, the voice one might expect from a shiny new earring. She'd written a poem once, for Langston Hughes Day, a poem brimming with all the teacher-winning ingredients—trees and oceans, sunsets and moons—but what cinched the poem for the grown-ups, snatching the win from Octavia's musical ode to Grandmaster Flash and the Furious Five, were Daphne's last lines:

> You are my father, the veteran
> When you cry in the dark
> It rains and rains and rains in my heart

She'd always worn clean, though faded, jumpers and dresses when Chic jeans were the fashion, but when she went up to the dais to receive her prize journal, pages trimmed in gold, she wore a new dress with a velveteen bodice and a taffeta skirt as wide as an umbrella. All the kids clapped, though none of them understood the poem. I'd read encyclopedias the way others read comics, and I didn't get it. But those last lines pricked me, they were so eerie, and as my father and I ate cereal, I'd whisper over my Froot Loops, like a mantra, *"You are my father, the veteran. You are my father, the veteran, the veteran, the veteran,"* until my father, who acted in plays as Caliban and Othello and was not a veteran, marched me up to my teacher one morning and said, "Can you tell me what's wrong with this kid?"

I thought Daphne and I might become friends, but I think she grew spooked by me whispering those lines to her, begging her to tell me what they meant, and I soon understood that two quiet people like us were better off quiet alone.

"Daphne? Didn't you hear them call you a nigger?" Arnetta asked, giving Daphne a nudge.

The sun was setting behind the trees, and their leafy tops formed a canopy of black lace for the flame of the sun to pass through. Daphne shrugged her shoulders at first, then slowly nodded her head when Arnetta gave her a hard look.

Twenty minutes later, when my restroom group returned to the cabin, Arnetta was still talking about Troop 909. My restroom group had passed by some of the 909 girls. For the most part, they deferred to us, waving us into the restrooms, letting us go even though they'd gotten there first.

We'd seen them, but from afar, never within their orbit enough to see whether their faces were the way all white girls appeared on TV—ponytailed and full of energy, bubbling over with love and money. All I could see was that some of them rapidly fanned their faces with their hands, though the heat of the day had long passed. A few seemed to be lolling their heads in slow circles, half purposefully, as if exercising the muscles of their necks, half ecstatically, like Stevie Wonder.

"We can't let them get away with that," Arnetta said, dropping her voice to a laryngitic whisper. "We can't let them get away with calling us niggers. I say we teach them a lesson." She sat down cross-legged on a sleeping bag, an embittered Buddha, eyes glimmering acrylic-black. "We can't go telling Mrs. Margolin, either. Mrs. Margolin'll say something about doing unto others and the path of righteousness and all. Forget that shit." She let her eyes flutter irreverently till they half closed, as though ignoring an insult not worth returning. We could all hear Mrs. Margolin outside, gathering the last of the metal campware.

Nobody said anything for a while. Usually people were quiet after Arnetta spoke. Her tone had an upholstered confidence that was somehow both regal and vulgar at once. It demanded a few moments of silence in its wake, like the ringing of a church bell or the playing of taps. Sometimes Octavia would ditto or dissent to whatever Arnetta had said, and this was the signal that others could speak. But this time Octavia just swirled a long cord of hair into pretzel shapes.

"*Well?*" Arnetta said. She looked as if she had discerned the hidden severity of the situation and was waiting for the rest of us to catch up. Everyone looked from Arnetta to Daphne. It was, after all, Daphne who had supposedly been called the name, but Daphne sat on the bare cabin floor, flipping through the pages of the Girl Scout handbook, eyebrows arched in mock wonder, as if the handbook were a catalogue full of bright and startling foreign costumes. Janice broke the silence. She clapped her hands to broach her idea of a plan.

"They gone be sleeping," she whispered conspiratorially, "then we gone sneak into they cabin, then we'll put daddy longlegs in they sleeping bags. Then they'll wake up. Then we gone beat 'em up till they're as flat as frying pans!" She jammed her fist into the palm of her hand, then made a sizzling sound.

Janice's country accent was laughable, her looks homely, her jumpy acrobatics embarrassing to behold. Arnetta and Octavia volleyed amused, arrogant smiles whenever Janice opened her mouth, but Janice never caught the hint, spoke whenever she wanted, fluttered around Arnetta and Octavia futilely offering her opinions to their departing backs. Whenever Arnetta and Octavia shooed her away, Janice loitered until the two would finally sigh and ask, "What *is* it, Miss Caucausoid? What do you *want*?"

"Shut up, Janice," Octavia said, letting a fingered loop of hair fall to her waist as though just the sound of Janice's voice had ruined the fun of her hair twisting.

Janice obeyed, her mouth hung open in a loose grin, unflappable, unhurt.

"All right," Arnetta said, standing up. "We're going to have a secret meeting and talk about what we're going to do."

Everyone gravely nodded her head. The word "secret" had a built-in importance, the modifier form of the word carried more clout than the noun. A secret meant nothing; it was like gossip: just a bit of unpleasant knowledge about someone who happened to be someone other than yourself. A secret *meeting,* or a secret *club* was entirely different.

That was when Arnetta turned to me as though she knew that doing so was both a compliment and a charity.

"Snot, you're not going to be a bitch and tell Mrs. Margolin, are you?"

I had been called "Snot" ever since first grade, when I'd sneezed in class and two long ropes of mucus had splattered a nearby girl.

"Hey," I said. "Maybe you didn't hear them right—I mean—"

"Are you gonna tell on us or not?" was all Arnetta wanted to know, and by the time the question was asked, the rest of our Brownie troop looked at me as though they'd already decided their course of action, me being the only impediment.

Camp Crescendo used to double as a high-school-band and field hockey camp until an arcing field hockey ball landed on the clasp of a girl's metal barrette, knifing a skull nerve and paralyzing the right side of her body. The camp closed down for a few years and the girl's teammates built a memorial, filling the spot on which the girl fell with hockey balls, on which they had painted—all in nail polish—get-well tidings, flowers, and hearts. The balls were still stacked there, like a shrine of ostrich eggs embedded in the ground.

On the second day of camp, Troop 909 was dancing around the mound of hockey balls, their limbs jangling awkwardly, their cries like the constant summer squeal of an amusement park. There was a stream that bordered the field hockey lawn, and the girls from my troop settled next to it, scarfing down the last of lunch: sandwiches made from salami and slices of tomato that had gotten waterlogged from the melting ice in the cooler. From the stream bank, Arnetta eyed the Troop 909 girls, scrutinizing their movements to glean inspiration for battle.

"Man," Arnetta said, "we could bumrush them right now if that damn lady would *leave.*"

The 909 troop leader was a white woman with the severe pageboy hairdo of an ancient Egyptian. She lay on a picnic blanket, sphinx-like, eating a banana, sometimes holding it out in front of her like a microphone. Beside her sat a girl slowly flapping one hand like a bird with a broken wing. Occasionally, the leader would call out the names of girls who'd attempted leapfrogs and flips, or of girls who yelled too loudly or strayed far from the circle.

"I'm just glad Big Fat Mama's not following us here," Octavia said. "At least we don't have to worry about her." Mrs. Margolin, Octavia assured us, was having her Afternoon Devotional, shrouded in mosquito netting, in a clearing she'd found. Mrs. Hedy was cleaning mud from her espadrilles in the cabin.

"I handled them." Arnetta sucked on her teeth and proudly grinned. "I told her we was going to gather leaves."

"Gather leaves," Octavia said, nodding respectfully. "That's a good one. Especially since they're so mad-crazy about this camping thing." She looked from ground to sky, sky to ground. Her hair hung down her back in two braids like a squaw's. "I mean, I really don't know why it's even called *camping*—all we ever do with Nature is find some twigs and say something like, 'Wow, this fell from a tree.'" She then studied her sandwich. With two disdainful fingers, she picked out a slice of dripping tomato, the sections congealed with red slime. She pitched it into the stream embrowned with dead leaves and the murky effigies of other dead things, but in the opaque water, a group of small silver-brown fish appeared. They surrounded the tomato and nibbled.

"Look!" Janice cried. "Fishes! Fishes!" As she scrambled to the edge of the stream to watch, a covey of insects threw up tantrums from the wheatgrass and nettle, a throng of tiny electric machines, all going at once. Octavia sneaked up behind Janice as if to push her in. Daphne and I exchanged terrified looks. It seemed as though only we knew that Octavia was close enough—and bold enough—to actually push Janice into the stream. Janice turned around quickly, but Octavia was already staring serenely into the still water as though she was gathering some sort of courage from it. "What's so funny?" Janice said, eyeing them all suspiciously.

Elise began humming the tune to "Karma Chameleon," all the girls joining in, their hums light and facile. Janice also began to hum, against everyone else, the high-octane opening chords of "Beat It."

"I love me some Michael Jackson," Janice said when she'd finished humming, smacking her lips as though Michael Jackson were a favorite meal. "I *will* marry Michael Jackson."

Before anyone had a chance to impress upon Janice the impossibility of this, Arnetta suddenly rose, made a sun visor of her hand, and watched Troop 909 leave the field hockey lawn.

"Dammit!" she said. "We've got to get them *alone*."

"They won't ever be alone," I said. All the rest of the girls looked at me, for I usually kept quiet. If I spoke even a word, I could count on someone calling me Snot. Everyone seemed to think that we could beat up these girls; no one entertained the thought that they might fight *back*. "The only time they'll be unsupervised is in the bathroom."

"Oh shut up, Snot," Octavia said.

But Arnetta slowly nodded her head. "The bathroom," she said. "The bathroom," she said, again and again. "The bathroom! The bathroom!"

According to Octavia's watch, it took us five minutes to hike to the rest-rooms, which were midway between our cabin and Troop 909's. Inside, the mirrors above the sinks returned only the vaguest of reflections, as though someone had taken a scouring pad to their surfaces to obscure the shine. Pine needles, leaves, and dirty, flattened wads of chewing gum covered the floor like a mosaic. Webs of hair matted the drain in the middle of the floor. Above the sinks and below the mirrors, stacks of folded white paper towels lay on a long metal counter. Shaggy white balls of paper towels sat on the sinktops in a line like corsages on display. A thread of floss snaked from a wad of tissues dotted with the faint red-pink of blood. One of those white girls, I thought, had just lost a tooth.

Though the restroom looked almost the same as it had the night before, it somehow seemed stranger now. We hadn't noticed the wooden rafters coming together in great V's. We were, it seemed, inside a whale, viewing the ribs of the roof of its mouth.

"Wow. It's a mess," Elise said.

"You can say that again."

Arnetta leaned against the doorjamb of a restroom stall. "This is where they'll be again," she said. Just seeing the place, just having a plan seemed to satisfy her. "We'll go in and talk to them. You know, 'How you doing? How long'll you be here?' That sort of thing. Then Octavia and I are gonna tell them what happens when they call any one of us a nigger."

"I'm going to say something, too," Janice said.

Arnetta considered this. "Sure," she said. "Of course. Whatever you want."

Janice pointed her finger like a gun at Octavia and rehearsed the line she'd thought up, "'We're gonna teach you a *lesson!*' That's what I'm going to say." She narrowed her eyes like a TV mobster. "'We're gonna teach you little girls a lesson!'"

With the back of her hand, Octavia brushed Janice's finger away. "You couldn't teach me to shit in a toilet."

"But," I said, "what if they say, 'We didn't say that? We didn't call anyone an N-I-G-G-E-R.'"

"Snot," Arnetta said, and then sighed. "Don't think. Just fight. If you even know how."

Everyone laughed except Daphne. Arnetta gently laid her hand on Daphne's shoulder. "Daphne. You don't have to fight. We're doing this for you."

Daphne walked to the counter, took a clean paper towel, and carefully unfolded it like a map. With it, she began to pick up the trash all around. Everyone watched.

"C'mon," Arnetta said to everyone. "Let's beat it." We all ambled toward the doorway, where the sunshine made one large white rectangle of light. We were immediately blinded, and we shielded our eyes with our hands and our forearms.

"Daphne?" Arnetta asked. "Are you coming?"

We all looked back at the bending girl, the thin of her back hunched like the back of a custodian sweeping a stage, caught in limelight. Stray strands of her hair were lit near-transparent, thin fiber-optic threads. She did not nod yes to the question, nor did she shake her head no. She abided, bent. Then she began again, picking up leaves, wads of paper, the cotton fluff innards from a torn stuffed toy. She did it so methodically, so exquisitely, so humbly, she must have been trained. I thought of those dresses she wore, faded and old, yet so pressed and clean. I then saw the poverty in them; I then could imagine her mother, cleaning the houses of others, returning home, weary.

"I guess she's not coming."

We left her and headed back to our cabin, over pine needles and leaves, taking the path full of shade.

"What about our secret meeting?" Elise asked.

Arnetta enunciated her words in a way that defied contradiction: "We just had it."

It was nearing our bedtime, but the sun had not yet set.

"Hey, your mama's coming," Arnetta said to Octavia when she saw Mrs. Hedy walk toward the cabin, sniffling. When Octavia's mother wasn't giving bored, parochial orders, she sniffled continuously, mourning an imminent divorce from her husband. She might begin a sentence, "I don't know what Robert will do when Octavia and I are gone. Who'll buy him cigarettes?" and Octavia would hotly whisper, *"Mama,"* in a way that meant: Please don't talk about our problems in front of everyone. Please shut up.

But when Mrs. Hedy began talking about her husband, thinking about her husband, seeing clouds shaped like the head of her husband, she couldn't be quiet, and no one could dislodge her from the comfort of her own woe. Only one thing could perk her up—Brownie songs. If the girls were quiet, and Mrs. Hedy was in her dopey, sorrowful mood, she would say, "Y'all know I like those songs, girls. Why don't you sing one?" Everyone would groan, except me and Daphne. I, for one, liked some of the songs.

"C'mon, everybody," Octavia said drearily. "She likes the Brownie song best."

We sang, loud enough to reach Mrs. Hedy:

"I've got something in my pocket;
It belongs across my face.
And I keep it very close at hand
 in a most convenient place.
I'm sure you couldn't guess it
If you guessed a long, long while.
So I'll take it out and put it on—
It's a great big Brownie smile!"

The Brownie song was supposed to be sung cheerfully, as though we were elves in a workshop, singing as we merrily cobbled shoes, but everyone except me hated the song so much that they sang it like a maudlin record, played on the most sluggish of rpms.

"That was good," Mrs. Hedy said, closing the cabin door behind her. "Wasn't that nice, Linda?"

"Praise God," Mrs. Margolin answered without raising her head from the chore of counting out Popsicle sticks for the next day's craft session.

"Sing another one," Mrs. Hedy said. She said it with a sort of joyful aggression, like a drunk I'd once seen who'd refused to leave a Korean grocery.

"God, Mama, get over it," Octavia whispered in a voice meant only for Arnetta, but Mrs. Hedy heard it and started to leave the cabin.

"Don't go," Arnetta said. She ran after Mrs. Hedy and held her by the arm. "We haven't finished singing." She nudged us with a single look. "Let's sing the 'Friends Song.' For Mrs. Hedy."

Although I liked some of the songs, I hated this one:

  Make new friends
  But keep the o-old,
  One is silver
  And the other gold.

If most of the girls in the troop could be any type of metal, they'd be bunched-up wads of tinfoil, maybe, or rusty iron nails you had to get tetanus shots for.

"No, no, no," Mrs. Margolin said before anyone could start in on the "Friends Song." "An uplifting song. Something to lift her up and take her mind off all these earthly burdens."

Arnetta and Octavia rolled their eyes. Everyone knew what song Mrs. Margolin was talking about, and no one, no one, wanted to sing it.

"Please, no," a voice called out. "Not 'The Doughnut Song.'"

"Please not 'The Doughnut Song,'" Octavia pleaded.

"I'll brush my teeth two times if I don't have to sing 'The Doughnut—'"

"Sing!" Mrs. Margolin demanded.

We sang:

> "Life without Jesus is like a do-ough-nut!
> Like a do-ooough-nut!
> Like a do-ooough-nut!
> Life without Jesus is like a do-ough-nut!
> There's a hole in the middle of my soul!"

There were other verses, involving other pastries, but we stopped after the first one and cast glances toward Mrs. Margolin to see if we could gain a reprieve. Mrs. Margolin's eyes fluttered blissfully. She was half asleep.

"Awww," Mrs. Hedy said, as though giant Mrs. Margolin were a cute baby, "Mrs. Margolin's had a long day."

"Yes indeed," Mrs. Margolin answered. "If you don't mind, I might just go to the lodge where the beds are. I haven't been the same since the operation."

I had not heard of this operation, or when it had occurred, since Mrs. Margolin had never missed the once-a-week Brownie meetings, but I could see from Daphne's face that she was concerned, and I could see that the other girls had decided that Mrs. Margolin's operation must have happened long ago in some remote time unconnected to our own. Nevertheless, they put on sad faces. We had all been taught that adulthood was full of sorrow and pain, taxes and bills, dreaded work and dealings with whites, sickness and death. I tried to do what the others did. I tried to look silent.

"Go right ahead, Linda," Mrs. Hedy said. "I'll watch the girls." Mrs. Hedy seemed to forget about divorce for a moment; she looked at us with dewy eyes, as if we were mysterious, furry creatures. Meanwhile, Mrs. Margolin walked through the maze of sleeping bags until she found her own. She gathered a neat stack of clothes and pajamas slowly, as though doing so was almost painful. She took her toothbrush, her toothpaste, her pillow. "All right!" Mrs. Margolin said, addressing us all from the threshold of the cabin. "Be in bed by nine." She said it with a twinkle in her voice, letting us know she was allowing us to be naughty and stay up till nine-fifteen.

"C'mon everybody," Arnetta said after Mrs. Margolin left. "Time for us to wash up."

Everyone watched Mrs. Hedy closely, wondering whether she would insist on coming with us since it was night, making a fight with Troop 909 nearly impossible. Troop 909 would soon be in the bathroom, washing their faces, brushing their teeth—completely unsuspecting of our ambush.

"We won't be long," Arnetta said. "We're old enough to go to the restrooms by ourselves."

Ms. Hedy pursed her lips at this dilemma. "Well, I guess you Brownies are almost Girl Scouts, right?"

"Right!"

"Just one more badge," Drema said.

"And about," Octavia droned, "a million more cookies to sell."

Octavia looked at all of us, *Now's our chance*, her face seemed to say, but our chance to do *what*, I didn't exactly know.

Finally, Mrs. Hedy walked to the doorway where Octavia stood dutifully waiting to say goodbye but looking bored doing it. Mrs. Hedy held Octavia's chin. "You'll be good?"

"Yes, Mama."

"And remember to pray for me and your father? If I'm asleep when you get back?"

"Yes, Mama."

When the other girls had finished getting their toothbrushes and washcloths and flashlights for the group restroom trip, I was drawing pictures of tiny birds with too many feathers. Daphne was sitting on her sleeping bag, reading.

"You're not going to come?" Octavia asked.

Daphne shook her head.

"I'm gonna stay, too," I said. "I'll go to the restroom when Daphne and Mrs. Hedy go."

Arnetta leaned down toward me and whispered so that Mrs. Hedy, who'd taken over Mrs. Margolin's task of counting Popsicle sticks, couldn't hear. "No, Snot. If we get in trouble, you're going to get in trouble with the rest of us."

We made our way through the darkness by flashlight. The tree branches that had shaded us just hours earlier, along the same path, now looked like arms sprouting menacing hands. The stars sprinkled the sky like spilled salt. They seemed fastened to the darkness, high up and holy, their places fixed and definite as we stirred beneath them.

Some, like me, were quiet because we were afraid of the dark; others were talking like crazy for the same reason.

"Wow!" Drema said, looking up. "Why are all the stars out here? I never see stars back on Oneida Street."

"It's a camping trip, that's why," Octavia said. "You're supposed to see stars on camping trips."

Janice said, "This place smells like my mother's air freshener."

"These woods are *pine*," Elise said. "Your mother probably uses *pine* air freshener."

Janice mouthed an exaggerated "Oh," nodding her head as though she just then understood one of the world's great secrets.

No one talked about fighting. Everyone was afraid enough just walking through the infinite deep of the woods. Even though I didn't fight to fight, was afraid of fighting, I felt I was part of the rest of the troop; like I was defending something. We trudged against the slight incline of the path, Arnetta leading the way.

"You know," I said, "their leader will be there. Or they won't even be there. It's dark already. Last night the sun was still in the sky. I'm sure they're already finished."

Arnetta acted as if she hadn't heard me. I followed her gaze with my flashlight, and that's when I saw the squares of light in the darkness. The bathroom was just ahead.

But the girls were there. We could hear them before we could see them.

"Octavia and I will go in first so they'll think there's just two of us, then wait till I say, 'We're gonna teach you a lesson,'" Arnetta said. "Then, bust in. That'll surprise them."

"That's what I was supposed to say," Janice said.

Arnetta went inside, Octavia next to her. Janice followed, and the rest of us waited outside.

They were in there for what seemed like whole minutes, but something was wrong. Arnetta hadn't given the signal yet. I was with the girls outside when I heard one of the Troop 909 girls say, "NO. That did NOT happen!"

That was to be expected, that they'd deny the whole thing. What I hadn't expected was *the voice* in which the denial was said. The girl sounded as though her tongue were caught in her mouth. "That's a BAD word!" the girl continued. "We don't say BAD words!"

"Let's go in," Elise said.

"No," Drema said, "I don't want to. What if we get beat up?"

"Snot?" Elise turned to me, her flashlight blinding. It was the first time anyone had asked my opinion, though I knew they were just asking because they were afraid.

"I say we go inside, just to see what's going on."

"But Arnetta didn't give us the signal," Drema said. "She's supposed to say, 'We're gonna teach you a lesson,' and I didn't hear her say it."

"C'mon," I said. "Let's just go in."

We went inside. There we found the white girls—about five girls huddled up next to one big girl. I instantly knew she was the owner of the voice we'd heard. Arnetta and Octavia inched toward us as soon as we entered.

"Where's Janice?" Elise asked, then we heard a flush. "Oh."

"I think," Octavia said, whispering to Elise, "they're retarded."

"We ARE NOT retarded!" the big girl said, though it was obvious that she was. That they all were. The girls around her began to whimper.

"They're just pretending," Arnetta said, trying to convince herself. "I know they are."

Octavia turned to Arnetta. "Arnetta. Let's just leave."

Janice came out of a stall, happy and relieved, then she suddenly remembered her line, pointed to the big girl, and said, "We're gonna teach you a lesson."

"Shut up, Janice," Octavia said, but her heart was not in it. Arnetta's face was set in a lost, deep scowl. Octavia turned to the big girl and said loudly, slowly, as if they were all deaf, "We're going to leave. It was nice meeting you, O.K.? You don't have to tell anyone that we were here. O.K.?"

"Why not?" said the big girl, like a taunt. When she spoke, her lips did not meet, her mouth did not close. Her tongue grazed the roof of her mouth, like a little pink fish. "You'll get in trouble. I know. *I* know."

Arnetta got back her old cunning. "If you said anything, then you'd be a tattletale."

The girl looked sad for a moment, then perked up quickly. A flash of genius crossed her face. "I *like* tattletale."

"It's all right, girls. It's gonna be all right!" the 909 troop leader said. All of Troop 909 burst into tears. It was as though someone had instructed them all to cry at once. The troop leader had girls under her arm, and all the rest of the girls crowded about her. It reminded me of a hog I'd seen on a field trip, where all the little hogs gathered about the mother at feeding time, latching on to her teats. The 909 troop leader had come into the bathroom, shortly after the big girl had threatened to tell. Then the ranger came, then, once the ranger had radioed the station, Mrs. Margolin arrived with Daphne in tow.

The ranger had left the restroom area, but everyone else was huddled just outside, swatting mosquitoes.

"Oh. They *will* apologize," Mrs. Margolin said to the 909 troop leader, but she said this so angrily, I knew she was speaking more to us than to the other troop leader. "When their parents find out, every one a them will be on punishment."

"It's all right, it's all right," the 909 troop leader reassured Mrs. Margolin. Her voice lilted in the same way it had when addressing the girls. She smiled the whole time she talked. She was like one of those TV-cooking-show women who talk and dice onions and smile all at the same time.

"See. It could have happened. I'm not calling your girls fibbers or anything." She shook her head ferociously from side to side, her Egyptian-style pageboy flapping against her cheeks like heavy drapes. "It *could* have happened. See. Our girls are *not* retarded. They are *delayed* learners." She said this in a syrupy instructional voice, as though our troop might be delayed learners as well. "We're from the Decatur Children's Academy. Many of them just have special needs."

"Now we won't be able to walk to the bathroom by ourselves!" the big girl said.

"Yes you will," the troop leader said, "but maybe we'll wait till we get back to Decatur—"

"I don't want to wait!" the girl said. "I want my Independence badge!"

The girls in my troop were entirely speechless. Arnetta looked stoic, as though she were soon to be tortured but was determined not to appear weak. Mrs. Margolin pursed her lips solemnly and said, "Bless them, Lord. Bless them."

In contrast, the Troop 909 leader was full of words and energy. "Some of our girls are echolalic—" She smiled and happily presented one of the girls hanging on to her, but the girl widened her eyes in horror, and violently withdrew herself from the center of attention, sensing she was being sacrificed for the village sins. "Echolalic," the troop leader continued. "That means they will say whatever they hear, like an echo—that's where the word comes from. It comes from 'echo.'" She ducked her head apologetically, "I mean, not all of them have the most *progressive* of parents, so if they heard a bad word, they might have repeated it. But I guarantee it would not have been *intentional*."

Arnetta spoke. "I saw her say the word. I heard her." She pointed to a small girl, smaller than any of us, wearing an oversized T-shirt that read: "Eat Bertha's Mussels."

The troop leader shook her head and smiled, "That's impossible. She doesn't speak. She can, but she doesn't."

Arnetta furrowed her brow. "No. It wasn't her. That's right. It was *her*."

The girl Arnetta pointed to grinned as though she'd been paid a compliment. She was the only one from either troop actually wearing a full uniform: the mocha-colored A-line shift, the orange ascot, the sash covered with badges, though all the same one—the Try-It patch. She took a few steps toward Arnetta and made a grand sweeping gesture toward the sash. "See," she said, full of self-importance, "I'm a Brownie." I had a hard time imagining this girl calling anyone a "nigger"; the girl looked perpetually delighted, as though she would have cuddled up with a grizzly if someone had let her.

On the fourth morning, we boarded the bus to go home.

The previous day had been spent building miniature churches from

Popsicle sticks. We hardly left the cabin. Mrs. Margolin and Mrs. Hedy guarded us so closely, almost no one talked for the entire day.

Even on the day of departure from Camp Crescendo, all was serious and silent. The bus ride began quietly enough. Arnetta had to sit beside Mrs. Margolin; Octavia had to sit beside her mother. I sat beside Daphne, who gave me her prize journal without a word of explanation.

"You don't want it?"

She shook her head no. It was empty.

Then Mrs. Hedy began to weep. "Octavia," Mrs. Hedy said to her daughter without looking at her, "I'm going to sit with Mrs. Margolin. All right?"

Arnetta exchanged seats with Mrs. Hedy. With the two women up front, Elise felt it safe to speak. "Hey," she said, then she set her face into a placid, vacant stare, trying to imitate that of a Troop 909 girl. Emboldened, Arnetta made a gesture of mock pride toward an imaginary sash, the way the girl in full uniform had done. Then they all made a game of it, trying to do the most exaggerated imitations of the Troop 909 girls, all without speaking, all without laughing loud enough to catch the women's attention.

Daphne looked down at her shoes, white with sneaker polish. I opened the journal she'd given me. I looked out the window, trying to decide what to write, searching for lines, but nothing could compare with what Daphne had written, *"My father, the veteran,"* my favorite line of all time. It replayed itself in my head, and I gave up trying to write.

By then, it seemed that the rest of the troop had given up making fun of the girls in Troop 909. They were now quietly gossiping about who had passed notes to whom in school. For a moment the gossiping fell off, and all I heard was the hum of the bus as we sped down the road and the muffled sounds of Mrs. Hedy and Mrs. Margolin talking about serious things.

"You know," Octavia whispered, "why did *we* have to be stuck at a camp with retarded girls? You know?"

"You know why," Arnetta answered. She narrowed her eyes like a cat. "My mama and I were in the mall in Buckhead, and this white lady just kept looking at us. I mean, like we were foreign or something. Like we were from China."

"What did the woman say?" Elise asked.

"Nothing," Arnetta said. "She didn't say nothing."

A few girls quietly nodded their heads.

"There was this time," I said, "when my father and I were in the mall and—"

"Oh shut up, Snot," Octavia said.

I stared at Octavia, then rolled my eyes from her to the window. As I watched the trees blur, I wanted nothing more than to be through with it all: the bus ride, the troop, school—all of it. But we were going home. I'd see the same girls in school the next day. We were on a bus, and there was nowhere else to go.

"Go on, Laurel," Daphne said to me. It seemed like the first time she'd spoken the whole trip, and she'd said my name. I turned to her and smiled weakly so as not to cry, hoping she'd remember when I'd tried to be her friend, thinking maybe that her gift of the journal was an invitation of friendship. But she didn't smile back. All she said was, "What happened?"

I studied the girls, waiting for Octavia to tell me to shut up again before I even had a chance to utter another word, but everyone was amazed that Daphne had spoken. The bus was silent. I gathered my voice. "Well," I said. "My father and I were in this mall, but *I* was the one doing the staring." I stopped and glanced from face to face. I continued. "There were these white people dressed like Puritans or something, but they weren't Puritans. They were Mennonites. They're these people who, if you ask them to do a favor, like paint your porch or something, they have to do it. It's in their rules."

"That sucks," someone said.

"C'mon," Arnetta said. "You're lying."

"I am not."

"How do you know that's not just some story someone made up?" Elise asked, her head cocked full of daring. "I mean, who's gonna do whatever you ask?"

"It's not made up. I know because when I was looking at them, my father said, 'See those people? If you ask them to do something, they'll do it. Anything you want.'"

No one would call anyone's father a liar—then they'd have to fight the person. But Drema parsed her words carefully. "How does your *father* know that's not just some story? Huh?"

"Because," I said, "he went up to the man and asked him would he paint our porch, and the man said yes. It's their religion."

"Man, I'm glad I'm a Baptist," Elise said, shaking her head in sympathy for the Mennonites.

"So did the guy do it?" Drema asked, scooting closer to hear if the story got juicy.

"Yeah," I said. "His whole family was with him. My dad drove them to our house. They all painted our porch. The woman and girl were in bonnets and long, long skirts with buttons up to their necks. The guy wore this weird hat and these huge suspenders."

"Why," Arnetta asked archly, as though she didn't believe a word, "would someone pick a *porch*? If they'll do anything, why not make them paint the whole *house*? Why not ask for a hundred bucks?"

I thought about it, and then remembered the words my father had said about them painting our porch, though I had never seemed to think about his words after he'd said them.

"He said," I began, only then understanding the words as they uncoiled from my mouth, "it was the only time he'd have a white man on his knees doing something for a black man for free."

I now understood what he meant, and why he did it, though I didn't like it. When you've been made to feel bad for so long, you jump at the chance to do it to others. I remembered the Mennonites bending the way Daphne had bent when she was cleaning the restroom. I remembered the dark blue of their bonnets, the black of their shoes. They painted the porch as though scrubbing a floor. I was already trembling before Daphne asked quietly, "Did he thank them?"

I looked out the window. I could not tell which were the thoughts and which were the trees. "No," I said, and suddenly knew there was something mean in the world that I could not stop.

Arnetta laughed. "If I asked them to take off their long skirts and bonnets and put on some jeans, would they do it?"

And Daphne's voice, quiet, steady: "Maybe they would. Just to be nice."

WHAT THE RIVER TOLD US TO DO

PETER MARKUS

We watched our father hammer and pound, into our front yard's ground, a hand-made sign that said, in letters big enough for us brothers to read what it said, all the way down from where we were watching, down by the muddy river's muddy shore: HOUSE FOR SALE. We'd seen signs like this sign before, sticking up from the front yards of other people's houses, but never in the front of ours. We knew what happened to those people who hammered those signs, down into the ground out front in the fronts of their houses' front yards. After a while, those people with signs out in the fronts of their houses left away from our town and were then replaced by new people who came to live on the insides of these kinds of houses. Us brothers, we did not want to be one of those people. We didn't want our house to be that kind of a house. Our house, we did not want it—our house—to be a house with any body but us living inside it. But us brothers both knew that this, us living in some other house, in some other town, in a town without a dirty river running through it, a town without so much mud and smoke and rust—this was what our mother said she wanted for us. We'd heard her say, to our father, that it was either this house and this dirty river town, or it was her that was leaving. Us, our mother's dirty boys, we listened close: we hoped we might hear the sound of footsteps, a door opening then closing shut. Later on that day, when us brothers saw our father working on the making and the painting and the nailing together of the sign that said on it, HOUSE FOR SALE, we asked our father what was he doing, then what was it, the sign, for? We stood by and watched our father's mouth move around to make such sounds as mother and river and town. We watched him raise up his hand and point with his first finger to where the mill was sitting quiet on the river's shore. But us brothers, we didn't want our ears to hear what it was that our father was wanting us to hear. And our eyes, when we looked upriver at the mill, it sitting quiet and still, what we saw was the moon rising big and white and glowing—the smokestacks holding it up. Us brothers said some words back to our father, words such as moon and mud and fish, but even these words, words that were the world to us brothers, these were sounds that our father did not hear. We watched him drop his head back down so that he could see his right hand holding his hammer: in his other he held a handful of nails. When our father did this with his hands, us brothers did this with ours. We each of us took the other one of us by the hand and went with each other to the river, to ask the river: what should we, us brothers, do? When the river told us what to do, we both knew it was the only thing we could do. So that night, while our mother and father both were in their room, with the lights turned off for sleeping, what we did was we climbed through our bedroom window. Only the moon and the stars were watching us as we walked out to our father's tool shed and got out his hammers and a box full of rusty, bent-back nails. We each of us brothers took up a fistful of nails and a hammer into each one of our hands and we walked out back to the back of our yard, back to where there was a telephone pole back there studded with the heads of fish. Brother, I said to Brother. You can go first. Brother, give me your hand, I told him. Hold your hand up against this pole. Brother did just what I told. We were brothers: we were each other's voice inside our own heads. This might sting, I warned, and then I raised back that hammer and I drove that rusty nail right through Brother's hand. Brother didn't even wince, or flinch with his body, or make with his mouth the sound of a brother crying out. Good, Brother, I said. I was hammering in a second nail into Brother's other hand when our father stepped out into the yard. Us, our father's sons, turned back with our heads toward the sound of our father. We stood waiting to hear what it was our father was going to say to us next. It was a long few seconds. The sky above the river where the steel mill stood—like some sort of a shipwreck—it was dark and quiet. Somewhere, I was sure, the sun was shining. You boys remember to clean up before you come back in, our father said to his boys. Our father turned back his back. Us brothers turned to face back with each other. I raised back the hammer. I lined up that rusted nail.

GOING FOR THE ORANGE JULIUS

MYLA GOLDBERG

It's not only about looking good. If you're just looking good, you'll probably be able to get a cone or a soft pretzel, but definitely not an Orange Julius.

"Carrie," Grandma says to me as we walk into the mall, "are you feeling like a lady?" The ceiling of the mall when you first walk in has mirrors on it, so you can look up and see yourself and whoever you're with.

"Yeah, Grandma," I say back. "I'm feeling like a lady."

Then we both look up at the ceiling so we can see each other and Grandma says,

"Well, here we are, two ladies going out to see the world."

Grandma only wears real gold and keeps her cigarettes in a genuine leather cigarette pack holder. She always wears dresses and panty hose and heels high enough to show she's got class and low enough to show she's no tramp. When we go out in her Caddy she lets me sit in front, which is one of the things I don't tell Mom. Grandma never wears a seat belt, but she always makes me wear one, which I pretend bothers me but which I don't really mind. With Grandma it's air-conditioning and no open windows because a lady must always look her best. At stoplights, Grandma turns to the car next to her and gives her best smile. Mom says it's the cigarettes that make Grandma's teeth yellow.

First thing in the morning, Grandma wakes me up and we go to her beauty chamber. Grandma puts her face on first, then mine. It's easier to look at Grandma once she's drawn in her eyebrows. When I ask why Mom doesn't shave her eyebrows too, Grandma says it's because Mom doesn't care enough to make the best out of what she has, which is why she can't keep a man and lives in a dump. Unless you watch Grandma put on her makeup, you won't know that the beauty mark above her lip isn't real. She says that when I'm older I'll have to pick a permanent place to put my beauty mark, but for now she lets me pick a different place every time. I have to hold very still when Grandma does my face. Sometimes the eyeliner brush tickles, but if I squirm it messes her up and we have to start all over again. I'm allowed to put on my own lipstick, which is pink instead of red like Grandma's because some things just aren't appropriate.

At McDonald's, I get hotcakes and hash browns and Grandma gets coffee, which she drinks with extra milk to keep her complexion creamy. Before we get back in the car, we go to the ladies room to refresh our makeup. I have a purse to carry my own makeup. In the beginning I lost the purse a lot, but I am much more mature now.

Grandma's favorite store is Lord & Taylor's, which she says if I ever manage not to walk like a cripple for a whole day she will buy me a present from, which is something I haven't managed to do yet. When we walk in, we go right to the perfume ladies, who squeeze their hands together and say,

"Why if it isn't Eleanor and her granddaughter, Carrie. How long has it been since we saw you last, Carrie?" and I tell them,

"A month," which I'm not really sure is true, but which is about how often Mom needs a break and calls Grandma to do the trade-off.

"Any longer and I don't know if I could undo the damage," Grandma says, which I wish she wouldn't say, but the perfume ladies laugh like it's a big joke so I pretend that it is.

The perfume ladies are extremely nice. Their hair is always perfect and their faces are on exactly right. I've never seen their feet, but I bet they wear heels the same height as Grandma's. Grandma won't buy me heels because I'm pigeon-toed and she's afraid I'll fall all over myself in heels. When we walk anywhere together I have to concentrate on walking toes pointed out. It's hard to walk just right, most of the time I am either walking like a cripple or like I'm wearing a diaper according to Grandma, who knows these things. The perfume ladies spritz me with something that smells like baby powder, which I definitely like better than smelling like flowers but not as much as smelling like peppermint.

We get to the Food Court around 2, after the serious lunch-eaters have gone because Grandma says it's important to make clear that this is not about being hungry. She always makes sure I eat really good before she sends me off so that it's the lady in me talking and not my stomach because guys can always tell the difference. Today I get the number #3 special at China Wok. I try to get my mouth around the egg roll in a way that won't mess up my lipstick, but Grandma makes me stop because she says it makes me look like a tramp.

When Grandma is driving, she puts her hand on my knee and says, "My knee." If I disagree she squeezes tighter and explains it really is her knee because I'm part of Mom and Mom is part of her, so I'm part of her too. When things get to be too much for Mom, she calls Grandma and they meet halfway for the trade-off at Howard Johnson's and I go from Mom's sticky seats to Grandma's cushy red leather.

We're sitting at the far corner of the Food Court by the Roy Rogers because that's where the best view is. The Food Court tables are on a raised platform with fake potted plants. The platform has six sides and reminds me of a musical jewelry box I have with a ballerina that spins when you open the lid. Grandma says the music they play in the Food Court is trashy. The Food Court plays Journey, Air Supply, Billy Joel, and Hall & Oates. I pretend the songs have been picked especially for me. That way, it's like the whole Food Court is rooting for me.

Grandma's Caddy has electric locks with master switches by the front seats that let you lock and unlock any door you want. I'm not allowed to play with the locks because what if I'm leaning against the door and it flies open or what if we're driving through a dark neighborhood and someone sees us and gets ideas? For a long time I thought dark meant no streetlights.

After I finish eating, I throw out my tray except for the soda and then I go to the bathroom to check my face. Grandma used to come with me, but now checking my face by myself is part of the whole thing. The Food Court bathroom isn't cleaned very often and smells like smoke. When I walk in, the girl from Candy World pretends like she's tucking her hair into her visor when the bag of jumbo malted milk balls is sitting right on top of her purse and her fingers have melted chocolate all over them. I can tell she's waiting for me to go, but when I don't she finally picks up her purse and leaves.

Even though I don't think I have to pee I make myself try because going to the bathroom in the middle of sitting with a guy is a signal and Grandma would get mad if I did it only because I had to pee. Since the Candy World girl is gone, I can turn on the water in the sinks, which helps. Grandma doesn't like me to sit on public toilet seats, so I don't because I know she's going to ask me when I come out and she can always tell when I'm lying. I do my best not to sprinkle, but it's hard and besides, there was some there already.

To check my face, first I stand really close to the mirror and then I back up three steps. Close for the details and further away for the full effect. I have to stand on a toilet with the stall door open to see my whole reflection, which is another reason why I waited for the Candy World girl to go. Today everything looks pretty good except for my lipstick, which is smeared because of the egg roll. Just to be safe, I also spray on a little more hair spray, which I do using Grandma's special method which she says is one of the dividing lines between ladies and tramps. Only tramps spray hair spray directly onto their heads, which gloms the hair together. Glommed hair is one thing guys notice without knowing they're noticing it when they first peg a girl for a tramp. So, I spray the hair spray next to my head and then step into it, sort of like I'm stepping into the shower. That way all the hair spray molecules settle evenly around my head and hold my hair without a single glommy spot.

Grandma says my skin is clear enough that I don't need to use foundation yet, but she's bought me my own bottle so that it'll be there for me when I'm ready. Grandma uses one a little darker than her own skin to make her look sun-kissed, but she never puts it on her neck, which makes her face a different color than the rest of her.

When I walk out of the bathroom and go back to the table, Grandma is waiting. She says,

"Are you ready?" in the same voice she uses when I've picked something to wear that she doesn't like. Except for one time, Grandma has always found something that needs fixing when I come out of the bathroom. Letting Grandma look me over and knowing she's going to find a mistake is the hardest part, harder than actually going up to a guy.

"I think so," I say, trying to sound all calm and sure of myself.

It's like Grandma is the sun through the magnifying glass and I'm the bug. The side of my head will burn a little and Grandma will tell me that my barrette is out of place, or my cheek will burn and Grandma will say that my blush is uneven. Even though she never says it, I know Grandma is doing all this so that I can do better in life than Mom, who can't keep a man and lives in a dump.

At Howard Johnson's I always get fried clam strips with French fries and extra tartar sauce and bubble gum ice cream for dessert. The great thing about bubble gum ice cream is saving the gum balls in your mouth until the ice cream is all gone and then chewing the gum, which there's so much of by then that it takes up your whole mouth. Grandma says that gum chewing is not ladylike and makes me look like a cow.

Sometimes Mom eats with us at the Howard Johnson's. I like it better when she doesn't because it's easier for me to think of her being a part of Grandma when they're not sitting across a table from each other not talking.

"Your blouse isn't tucked in right," Grandma says, and I look and it's true. "Show me how a lady's blouse should be tucked in," she says.

I retuck in my blouse so that the creases are slanting down in front. Grandma once described it as the creases coming toward each other like roads converging at the Promised Land.

I say,

"Is that better?" and she looks me over again and says,

"Much better," and I know that it's time to get started.

Grandma has taught me that the right way to put on a bra is to place each bosom inside the cup like you're scooping up a baby chick. Mine are so small that it's impossible to scoop anything up yet, so what I do is I pretend there is something to scoop, which Grandma says I do so well she can almost see my young bosoms. Grandma is the only person I know who says bosom, which for a long time I didn't know was the same as titty. I have matching bras and undies that Grandma keeps special for me in a drawer at her house that I can only wear when we're going out to see the world.

Grandma starts looking for my assignment, and we both sip our sodas like we're taking a break from shopping. "Love Is a Battlefield," by Pat Benatar, is coming through the Food Court speakers, which makes me feel totally prepared and like the songs really aren't a tape that plays over and over. I sip my soda by holding my cup with one hand and casually putting my lips just at the very tip of the straw and sucking on the straw until only the slightest bit of soda comes up and then taking the straw out of my mouth and starting all over again. Grandma and I are experts at looking around the Food Court like we're not looking at anything in particular when we're really noticing everything.

At first glance it seems like there are a lot of ladies around, but mostly the Food Court is full of tramps. I can tell a tramp by their makeup or their clothes, or by the way they eat their food. Even when I think I've found a lady, Grandma usually points out something I've missed that makes her a tramp, like the way she wears her hair, or the kind of purse she has. It's incredibly difficult to be a lady. I don't really blame Mom for not being able to do it.

Mom always asks me when I come back from Grandma's, How was your stay and I always say Fine. Then she says Don't let her turn you into something you're not, and I say Okay. Once, I forgot to take off my nails with the fake tips and Mom started crying in the Howard Johnson's parking lot and saying She's only a baby and You promised you wouldn't do this to her and Grandma said I'm not doing anything, it was only a little mani-cure and Mom made me peel the nails off before getting into her car. I knew after that it would be better not to tell about the matching bras and undies. Or about Grandma showing me how, when I got hair down there, it should be a nice, neat triangle with no Goody Trail, which is the hairs that lead from under the belly button to the Promised Land.

I'm watching the girl at Candy World and counting up all her tramp qualities when Grandma says,

"There's someone who looks like he could use the presence of a lady," and she's pointing at a guy in line for China Wok. When I first started out, Grandma would only assign me guys my age, but now that I'm more advanced, she sometimes gives me guys a little older. I was really shy at first about going to older ones, but they usually end up being easier because they have more money. This guy looks maybe three years older than me and I'm surprised that he's the one Grandma picked because he's wearing parachute pants, which Grandma says are trashy. I actually have a pair of parachute pants that I never take to Grandma's because she would throw them away. Then I realize that Grandma might not be able to tell they're parachute pants because they're black and China Wok is all the way across the Food Court.

Grandma says that in order to keep a man it's important to act inter-ested and to give him a little taste and that the reason Mom can't keep a man is because she gives him the whole seven-course meal, but I never see Grandma using her advice on Grandpa who's always watching golf in his recliner with the volume turned up really loud. Grandpa has the hairiest arms I've ever seen, which I'm glad for that reason he's not the hugging type. He and Grandma say as little to each other as Mom and Grandma, which makes me think that Mom must have had the quietest childhood in childhood history.

Grandpa used to be a doctor but he had to retire early on account of his heart. When Grandma picked him, he was only fifteen and the son of a grocer who drank too much, but Grandma says she could tell by the way he carried himself that he had motivation. She got him to notice her and the rest, she says, is history. Grandpa has a Cadillac with brown seats that aren't soft like Grandma's. Every time we drive to dinner at the Italian restaurant he shows me the doctor's card clipped to his sun visor that proves he's got more important things to do than stop for a damn red light. Then Grandma says Watch your language, I'm bringing someone up to be a lady and Grandpa says Aw, shut up, what do you know about being a lady? which makes Grandma's lips crinkle like she's just sucked on something sour. If my knee is Grandma's, then I guess a part of me has to be Grandpa's too.

Instead of going in a straight line from our table to China Wok, I walk around the outside of the whole platform so it will look more like I found the guy in the parachute pants by accident and not like I have set plans. By the time I get to China Wok, he's actually leaving with his tray, so I follow him to where the napkins and plastic forks are.

I stand next to the guy in the parachute pants while he's getting napkins and pretend I'm waiting for a napkin while I look straight at him. When he looks at me, I look away but not until after we've looked at each other for a split second.

"Hi," he says, which makes him at least soda material because a lot of the time I'm the one who has to talk first. I relax then, because chances are I'm going to get it on my first try and Grandma won't have to find me another one.

"Hi," I say back and this time I look straight at him without turning away. He's pretty okay looking and I understand now why Grandma picked him. I haven't seen pictures of Grandpa before he got old, but I'm pretty sure he'd look a lot like this guy. This guy has Grandpa's dark hair although, lucky for me, not on his arms, and also maybe Grandpa's nose. He's also built kind of big like Grandpa—not fat, but with big shoulders and arms and I bet he plays football. So that's what I ask him next,

"Do you play football?" I say, because they like it when you ask them questions about themselves.

"Yeah," he says, "I'm the only sophomore on varsity," which makes him just the third high school guy I've done this with, which makes me a little nervous but also excited because it means I can definitely skip gum or candy or a soft pretzel.

"Do you go to Larchdale," the guy says, "'cause I ain't seen you at Pulaski." When I nod he says,

"You look a little young for high school," but with a grin that means he doesn't really mind. He's done getting his napkins and his plasticware now, but he hasn't made a move to walk away or anything, so we're both just standing there. I happen to be standing under an air-conditioning vent, so there's a breeze blowing my hair back in this really cool way that I couldn't have planned even if I tried.

"Yeah," I say. "I skipped kindergarten, so I guess I'm a little young."

Grandma says that being smart or stupid doesn't matter as much as motivation, meaning how hard will you work to get what you want, which it seems to me that being on varsity when you're only a sophomore is a pretty good sign of that so I say,

"Look, you want to buy me some fries?" because I can tell he's the kind of guy who likes to get to the point. He just smiles then, he doesn't even need to say anything, and when he turns around with his tray I know we're heading to Boardwalk Fries.

I'm not ever supposed to ask for lunch, even if the guy looks like he can handle it. With lunch come obligations, Grandma says, and I'm too young for that. Like, for instance, I know this guy with the parachute pants would have bought me a turkey club. This is a guy who if I ask for a turkey club, he's going to buy it just so I won't think that he can't. And guys like that make me want to push them, just a little bit, just a little bit further than they were thinking they were going to go.

We get to Boardwalk Fries and before I even tell him what size I want he orders me a large, which is really huge, and more fries than I could eat even if I was hungry, which I'm not. I know that Grandma is watching the whole thing and that as soon as she sees the size of the fries she's going to get peeved because I'm only ever supposed to ask for a small because 1) it's unattractive to eat too much and 2) I'm too young to ask for any one item costing more than $2.50 or multiple items costing more than $5.00. And a large fries costs $3.75, which messes up my plan because after the fries I was going to ask for an Orange Julius, which costs $2.50 and is my trademark drink.

The guy's tray is already full with his stuff from China Wok, but he insists on putting the fries on his tray too, and a couple of fries fall into his wonton soup.

"Your fries just fell into my soup," he says, wiggling his eyebrows. "I think that's a pretty good sign," and I giggle because I know I'm supposed to.

At home, I have guys who are friends and who I would never let buy me anything. In fact, when we go to the arcade, we make fun of the girls who giggle at everything and wear pink all the time and are always changing their lipgloss. But it worries me because I look at Mom and our dump of a house and at how unhappy she is all the time and I know I don't want to be like that when I get old.

"Why don't we get a table?" I say and lead the guy up to the platform so that Grandma can see everything. I can't sit too close to Grandma or I'll get distracted. So instead I pick a table right in the middle of the plat-form, where she can see me but where I won't be able to tell how she's reacting to everything. I make sure to sit not facing her so that I don't start looking at Grandma instead of this guy, who's supposed to be the center of my universe.

I know that because of the large fries, Grandma's going to be paying close attention to make sure this guy doesn't get fresh and that I don't do anything trampy. I'm extra-careful to bite the fries in a way that doesn't mess up my lipstick, which means eating them one at a time and biting into them with my front teeth only and with my lips kind of raised up like I'm growling. The guy doesn't eat his food at all while I'm doing this, he just stares and I get scared that I'm doing something wrong, so I peek over at Grandma to see if I can tell what she's thinking, but her face is totally blank and I realize she's not going to give me any hints.

"Babe, you eat those fries sexier than any girl I've ever seen," the guy says, which makes me blush real hard which I know Grandma is going to notice.

"I don't know what you're talking about," I say. "All girls eat fries like this."

"Not where I come from," the guy says and he laughs this low, *heh-heh* laugh that sounds a lot older than I thought he was and which makes me wonder if he's been a sophomore more than once.

"So, you play video games?" I ask, because it's good to find something you have in common and it's a subject I'm pretty good at.

"Nah," he says, sucking up a lo mein noodle real slow, "video games are for dorks."

"Yeah," I say.

"You ever play poker?" he says. The song coming through the speakers is "Maneater," by Hall & Oates, which I use to remind myself to be brave.

"All the time," I say, trying to come up with another way to eat my fries.

"You should come over to my house and play poker with me and my friends some time," he says. "They would like you a lot," he says, "but don't worry. They'd know that you were with me and they wouldn't mess with you."

I can't eat any more fries because I can't think of another way to eat them without messing up my makeup. The guy reaches under the table and touches my knee.

If they touch me, I'm supposed to say I have to go to the bathroom and wait in there until Grandma comes in to tell me they're gone.

Instead I move my knee away and say,

"Buy me an Orange Julius," and he says,

"Sure thing, babe," but takes a few sips of his soup before getting up.

I know if I looked over at Grandma now, we could get out of the Food Court and into her Caddy before the guy in the parachute pants had any idea what was going on. We would laugh like we do sometimes when a guy gets too fresh. Grandma would say, What a scoundrel he was! and I would say Oh, yes, a real scoundrel, and we would go back to Grandma's house and get changed for dinner and by the time we got to the Italian restaurant, it would be like nothing had happened. But I know if I did that today, Grandma would blame me for the fries. Even if I told her that I hadn't asked for a large, she would tell me I must have asked somehow because why else would a guy buy that many fries? But with the Orange Julius, which is my trademark, she'll know that everything went okay despite the fries. She might even decide I'm ready for lunches, because from where Grandma's sitting there's no way she could have seen under the table. So instead of looking at Grandma, I fix my lipstick, which I do so well and so fast that my mouth is perfect by the time the guy in the parachute pants gets back with an extra-large cup.

If I'd thought about it I probably could have guessed he'd get the extra-large, but my eyes get a little wide when I see the cup. Then the guy gives the *heh-heh* smile and says,

"Only the best for you, babe," and there's no way I'm going to be able to drink all that. He puts it in front of me and sits down and pushes his own tray away and says,

"Show me how you drink through a straw," which makes me blush real hard again.

By now, the Food Court is playing "Hot Blooded," by Foreigner, and I know I've got to do this, at least sip a little of it because the Orange Julius is my trademark drink. I hold the cup with one hand and casually put my lips just at the very tip of the straw and suck on the straw until only the slightest bit of it comes up. The guy puts his hand on my knee under the table. I want to say,

"My knee," but I know that it's not.

LONGINGS

The course of true love seldom runs smoothly; often it's more like a wild ride down rapids strewn with jagged rocks. Yet the longing for romance is so potent we risk shattering heartbreak time and again to find our mate. Sometimes it ends with happily-ever-after, but most of the time it leads to a complicated situation that leaves us wondering: what is love, anyway? Nevertheless, romantic love is what we're meant for, what we sing about, and, yes, it is a many splendored thing.

In Claire Davis's "Labors of the Heart," we meet a lonely and overweight janitor who long ago realized love was not for him. When this big man takes a hard fall for a woman in the aisle of a grocery store, he lumbers into uncharted territory. He knows nothing about romance; she's done with men for good. Do they have a chance? Of course not. But never underestimate the tenacity of the human heart.

Lou Mathews's "Crazy Life" makes us wonder why an intelligent and headstrong girl in the barrio would stand by her man—a gang member with dangerous friends, a drug habit, and a murder rap. Well, she loves him, which may nor may not be enough to protect him from the impending doom. Is her lasting affection for this boy noble or foolish or so many fathoms deep it can't be explained?

Dating is a big part of the modern-day mating dance, but the steps can be daunting. In Pam Houston's "Sometimes We Talk About Idaho," a woman faces that most nerve-racking of first encounters, a blind date. She does it mostly to please her father, but this happily independent woman faces an even greater challenge when—yikes—she actually likes the guy.

Romance ought to be simpler in T. C. Boyle's "After the Plague," seeing as how the region has been reduced by disease to only one man and one woman (or close to it). Still, things are stormy. Sure, most of the competition and options have been wiped away, along with all the divorce courts, but people still get on each other's nerves. If the couple in this story had been Adam and Eve, we might none of us be here right now.

LABORS OF THE HEART

CLAIRE DAVIS

The remarkable thing in dreams: people say what he never hears in waking. Fat. They say it to his face, not behind his back, or clear of earshot. The word is succulent in their mouths—"faaat"—stretching out like the waist on his Sansabelt pants. Nothing derogatory about it, only an unabashed honesty. On these mornings, for a few moments, he wakes feeling curiously relieved.

Clarence John Softitch, Pinky to his friends, at five foot eight and 482 pounds on a good day, *is* fat, not large, big, or big-boned. Not hefty, husky, generous, or oversized. Nor robust, portly, or pleasingly plump. He is fat. Enormous. Corpulent. And no delicate euphemisms or polite evasions can relieve him of this knowledge when every movement, whether tying a shoe or climbing a short flight of stairs, becomes a labor of the heart.

Not that he has much to do with people in general. He lives in Clarkston, Washington, a scrappy town of twenty-odd thousand on the eastern edge of the state where the paltry rainfall encourages prickly pear in lawns and 12 percent of the population is on welfare. He works as night janitor at Loyola High School, and when most of the town's folk are gathered in families for dinner, or socially at Hogan's Bar, Pinky's company is the clatter of scrub bucket, mop, and brush. For solace he has his voice— a fine, clear tenor to fill the empty rooms. He sings, "When the moon hits your eye like a big-a pizza pie, that's *amore*."

Not that he knows anything about that. *Amore*, that is.

For he is virginal, a moderate embarrassment at his age, having come

to terms, he believes, with the reality that no one loves a fat man. And so
he has given up on love, the daydreams, the hope, the mooning about, the
unsightly chase and precipitous rejections. Until this Monday, that is, on
one of his twice-weekly food shopping trips, when he sees *her* in the produce
aisle of the northside A & B grocery, a rutabaga under her nose, a peckish
look about her mouth. She's little. A narrow, neatly planed body. There is
about her the solidity, the starkness of a lightning rod.

He finds this fascinating; more than that, it stirs him in a way he's
never imagined, his feet locked like a stammer, his breast tightening unlike
the usual angina. But what is it about this woman? Her shoulders pinned
at attention—the fierce way she sniffs out the proper rutabaga, so that he
feels intimidated. Dwarfed, really. For although Pinky *knows* himself to be
large—talcums each pant leg to keep his thighs from chafing, avoids chairs
with arms—he's always *believed* himself small, just a tiny voice chirping
on the horizon, flotsam in an ocean of flesh. He's amazed at how his vessel
sloshes and wags, jiggles and rolls. The *real him* adrift inside like a buoy
at high tide. He cannot imagine being of consequence in the larger world
beyond bumped tables and broken chairs, the numerous bruises and
insulted flesh so common that he has ceased to wonder at the many ways
the world is rigged against the fat.

But standing in the grocery aisle, he knows for the first time in his
forty-odd years what it means to be *struck* by love.

She passes on the rutabagas, and even as she's whisking out of produce,
he's slipping the vegetable under his nose and then into his cart, perhaps
as a keepsake, as he's never actually eaten one, doesn't know what to do
with the thing bowling down the cart's length, tippling stacked frozen
dinners—breaded fish sticks; Hungry Man slabs of Salisbury steak, mashed
potatoes, and gravy; lasagna; chicken Kiev—and the comfort foods:
doughnut holes, potato chips, a baker's dozen Hostess Ho-Hos, chocolate
cheesecake as a chaser. A front wheel turned sideways thumps, ba bump,
ba bump, ba bump, calling everyone's attention, he thinks, as he trails her
to the checkout lane before he's actually ready.

He tries not to stare, but admires the efficiency of her moves. She
retrieves each item with a lean elegance, and he hangs on to the cart
handle, dizzy with love, half hopes she notices the rutabaga. When she
leaves the store, she's burdened by six plastic sacks hanging plumb from
her fists. She staggers out and pauses in the sunlight, the door frozen open

at her back so that the heat wafts in, and he imagines her body, that small dark column, immune to the glare of sun on concrete, her clothes dry, armpits forever fresh.

By the time he's checked out, she's gone, and as he pulls onto the street he sees her struggling down the block. He closes his teeth against the knocking of his heart and idles behind her, the wide-body Chevy wallowing like a whale in the shallows as he leans across the seat to roll down the window.

"Can I give you a lift?" he asks.

She angles a suspicious look at him—the friendly stranger—but then she stiffens her back along with her upper lip and marches on.

"Just a ride. I'm safe," he says and has to steer around a parked car.

She glances over her shoulder. "Do I look like I need help?" she says. She crooks her elbows and flexes tidy biceps, causing the plastic bags to twist in slow revolutions, and from the cottonwoods white duff spindles down into curbside drifts, a goldfinch flits overhead—a stab of yellow and gone—and still she holds the bags high, until Pinky begins to feel *he* is that assortment of odd bulges and bumps bundled in an unsightly sack turning this way, then that.

Of course she doesn't need help, certainly not from him, and he ducks his head in apology, cheeks flushing with an old but familiar heat. What is left him is this small dignity—he touches a finger to his forehead, as if to tip a cap, and accelerates down the street as though his heart were still intact.

It's a full week before he sees her again, which is odd, because it turns out she's his new neighbor, rents the old Grieger house kitty-corner. Though given his daytime schedule of sleep and hermitage he hasn't noticed the lights on, the mail delivery, the mowed lawn, before this moment. Curious also is how he recognizes her, half concealed as she is beneath the draped branches of a weeping birch, her back to him, head tilted so that the short nap of hair twists into something like a question mark against her neck. No more clue than the spine's rigidity, the belligerence in her stance, and still Pinky's heart begins to toll. He wishes he were driving, but these last three nights he's begun an exercise program—walking the three blocks to work and back. *Morbidly obese*, he's been categorized. Morbidly. As in deadly, not sadly, which is the way he's preferred to construe it. Midway second block, he'll be winded, and by the time he reaches the school door the back of his shirt will be sweated in the early evening cool. He'd walk by her house without stopping, but she's noticed him, turns, and by the look on her face he can tell she can't place him. He tries not to waddle, wishes he were wearing something other than Carhartt coveralls. He tips his finger to his forehead and gives it away.

"The man in the car," she says.

He nods, pleased in spite of himself. He toes up to the lawn to extend a hand. Her own hand disappears in his, but her grip shakes him. "I live in the yellow house." He points over his shoulder. He tells her his name, says, "Call me Pinky," and he wants to say, *All my friends do*, but thinks, *What friends?* and feels a surge of despair. What folly. What gall. What enormous odds. It's overwhelming, this business of love.

"Pinky." Her voice rises. "Rose. I'm Rose Spencer." She doesn't release his fingertips, instead stalks up the lawn with Pinky in tow. "Tell me, what this is?" Rose disengages her hand to point at a branch. In the upper reaches there is a cocoon, a tented web, with freckled bits splotted here and there. In yet another branch, he sees the start of another, and how is it that he hasn't noticed them before? He sights down the row of cottonwoods streetside, the upper reaches. He sighs.

"Tent caterpillars," he says. He hopes she doesn't register the way his flesh quivers as he thinks of the frantic shivering of worms overhead. A phobia, like some folks have for snakes, spiders.

"Are they bad? For the tree?" she asks.

He knows they'll eat their way down a branch, mature, and drop like fruit. He backs up a pace. No more than a couple tents. Not so bad. "We'll keep an eye on them." And suddenly he's using "we," and such audacity stuns him. But she lets him get away with it, nodding her head and escorting him off her lawn.

"If you need anything," he says. "I have a car," he says, "for groceries, anything." She's watching, and he has the sense she's backing away, though her feet are still rooted to the edge of the lawn. "I'm safe," he says, ducks his head.

"How's that?" she asks.

He flushes. Can't believe he's saying this. "Well, you can probably run faster than I can." He laughs as he's always had to.

Rose arches an eyebrow at him. "I don't know what you expect from me." She crosses her arms, cups an elbow in each palm. "But I'm tapped out when it comes to men. Pity, love, anger, compassion—you name it, and I've exhausted it."

"I'm sorry," Pinky says, and he means it. He wonders what could have hurt her so deeply, briefly envies her pain, the experience of being close enough to wound or be wounded. And then, of course, he realizes that's nonsense. Believes he has the perfect vantage for sympathy, from behind this great bulwark of flesh. He's thinking of himself now—the lifetime alone, avoiding pain. He runs a hand down his chest, down the globe of his belly, a gesture he's developed over the years, familiarizing himself with the expanding boundaries of his body. "We're neighbors," he says, and she seems puzzled, but there's something in his face, or his tone, that puts her at ease.

She relaxes the grip on her arms, and says, "Neighbors. I can handle that."

It's his turn to be confused now. He checks his watch, then looks west, to the sunset, as though that might be more accurate. "I have to get on to work—over at the school? I'm the maintenance technician." A smile sweeps across his face. "Night janitor." He avoids her eyes, looks over her shoulder, and the hills rising above the town turn amber, then the color of autumn rushes, and where the light catches the grasses, the bunched sage, it is a luminous fire. It occurs to him just how long it's been since he's *seen* the hills, wonders how it is that he could have moved through these days, these months without noticing how the crowns levitate with light above the rim rock, the dimming crevasses. He backs up a step, and as she turns her attention once again on the yard, he starts away, first one foot and then the other until he finds himself three blocks gone and on the steps of school. He unlocks the door with a jangle of keys, lets them loose to the satisfying snatch and click of the takeup reel, then enters the building. He clamps the door shut, and, flipping on hall lights, he breaks into his best Johnny Mathis voice, *"Chances are . . ."*

They shop together now. One day a week. Separate carts. He's taken it upon himself to keep Rose advised on lawn maintenance. "It's the first yard I've ever taken care of," she confides, and so he understands she's always had a man, and no, he won't infringe because it's obvious she takes delight in adding oil to the lawn mower gasoline and pruning the boxwood hedges, regards each task as an indication of competence in the larger world. "I believe a person could fix anything," she says in the house utensils aisle, "given proper instruction and duct tape." Then she adds, "Except trust." And this is the first hint she's given of what keeps her so clearly focused on staying "neighborly."

Not that he's done much more than buddy his grocery cart up to hers, and although it's true, the contents have more and more begun to resemble hers, still he keeps a cautious distance. He's at a standstill, and all the month of long hours mulling over the mop handle at work, dreaming up ways to woo and win her, have yielded nothing more than any neighbor could claim.

Until today, when she lets slip the tidbit about trust. And then the store manager, Ray Tipp, an old classmate—a starved-looking man who keeps himself anxious with coffee—checks out Pinky's groceries, says, "Got a sale on Hostess Ho-Hos." He lifts a head of broccoli and Roman Meal bread. "You on a diet?"

Pinky can't even run. He feels Rose, next in line, caught up in his embarrassment. He shuffles between the checkout stands, the backside of his trousers snag on a magazine rack, and he endures Ray's curiosity while he frees himself without spilling *Vogue* and *Look* into the aisle. He pays Ray, lifts his bagged groceries from the grinning stock boy. He knows that this too Rose must see, how the young boy's eyes widen and the whites shine like twin moons, roll in their sockets.

Stupid. Stupid to have invited her along. To see this. Still stupid—after all these years—to aim yourself at inevitable hurt. But the damage is done. Rose, after all, is guilty by association, and so he pivots on his heel, the great slowing mass of him, to face this small woman and take her disgust in stride.

She's handing money to Ray. Two twenties, a ten. She fishes out a single and another. Some change. She takes her bags from the boy and waits for Pinky to lead the way, which he does with all the grace he can muster. When he breaks out into the sunshine, his heart is cluttering his chest, so huge, so full it's become. He puffs crossing the parking lot, the bags swinging at his sides, and he sets them on the ground to open the car door for her.

Two blocks from the store, she says, "Why don't you pull into the park? I've bought a melon. We can have a bite."

Just like that.

And why not? he thinks. A picnic, something he hasn't done since his mother passed on, and for a brief moment he can almost hear her, see the woman she was, all comfort—bosomy and dimpled elbows—pressing food onto him, the sound of other children chasing and laughing. He is hiccuping tears. "Eat," she says. "Like a good boy. Never mind those others. They're jealous you gotta momma can cook." She chucks a finger under his chin. "Your daddy was a *big* man." By this he understands that he too would be . . . large . . . and in her eyes that was good.

Rose directs him onto River Street and down to the small riverside park. He used to come here as a younger man, walked the levee at night to imagine himself with a woman, strolling the paths or swooning on a bench in the grip of passion and the moony night, like any one of a number of couples whispering from behind the willows' curtains or lolling in the tall blue grasses riverside.

He follows Rose's lead, carrying the plastic-sacked melon in both hands like a gift, an offering of the magi, and she brings them to the base of a cottonwood. He is breaking a sweat, and the air is brilliant with light on water so that he squints the moisture from his eyes, releases a great round sigh, "Aaah," and he's just so damned grateful for these simple pleasures—river, melon, woman—that he's unlikely to recover his voice anytime soon, so he sighs again.

Rose has seated herself in the grass. He wishes she were wearing a flowing skirt, a frilly blouse, a wide-brimmed straw hat, instead of the baggy jeans and T-shirt that slouch on her tiny frame, and then he feels an ingrate. Clothes. What do they signify? Certainly not the moment. She takes the melon from him, plops it in her lap like a placid child, then pats the grass beside her, and he faces the task of lowering himself. Pinky thinks to remain standing, strike a noble pose, but she's already gazing off across the wide blue river to the hills opposite. He braces one hand against the tree, crooks a knee, stretches the other leg behind, and bends cautiously forward and down and down some more. It's a struggle against mass, gravity. His joints pop in series. He tries not to gasp or puff, and that's nearly as much effort as kneeling. His crotch feels like a wishbone, ready to snap, and then he's down without having fallen. His face is red; he can tell. He filches a handkerchief out of his rear pocket and towels off his forehead, neck, the skinny V of flesh in the unbuttoned top of his button-up shirt.

"Do you have a knife?" she asks.

And he does, though he must lean back, lift his stomach, and squeeze his hand into the narrow flap of cloth, cutting the blood to his fingers as he feels for the knife. Finally he frees it, a pocket Buck knife with all the appointments—even a corkscrew. But she lifts the knife away, slaps the screw back into its steel nest, and locks open the large blade. She stabs into the melon's meat, saws a chunk free, and scrapes the seeds back into the exposed heart of the fruit. She hands the wedge to him, and he waits for her to join him.

"People on the whole are an unlikable bunch," she says, sinks the knife to the hilt into the melon's rind. "Take my advice. Never fall in love with them."

Pinky laughs, but it's a squeezed little thing, his chest constricting.

"You think you know cruelty, I know you do." She saws into the melon. "But the cruelty of strangers, or friends, is nothing"—she wags a finger in his face—"compared to what love can do." She is tight-lipped. Her brows beetle, and the air about her seems charged with a static energy. She bites into the melon, tells him about her first husband, his one-night stands, moves on to her second husband and his affairs. Tells it all in four short sentences, as if she can't bite off the ends of words hard enough, spit it out fast enough.

"What did I learn from it, you want to know . . ."

She dabbles at the corner of her mouth with a fingertip, where some melon juice drips down, and Pinky thinks he has never seen anything more delectable. He'd like to take her finger into his mouth and suck it dry.

She stretches her legs out, leans against the tree, and tells him of her third and last husband's affairs. How she then called the woman, wanted to see her. "Couldn't help myself. Called a complete stranger—though it seemed I had the right, we'd shared so much. I don't know what I expected. She came to my house. Not the first time, I could tell that right off—the way she found her way to his chair."

Rose rubbed the back of her head against the tree's bark, a leisurely scratching. "She was a short, stumpy-legged little thing, not cute, no, not even handsome. But interesting. Perky. She says, 'I didn't mean to ruin your life.' She was being sincere, but of course she was flattering herself. After all, my life wasn't ruined. Merely changed. I told her that."

She looked over at Pinky. "Don't you wonder at how I could be so collected? So smug?"

"I can't imagine," Pinky says.

"No." She leans over, pats his hand. "Of course you can't. And of course I was full of crap." She sighed. "If my life wasn't ruined, it was the next thing to it. Rubble. That's what I was left with. Rubble."

She squeezes her left breast, and Pinky knows it is her heart she means, but all he can picture is the tender flesh crumpled in her fist, and he wants to loosen her fingers, cradle her breast and heart in the palm of his hand, which he discovers is sweating, so he swipes it down his pant leg. And then, wonder of all wonders, he reaches over with his newly dried hand and takes the melon from her, lifts the knife away, slices another piece, skins and offers it to her.

Which she declines.

"Three strikes, you're out. Isn't that right?" she asks.

"In baseball," Pinky says, and he wants to sound decisive but hears how his voice trails off. He's stuck with the melon wedge, dripping through his fingers onto his pant leg.

"Yes," she agrees. "In baseball *and in men.*"

And what can Pinky say? He eats the melon slice, wipes his hand on the grass. On the river, a pair of Canada geese paddle upstream, six goslings drifting in their wake. Sunlight crooks across the water's surface, and shadows swim the face of the hills opposite. Pinky blinks, feels moisture budding behind his eyes, and blinks again. He begins to comprehend the scale of his task—wooing this woman—even if he weren't hobbled by his own body. He's still holding the knife, and he looks down at his belly, wishes he could slice away the flesh, pare down to some more supple version of himself that would be capable of the acrobatics—walking, sitting, bending over—that normal, everyday people perform in everyday courtship. He wants to be handsome for her.

A pair of young girls roller-blade down the sidewalk, the wheels buzzing with the sound of enormous hummingbirds. They wind down the path, skinny legs and arms knotted in protective pads. Their laughter is a shouting, and Pinky admires the honesty of it. He wonders what Rose sounds like when she laughs. He wonders if she laughs.

Rubble, she'd said, and he questions the state her heart's in now. "I'm not like those men," he says.

"Why?" she asks. "Because you're fat?" And it's just a statement. "Because you think other women wouldn't find you attractive?"

Truth is he hadn't thought of it that way, but he begins to see this could work for him. He nods.

"Another way that you're safe?" she asks.

He nods again, though he feels like he's stepping into something unseen, something with teeth.

She stares across the river. "Do you think that little of yourself, or me?"

It's worse than he'd feared, certain now that she despises him for his clumsiness, his transparent eagerness. He blames himself and his lack of experience; he blames the hour of the day and the bristling grass that torments his ankles. He tells her he's a fool and that he respects her and her friendship. Those are the words he uses, *respect* and *friendship*, and she continues to stare out across the river. He asks her to understand, he's not used to . . . to . . . picnics.

Her brows furrow, and she says, as if she hasn't heard him, "My last husband was different. Where the others'd been tall, he was short. A bookish man with a sense of humor. He couldn't change the oil in the car, but he was mad for opera. I believed he was different, as day is to night." She wags her head. "But finally he was only a different kind of night. And this is much too lovely a day"—she leans back on her elbows—"to quibble. I'm done with men." Rose rolls onto her side, facing Pinky. "Except as friends. Take it or leave it."

Pinky nods and heaves a sigh, but even as she pats his hand and closes her eyes to rest, he is studying the logistics of getting back on his feet.

Late at night, in the gym, Pinky plots strategy. He turns on the overheads, and the constellation of bulbs shine from the floor's mirror finish. He has cleaning down to an art, dry-mopping the area in under an hour, starting at the foot of the bleachers, left to right, and threading his way in overlapping lanes down and back until he's dusted his way into the boys' locker room, where the real work begins. Though, as it is summer, this chore is reduced to a twice-weekly touchup instead of the nightly tour during the school year. He switches to a wet mop, fills the big steel bucket on casters with hot water, a splash of disinfectant Sparkle, and bleach. He works backward, kicking the bucket ahead of him like a troublesome dog. The mop bangs against lockers, and Pinky loves the rat-a-tat-tat off the empty doors. Sings "Frankie and Johnny" to their machine-gun accompaniment.

Sees himself as Johnny, but can't imagine doing her wrong, can't conceive of such discontent. He rolls the bucket into the boys' bathroom. Lifts his voice to the tiled walls. *At least that's the way the story goes. Frankie bought everything for Johnny, from his sports car to his Ivy League clothes.* He buffs the floor, glances in the mirror.

His face seems different, and maybe it's just love has transformed him. Or has he lost weight? He lifts the putty knife from the cart, scrapes at a wad of paper toweling glommed to the underside of a sink. When he straightens up, he fidgets a finger into his waistband, snugs in two. Yes. Oh yes. He's lost weight. *Friend came running to Frankie, said, You know I wouldn't tell you no lie. I saw your man driving that sports car with a chick named Nellie Bly—*

And this is the tough part. He enters a stall. How can he convince Rose of his own true heart? And damn it. He slaps the brush in the toilet bowl, squirts in blue disinfectant, swabs, and flushes. He deserves one good shot at it, doesn't he? He slaps the cover up, scrubs—cover down—scrubs—backs out of the stall, then moves on to the next and the next. Patience, he tells himself, and though he's only known Rose as a friend and neighbor a little over two months, he's got a forty-year backlog of empty nights, and Pinky stops, envisions the calamity of another forty empty years, and finds himself doubled over one of the toilets. When his heart calms in his chest and the angina eases under his left wing bone, he backs out of the stall. The room is bright, as only locker-room bathrooms can be, with the high banks of fluorescent lights buzzing and reflecting off the mirrors and stainless steel doors, the white porcelain sinks and urinals all ablaze, so that when he looks in the mirror this time what he sees is his forehead shining with sweat and the enormous bell of his body overexposed in white overalls, and for a moment he loses himself against the white wall tiles.

He leaves the bucket and mop, the toilet brush and disinfectant, and crosses back through the locker room, turning off lights as he goes, through the gym and out the side door. He stands on the asphalt stoop. In the school parking lot, the arc lamp's cone of light seethes with winged insects—swirling, bumping, a luminous feast that the nighthawks scoop through. Pinky breathes deeply, feels the moist back of his shirt cooling. Crickets pick up where they'd left off. He steps away from the building and walks until the locked school folds into the night. He walks slow and steady, his heart easing, chest lightening. He knows he will have to return to work, but for now he turns up a side street where lamplight streams out onto porches and grass.

He stays to the sidewalk but glances in each house. Where drapes are open, it's the furniture he notices—which place has a piano, or a lamp centered in the window like a beacon. Then there are all the dining rooms with tables bunkered by chairs. So many chairs. Seascapes over the sofa, mounted deer, or the grouping of family pictures like a lineup in the post office. Once in a while he glimpses the people. Sometimes he believes he can smell their dinner: chicken, hamburger, barbecued ribs. Or, more vaguely, Italian cuisine, Oriental, Middle Eastern. He feels a stirring of hunger, but he tucks his two fingers into his waistband again and thinks apple instead of apple pie. He journeys down another side street and exchanges greetings with a man smoking a pipe on his front porch. He passes a young couple and the woman titters, but they don't notice Pinky, so wrapped up are they, and he finds that utterly disarming. He meets more people strolling under the streetlamps. Why, it seems to him that the whole town must be spilling out into the warm night. Or maybe this is the way the world congregates when he's alone, in his school, his home. And there it is. His house. Locked tight and shuttered close. He opens the front door, the drapes, turns on all the lights. Then he steps back out on the sidewalk to see what he can of himself. He's reluctant to look, but discovers he doesn't fare so badly. Tomorrow, first thing, he will dig out the old photos, frame the one of his mother and father's wedding, the portrait of his grandfather—big-chested, with thighs like a Percheron. It will take so little, he thinks, and he pivots on his heel to look across the street, to the house of his beloved. The lights behind the drapes are a wan glow, and he's stricken with how tidy the place is, how self-contained. He feels . . . what is it? Not exactly love, but a stirring that is equally unfamiliar from his end of things, and . . . disconcerting—call it pity. He wishes he could step into her life as easily as into his home, open it wide to this sweet night. He heaves a sigh and looks up, over the trees and over the tops of houses to where the distant hills shoulder the dark beneath the quickening stars.

He means to take her on a date, but he doesn't call it that. He doesn't dare. He mentions the movie, casually, over groceries. He tells Rose, "Dutch treat," to allay her suspicion. It's a love story, but he doesn't mention that either. She offers to buy the popcorn. "Only fair," she says. "All the gas you've used on grocery trips."

Pinky accepts. He feels pretty smart. Of course he hasn't thought about the theater seats, and though his pants are looser now and sitting upright no longer cuts off his wind, still it's a tight, tight squeeze, but he manages. He's appreciative for her small kindness of unbuttered popcorn. She'd noticed his weight loss a couple days ago. "Hope you're not doing this for me," she'd said, and when he replied, "No," he could see she was unprepared for the truth, some small part of her stung by his admission. He felt encouraged.

It *was* a sappy film. Any other time he would have been the first to ridicule the sentimentality. Except now it is Rose scoffing, and that provokes in him a desire to defend it. She curls her lip, and Pinky lets his heart go soft. Walking back to the car, she recaps some of the *lowlights*. When she snorts at the dialogue, Pinky taps her arm with a finger, says, "You could give it a chance."

"You can't mean it."

"It had heart," he says.

She pinches his arm. "It had a lobotomy. Not the same thing."

"Ouch," he says.

She goes on. "What you don't know"—she shakes a finger at him—"is that this kind of willful ignorance about the *realities* of love wearies me sometimes."

They drive away from the theater in silence. He wants to talk but is embarrassed to admit that there's little willful about his ignorance. Inexperience, certainly.

He suggests the 410 Drive-In for a bite, and she agrees. Rose's hamburger fills her hands, drapes over her fingers, lobs chunks of lettuce and pickle into the napkin covering her lap, while Pinky's grilled chicken breast sandwich is a pale, insignificant thing in comparison. It hardly seems worth the effort. He takes baby bites to stretch it out. She offers him a sip of her malt, and it's so intimate a gesture he's dumbfounded. He accepts the plastic cup from her hands and takes the straw—squeezed between her lips just moments earlier—into his mouth, tongues the tip tenderly. It is a jolt of pure chocolate, cold and clean and sweet. His eyes close.

So this is what it's like—the taste of a woman—and there's a curious quivering at the base of his spine. And of course he *knows* that's not the case, but he enjoys the *idea* of it and has to stop himself from draining her malt.

"You think I'm harsh," she says, "about the movie. But the point is"— she crumples the emptied hamburger wrapping—"romantic love suggests we are incomplete without another, in need of salvation. You're led to believe that you'll be a better person if there's someone around to expect it. But somewhere down the line, you find the cost of these expectations too dear. What? you say. Eat the same cooking? Sleep on the same side of the bed? Give up variety? Implausible, if not impossible. All you will *ask* for is a little kindness, but what you will *want* is more than anybody can give— their undivided attention for the rest of their life—and so you struggle and struggle and hurt each other endlessly.

"Three marriages, over twenty-five years' worth. Imagine—twenty-five years attempting love. Trust me. It's a complication you're better off without."

Rose sighs, pats her lips dry, then sets the soiled napkin and empty malt cup back on the serving tray. "Take me home," she says. She sounds utterly weary.

Pinky takes a deep breath, resettles in the seat. His stomach bumps the steering wheel. He drives the long way, down Bridge Street, over to Riverside, up to Highland, slowly. How painful she makes it sound, *twenty-five years,* but all he can think of is turning over in bed to find someone there, of eating someone else's cooking, and it sounds grand to Pinky, worth the risk, the heartache. He *knows* what it's like to be alone—the long haul of it, not the early phase, when the day winds down because *you've* nothing better to do and stretching across an empty bed still seems a luxury.

It's coming on to seven in the evening, and the sky is yet bright with daylight. He stops at the school, invites her in. He shows her the broom closet, the mops. He shows her classrooms, the new computer lab—shakes his head; feather dusting, he explains. He takes her into the gym, throws on the lights just to show her how the floor shines. He stands center court and lobs a high A at her. He could almost swear she blushes. He proceeds to sing the only song he can think of with her name in the title, "The Yellow Rose of Texas."

On the way out of the building, she says, "A most unlikely but lovely serenade. Thank you." They leave the car there to walk the three blocks home. He knows she slows her pace to match his. It is early evening, and the shortening daylight lapses into a dim gloaming. Dusky-winged ash aphids are swarming—bumbling clouds of blue-bodied mites that rise like yeast from the grass. Late summer, they come down from the Camas and Palouse prairies to swim in the warmer valley air. By full evening, they will web together in gray winding sheets around the south side of the ash tree trunks, where they will shiver into their final, short-lived ecstasy. But now they are a squall, riding the turmoil of heat convections and cooling drafts. They speckle the couple's clothes, dust their hair. Pinky is enthralled with the tiny creatures, the enormous bulb of their bodies and improbable flight. They bobble and fall, rise and fumble. This is not a matter of grace.

Rose waves a hand through the air in front of her. They stop on the far edge of the cloud, and Rose ducks her head, swipes at an eye. Pinky can see a bead of aphids riding her eyelashes.

"Ow," she says, her eye tearing.

"Here," he comforts, nips her chin between thumb and forefinger, lifts her face to what is left of the light. Rose is a woman who has little truck with makeup. There's no attempt to disguise the lines, the thinning skin. He is captivated, as he was the first time he saw her, by the static energy of this woman, her relentless honesty, all her life available in her face, her eyes. And this is the thing he both fears and admires, how she has been pared down to the bone, tried and fired as he never has been. Though his fingers barely grace her chin, he feels her energy, some galvanic current of old doubts running through her, and she sidesteps under his hand. He takes a steadying breath, says, "Hold still." He spits on his free thumb, touches that small drop of moisture to the corner of her eye. The speck of blue floats off the white, onto Pinky's thumb, and he neatly lifts it away.

Up and down the block, house lights come on, and children shoo cats out of front doors. The hills over the town flatten, grow larger with the dark. There's no help for it, but Pinky feels a melancholy he's hard put to explain, and it has to do with the onset of dark and the sudden still. It has to do with the small woman at his side, her mistrust, and his own lifetime of hiding, in his house, his work, and foremost his own flesh. And he sees it has to do with fear—the way we run through our lives in terror of it—and everything to do with despair, and perhaps, he thinks, that is what despair is, finally, a lack of daring. He feels savvy. Overhead, a crow lifts from the treetop, banks toward the river with a hard laugh—ha, ha, ha.

In another block they stop again so that Pinky can catch his breath. He pants in the quiet, shakes his head. He will lose weight—he will because he cannot go on as he always has, he understands this now—but he also knows he will always be big. Not small, or even trim, and he is struck by this. It has been with him so long, this ocean of flesh. Pinky feels he must tell Rose. Warn her. "I will always be fat," he says.

"Yes," she agrees. She lays a hand on his forearm. "As I will always be bitter," she says.

They stand that way in the new dark, and he thinks, should a young husband look out from his living room window, or should the young wife hurrying home from errands come across them standing so, they would think Rose and Pinky some middle-aged couple of long years—the way Rose's hand is anchored on his arm. And he wonders about the couples he has so long envied, how much is illusion—a public face for the private griefs and hurts they harbor? He thinks of the depth of Rose's bitterness, the earnest way in which she confirms it, and he understands it's as deep and abiding as the bones seated in the continent of his flesh. It humbles him, how fiercely she is grounded in her resolve.

And he does not feel up to the task. Sees himself as the light-weight in this struggle. His stomach gripes, and will not be consoled by the pat of his hand. How he already misses the easy comfort of food, the anonymity. He feels a nervousness, an anxiousness like a missed meal, or the temptation of chocolate before sleep. He sways from foot to foot, rocking in place. A terror steals upon him that he cannot fathom, so that his feet are seized in place and his fat plumbs him to the earth while she stands stark and quiet at his side as if forged of consequences larger than his imagining. He sees she is not the rod but the lightning itself, flinty bits striking off—old loves, grudges, misfortunes, a hundred errors in judgment, and more—quizzing his friable heart. He should run. He should bolt, for he senses this is a struggle deeper than the naive courtship he'd embarked on. Not the territory of novices. Not for the uninitiated. It is a journey of days, years, a chronic case of heartache, the relentless wooing to win and lose, again and again. He almost laughs, for all his assurances to Rose of how safe he is—he sees now that it is *she* who is the danger . . . always has been.

Overhead, the clouds quail beneath the rising moon. He turns his face away. He slows his panic by imagining the imaginable: the march of days, the orderliness of work—nights, cleaning, trips to the grocery store, lawn care, and diets. Conversation that spills over from day to day, and running jokes. He wonders how they will look in a year, two, five. Will she grow generous as he grows slight? He steadies, takes a deep breath. What he wants, he realizes, more than anything, is to imagine a time when fear will carry no weight in his heart. When love will need no proof. He squints into the dark, as if to make out the features of that distant time—the heel of a foot striking the floor as she steps down from her side of his bed, the shape of her face, is it Rose? But he cannot know this. Not now. Not yet. And perhaps for now the question is enough. He quashes the impulse to push back his sleeves. Instead, he leads them arm in arm, their bodies swaying each its own way, beneath the steepled canopy of sycamore where the first flush of moonrise swims the wavering shadows in a school of light.

CRAZY LIFE

LOU MATHEWS

Chuey called me from the jail. He said it was all a big mistake. I said, Sure Chuey, like always, que no? What is it this time, weed or wine? He said it was something different this time. I said, You mean like reds, angel dust, what? Chuey says, No Dulcie, something worse.

I said, So? Why call me? Why don't you call that Brenda who was so nice to you at the party. He said Dulcie. Listen. It's a lot worse. I got to get a lawyer. Then he like started to cry or something. Not crying—Chuey wouldn't cry—but it was like he had a hard time breathing, like he was scared. I couldn't believe it. I didn't do it, Dulcie, he told me. I didn't do nothing. I was just in the car.

I got scared then. Chuey, I said, Can anybody hear you? He said there was a chota—a cop—around and some dude from the D.A.'s office, but not close. I told him, Shut up Chuey. Just shut up. Don't say nothing to nobody. I'll come down. Chuey said, I don't know if they'll let you see me.

They'll let me, I said, Hang on.

I skipped school, fifth and sixth periods, just gym and home wreck, and hitchhiked up to Highland Park. I been there before, the Highland Park cop shop. Chuey's been busted there three or four times. Nothing bad, just drunk and one time a joint in the car.

This time it looked bad. They had a bunch of reporters there. This T.V. chick was on the steps when I come up, standing in front of the bright lights saying about the police capturing these guys. She kept saying the same words, Drive-by murders. Drive-by murders. There was these two kids, brothers, and one was dead and the other was critical.

I walked up the steps and all these people started yelling. This one guy tells me, You can't come up here while we're shooting. I told him, You don't own the steps. The T.V. lights go out and the chick with the microphone says, Fuck. Then she turns around to me, real sarcastic and says, Thanks a lot honey. I told her, Chinga tu madre, Bitch, I got rights too. My boyfriend's in there. I got more business here than you. She gave me the big eyes and went to complain.

I went on inside, up to the desk and said I'm here to see Chuey Medina. Who? he says and he looks at the list, We got a Jesus Medina. That's Chuey, I tell him.

He looks at me, up and down, this fat Paddy with the typical little cop moustache. What's your name, he says. Dulcie Medina, I tell him. It's not, but if they don't think we're related they won't let me see Chuey. Dulcie? he says, does that mean Sugar? Sweet, I tell him it means sweet.

You related? he says. What the hell, I'm thinking, God can't get me till I get outside. I tell him, I'm his wife.

Well, sweetheart, he says, nobody gets to see Jesus Medina until he's been booked. He says it Jeezus, not Hayzhoos the way it's supposed to be pronounced, like he's making a big point.

He's *been* booked, I say. He called me. They wouldn't have let him call me if he hadn't been booked already. The cop looks real snotty at me but he knows I'm right. Just a minute, he says. He gets on the phone. When he gets off he says, You'll have to wait. You can wait over there.

How long? I say. He gets snotty again, I don't know, sweetheart. They'll call me.

Cops, when they don't know what to do, they know to make you wait. I hung out, smoking, for awhile. Outside on the steps, the lights are on and that same blonde T.V. bitch is holding a microphone up to a guy in a suit; he's banging his briefcase against his knee while he talks. I come out the door as the guy is saying about We have to send a message to gang members that we will no longer tolerate—blah, blah, blah, like that—and then all this stuff about the Community.

Hey, I tell him, are you the D.A.? They won't let me see my husband, Chuey Medina. He turns around. The blondie is mouthing at me GO AWAY. I tell the D.A. guy, They won't let him talk to a lawyer. Isn't he entitled to legal representation? Those are the magic words. He grabs me by the arm, Mrs. Medina, he says, let's talk inside. The blondie jerks a thumb across her throat and the lights go out. She looks at me and thinks of something. Keep rolling, she says, and the lights go on again. Mrs. Medina, she says, Mrs. Medina. Could we talk with you a moment? The D.A. still has hold of my arm and he pulls me through the door. She gives him a nasty look and then turns around to the lights again, I can hear her as we're going through the door.

In a dramatic development, she says, here at the Highland Park Police Station, the wife of alleged drive-by murderer Jesús-Chuey-Medina has accused the district attorney's office . . . The D.A. says, Goddammit. I don't hear what she says after that, my legs get like water and he has to help me over to the bench. Chuey didn't kill nobody, I tell him, he wouldn't. He looks at me funny and I remember I'm supposed to already know everything. I straighten up and tell him, Chuey wants a lawyer.

That's simply not a problem, Mrs. Medina, he tells me, an attorney will be provided. I *know* Mr. Medina has been offered an attorney.

No, I say, he wanted a certain one. He told me on the phone, but your chingadera phone is such junk that I couldn't hear the name. I have to talk to him.

He gives me another funny look and goes over to the guy at the desk. Look, he tells the cop, I don't know what's going on here, but I don't want *any* procedural fuckups on this one.

The cop says, Big case huh? and the D.A. tells him, This is the whole enchilada, Charlie. Where are you holding Medina?

Second floor tank.

Okay, he says, We'll use the conference room there. Call ahead. The cop looks at me and tells the D.A., We'll need a matron.

I know what that means. One time before, when I went to see my brother Carlos in jail, they gave me a strip search. It was some ugly shit. They put their fingers everywhere, and I mean everywhere, and the lady who did it, she got off on it. You could tell. My ass was sore for a week. I swore to God then that I'd never let anybody do that to me again.

Bullshit, I yell. No strip search. The D.A. guy whirls around. The cop says, If it's a face to face meeting with a prisoner, the Captain says skin search. That's the way we play it.

The D.A. tells him, I'll take responsibility on this one. We'll do a pat search and I'll be with her every step after that. I'm going to walk this one through. He holds the cop on the arm, We got cameras out there Charlie, he says.

The matron is waiting for me in this little room. Undo your blouse, is the first thing she tells me. I already told them, I say, I ain't going to strip. Just the top two buttons, she says, visual inspection, honey. I have to make sure your bra's not loaded.

I undo the buttons and hold the blouse open. Just some kleenex, I tell her. She checks me out and then pats me down. Then she starts poking in my hair. They always do that. Some pachuca thirty years ago supposedly had a razor blade in her beehive and they're still excited about it. They never do it to any Anglo chicks.

The D.A. guy meets me outside and we walk through the first floor jail. It's like walking through the worst party you ever been to in your life. All these guys checking me out. Putting their hands through the bars and yelling. Ola, Chica. Hey, Chica, over here, they keep saying, and worse stuff. This one dude keeps making these really disgusting kissing noises. Guys can be weird. I give the dude making the kissing sounds the finger and make my walk all sexy on the way out, shaking my ass. They all go wild. Serves them right.

Chuey is in this big cell, all by himself except for one other guy. When I see who that is, I know why Chuey's in trouble. Sleepy Chavez is sitting next to him. I don't know why they call him Sleepy. He's wired most of the time. I think he might have been a red freak once. Sleepy is one vato loco. The craziest I know. Everything bad that happens on 42nd Avenue starts with Sleepy Chavez.

There's this guy that shines shoes outside Jesse's Barber Shop. I thought he was retarded but it turns out he got in a fight with Sleepy in like sixth grade and Sleepy kicked him so hard in the huevos that the guy ain't been right since. And what's really sick is that Sleepy *loves* getting his shoes shined there.

Chuey doesn't look so good. He's got bruises on his cheeks, a cut on his forehead and his hand's bandaged up. He looks like what the 42nd Flats, that's his gang, call resisting arrest. He looks sick too, pale and his eyes are all red. Sleepy sees me first. He's chewing on his fingers, looks up and spits out a fingernail. Sleepy can't leave his fingers alone. When he was little, his sister told me, his mom used to put chili juice on them.

He's always poking them in his ears or picking his nose or something. You don't want to be alone with him.

Chuey stands up while the cop is unlocking the door. He just looks at me and his eyes are so sad it makes me feel sick. He looks worse than when his father died or even when the guys from White Fence burned his car and laughed at him. Sleepy Chavez looks at me and chucks his head at Chuey. Watch your mouth, Medina, he says.

They take us in this big room. The cop stands by the door. The D.A. guy sits down at the end of this long table and we go down to the other. Chuey reaches out and touches my face. Dulcie, he says, Mi novia. Chuey only calls me that when he's really drunk or sentimental, he never has asked me to marry him. No touching, the cop says. Keep your hands on the table. I figure Chuey needs cheering up so I slip off my shoe and slide my foot up on the inside of his leg and rub him under the table.

Aye, Chuey, I tell him, all happy, que problemas you have, Chuey. My toes are rubbing a certain place, but Chuey surprises me he doesn't even push back.

Dulcie, he says, They think I was the shooter.

Keep your voice down, I say, What did you tell them? Exactamente.

We didn't say nothing. We got to stick together, like Sleepy says. They haven't got any witnesses.

Chuey, I say, one of those guys is still alive.

He sits up when I tell him that.

It doesn't matter, Chuey says, neither of them saw us. All the cops got is Sleepy's car. They ain't got the gun. Sleepy threw it out when they were chasing us. Chuey, I said, were you driving? he just looks at me for awhile and then he says, yeah. I ask, How come you were driving?

He had the shotgun, Chuey said, I had to drive.

I can tell when Chuey's lying, which is most of the time; I think he was telling the truth. Chuey, I said, you're crazy. They'll put you both away. You don't owe Sleepy nothing.

Chuey looks mean at me, his eyes get all skinny. It was my fault we got caught, he says. We should have got away. I hit another car and wrecked Sleepy's Mustang. We tried to hide and the cops found us. I owe Sleepy, so just shut up Dulcie.

It's hopeless to argue with Chuey when he gets like this. Muy macho. You can't talk to him about his friends, even the jerks. He won't believe me over them. Chuey says, I'm gonna need a good lawyer. Get me Nardoni.

Tony Nardoni is this big lawyer all the drug dealers in East L.A. use. Chuey I say, I don't think Nardoni does this kind of stuff. I think he just does the drugs.

Yeah he does, Chuey says, he's a lawyer isn't he? Sometimes Chuey can be just as dumb as his friends; it's not even worth telling him. Now he's all puffed up. You call Nardoni, Chuey says, Tell him I'm a compañero of Flaco Valdez. Tell him we're like this, Chuey holds up two crossed fingers, Tight. Flaco Valdez is like the heavy duty drug dealer in Highland Park and Shaky Town. As usual, Chuey's bullshitting. Flaco never ran with 42nd Flats and he deals mostly smack, so Chuey isn't even one of his customers. It's just that Flaco Valdez is the biggest name that Chuey can think of. O.K., I tell him, I'll call Nardoni. Now what about your mom?

Don't call her, Chuey says, all proud, I don't want her to know about this. Chuey, I say, Chuey you big estupido, she *is* going to hear about this. It's going to be in the papers and on T.V.

O.K., Chuey says, like he's doing me this big favor, You can call her. Tell her they made a big mistake. Right Chuey, I'm thinking. Smart, Chuey. Pretend it didn't happen, like always. That's going to be a fun phone call for me. His mom is going to go crazy.

I know better, but I have to ask. Chuey?, I say. Why did you do such a stupid thing?

They was on our turf!, Chuey says. They challenged us. Like we didn't have any huevos, Chica. We got huevos!

And whose smart idea was it to shoot those boys? As if I didn't know. Chuey just looks at me, he doesn't say nothing.

Chuey, I say, was you high? He looks down at the table, when he looks up again, I can't believe it, his eyes are wet. He sees me looking so he closes them. He just sits there, with his eyes closed, pulling on his little chin beard. God, he's such a pretty dude. Ay, Dulcie, he says. His eyes open and he gives me that smile, the one I have to argue to get, the one I love him for. What can I say?, Chuey tells me, La Vida Loca, no? La Vida Loca.

Right Chuey, I think, La Vida Loca. The Crazy Life. It's the explanation for everything on 42nd Ave.

The D.A. knocks on the table. Time, he says. I look right at him, I got to talk to you. Chuey cuts his eyes at me but I don't care. I never done anything like this, I never gone against him but now I have to. Sleepy

Chavez could give a shit if Chuey takes the fall. Chuey doesn't get it, he thinks he's tough. If he goes to a real jail, they'll bend him over. They'll fry those huevos of his that he's always talking about.

I walk over to the D.A. and sit down. I tell him, Sleepy Chavez was the shooter. Chuey was driving and he was stoned. If Chuey testifies what will he get? That D.A. sees me for the first time. The numbers turn over in his eyes like a gas pump.

Mrs. Medina, he says, You are not a lawyer, I cannot plea bargain with you. If you were a lawyer I would probably tell you that your client is guilty and that we can prove it.

You got some witnesses? I tell him. He doesn't say nothing but the numbers start rolling again.

Chuey stands up and yells at me, Dulcie you stupid bitch, just shut up. He's all pale and scared. The cop walks over and sits him down.

I'm going to get him a lawyer, I say. The D.A. tells me, If you get a lawyer, we will talk. I would say better sooner than later—he has this little smile—before a witness shows up.

One other thing, I tell him, if I was you I'd put Chuey in a different cell from Sleepy Chavez.

Chuey won't kiss me goodbye. He pushed me away, all cold. He won't look at me. Out in the hall, he won't look at Sleepy Chavez either. Sleepy checks that out good and then when he sees that the cop is taking Chuey someplace else, he starts banging on the bars and screaming in Spanish. Hombre muerto, he's screaming, Hombre muerto. The D.A. looks at me and asks, What's he saying? Dead man, I tell him, he says dead man.

The D.A. walks me back downstairs to the desk and shakes my hand. Thank you Mrs. Medina, he says.

I tell him, Look, don't call me Mrs. Medina no more. O.K.? They're going to check and find out anyway and it doesn't make any difference. It's not Mrs. Medina, I tell him, It's Dulcie Gomez. I'm only married in my mind.

I got what I wanted, I guess. Chuey's lawyer who was this woman from the Public Defender's office, and Chuey's mom, and me, we all worked on Chuey. We worked on him real good. Chuey testified against Sleepy Chavez. We talked him into it.

The D.A. wouldn't make any deals. The brother that was on the critical list recovered but he never came to court. He hadn't seen nothing and they didn't need him anyway. They done this test that showed Sleepy fired a gun and then they found the gun. Some tow truck driver brought it in. It was under a car he towed away. Sleepy's fingerprints was all over it. The only thing the D.A. said he would do, if Chuey testified, was talk to the judge when it was time for the sentencing. Ms. Bernstein, Chuey's lawyer, said it was probably as good a deal as we could get.

Chuey had to stand trial next to Sleepy. Every day Sleepy blew him kisses and told him he was a pussy and a maricon. Ms. Bernstein never complained about it. She said it might help with the jury.

I was surprised at the judge. I didn't think she would let that stuff go on. Every day Sleepy did something stupid. There was all this yelling and pointing, and she never said nothing. The judge was this black chick about forty. She wore a different wig and different nails every day. She sat there playing with her wooden hammer. It didn't seem like she was listening. If you ask me, she was losing it. She called a recess once when one of her nails broke. Ms. Bernstein was real polite to her. She said this was the best judge we could get because she was known for her light sentences.

Ms. Bernstein didn't even try to prove that Chuey was innocent. All she did was show that he didn't know what he was doing. She said that he was stoned that day and she said that he was easily led. Even Chuey's mom got up and said that Chuey was easily led, from when he was a little boy.

It was weird to watch. They talked about him like he wasn't there. Ms. Bernstein would show that Chuey was a fool and then Sleepy's lawyer would try to show that Chuey wasn't a fool. He couldn't do it. Everybody in that courtroom thought Chuey was a fool by the time they got done. Chuey sat at that table listening and he got smaller and smaller, while Sleepy Chavez kept showing off for all the vatos locos and got bigger and bigger.

The jury said that Sleepy Chavez was guilty but they couldn't make their minds up about Chuey. They didn't think he was innocent but they didn't think he was guilty either. They didn't know what to do. The judge talked to them some more and they came back in ten minutes and said Chuey was guilty but with like mitigating circumstances.

The D. A. did stand up for Chuey when it came to the sentencing. The judge sent Sleepy Chavez to the C.Y.A., the California Youth Authority, until he turned twenty-one, and then after that he had to go to prison. The judge said she wanted to give Sleepy a life sentence but she couldn't because of his age. She gave Chuey probation and time served.

The courtroom went crazy. All the gangs from Shaky Town were there. 42nd Flats, The Avenues and even some from White Fence. They all started booing the judge, who finally bangs her hammer. Sleepy Chavez stands up. He makes a fist over his head and yells, Flats! La Raza Unida, and the crowd goes crazy some more.

I couldn't believe it. Sleepy Chavez standing there with both arms in the air, yelling, Viva!, like he just won something and Chuey sits there with his head down like he was the one going to prison.

I go down to kiss Chuey and Sleepy spits at my feet. Hey, Puta, he tells me, Take your sissy home.

I can't stand it. I tell him, Sleepy, those guys in prison are gonna fuck you in the ass and I'm glad.

Sleepy says, Bullshit. I'll be in the Mexican Mafia before I get out of C.Y.A. I'll tell you who gets fucked in the ass, Puta, your sissy, li'l Chuey. He yells at Chuey, Hey maricon. Hombre muerto. Chuey don't never raise his head.

I talked to the D.A. afterward. I said, You saw those guys. Chuey needs help. He helped you, you should help him. What about those relocation programs? The D.A. could give a shit. He cares for Chuey about as much as Sleepy Chavez. He just packs his briefcase and walks away, shaking hands with everybody. The T.V. is waiting for him outside.

Ms. Bernstein says she'll see what she can do about police protection. I tell her that ain't going to make it. The only thing that will make it is if Chuey gets out of East L.A. She says there's nothing to keep Chuey from moving, as long as he tells his probation officer and keeps his appointments. She doesn't understand, the only way Chuey will move is if they make him. She says they can't do that.

I tried to make him move. I tell him, Chuey, they going to kill you. Sooner or later. He doesn't want to talk about it, all he'll say is, Forget it. Flats is my home.

The night he got out, Chuey came to my sister's house where I was babysitting. I wanted him so bad. After I put the kids to bed we made love. He looked so fine, even pale and too skinny, but it wasn't any good. It wasn't like Chuey at all. He hardly would kiss me. It was like I could have been anyone. After we made it all he wanted to do was drink wine and listen to records. Every time I tried to talk he got mad.

On the street, the first month after the trial, the cops were doing heavy duty patrols. It seemed like there was a black and white on every corner. They sent the word out through the gang counselors that Shaky Town was going to stay cool or heads would get broken. They busted the warlords from the 42nd Flats and The Avenues for like jay-walking or loitering.

None of the 42nd Flats would talk to Chuey. They cruised his house and gave him cold looks but there was too many cops to do anything. Chuey went back to work at Raul's Body Shop. Raul said he didn't care about the gang stuff and Chuey was a good worker, but then things started happening. Chuey was getting drunk and stoned every night and then he started smoking at work too. Plus windows got broken at the body shop, then there were fires in the trash cans and over the weekend someone threw battery acid on a bunch of customers' cars. Raul told Chuey he'd have to let him go. He didn't fire Chuey, he just laid him off so Chuey could collect unemployment.

The night that he got laid off I took him to dinner and a movie, Rocky something, I forget the number. I didn't want him to get down. After the movie I took Chuey to the Notell Motel in Eagle Rock. It cost me all my tips from two weekends. They had adult movies there and a mirror over the water bed.

Chuey got into it a little. He'd been smoking weed at the movie and he was real relaxed. He lasted a long time. It wasn't great for me. I was too worried about what I wanted to ask and also he wasn't really there. Maybe because of the weed, but it was like that time when he first got out of jail. I could have been anyone.

When he was done I turned off the T.V. and laid down next to him with my head on his chest. We had a cigarette. When I put it out, I kissed his ear and whispered, Chuey, let's get out of this place. You got a trade, I said. We could move anyplace. We could get married. We could go to San Francisco or San Diego. We could just live together if you want. I don't care. But we got to get out of here.

Chuey sat up. He pushed me down off his chest. Flats is my home, he said. Chuey, I said, They're going to kill you. He looked at me like I was a long way away and then he nodded and his eyes were just like that D.A.'s. With the numbers. That's right, Chuey said. They're going to kill me. The numbers flamed up in his eyes like a match. You did this to me, bitch.

Chuey, I said, I love you. He said it again, You did this to me, bitch, and after that he wouldn't talk. We didn't even spend the night.

After he got on unemployment, he filled up his day with weed and wine. I seen him walking right on the street with a joint in one hand and a short dog of white port in the other. Chuey's color T.V., he calls it. I had to be in school, I couldn't babysit him. On the street, none of his old friends would talk to him and there was no place he could hang out. Even people who didn't know him didn't like him around. White Fence had put out the word that they were going to do him as a favor to 42nd Flats. No one wanted to be near Chuey in case there was shooting.

When I got out of school every day, I'd go find him. I tried to get him interested in other stuff, like school, so he could get his high school diploma, or a car. I was even going to front him some of the money, but he didn't want it. All he wanted was his weed and his wine. I even set him up for a job with my cousin who's a plumber but Chuey said no, unemployment was enough. He just kept slipping, going down, and I couldn't pull him up. There wasn't nothing I could do.

He started hanging out with the junkies. They were the only ones, except his family and me, that would talk to him. The junkies hang out in this empty lot across from Lupé's Grocery Store. A Korean guy owns the store but he's afraid to change the name. He's afraid of the junkies too. They steal him blind and shoot up in his alley. They got some old chairs and a sofa in the lot and they sit there, even when it rains. It wasn't too long before Chuey started doing reds. If you ask me, reds are the worst pill around. Red freaks are like zombies. They talk all slurred and spill things. The only thing that's good about them is they don't fight too much, like a white freak, and if they do, they don't hurt each other.

It was hard to be around Chuey once he started doing reds. He'd want to kiss me and his mouth was always full of spit and then he'd try to feel me up right in front of other guys. I hated it, even if they were just junkies.

Then I heard he was doing smack. Chuey didn't tell me, his uncle did. They were missing money from the house and a stereo. They found out Chuey had done it and they found his kit. The only thing I'd noticed was that he wasn't drinking so much and he was eating a lot of candy bars.

The weird thing was that once he got to be a junkie, the 42nd Flats stopped hassling him so much. Gangs are funny that way. They treat junkies like they was teachers or welfare workers. They don't respect them. It's like a truce or like they're invisible. I don't know now whether they're going to kill him or not. Maybe they think the smack will do it for them or maybe they're just waiting for the cops to go away or maybe they're saving him for Sleepy Chavez's little brother who gets paroled out of Juvie next month. I don't know. They still come by the junkie lot. We'll be sitting there and a cruiser will pull up with like four or five dudes inside and you'll see the gun on the window. They call him names, Calavera, which is like a skeleton, or they whisper Muerto, hombre muerto. But it's like they're playing with him. The other junkies think it's funny. They started calling him Muerto Medina. Chuey don't care.

Sometimes I skip sixth period and come down and sit with him. That's the best time of day. He's shot up and mellow by then. I cut out coming by in the morning 'cause he'd be wired and shaky and if he'd just scored he'd want me to shoot up with him. But by late afternoon he's cool. It's real peaceful there in the lot. The sun is nice. We sit on the sofa and I hold his hand. I like to look at him. He's getting skinny but he's still a pretty dude. Chuey nods and dreams, nods and dreams, and I sit there as long as I can. It's what I can do.

SOMETIMES YOU TALK ABOUT IDAHO

PAM HOUSTON

You've come, finally, to a safe place. It could be labeled *safe place*, marquee-style in bright glittering letters. You've put the time in to get there. You've read all the books. You have cooked yourself elaborate gourmet meals. You have brought home fresh-cut flowers. You love your work. You love your friends. It's the single life in the high desert. No booze, no drugs. It isn't just something you tell yourself. It's something you believe.

The man you admire most in the world calls you and asks you out to lunch. He is your good father, the one you trust, the one you depend on. The only one, besides your agent and the editors, who still sees your work.

You have lunch with him often because he is honest and rare, and because he brings a certain manic energy to your life. He is the meter of your own authenticity, the way his eyes drop when you say even the most marginally ingenuous thing. He lives in a space you can only pretend to imagine. When he talks about his own life there seem to be no participants and no events, just a lot of energy moving and spinning and changing hands. It's dizzying, really; sex becomes religion, and religion becomes art.

Sometimes you talk about Idaho: the smell of spruce trees, the snap of a campfire, the arc of a dry fly before it breaks the surface of the water. Idaho is something he can speak about concretely.

He always asks about your love life. No, you say, there's no one at all.

"The problem," he says, "with living alone is that you have to go so far away to the place you can do your work, and when you're finished there's no one there to tell you whether or not you've gotten back."

Your good father smiles a smile of slight embarrassment which is as uncomfortable as new shoes on his soft face. He has a friend, he says, that he'd like you to meet.

"He is both smart and very masculine," your good father says, something in his voice acknowledging that this is a rare combination because he wants you to know he's on your side here. "Our friendship," he says, "is ever new."

"Imagine a first date," your good father says, "where you don't have to watch your vocabulary. Imagine a man," he says, "who might be as intense as you."

Your good father's friend lives in Manhattan, twenty-two hundred miles from the place you've learned to call home. He's a poet, a concert pianist, a soap opera star. He's translated plays from five different Native American languages. He's an environmentalist, a humanist, he's hard to the left.

"He's been through a lot of self-evaluation. He wants a relationship," your good father says, "and he's a dog person. Now that you fly back to New York so often, it could be just the right thing."

You watch him wait for your reaction. You look at the lines that pain has made on his face and realize that you love your good father more than anyone you have slept with in the last five years. You would do anything he told you to do.

"Sounds like fun," you say, without blinking. You are pure nonchalance. A relationship, you've decided, is not something you need like a drug, but a journey, a circumstance, a choice you might make on a particular day.

"My friend loves the mountains, and the desert," your good father says. "He comes out here as often as he can. His real name is Evan, but he's played the same part on the soap for so many years now, everyone we know just calls him Tex."

"Tex?" you say.

"I didn't tell you," he says. "My friend plays a cowboy." Your good father smiles his embarrassed smile. "That's the best part."

You fly to the East Coast on an enormous plane that is mostly empty. You watch the contours of the land get steadily greener, badlands to prairies to cornfields, till the clouds close your view and water runs off the wing.

Somehow you have lived to be twenty-nine years old without ever having gone on a blind date. You don't let yourself admit it, but you are excited beyond words.

You let your mother dress you. She lives in New Jersey and is an actress and you think it's her privilege. She makes you do the following things you are not accustomed to doing: wear foundation, curl your eyelashes, part your hair on the side. Even the Mona Lisa, she says, doesn't look pretty with her hair parted in the middle. She gives you her car so you don't have to take the bus into New York, and in exchange you leave her a phone number where she can reach you. She promises not to call.

It's a little dislocating in New Jersey, where there are cars on the road at all hours and it never really gets dark at night. On the freeway, four miles outside of Newark, you see a deer walking across a cement overpass that's been planted with trees. This seems more amazing to you than it probably is. A sign from your homeland, safe passage, good luck.

It works. You make it through the improbable fact of the Lincoln Tunnel and it doesn't cave in. You find a twenty-four-hour garage four blocks from Moran's Seafood, the meeting place for your date. On the way there you see a woman who looks very happy carrying a starfish in a translucent Tupperware bowl. You only have to walk down one street that scares you a little bit. You get to the restaurant first, and your wide-eyed reflection in the glass behind the car startles you a little. You resist the urge to tell the bartender that you have a blind date.

When he walks in the door there's no mistaking him. He's the soap opera star with the umbrella, the strong back and shoulders, the laugh lines America loves. As he scans the bar it occurs to you for the first time to wonder what kind of a sales job your good father has done on him about you. Then you are shaking hands, then he is picking up your umbrella, one arm hooked in yours guiding you to the table for two.

It is only awkward for the first ten minutes. He is a great mass of charisma moving forward to ever more entertaining subjects. You are both so conscious of keeping the conversation going that you don't look at the menu till the waiter has come back for the fifth time.

Of all the things on the menu, you pick the only one that's difficult to pronounce. You have just passed a fluency exam in French that is one of the requirements of your Ph.D., but saying *en papillote* to the waiter is something that is beyond your power to do. So you describe the dish in English and when the waiter has watched you suffer to his satisfaction, he moves his pen and nods his head.

During dinner, you cover all the required topics for first dates in the nineties: substance abuse, failed marriage, hopes, dreams, and aspirations. You talk about your dogs so much he gets confused and thinks they are your children. He uses emotion words when he talks, sometimes more than one in a sentence: *ache, frightened, rapture.* And something else: He is listening, not only to the words you are saying, but to your rhythms, your reverberations, he picks them up like a machine. Something in his manner is so much like your good father that a confusion which is not altogether unpleasant settles in behind your heart.

Between the herbal tea and the triple fudge decadence he's ordered so that you can have one bite, he reaches across the table and takes your hand in both of his. Then he calls you a swell critter.

You feel a hairline fracture easing through your structure the way snow separates before an avalanche on a too-warm winter day. Something in the air smells a little like salvation, and you breathe deeper every minute but you can't fill your lungs. When all the tables are empty and every restaurant employee is staring at you in disgust, you finally let go of his hand.

Then you go walking. One end of Chelsea to the other, all the time circumventing the block with your garage. He knows about the architecture. He reads from the historic plaques. He shows you nooks and crannies, hidden doorways, remnants of the Latinate style.

It's been raining softly for the hours since dinner and you can feel your hair creeping back over to its comfortable middle part. You smile at him like the Mona Lisa, and he looks as though he's going to kiss you, but doesn't. Then the sky opens up and you duck into a café for more herbal tea.

The café is crowded and the streets are full of people and it makes no sense to you when he tells you it's three o'clock in the morning. You can't possibly, he says, drive all the way back to New Jersey tonight. It's your first real chance to size him up and you do. From the empty next table your good father gives you a wink. "It would be foolish," you say, "to drive in the middle of the night."

When you look back on this date it's the cab ride you'll remember. Broadway going by in a wild blur of green lights, the tallest buildings all lit up like daytime. Your driver and another in a cab next to yours hang heads out their windows and converse at fifty miles an hour in a tongue that sounds a little like Portuguese, a little like music. It's pure unburdened anticipation: you both know sex is imminent, but you don't yet hold the fact of it in your hand. You are laughing and leaning against him. You are watching yourself on the giant screen, western woman finds daytime cowboy in the big city, where even if it wasn't raining, you couldn't see a single star.

His building is a West Side co-op, a name that sounds happy to you, like a place where everyone should get along. In his apartment there are the black-and-white photos you expected, the vertical blinds, the tiny kitchen and immense workplace, the antique rolltop desk.

Some tea without caffeine? he says. And you nod. You count. This is your eleventh cup of herbal tea today. You have never done a first date without alcohol. Now you know why.

You watch him move around the room like a soap opera star. Take one: western woman's seduction: a smile, a touch, a glance. You're still waiting for the big one-liner when he starts kissing you, his hand cupped around your chin, one on the back of your head. Procter and Gamble Industries has taught him how to do this. "Slowly now," the director says, "a little softer. Turn the chin, turn the chin, we can't see her face." You aren't fooling anybody. It's way better than TV.

"Let's forget the herbal tea," he says, which is a disappointment. You want to see the script. You want to make a big red X over that line and write in another, but he has your hand and is leading you to the bedroom with the queen-size bed and the wrought-iron headboard with the sunset over the mountains and there are so many things to think about. Like how many days since your last period and the percentage of people in New York with AIDS, and what you can say to make him realize, if it matters anymore, that going to bed on first dates is not something you do with great regularity. Something needs to be said here, not exactly to defend your virtue, but to make it clear that the act needs to be meaningful, to make it matter, not for all time or forever but for right now, because that's what you've decided it needs to be with sex—after discarding all those other requirements over the years—something that matters right now.

"I'm feeling a little strange," you begin, and you realize this isn't just about you but you're testing him to see if he'll let you talk. "I seem to be violating my own code of dating," you say. "If I have one, that is. I mean, I wanted to come here with you, I didn't want this to end just now, and then we have this other person in common, and because we both love him, there's this closeness between us, this trust which may be totally inappropriate, and so," you wind up, "I'm just feeling a little strange."

This is what happens, you realize, when you begin to get mentally healthy. Instead of letting yourself be whisked silently off to bed you feel compelled to say a lot of mostly incoherent things in run-on sentences.

"I know how you feel," he says. "Me too. But I want this closeness. I don't want you to go back home without us having had it."

It's not exactly a declaration, but it's good enough for you. You fall into the ocean that banks the sunset over mountains. It's a thunderstorm in the desert. It's warm wind on snow. You lose count of orgasms under the smoky city lighting, first streetlight and then daylight, the contours always changing.

"Having fun?" he says, at one point or another. And you nod because fun is one of the things you are having.

He does something to the back of your neck that is closer, more intimate, somehow, even than having him inside you. You read an article once on craniosacral massage, where the body's task of pumping blood to the brain is performed by another person, giving the patient's body the closest thing it's ever had to total rest.

At eight-thirty your mother calls and you take a break long enough to mumble a few words into the phone. "I'm perfectly safe," you tell her, and laugh all the way back to the bedroom at the absurdity of your lie.

It is noon before you emerge, still not having slept, your body feeling numb and tingling and drenched, weightless, rain-soaked, rejuvenated.

But like it or not, it's the next day. You both have appointments. He kisses you twice. "Dinner?" he says. "It'll be late," you say. "That's okay," he says, "call me."

You go to meeting after meeting, and finally to a party with people who mean everything to your career. You are wearing the same clothes as yesterday, walking a little tender, and bowlegged as a bear. Your editor, by some miracle of perception, takes your hand and doesn't let it go all night, even when you are involved in two separate conversations.

Later, you call the soap opera star. He tries to give you directions. "You," he says, "are on the East Side. I am on the West Side."

You tell him you've been to New York before. You hang up.

On the way to his house you get lost. It is raining the kind of rain it never rains in the high desert. A saturating rain where the air spaces between the raindrops contain almost as much moisture as the raindrops themselves. You drive your mother's car through running canals deeper than your wheel wells. You have never been to this part of Manhattan before. Street after street bears a name you don't recognize. Dark figures loom in dark doorways, and the same series of parks seems to have you boxed in. Your defroster can't keep up with your anxiety. Then suddenly you are back on Broadway. You find his house.

"I had a learning experience," you say. What should have taken fifteen minutes has taken an hour and a half. He isn't angry, but he takes the keys from your hand. Together you look for an open garage.

"Dinner?" he says. You shake your head either no you haven't had it or no you don't want it.

"If you're not sleeping," he says, "you need to eat." The two of you look like war-zone survivors. You both try to be charming and fail. Even the simplest conversation is beyond your power. Finally you eat in silence. You fall into bed. It's sleep you both need, but there's the fact of what's insatiable between you. All night you keep reaching, tumbling, waiting for the bell to ring to let you know you've found each other, to let you know it's okay to sleep.

In what seems like minutes, it's time to say goodbye, way too early, not even light out, dusky gray New York morning, clear or cloudy, who can tell without the stars? He has to go to the studio and put on his cowboy boots and court somebody named Hannah, so that all of America can sigh.

"So is Tex nice?" you say, sleepy-eyed as he kisses you goodbye.

"Darlin'," he says, "they don't come any nicer than Tex. Drop the keys in the mail slot. Take care."

When he's gone the phone rings and the machine gets it. Past experience has taught you to expect a woman's voice, but it's your good father, wanting Evan to tell him how everything went. You imagine your good father in the desert, bright sunshine, sage and warm wind. When you hear his laugh crackle over the answering machine your dislocation is complete.

You wander around New York until your lunch date. One of the polished magazines you have written a few short pieces for wants to send you to Yugoslavia. This is not something you can immediately comprehend. They keep talking about it, airfare and train passes and what time of year is the most beautiful, and even though they have said they want you to go you keep thinking, But why are they saying this to me?

It's Wednesday, a matinee day, so you stand in line to get half-priced tickets to a musical, even though you prefer drama, but you know you aren't up for anything that requires you to think. You pick the wrong musical anyway. The first words delivered onstage are "Love changes everything," and it's downhill from there. You leave feeling like you've been through three and a half hours of breath work. On the way up Fifty-seventh Street you realize a valuable and frightening thing: Today you want to be in love more than you want anything; the National Book Award, say, or a Pulitzer Prize.

You've left something at the soap opera star's apartment; a contact lens, a computer disk, your forty-dollar Oscar de la Renta underwear. It takes several phone calls to determine a time to retrieve them. He is short on the phone, on the other line to a director in London, and you realize you've stepped across some kind of a boundary into his space. You have forgotten how New Yorkers can be about their space. You are overly hard on yourself. Where you live, there is plenty of space. There is so much goddam space you can hardly believe it. Finally, it's the doorman who lets you into his empty apartment.

And then you go home, on another enormous airplane, and sit next to a fat woman who is reading a book called *Why Women Confuse Love with Sex*. It's not her you're mad at, but you glare at her so she won't speak to you because you know that anything—anything—anybody says to you will make you cry and cry.

For two days you catch up on sleep and expect him to call. On the third day you come to your senses enough to go hiking, to get out into the landscape that heals you. There is a dynamic in the desert that you understand perfectly: the dry, dry earth and the plants designed to live almost forever without the simple and basic ingredients they need the most. After five days you know he isn't going to call, which is okay, because out of the rubble you carried back from the city you have resurrected your independence. Your work surrounds you like a featherbed and things almost go back to how they were before. But now desire grows inside you like a plant, a big green leafy thing that has been fed only once, but now that it's growing, it won't be still. You sit in your own house and talk to your dogs. More often than not, you answer back.

Your good father calls and asks you out to breakfast. It's an early appointment but you get up even earlier to bathe and dress. It's breakfast at Howard Johnson's but you wear what you wore at Moran's. You even curl your eyelashes. You tell your good father that Evan was everything he said he would be. You run down the weekend with more facts than innuendo. He gets the picture. He is, he says, a lonely man himself.

You tell him about the leafy thing in your stomach, how you have detached it from Evan, how your desire has become something you own, after all. When you get to that part, tears spring into your eyes. It's your turn to give the performance, and its authenticity doesn't make it any less theatrical. It's honesty you are striving for, and still, you're a little bigger than life. Your good father's eyes tell you you've succeeded, and yet your motives are too suspect for even you to explore. You choose to boil it down to what's simple: You perform for your good father because you love him. Anything else is beside the point. Your good father reaches across the table and takes your hand in both of his. "Evan will call you," he says. "I know him. He will."

You wonder what Evan has said to your good father on the phone. You wonder why there's no word for the opposite of lonely. You wonder if there's a difference between whatever might be truth and a performance that isn't a lie. In your life right now, you can't find one.

AFTER THE PLAGUE

T. C. BOYLE

After the plague—it was some sort of Ebola mutation passed from hand to hand and nose to nose like the common cold—life was different. More relaxed and expansive, more natural. The rat race was over, the freeways were clear all the way to Sacramento, and the poor dwindling ravaged planet was suddenly big and mysterious again. It was a kind of miracle really, what the environmentalists had been hoping for all along, though of course even the most strident of them wouldn't have wished for his own personal extinction, but there it was. I don't mean to sound callous—my parents are long dead and I'm unmarried and siblingless, but I lost friends, colleagues and neighbors, the same as any other survivor. What few of us there are, that is. We're guessing it's maybe one in ten thousand, here in the States anyway. I'm sure there are whole tribes that escaped it some-where in the Amazon or the interior valleys of Indonesia, meteorologists in isolated weather stations, fire lookouts, goatherds and the like. But the president's gone, the vice president, the cabinet, Congress, the joint chiefs of staff, the chairmen of the boards and CEOs of the Fortune 500 compa-nies, along with all their stockholders, employees and retainers. There's no TV. No electricity or running water. And there won't be any dining out anytime soon.

Actually, I'm lucky to be here to tell you about it—it was sheer serendipity, really. You see, I wasn't among my fellow human beings when it hit—no festering airline cabins or snaking supermarket lines for me, no concerts, sporting events or crowded restaurants—and the closest I came to intimate contact was a telephone call to my on-and-off girlfriend, Danielle, from a gas station in the Sierra foothills. I think I may have made a kissing noise over the wire, my lips very possibly coming into contact with the molded plastic mouthpiece into which hordes of strangers had breathed before me, but this was a good two weeks before the first victim carried the great dripping bag of infection that was himself back from a camcorder safari to the Ngorongoro Crater or a conference on economic development in Malawi. Danielle, whose voice was a drug I was trying to kick, at least temporarily, promised to come join me for a weekend in the cabin after my six weeks of self-imposed isolation were over, but sadly, she never made it. Neither did anyone else.

I *was* isolated up there in the mountains—that was the whole point—and the first I heard of anything amiss was over the radio. It was a warm, full-bodied day in early fall, the sun caught like a child's ball in the crown of the Jeffrey pine outside the window, and I was washing up after lunch when a smooth melodious voice interrupted *Afternoon Classics* to say that people were bleeding from the eyeballs and vomiting up bile in the New York subways and collapsing en masse in the streets of the capital. The authorities were fully prepared to deal with what they were calling a minor outbreak of swine flu, the voice said, and people were cautioned not to panic, but all at once the announcer seemed to chuckle deep in his throat, and then, right in the middle of the next phrase, he sneezed—a controlled explosion hurtling out over the airwaves to detonate ominously in ten million trembling speakers—and the radio fell silent. Somebody put on a CD of Richard Strauss' *Death and Transfiguration*, and it played over and over through the rest of the afternoon.

I didn't have access to a telephone—not unless I hiked two and a half miles out to the road where I'd parked my car and then drove another six to Fish Fry Flats, pop. 28, and used the public phone at the bar/restaurant/gift shop/one-stop grocery/gas station there—so I ran the dial up and down the radio to see if I could get some news. Reception is pretty spotty up in the mountains—you never knew whether you'd get Bakersfield, Fresno, San Luis Obispo or even Tijuana—and I couldn't pull in anything but white noise on that particular afternoon, except for the aforementioned tone poem, that is. I was powerless. What would happen would happen, and I'd find out all the sordid details a week later, just as I found out about all the other crises, scandals, scoops, coups, typhoons, wars and cease-fires that held the world spellbound while I communed with the ground squirrels and woodpeckers. It was funny. The big events didn't seem to mean much up here in the mountains, where life was so much more elemental and immediate and the telling concerns of the day revolved around priming the water pump and lighting the balky old gas stove without blowing the place up. I picked up a worn copy of John Cheever's stories somebody had left in the cabin during one of its previous incarnations and forgot all about the news out of New York and Washington.

Later, when it finally came to me that I couldn't live through another measure of Strauss without risk of permanent impairment, I flicked off the radio, put on a light jacket and went out to glory in the way the season had touched the aspens along the path out to the road. The sun was leaning way over to the west now, the shrubs and ground litter gathering up the night, the tall trees trailing deep blue shadows. There was the faintest breath of a chill in the air, a premonition of winter, and I thought of the simple pleasures of building a fire, preparing a homely meal and sitting through the evening with a book in one hand and a scotch and Drambuie in the other. It wasn't until nine or ten at night that I remembered the bleeding eyeballs and the fateful sneeze, and though I was half-convinced it was a hoax or maybe one of those fugitive terrorist attacks with a colorless, odorless gas—sarin or the like—I turned on the radio, eager for news.

There was nothing, no Strauss, no crisp and efficient NPR correspondent delivering news of riots in Cincinnati and the imminent collapse of the infrastructure, no right-wing talk, no hip-hop, no jazz, no rock. I switched to AM, and after a painstaking search I hit on a weak signal that sounded as if it were coming from the bottom of Santa Monica Bay. *This is only a test*, a mechanical voice pronounced in what was now just the faintest whispering squeak, *in the event of an actual emergency please stay tuned to* . . . and then it faded out. While I was fumbling to bring it back in, I happened upon a voice shouting something in Spanish. It was just a single voice, very agitated, rolling on tirelessly, and I listened in wonder and dread until the signal went dead just after midnight.

I didn't sleep that night. I'd begun to divine the magnitude of what was going on in the world below me—this was no hoax, no casual atrocity or ordinary attrition; this was the beginning of the end, the Apocalypse, the utter failure and ultimate demise of all things human. I felt sick at heart. Lying there in the fastness of the cabin in the absolute and abiding dark of the wilderness, I was consumed with fear. I lay on my stomach and listened to the steady thunder of my heart pounding through the mattress, attuned to the slightest variation, waiting like a condemned man for the first harrowing sneeze.

Over the course of the next several days, the radio would sporadically come to life (I left it switched on at all times, day and night, as if I were going down in a sinking ship and could shout "Mayday!" into the receiver at the first stirring of a human voice). I'd be pacing the floor or spooning sugar into my tea or staring at a freshly inserted and eternally blank page in my ancient manual typewriter when the static would momentarily clear and a harried newscaster spoke out of the void to provide me with the odd and horrific detail: an oceanliner had run aground off Cape Hatteras and nothing left aboard except three sleek and frisky cats and various puddles of flesh swathed in plaid shorts, polo shirts and sunglasses; no sound or signal had come out of South Florida in over thirty-six hours; a group of survivalists had seized Bill Gates' private jet in an attempt to escape to Antarctica, where it was thought the infection hadn't yet reached, but everyone aboard vomited black bile and died before the plane could leave the ground. Another announcer broke down in the middle of an unconfirmed report that every man, woman and child in Minneapolis was dead, and yet another came over the air early one morning shouting, "It kills! It kills! It kills in three days!" At that point, I jerked the plug out of the wall.

My first impulse, of course, was to help. To save Danielle, the frail and the weak, the young and the old, the chairman of the social studies department at the school where I teach (or taught), a student teacher with cropped red hair about whom I'd had several minutely detailed sexual fantasies. I even went so far as to hike out to the road and take the car into Fish Fry Flats, but the bar/restaurant/gift shop/one-stop grocery/gas station was closed and locked and the parking lot deserted. I drove round the lot three times, debating whether I should continue on down the road or not, but then a lean furtive figure darted out of a shed at the corner of the lot and threw itself—himself—into the shadows beneath the deck of the main building. I recognized the figure immediately as the splay-footed and pony-tailed proprietor of the place, a man who would pump your gas with an inviting smile and then lure you into the gift shop to pay in the hope that the hand-carved Tule Indian figurines and Pen-Lite batteries would prove irresistible. I saw his feet protruding from beneath the deck, and they seemed to be jittering or trembling as if he were doing some sort of energetic new contra-dance that began in the prone position. For a long moment I sat there and watched those dancing feet, then I hit the lock button, rolled up the windows and drove back to the cabin.

What did I do? Ultimately? Nothing. Call it enlightened self-interest. Call it solipsism, self-preservation, cowardice, I don't care. I was terrified—who wouldn't be?—and I decided to stay put. I had plenty of food and firewood, fuel for the generator and propane for the stove, three reams of twenty-five percent cotton fiber bond, correction fluid, books, board games—Parcheesi and Monopoly—and a complete set of *National Geographic*, 1947–1962. (By way of explanation, I should mention that I am—or was—a social studies teacher at the Montecito School, a preparatory academy in a pricey suburb of Santa Barbara, and that the serendipity that spared me the fate of nearly all my fellow men and women was as simple and fortuitous a thing as a sabbatical leave. After fourteen years of unstinting service, I applied for and was granted a one-semester leave at half-salary for the purpose of writing a memoir of my deprived and miserable Irish-Catholic upbringing. The previous year a high school teacher from New York—the name escapes me now—had enjoyed a spectacular *succès d'estime*, not to mention *d'argent*, with a memoir about his own miserable and deprived Irish-Catholic boyhood, and I felt I could profitably mine the same territory. And I got a good start on it too, until the plague hit. Now I ask myself what's the use—the publishers are all dead. Ditto the editors, agents, reviewers, book-sellers and the great congenial book-buying public itself. What's the sense of writing? What's the sense of anything?)

At any rate, I stuck close to the cabin, writing at the kitchen table through the mornings, staring out the window into the ankles of the pines and redwoods as I summoned degrading memories of my alcoholic mother, father, aunts, uncles, cousins and grandparents, and in the afternoons I hiked up to the highest peak and looked down on the deceptive tranquillity of the San Joaquin Valley spread out like a continent below me. There were no planes in the sky overhead, no sign of traffic or movement anywhere, no sounds but the calling of the birds and the soughing of the trees as the breeze sifted through them. I stayed up there past dark one night and felt as serene and terrible as a god when I looked down at the velvet expanse of the world and saw no ray or glimmer of light. I plugged the radio back in that night, just to hear the fading comfort of man-made noise, of the static that emanates from nowhere and nothing. Because there was nothing out there, not anymore.

It was four weeks later—just about the time I was to have ended my hermitage and enjoyed the promised visit from Danielle—that I had my first human contact of the new age. I was at the kitchen window, beating powdered eggs into a froth for dinner, one ear half-attuned to the perfect and unbroken static hum of the radio, when there was a heavy thump on the deteriorating planks of the front deck. My first thought was that a branch had dropped out of the Jeffrey pine—or worse, that a bear had got wind of the corned beef hash I'd opened to complement the powdered eggs—but I was mistaken on both counts. The thump was still reverberating through the floorboards when I was surprised to hear a moan and then a curse—a distinctly human curse. "Oh, shit-fuck!" a woman's voice cried. "Open the goddamned door! Help, for shit's sake, help!"

I've always been a cautious animal. This may be one of my great failings, as my mother and later my fraternity brothers were always quick to point out, but on the other hand, it may be my greatest virtue. It's kept me alive when the rest of humanity has gone on to a quick and brutal extinction, and it didn't fail me in that moment. The door was locked. Once I'd got wind of what was going on in the world, though I was devastated and the thought of the radical transformation of everything I'd ever known gnawed at me day and night, I took to locking it against just such an eventuality as this. "Shit!" the voice raged. "I can hear you in there, you son of a bitch—I can *smell* you!"

I stood perfectly still and held my breath. The static breathed dismally through the speakers and I wished I'd had the sense to disconnect the radio long ago. I stared down at the half-beaten eggs.

"I'm dying out here!" the voice cried. "I'm starving to death—hey, are you deaf in there or what? I said, I'm *starving!*"

And now of course I was faced with a moral dilemma. Here was a fellow human being in need of help, a member of a species whose value had just vaulted into the rarefied atmosphere occupied by the gnatcatcher, the condor and the beluga whale by virtue of its rarity. Help her? Of course I would help her. But at the same time, I knew if I opened that door I would invite the pestilence in and that three days hence both she and I would be reduced to our mortal remains.

"Open up!" she demanded, and the tattoo of her fists was the thunder of doom on the thin planks of the door.

It occurred to me suddenly that she couldn't be infected—she'd have been dead and wasted by now if she were. Maybe she was like me, maybe she'd been out brooding in her own cabin or hiking the mountain trails, utterly oblivious and immune to the general calamity. Maybe she was beautiful, nubile, a new Eve for a new age, maybe she would fill my nights with passion and my days with joy. As if in a trance, I crossed the room and stood at the door, my fingers on the long brass stem of the bolt. "Are you alone?" I said, and the rasp of my own voice, so long in disuse, sounded strange in my ears.

I heard her draw in a breath of astonishment and outrage from the far side of the thin panel that separated us. "What the hell do you think, you son of a bitch? I've been lost out here in these stinking woods for I don't know how long and I haven't had a scrap for days, not a goddamn scrap, not even bark or grass or a handful of soggy trail mix. *Now will you fucking open this door?!*"

Still, I hesitated.

A rending sound came to me then, a sound that tore me open as surely as a surgical knife, from my groin to my throat: she was sobbing. Gagging for breath, and sobbing. "A frog," she sobbed, "I ate a goddamn slimy little putrid *frog!*"

God help me. God save and preserve me. I opened the door.

Sarai was thirty-eight years old—that is, three years older than I—and she was no beauty. Not on the surface, anyway. Even if you discounted the twenty-odd pounds she'd lost and her hair that was like some crushed rodent's pelt and the cuts and bites and suppurating sores that made her skin look like a leper's, and tried, by a powerful leap of the imagination, to see her as she once might have been, safely ensconced in her condo in Tarzana and surrounded by all the accoutrements of feminine hygiene and beauty, she still wasn't much.

This was her story: she and her live-in boyfriend, Howard, were nature enthusiasts—at least Howard was, anyway—and just before the plague hit they'd set out to hike an interlocking series of trails in the Golden Trout Wilderness. They were well provisioned, with the best of everything—Howard managed a sporting goods store—and for the first three weeks everything went according to plan. They ate delicious freeze-dried fettuccine Alfredo and shrimp couscous, drank cognac from a bota bag and made love wrapped in propylene, Gore-Tex and nylon. Mosquitoes and horseflies sampled her legs, but she felt good, born again, liberated from the traffic and the smog and her miserable desk in a miserable corner of the electronics company her father had founded. Then one morning, when they were camped by a stream, Howard went off with his day pack and a fly rod and never came back. She waited. She searched. She screamed herself hoarse. A week went by. Every day she searched in a new direction, following the stream both ways and combing every tiny rill and tributary, until finally she got herself lost. All streams were one stream, all hills and ridges alike. She had three Kudos bars with her and a six-ounce bag of peanuts, but no shelter and no freeze-dried entrées—all that was back at the camp she and Howard had made in happier times. A cold rain fell. There were no stars that night, and when something moved in the brush beside her she panicked and ran blindly through the dark, hammering her shins and destroying her face, her hair and her clothes. She'd been wandering ever since.

I made her a package of Top Ramen, gave her a towel and a bar of soap and showed her the primitive shower I'd rigged up above the ancient slab of the tub. I was afraid to touch her or even come too close to her. Sure I was skittish. Who wouldn't be when ninety-nine percent of the human race had just died off on the tailwind of a simple sneeze? Besides, I'd begun to adopt all the habits of the hermit—talking to myself, performing elaborate rituals over my felicitous stock of foodstuffs, dredging bursts of elementary school songs and beer jingles out of the depths of my impacted brain—and I resented having my space invaded. *Still.* Still, though, I felt that Sarai had been delivered to me by some higher power and that she'd been blessed in the way that I was—we'd escaped the infection. We'd survived. And we weren't just errant members of a selfish, suspicious and fragmented society, but the very foundation of a new one. She was a woman. I was a man.

At first, she wouldn't believe me when I waved a dismissive hand at the ridge behind the cabin and all that lay beyond it and informed her that the world was depeopled, that the Apocalypse had come and that she and I were among the solitary survivors—and who could blame her? As she sipped my soup and ate my flap-jacks and treated her cuts and abrasions with my Neosporin and her hair with my shampoo, she must have thought she'd found a lunatic as her savior. "If you don't believe me," I said, and I was gloating, I was, sick as it may seem, "try the radio."

She looked up at me out of the leery brooding eyes of the one sane woman in a madhouse of impostors, plugged the cord in the socket and calibrated the dial as meticulously as a safecracker. She was rewarded by static—no dynamics even, just a single dull continuum—but she glared up at me as if I'd rigged the thing to disappoint her. "So," she spat, skinny as a refugee, her hair kinked and puffed up with my shampoo till it devoured her parsimonious and disbelieving little sliver of a face, "that doesn't prove a thing. It's broken, that's all."

When she got her strength back, we hiked out to the car and drove into Fish Fry Flats so she could see for herself. I was half-crazy with the terrible weight of the knowledge I'd been forced to hold inside me, and I can't describe the irritation I felt at her utter lack of interest—she treated me like a street gibberer, a psychotic, Cassandra in long pants. She condescended to me. She was *humoring* me, for God's sake, and the whole world lay in ruins around us. But she would have a rude awakening, she would, and the thought of it was what kept me from saying something I'd regret—I didn't want to lose my temper and scare her off, but I hate stupidity and willfulness. It's the one thing I won't tolerate in my students. Or wouldn't. Or didn't.

Fish Fry Flats, which in the best of times could hardly be mistaken for a metropolis, looked now as if it had been deserted for a decade. Weeds had begun to sprout up through invisible cracks in the pavement, dust had settled over the idle gas pumps and the windows of the main building were etched with grime. And the animals—the animals were everywhere, marmots waddling across the lot as if they owned it, a pair of coyotes asleep in the shade of an abandoned pickup, ravens cawing and squirrels chittering. I cut the engine just as a bear the color of cinnamon toast tumbled stupendously through an already shattered window and lay on his back, waving his bloodied paws in the air as if he were drunk, which he was. As we discovered a few minutes later—once he'd lurched to his feet and staggered off into the bushes—a whole host of creatures had raided the grocery, stripping the candy display right down to the twisted wire rack, scattering Triscuits and Doritos, shattering jars of jam and jugs of port wine and grinding the hand-carved Tule Indian figurines underfoot. There was no sign of the formerly sunny proprietor or of his dancing feet—I could only imagine that the ravens, coyotes and ants had done their work.

But Sarai—she was still an unbeliever, even after she dropped a quarter into the public telephone and put the dead black plastic receiver to her ear. For all the good it did her, she might as well have tried coaxing a dial tone out of a stone or a block of wood, and I told her so. She gave me a sour look, the sticks of her bones briefly animated beneath a sweater and jacket I'd loaned her—it was the end of October and getting cold at seventy-two hundred feet—and then she tried another quarter, and then another, before she slammed the receiver down in a rage and turned her seething face on me. "The lines are down, that's all," she sneered. And then her mantra: "It doesn't prove a thing."

While she'd been frustrating herself, I'd been loading the car with canned goods, after entering the main building through the broken window and unlatching the door from the inside. "And what about all this?" I said, irritated, hot with it, sick to death of her and her thick-headedness. I gestured at the bloated and lazy coyotes, the hump in the bushes that was the drunken bear, the waddling marmots and the proprietary ravens.

"I don't know," she said, clenching her jaws. "And I don't care." Her eyes had a dull sheen to them. They were insipid and bovine, exactly the color of the dirt at her feet. And her lips—thin and stingy, collapsed in a riot of vertical lines like a dried-up mud puddle. I hated her in that moment, godsend or no. Oh, how I hated her.

"What are you *doing?*" she demanded as I loaded the last of the groceries into the car, settled into the driver's seat and turned the engine over. She was ten feet from me, caught midway between the moribund phone booth and the living car. One of the coyotes lifted its head at the vehemence of her tone and gave her a sleepy, yellow-eyed look.

"Going back to the cabin," I said.

"You're *what?*" Her face was pained. She'd been through agonies. I was a devil and a madman.

"Listen, Sarai, it's all over. I've told you time and again. You don't have a job anymore. You don't have to pay rent, utility bills, don't have to make car payments or remember your mother's birthday. It's over. Don't you get it?"

"You're insane! You're a shithead! I hate you!"

The engine was purring beneath my feet, fuel awasting, but there was infinite fuel now, and though I realized the gas pumps would no longer work, there were millions upon millions of cars and trucks out there in the world with full tanks to siphon, and no one around to protest. I could drive a Ferrari if I wanted, a Rolls, a Jag, anything. I could sleep on a bed of jewels, stuff the mattress with hundred-dollar bills, prance through the streets in a new pair of Italian loafers and throw them into the gutter each night and get a new pair in the morning. But I was afraid. Afraid of the infection, the silence, the bones rattling in the wind. "I know it," I said. "I'm insane. I'm a shithead. I admit it. But I'm going back to the cabin and you can do anything you want—it's a free country. Or at least it used to be."

I wanted to add that it was a free world now, a free universe, and that God was in the details, the biblical God, the God of famine, flood and pestilence, but I never got the chance. Before I could open my mouth she bent for a stone and heaved it into the windshield, splintering me with flecks and shards of safety glass. "Die!" she shrieked. "*You* die, you shit!"

That night we slept together for the first time. In the morning, we packed up a few things and drove down the snaking mountain road to the charnel house of the world.

I have to confess that I've never been much of a fan of the apocalyptic potboiler, the doomsday film shot through with special effects and asinine dialogue or the cyberpunk version of a grim and relentless future. What these entertainments had led us to expect—the roving gangs, the inhumanity, the ascendancy of machines and the redoubled pollution and ravaging of the earth—wasn't at all what it was like. There were no roving gangs—they were all dead, to a man, woman and tattooed punk— and the only machines still functioning were the automobiles and weed whippers and such that we the survivors chose to put into prosaic action. And a further irony was that the survivors were the least likely and least qualified to organize anything, either for better or worse. We were the fugitive, the misfit, the recluse, and we were so widely scattered we'd never come into contact with one another, anyway—and that was just the way we liked it. There wasn't even any looting of the supermarkets—there was no need. There was more than enough for everybody who ever was or would be.

Sarai and I drove down the mountain road, through the deserted small town of Springville and the deserted larger town of Porterville, and then we turned south for Bakersfield, the Grapevine and Southern California. She wanted to go back to her apartment, to Los Angeles, and see if her parents and her sisters were alive still—she became increasingly vociferous on that score as the reality of what had happened began to seep through to her—but I was driving and I wanted to avoid Los Angeles at all costs. To my mind, the place had been a pit before the scourge hit, and now it was a pit heaped with seven million moldering corpses. She carped and moaned and whined and threatened, but she was in shock too and couldn't quite work herself up to her usual pitch, and so we turned west and north on Route 126 and headed toward Montecito, where for the past ten years I'd lived in a cottage on one of the big estates there—the DuPompier place, *Mírame*.

By the way, when I mentioned earlier that the freeways were clear, I was speaking metaphorically—they were free of traffic, but cluttered with abandoned vehicles of all sorts, take your pick, from gleaming choppers with thousand-dollar gold-fleck paint jobs to sensible family cars, Corvettes, Winnebagos, eighteen-wheelers and even fire engines and police cruisers. Twice, when Sarai became especially insistent, I pulled alongside one or another of these abandoned cars, swung open her door and said, "Go ahead. Take this Cadillac"—or BMW or whatever—"and drive yourself any damn place you please. Go on. What are you waiting for?" But her face shrank till it was as small as a doll's and her eyes went stony with fear: those cars were catacombs, each and every one of them, and the horror of that was more than anybody could bear.

So we drove on, through a preternatural silence and a world that already seemed primeval, up the Coast Highway and along the frothing bright boatless sea and into Montecito. It was evening when we arrived, and there wasn't a soul in sight. If it weren't for that—and a certain creeping untended look to the lawns, shrubs and trees—you wouldn't have noticed anything out of the ordinary. My cottage, built in the twenties of local sandstone and draped in wisteria till it was all but invisible, was exactly as I'd left it. We pulled into the silent drive with the great house looming in the near distance, a field of dark reflective glass that held the blood of the declining sun in it, and Sarai barely glanced up. Her thin shoulders were hunched and she was staring at a worn place on the mat between her feet.

"We're here," I announced, and I got out of the car.

She turned her eyes to me, stricken, suffering, a waif. "Where?"

"Home."

It took her a moment, but when she responded she spoke slowly and carefully, as if she were just learning the language. "I have no home," she said. "Not anymore."

So. What to tell you? We didn't last long, Sarai and I, though we were pioneers, though we were the last hope of the race, drawn together by the tenacious glue of fear and loneliness. I knew there wouldn't be much opportunity for dating in the near future, but we just weren't suited to each other. In fact, we were as unsuited as any two people could ever be, and our sex was tedious and obligatory, a ballet of mutual need and loathing, but to my mind at least, there was a bright side—here was the chance to go forth and be fruitful and do what we could to repopulate the vast and aching sphere of the planet. Within the month, however, Sarai had disabused me of that notion.

It was a silky, fog-hung morning, the day deepening around us, and we'd just gone through the mechanics of sex and were lying exhausted and unsatisfied in the rumple of my gritty sheets (water was a problem and we did what laundry we could with what we were able to haul down from the estate's swimming pool). Sarai was breathing through her mouth, an irritating snort and burble that got on my nerves, but before I could say anything, she spoke in a hard shriveled little nugget of a voice. "You're no Howard," she said.

"Howard's dead," I said. "He deserted you."

She was staring at the ceiling. "Howard was gold," she mused in a languid, reflective voice, "and you're shit."

It was childish, I know, but the dig at my sexual performance really stung—not to mention the ingratitude of the woman—and I came back at her. "You came to me," I said. "I didn't ask for it—I was doing fine out there on the mountain without you. And where do you think you'd be now if it wasn't for me? Huh?"

She didn't answer right away, but I could feel her consolidating in the bed beside me, magma becoming rock. "I'm not going to have sex with you again," she said, and still she was staring at the ceiling. "Ever. I'd rather use my finger."

"You're no Danielle," I said.

She sat up then, furious, all her ribs showing and her shrunken breasts clinging to the remains of them like an afterthought. "Fuck Danielle," she spat. "And fuck you."

I watched her dress in silence, but as she was lacing up her hiking boots I couldn't resist saying, "It's no joy for me either, Sarai, but there's a higher principle involved here than our likes and dislikes or any kind of animal gratification, and I think you know what I'm talking about—"

She was perched on the edge of a leather armchair I'd picked up at a yard sale years ago, when money and things had their own reality. She'd laced up the right boot and was working on the left, laces the color of rust, blunt white fingers with the nails bitten to the quick. Her mouth hung open slightly and I could see the pink tip of her tongue caught between her teeth as she worked mindlessly at her task, reverting like a child to her earliest training and her earliest habits. She gave me a blank look.

"Procreation, I mean. If you look at it in a certain way, it's—well, it's our duty."

Her laugh stung me. It was sharp and quick, like the thrust of a knife. "You idiot," she said, and she laughed again, showing the gold in her back teeth. "I hate children, always have—they're little monsters that grow up to be uptight fussy pricks like you." She paused, smiled, and released an audible breath. "I had my tubes tied fifteen years ago."

That night she moved into the big house, a replica of a Moorish castle in Seville, replete with turrets and battlements. The paintings and furnishings were exquisite, and there were some twelve thousand square feet of living space, graced with carved wooden ceilings, colored tiles, rectangular arches, a loggia and formal gardens. Nor had the DuPompiers spoiled the place by being so thoughtless as to succumb inside—they'd died, Julius, Eleanor and their daughter, Kelly, under the arbor in back, the white bones of their hands eternally clasped. I wished Sarai good use of the place. I did. Because by that point I didn't care if she moved into the White House, so long as I didn't have to deal with her anymore.

Weeks slipped by. Months. Occasionally I would see the light of Sarai's Coleman lantern lingering in one of the high windows of *Mirame* as night fell over the coast, but essentially I was as solitary—and as lonely—as I'd been in the cabin in the mountains. The rains came and went. It was spring. Everywhere the untended gardens ran wild, the lawns became fields, the orchards forests, and I took to walking round the neighborhood with a baseball bat to ward off the packs of feral dogs for which Alpo would never again materialize in a neat bowl in the corner of a dry and warm kitchen. And then one afternoon, while I was at Von's, browsing the aisles for pasta, bottled marinara and Green Giant asparagus spears amid a scattering of rats and the lingering stench of the perished perishables, I detected movement at the far end of the next aisle over. My first thought was that it must be a dog or a coyote that had somehow managed to get in to feed on the rats or the big twenty-five-pound bags of Purina Dog Chow, but then, with a shock, I realized I wasn't alone in the store.

In all the time I'd been coming here for groceries, I'd never seen a soul, not even Sarai or one of the six or seven other survivors who were out there occupying the mansions in the hills. Every once in a while I'd see lights shining in the wall of the night—someone had even managed to fire up a generator at Las Tejas, a big Italianate villa half a mile away— and every so often a car would go helling up the distant freeway, but basically we survivors were shy of one another and kept to ourselves. It was fear, of course, the little spark of panic that told you the contagion was abroad again and that the best way to avoid it was to avoid all human contact. So we did. Strenuously.

But I couldn't ignore the squeak and rattle of a shopping cart wheeling up the bottled water aisle, and when I turned the corner, there she was, Felicia, with her flowing hair and her scared and sorry eyes. I didn't know her name then, not at first, but I recognized her—she was one of the tellers at the Bank of America branch where I cashed my checks. Formerly cashed them, that is. My first impulse was to back wordlessly away, but I mastered it—how could I be afraid of what was human, so palpably human, and appealing? "Hello," I said, to break the tension, and then I was going to say something stupid like "I see you made it too" or "Tough times, huh?" but instead I settled for "Remember me?"

She looked stricken. Looked as if she were about to bolt—or die on the spot. But her lips were brave and they came together and uttered my name. "Mr. Halloran?" she said, and it was so ordinary, so plebeian, so real.

I smiled and nodded. My name is—was—Francis Xavier Halloran III, a name I've hated since Tyrone Johnson (now presumably dead) tormented me with it in kindergarten, chanting "Francis, Francis, Francis" till I wanted to sink through the floor. But it was a new world now, a world burgeoning and bursting at the seams to discover the lineaments of its new forms and rituals. "Call me Jed," I said.

Nothing happens overnight, especially not in plague times. We were wary of each other, and every banal phrase and stultifying cliché of the small talk we made as I helped her load her groceries into the back of her Range Rover reverberated hugely with the absence of all the multitudes who'd used those phrases before us. Still, I got her address that afternoon— she'd moved into Villa Ruscello, a mammoth place set against the mountains, with a creek, pond and Jacuzzi for fresh water—and I picked her up two nights later in a Rolls Silver Cloud and took her to my favorite French restaurant. The place was untouched and pristine, with a sweeping view of the sea, and I lit some candles and poured us each a glass of twenty-year-old Bordeaux, after which we feasted on canned crab, truffles, cashews and marinated artichoke hearts.

I'd like to tell you that she was beautiful, because that's the way it should be, the way of the fable and the fairy tale, but she wasn't—or not conventionally, anyway. She was a little heavier than she might have been ideally, but that was a relief after stringy Sarai, and her eyes were ever so slightly crossed. Yet she was decent and kind, sweet even, and more important, she was available.

We took walks together, raided overgrown gardens for lettuce, tomatoes and zucchini, planted strawberries and snow peas in the middle of the waist-high lawn at Villa Ruscello. One day we drove to the mountains and brought back the generator so we could have lights and refrigeration in the cottage—ice cubes, now there was a luxury—and begin to work our way through the eight thousand titles at the local video store. It was nearly a month before anything happened between us—anything sexual, that is. And when it did, she first felt obligated, out of a sense of survivor's guilt, I suppose, to explain to me how she came to be alive and breathing still when everyone she'd ever known had vanished off the face of the earth. We were in the beamed living room of my cottage, sharing a bottle of Dom Pérignon 1970, with the three-hundred-ten-dollar price tag still on it, and I'd started a fire against the gathering night and the wet raw smell of rain on the air. "You're going to think I'm an idiot," she said.

I made a noise of demurral and put my arm round her.

"Did you ever hear of a sensory deprivation tank?" She was peering up at me through the scrim of her hair, gold and red highlights, health in a bottle.

"Yeah, sure," I said. "But you don't mean—?"

"It was an older one, a model that's not on the market anymore—one of the originals. My roommate's sister—Julie Angier?—she had it out in her garage on Padaro, and she was really into it. You could get in touch with your inner self, relax, maybe even have an out-of-body experience, that's what she said, and I figured why not?" She gave me a look, shy and passionate at once, to let me know that she was the kind of girl who took experience seriously. "They put salt water in it, three hundred gallons, heated to your body temperature, and then they shut the lid on you and there's nothing, absolutely nothing there—it's like going to outer space. Or inner space. Inside yourself."

"And you were in there when—?"

She nodded. There was something in her eyes I couldn't read—pride, triumph, embarrassment, a spark of sheer lunacy. I gave her an encouraging smile.

"For days, I guess," she said. "I just sort of lost track of everything, who I was, where I was—you know? And I didn't wake up till the water started getting cold"—she looked at her feet—"which I guess is when the electricity went out because there was nobody left to run the power plants. And then I pushed open the lid and the sunlight through the window was like an atom bomb, and then, then I called out Julie's name, and she . . . well, she never answered."

Her voice died in her throat and she turned those sorrowful eyes on me. I put my other arm around her and held her. "Hush," I whispered, "it's all right now, everything's all right." It was a conventional thing to say, and it was a lie, but I said it, and I held her and felt her relax in my arms.

It was then, almost to the precise moment, that Sarai's naked sliver of a face appeared at the window, framed by her two uplifted hands and a rock the size of my Webster's unabridged. "What about *me*, you son of a bitch!" she shouted, and there it was again, everlasting stone and frangible glass, and not a glazier left alive on the planet.

I wanted to kill her. It was amazing—three people I knew of had survived the end of everything, and it was one too many. I felt vengeful. Biblical. I felt like storming Sarai's ostentatious castle and wringing her chicken neck for her, and I think I might have if it weren't for Felicia. "Don't let her spoil it for us," she murmured, the gentle pressure of her fingers on the back of my neck suddenly holding my full attention, and we went into the bedroom and closed the door on all that mess of emotion and glass.

In the morning, I stepped into the living room and was outraged all over again. I cursed and stomped and made a fool of myself over heaving the rock back through the window and attacking the shattered glass as if it were alive—I admit I was upset out of all proportion to the crime. This was a new world, a new beginning, and Sarai's nastiness and negativity had no place in it. Christ, there were only three of us—couldn't we get along?

Felicia had repaired dozens of windows in her time. Her little brothers (dead now) and her fiancé (dead too) were forever throwing balls around the house, and she assured me that a shattered window was nothing to get upset over (though she bit her lip and let her eyes fill at the mention of her fiancé, and who could blame her?). So we consulted the Yellow Pages, drove to the nearest window glass shop and broke in as gently as possible. Within the hour, the new pane had been installed and the putty was drying in the sun, and watching Felicia at work had so elevated my spirits I suggested a little shopping spree to celebrate.

"Celebrate what?" She was wearing a No Fear T-shirt and an Anaheim Angels cap and there was a smudge of off-white putty on her chin.

"You," I said. "The simple miracle of you."

And that was fine. We parked on the deserted streets of downtown Santa Barbara and had the stores to ourselves—clothes, the latest (and last) bestsellers, CDs, a new disc player to go with our newly electrified house. Others had visited some of the stores before us, of course, but they'd been polite and neat about it, almost as if they were afraid to betray their presence, and they always closed the door behind them. We saw deer feeding in the courtyards and one magnificent tawny mountain lion stalking the wrong way up a one-way street. By the time we got home, I was elated. Everything was going to work out, I was sure of it.

The mood didn't last long. As I swung into the drive, the first thing I saw was the yawning gap where the new window had been, and beyond it, the undifferentiated heap of rubble that used to be my living room. Sarai had been back. And this time she'd done a thorough job, smashing lamps and pottery, poking holes in our cans of beef stew and chili con carne, scattering coffee, flour and sugar all over everything and dumping sand in the generator's fuel tank. Worst of all, she'd taken half a dozen pairs of Felicia's panties and nailed them to the living room wall, a crude X slashed across the crotch of each pair. It was hateful and savage—human, that's what it was, human— and it killed all the joy we'd taken in the afternoon and the animals and the infinite and various riches of the mall. Sarai had turned it all to shit.

"We'll move to my place," Felicia said. "Or any place you want. How about an oceanfront house—didn't you say you'd always wanted to live right on the ocean?"

I had. But I didn't want to admit it. I stood in the middle of the desecrated kitchen and clenched my fists. "I don't want any other place. This is my home. I've lived here for ten years and I'll be damned if I'm going to let *her* drive me out."

It was an irrational attitude—again, childish—and Felicia convinced me to pack up a few personal items (my high school year-book, my reggae albums, a signed first edition of *For Whom the Bell Tolls*, a pair of deer antlers I'd found in the woods when I was eight) and move into a place on the ocean for a few days. We drove along the coast road at a slow, stately pace, looking over this house or that, until we finally settled on a grand modern place that was all angles and glass and broad sprawling decks. I got lucky and caught a few perch in the surf, and we barbecued them on the beach and watched the sun sink into the western bluffs.

The next few days were idyllic, and we thought about little beyond love and food and the way the water felt on our skin at one hour of the day or another, but still, the question of Sarai nagged at me. I was reminded of her every time I wanted a cold drink, for instance, or when the sun set and we had to make do with candles and kerosene lanterns—we'd have to go out and dig up another generator, we knew that, but they weren't exactly in demand in a place like Santa Barbara (in the old days, that is) and we didn't know where to look. And so yes, I couldn't shake the image of Sarai and the look on her face and the things she'd said and done. And I missed my house, because I'm a creature of habit, like anybody else. Or more so. Definitely more so.

Anyway, the solution came to us a week later, and it came in human form—at least it appeared in human form, but it was a miracle and no doubt about it. Felicia and I were both on the beach—naked, of course, as naked and without shame or knowledge of it as Eve and Adam—when we saw a figure marching resolutely up the long curving finger of sand that stretched away into the haze of infinity. As the figure drew closer, we saw that it was a man, a man with a scraggly salt-and-pepper beard and hair the same color trailing away from a bald spot worn into his crown. He was dressed in hiking clothes, big-grid boots, a bright blue pack riding his back like a second set of shoulders. We stood there, naked, and greeted him.

"Hello," he said, stopping a few feet from us and staring first at my face, then at Felicia's breasts, and finally, with an effort, bending to check the laces of his boots. "Glad to see you two made it," he said, speaking to the sand.

"Likewise," I returned.

Over lunch on the deck—shrimp salad sandwiches on Felicia-baked bread—we traded stories. It seems he was hiking in the mountains when the pestilence descended—"The mountains?" I interrupted. "Whereabouts?"

"Oh," he said, waving a dismissive hand, "up in the Sierras, just above this little town—you've probably never heard of it—Fish Fry Flats?"

I let him go on a while, explaining how he'd lost his girlfriend and wandered for days before he finally came out on a mountain road and appropriated a car to go on down to Los Angeles—"One big cemetery"— and how he'd come up the coast and had been wandering ever since. I don't think I've ever felt such exhilaration, such a rush of excitement, such perfect and inimitable a sense of closure.

I couldn't keep from interrupting him again. "I'm clairvoyant," I said, raising my glass to the man sitting opposite me, to Felicia and her breasts, to the happy fishes in the teeming seas and the birds flocking without number in the unencumbered skies. "Your name's Howard, right?"

Howard was stunned. He set down his sandwich and wiped a fleck of mayonnaise from his lips. "How did you guess?" he said, gaping up at me out of eyes that were innocent and pure, the newest eyes in the world.

I just smiled and shrugged, as if it were my secret. "After lunch," I said, "I've got somebody I want you to meet."

THOSE WE KNOW

No one is an island. Our lives are dramatically affected by the people around us, especially those who dwell in our families. Whether they've entered our borders by fate or choice, family members are usually the source of our most profound joy and greatest aggravation. Often the same person provides both. The inner workings of these relationships can be as labyrinthine as a late-night session of the UN Security Council. And sometimes we discover that those we know best aren't known so well to us after all.

In Dorothy Parker's "Here We Are," we observe a newlywed couple en route to their honeymoon. They are traveling the first adventurous miles of a lifetime partnership. At least that's the way it's supposed to go. Nobody expects the honeymoon to last forever, but what happens when it ends before it even starts? The styles in this story may now be out of fashion, but not the foibles of the people wearing them.

The honeymoon is long over for the married couple in Raymond Carver's "Whoever Was Using This Bed." They're holding together pretty well but they've simply become a fact of each other's reality; every day they eat, sleep, smoke, drink, whine, and argue together. No real surprises here. Or so they think. When they get to talking in bed one sleepless night, the concept of "till death do us part" takes on a startling new meaning.

Siblings are natural rivals, and that's certainly true of the two sisters in Anthony Doerr's "For a Long Time This Was Griselda's Story." One is the star, a tall attention-grabber destined for fame; the other is the drab understudy, trudging toward a predictable life. Through a mythlike lens, we see the sisters following drastically different orbits, then reuniting for a grand collision remembered in town for years after.

In Hannah Tinti's "Home Sweet Home," two homes are turned upside down one calm evening by a double murder. We follow the chain of events and relationships surrounding the crime, combing for clues to who did it and why. Every character becomes an open book to the reader, though not to the detective investigating the crime. You'll want to know the killer's identity, of course, but you'll be even more intrigued by the various people you meet.

HERE WE ARE

DOROTHY PARKER

The young man in the new blue suit finished arranging the glistening luggage in tight corners of the Pullman compartment. The train had leaped at curves and bounced along straightaways, rendering balance a praiseworthy achievement and a sporadic one; and the young man had pushed and hoisted and tucked and shifted the bags with concentrated care.

Nevertheless, eight minutes for the settling of two suitcases and a hat-box is a long time.

He sat down, leaning back against bristled green plush, in the seat opposite the girl in beige. She looked as new as a peeled egg. Her hat, her fur, her frock, her gloves were glossy and stiff with novelty. On the arc of the thin, slippery sole of one beige shoe was gummed a tiny oblong of white paper, printed with the price set and paid for that slipper and its fellow, and the name of the shop that had dispensed them.

She had been staring raptly out of the window, drinking in the big weathered signboards that extolled the phenomena of codfish without bones and screens no rust could corrupt. As the young man sat down, she turned politely from the pane, met his eyes, started a smile and got it about half done, and rested her gaze just above his right shoulder.

"Well!" the young man said.

"Well!" she said.

"Well, here we are," he said.

"Here we are," she said. "Aren't we?"

"I should say we were," he said. "Eeyop. Here we are."

"Well!" she said.

"Well!" he said. "Well. How does it feel to be an old married lady?"

"Oh, it's too soon to ask me that," she said. "At least—I mean. Well, I mean, goodness, we've only been married about three hours, haven't we?"

The young man studied his wrist-watch as if he were just acquiring the knack of reading time.

"We have been married," he said, "exactly two hours and twenty-six minutes."

"My," she said. "It seems like longer."

"No," he said. "It isn't hardly half-past six yet."

"It seems like later," she said. "I guess it's because it starts getting dark so early."

"It does, at that," he said. "The nights are going to be pretty long from now on. I mean. I mean—well, it starts getting dark early."

"I didn't have any idea what time it was," she said. "Everything was so mixed up, I sort of don't know where I am, or what it's all about. Getting back from the church, and then all those people, and then changing all my clothes, and then everybody throwing things, and all. Goodness, I don't see how people do it every day."

"Do what?" he said.

"Get married," she said. "When you think of all the people, all over the world, getting married just as if it was nothing. Chinese people and everybody. Just as if it wasn't anything."

"Well, let's not worry about people all over the world," he said. "Let's don't think about a lot of Chinese. We've got something better to think about. I mean. I mean—well, what do we care about them?"

"I know," she said. "But I just sort of got to thinking of them, all of them, all over everywhere, doing it all the time. At least, I mean—getting married, you know. And it's—well, it's sort of such a big thing to do, it makes you feel queer. You think of them, all of them, all doing it just like it wasn't anything. And how does anybody know what's going to happen next?"

"Let them worry," he said. "We don't have to. We know darn well what's going to happen next. I mean. I mean—well, we know it's going to be great. Well, we know we're going to be happy. Don't we?"

"Oh, of course," she said. "Only you think of all the people, and you have to sort of keep thinking. It makes you feel funny. An awful lot of people that get married, it doesn't turn out so well. And I guess they all must have thought it was going to be great."

"Come on, now," he said. "This is no way to start a honeymoon, with all this thinking going on. Look at us—all married and everything done. I mean. The wedding all done and all."

"Ah, it was nice, wasn't it?" she said. "Did you really like my veil?"

"You looked great," he said. "Just great."

"Oh, I'm terribly glad," she said. "Ellie and Louise looked lovely, didn't they? I'm terribly glad they did finally decide on pink. They looked perfectly lovely."

"Listen," he said. "I want to tell you something. When I was standing up there in that old church waiting for you to come up, and I saw those two bridesmaids, I thought to myself, I thought, 'Well, I never knew Louise could look like that!' Why, she'd have knocked anybody's eye out."

"Oh, really?" she said. "Funny. Of course, everybody thought her dress and hat were lovely, but a lot of people seemed to think she looked sort of tired. People have been saying that a lot, lately. I tell them I think it's awfully mean of them to go around saying that about her. I tell them they've got to remember that Louise isn't so terribly young any more, and they've got to expect her to look like that. Louise can say she's twenty-three all she wants to, but she's a good deal nearer twenty-seven."

"Well, she was certainly a knock-out at the wedding," he said. "Boy!"

"I'm terribly glad you thought so," she said. "I'm glad someone did. How did you think Ellie looked?"

"Why, I honestly didn't get a look at her," he said.

"Oh, really?" she said. "Well, I certainly think that's too bad. I don't suppose I ought to say it about my own sister, but I never saw anybody look as beautiful as Ellie looked today. And always so sweet and unselfish, too. And you didn't even notice her. But you never pay attention to Ellie, anyway. Don't think I haven't noticed it. It makes me feel just terrible. It makes me feel just awful, that you don't like my own sister."

"I do like her!" he said. "I'm crazy for Ellie. I think she's a great kid."

"Don't think it makes any difference to Ellie!" she said. "Ellie's got enough people crazy about her. It isn't anything to her whether you like her or not. Don't flatter yourself she cares! Only, the only thing is, it makes it awfully hard for me you don't like her, that's the only thing. I keep thinking, when we come back and get in that apartment and everything, it's going to be awfully hard for me that you won't want my own sister to come and see me. It's going to make it awfully hard for me that you won't ever want my family around. I know how you feel about my family. Don't think I haven't seen it. Only, if you don't ever want to see them, that's your loss. Not theirs. Don't flatter yourself!"

"Oh, now, come on!" he said. "What's all this talk about not wanting your family around? Why, you know how I feel about your family. I think your old lady—I think your mother's swell. And Ellie. And your father. What's all this talk?"

"Well, I've seen it," she said. "Don't think I haven't. Lots of people they get married, and they think it's going to be great and everything, and then it all goes to pieces because people don't like people's families, or something like that. Don't tell me! I've seen it happen."

"Honey," he said, "what is all this? What are you getting all angry about? Hey, look, this is our honeymoon. What are you trying to start a fight for? Ah, I guess you're just feeling sort of nervous."

"Me?" she said. "What have I got to be nervous about? I mean. I mean, goodness, I'm not nervous."

"You know, lots of times," he said, "they say that girls get kind of nervous and yippy on account of thinking about—I mean. I mean—well, it's like you said, things are all so sort of mixed up and everything, right now. But afterwards, it'll be all right. I mean. I mean—well, look, honey, you don't look any too comfortable. Don't you want to take your hat off? And let's don't ever fight, ever. Will we?"

"Ah, I'm sorry I was cross," she said. "I guess I did feel a little bit funny. All mixed up, and then thinking of all those people all over everywhere, and then being sort of 'way off here, all alone with you. It's so sort of different. It's sort of such a big thing. You can't blame a person for thinking, can you? Yes, don't let's ever, ever fight. We won't be like a whole lot of them. We won't fight or be nasty or anything. Will we?"

"You bet your life we won't," he said.

"I guess I will take this darned old hat off," she said. "It kind of presses. Just put it up on the rack, will you, dear? Do you like it, sweetheart?"

"Looks good on you," he said.

"No, but I mean," she said, "do you really like it?"

"Well, I'll tell you," he said. "I know this is the new style and everything like that, and it's probably great. I don't know anything about things like that. Only I like the kind of a hat like that blue hat you had. Gee, I liked that hat."

"Oh, really?" she said. "Well, that's nice. That's lovely. The first thing you say to me, as soon as you get me off on a train away from my family and everything, is that you don't like my hat. The first thing you say to your wife is you think she has terrible taste in hats. That's nice, isn't it?"

"Now, honey," he said, "I never said anything like that. I only said—"

"What you don't seem to realize," she said, "is this hat cost twenty-two dollars. Twenty-two dollars. And that horrible old blue thing you think you're so crazy about, that cost three ninety-five."

"I don't give a darn what they cost," he said. "I only said—I said I liked that blue hat. I don't know anything about hats. I'll be crazy about this one as soon as I get used to it. Only it's kind of not like your other hats. I don't know about the new styles. What do I know about women's hats?"

"It's too bad," she said, "you didn't marry somebody that would get the kind of hats you'd like. Hats that cost three ninety-five. Why didn't you marry Louise? You always think she looks so beautiful. You'd love her taste in hats. Why didn't you marry her?"

"Ah, now, honey," he said. "For heaven's sakes!"

"Why didn't you marry her?" she said. "All you've done, ever since we got on this train, is talk about her. Here I've sat and sat, and just listened to you saying how wonderful Louise is. I suppose that's nice, getting me all off here alone with you, and then raving about Louise right in front of my face. Why didn't you ask her to marry you? I'm sure she would have jumped at the chance. There aren't so many people asking her to marry them. It's too bad you didn't marry her. I'm sure you'd have been much happier."

"Listen, baby," he said, "while you're talking about things like that, why didn't you marry Joe Brooks? I suppose he could have given you all the twenty-two-dollar hats you wanted, I suppose!"

"Well, I'm not so sure I'm not sorry I didn't," she said. "There! Joe Brooks wouldn't have waited until he got me all off alone and then sneered at my taste in clothes. Joe Brooks wouldn't ever hurt my feelings. Joe Brooks has always been fond of me. There!"

"Yeah," he said. "He's fond of you. He was so fond of you he didn't even send a wedding present. That's how fond of you he was."

"I happen to know for a fact," she said, "that he was away on business, and as soon as he comes back he's going to give me anything I want, for the apartment."

"Listen," he said. "I don't want anything he gives you in our apartment. Anything he gives you, I'll throw right out the window. That's what I think of your friend Joe Brooks. And how do you know where he is and what he's going to do, anyway? Has he been writing to you?"

"I suppose my friends can correspond with me," she said. "I didn't hear there was any law against that."

"Well, I suppose they can't!" he said. "And what do you think of that? I'm not going to have my wife getting a lot of letters from cheap traveling salesmen!"

"Joe Brooks is not a cheap traveling salesman!" she said. "He is not! He gets a wonderful salary."

"Oh yeah?" he said. "Where did you hear that?"

"He told me so himself," she said.

"Oh, he told you so himself," he said. "I see. He told you so himself."

"You've got a lot of right to talk about Joe Brooks," she said. "You and your friend Louise. All you ever talk about is Louise."

"Oh, for heaven's sakes!" he said. "What do I care about Louise? I just thought she was a friend of yours, that's all. That's why I ever even noticed her."

"Well, you certainly took an awful lot of notice of her today," she said. "On our wedding day! You said yourself when you were standing there in the church you just kept thinking of her. Right up at the altar. Oh, right in the presence of God! And all you thought about was Louise."

"Listen, honey," he said, "I never should have said that. How does anybody know what kind of crazy things come into their heads when they're standing there waiting to get married? I was just telling you that because it was so kind of crazy. I thought it would make you laugh."

"I know," she said. "I've been all sort of mixed up today, too. I told you that. Everything so strange and everything. And me all the time thinking about all those people all over the world, and now us here all alone, and everything. I know you get all mixed up. Only I did think, when you kept talking about how beautiful Louise looked, you did it with malice and forethought."

"I never did anything with malice and forethought!" he said. "I just told you that about Louise because I thought it would make you laugh."

"Well, it didn't," she said.

"No, I know it didn't," he said. "It certainly did not. Ah, baby, and we ought to be laughing, too. Hell, honey lamb, this is our honeymoon. What's the matter?"

"I don't know," she said. "We used to squabble a lot when we were going together and then engaged and everything, but I thought everything would be so different as soon as you were married. And now I feel so sort of strange and everything. I feel so sort of alone."

"Well, you see, sweetheart," he said, "we're not really married yet. I mean. I mean—well, things will be different afterwards. Oh, hell. I mean, we haven't been married very long."

"No," she said.

"Well, we haven't got much longer to wait now," he said. "I mean— well, we'll be in New York in about twenty minutes. Then we can have dinner, and sort of see what we feel like doing. Or I mean. Is there anything special you want to do tonight?"

"What?" she said.

"What I mean to say," he said, "would you like to go to a show or something?"

"Why, whatever you like," she said. "I sort of didn't think people went to theaters and things on their—I mean, I've got a couple of letters I simply must write. Don't let me forget."

"Oh," he said. "You're going to write letters tonight?"

"Well, you see," she said. "I've been perfectly terrible. What with all the excitement and everything. I never did thank poor old Mrs. Sprague for her berry spoon, and I never did a thing about those book ends the McMasters sent. It's just too awful of me. I've got to write them this very night."

"And when you've finished writing your letters," he said, "maybe I could get you a magazine or a bag of peanuts."

"What?" she said.

"I mean," he said, "I wouldn't want you to be bored."

"As if I could be bored with you!" she said. "Silly! Aren't we married? Bored!"

"What I thought," he said, "I thought when we got in, we could go right up to the Biltmore and anyway leave our bags, and maybe have a little dinner in the room, kind of quiet, and then do whatever we wanted. I mean. I mean—well, let's go right up there from the station."

"Oh, yes, let's," she said. "I'm so glad we're going to the Biltmore. I just love it. The twice I've stayed in New York we've always stayed there, Papa and Mamma and Ellie and I, and I was crazy about it. I always sleep so well there. I go right off to sleep the minute I put my head on the pillow."

"Oh, you do?" he said.

"At least, I mean," she said. "Way up high it's so quiet."

"We might go to some show or other tomorrow night instead of tonight," he said. "Don't you think that would be better?"

"Yes, I think it might," she said.

He rose, balanced a moment, crossed over and sat down beside her.

"Do you really have to write those letters tonight?" he said.

"Well," she said, "I don't suppose they'd get there any quicker than if I wrote them tomorrow."

There was a silence with things going on in it.

"And we won't ever fight any more, will we?" he said.

"Oh, no," she said. "Not ever! I don't know what made me do like that. It all got so sort of funny, sort of like a nightmare, the way I got thinking of all those people getting married all the time; and so many of them, everything spoils on account of fighting and everything. I got all mixed up thinking about them. Oh, I don't want to be like them. But we won't be, will we?"

"Sure we won't," he said.

"We won't go all to pieces," she said. "We won't fight. It'll all be different, now we're married. It'll all be lovely. Reach me down my hat, will you, sweetheart? It's time I was putting it on. Thanks. Ah, I'm so sorry you don't like it."

"I do so like it!" he said.

"You said you didn't," she said. "You said you thought it was perfectly terrible."

"I never said any such thing," he said. "You're crazy."

"All right, I may be crazy," she said. "Thank you very much. But that's what you said. Not that it matters—it's just a little thing. But it makes you feel pretty funny to think you've gone and married somebody that says you have perfectly terrible taste in hats. And then goes and says you're crazy, beside."

"Now, listen here," he said. "Nobody said any such thing. Why, I love that hat. The more I look at it the better I like it. I think it's great."

"That isn't what you said before," she said.

"Honey," he said. "Stop it, will you? What do you want to start all this for? I love the damned hat. I mean, I love your hat. I love anything you wear. What more do you want me to say?"

"Well, I don't want you to say it like that," she said.

"I said I think it's great," he said. "That's all I said."

"Do you really?" she said. "Do you honestly? Ah, I'm so glad. I'd hate you not to like my hat. It would be—I don't know, it would be sort of such a bad start."

"Well, I'm crazy for it," he said. "Now we've got that settled, for heaven's sakes. Ah, baby. Baby lamb. We're not going to have any bad starts. Look at us—we're on our honeymoon. Pretty soon we'll be regular old married people. I mean. I mean, in a few minutes we'll be getting in to New York, and then we'll be going to the hotel, and then everything will be all right. I mean—well, look at us! Here we are married! Here we are!"

"Yes, here we are," she said. "Aren't we?"

WHOEVER WAS
USING THIS BED

RAYMOND CARVER

The call comes in the middle of the night, three in the morning, and it nearly scares us to death.

"Answer it, answer it!" my wife cries. "My God, who is it? Answer it!"

I can't find the light, but I get to the other room, where the phone is, and pick it up after the fourth ring.

"Is Bud there?" this woman says, very drunk.

"Jesus, you have the wrong number," I say, and hang up.

I turn the light on, and go into the bathroom, and that's when I hear the phone start again.

"Answer that!" my wife screams from the bedroom. "What in God's name do they want, Jack? I can't take any more."

I hurry out of the bathroom and pick up the phone.

"Bud?" the woman says. "What are you doing, Bud?"

I say, "Look here. You have a wrong number. Don't ever call this number again."

"I have to talk to Bud," she says.

I hang up, wait until it rings again, and then I take the receiver and lay it on the table beside the phone. But I hear the woman's voice say, "Bud, talk to me, please." I leave the receiver on its side on the table, turn off the light, and close the door to the room.

In the bedroom I find the lamp on and my wife, Iris, sitting against the headboard with her knees drawn up under the covers. She has a pillow behind her back, and she's more on my side than her own side. The covers are up around her shoulders. The blankets and the sheet have been pulled out from the foot of the bed. If we want to go back to sleep—I want to go back to sleep, anyway—we may have to start from scratch and do this bed over again.

"What the hell was that all about?" Iris says. "We should have unplugged the phone. I guess we forgot. Try forgetting one night to unplug the phone and see what happens. I don't believe it."

After Iris and I started living together, my former wife, or else one of my kids, used to call up when we were asleep and want to harangue us. They kept doing it even after Iris and I were married. So we started unplugging our phone before we went to bed. We unplugged the phone every night of the year, just about. It was a habit. This time I slipped up, that's all.

"Some woman wanting *Bud*," I say. I'm standing there in my pajamas, wanting to get into bed, but I can't. "She was drunk. Move over, honey. I took the phone off the hook."

"She can't call again?"

"No," I say. "Why don't you move over a little and give me some of those covers?"

She takes her pillow and puts it on the far side of the bed, against the headboard, scoots over, and then she leans back once more. She doesn't look sleepy. She looks fully awake. I get into bed and take some covers. But the covers don't feel right. I don't have any sheet; all I have is blanket. I look down and see my feet sticking out. I turn onto my side, facing her, and bring my legs up so that my feet are under the blanket. We should make up the bed again. I ought to suggest that. But I'm thinking, too, that if we kill the light now, this minute, we might be able to go right back to sleep.

"How about you turning off your light, honey?" I say, as nice as I can.

"Let's have a cigarette first," she says. "Then we'll go to sleep. Get us the cigarettes and the ashtray, why don't you? We'll have a cigarette."

"Let's go to sleep," I say. "Look at what time it is." The clock radio is right there beside the bed. Anyone can see it says three-thirty.

"Come on," Iris says. "I need a cigarette after all that."

I get out of bed for the cigarettes and ashtray. I have to go into the room where the phone is, but I don't touch the phone. I don't even want to look at the phone, but I do, of course. The receiver is still on its side on the table.

I crawl back in bed and put the ashtray on the quilt between us. I light a cigarette, give it to her, and then light one for myself.

She tries to remember the dream she was having when the phone rang. "I can just about remember it, but I can't remember exactly. Something about, about—no, I don't know what it was about now. I can't be sure. I can't remember it," she says finally. "God damn that woman and her phone call. '*Bud*,'" she says. "I'd like to punch her." She puts out her cigarette and immediately lights another, blows smoke, and lets her eyes take in the chest of drawers and the window curtains. Her hair is undone and around her shoulders. She uses the ashtray and then stares over the foot of the bed, trying to remember.

But, really, I don't care what she's dreamed. I want to go back to sleep is all. I finish my cigarette and put it out and wait for her to finish. I lie still and don't say anything.

Iris is like my former wife in that when she sleeps she sometimes has violent dreams. She thrashes around in bed during the night and wakes in the morning drenched with sweat, the nightgown sticking to her body. And, like my former wife, she wants to tell me her dreams in great detail and speculate as to what this stands for or that portends. My former wife used to kick the covers off in the night and cry out in her sleep, as if someone were laying hands on her. Once, in a particularly violent dream, she hit me on the ear with her fist. I was in a dreamless sleep, but I struck out in the dark and hit her on the forehead. Then we began yelling. We both yelled and yelled. We'd hurt each other, but we were mainly scared. We had no idea what had happened until I turned the lamp on; then we sorted it out. Afterward, we joked about it—fistfighting in our sleep. But then so much else began to happen that was far more serious we tended to forget about that night. We never mentioned it again, even when we teased each other.

Once I woke up in the night to hear Iris grinding her teeth in her sleep. It was such a peculiar thing to have going on right next to my ear that it woke me up. I gave her a little shake, and she stopped. The next morning she told me she'd had a very bad dream, but that's all she'd tell me about it. I didn't press her for details. I guess I really didn't want to know what could have been so bad that she didn't want to say. When I told her she'd been grinding her teeth in her sleep, she frowned and said she was going to have to do something about that. The next night she brought home something called a Niteguard—something she was supposed to wear in her mouth while she slept. She had to do something, she said. She couldn't afford to keep grinding her teeth; pretty soon she wouldn't have any. So she wore this protective device in her mouth for a week or so, and then she stopped wearing it. She said it was uncomfortable and, anyway, it was not very cosmetic. Who'd want to kiss a woman wearing a thing like that in her mouth, she said. She had something there, of course.

Another time I woke up because she was stroking my face and calling me Earl. I took her hand and squeezed her fingers. "What is it?" I said. "What is it, sweetheart?" But instead of answering she simply squeezed back, sighed, and then lay still again. The next morning, when I asked her what she'd dreamed the night before, she claimed not to have had any dreams.

"So who's Earl?" I said. "Who is this Earl you were talking about in your sleep?" She blushed and said she didn't know anybody named Earl and never had.

The lamp is still on and, because I don't know what else to think about, I think about that phone being off the hook. I ought to hang it up and unplug the cord. Then we have to think about sleep.

"I'll go take care of that phone," I say. "Then let's go to sleep."

Iris uses the ashtray and says, "Make sure it's unplugged this time."

I get up again and go to the other room, open the door, and turn on the light. The receiver is still on its side on the table. I bring it to my ear, expecting to hear the dial tone. But I don't hear anything, not even the tone.

On an impulse, I say something. "Hello," I say.

"Oh, Bud, it's you," the woman says.

I hang up the phone and bend over and unplug it from the wall before it can ring again. This is a new one on me. This deal is a mystery, this woman and her Bud person. I don't know how to tell Iris about this new development, because it'll just lead to more discussion and further speculation. I decide not to say anything for now. Maybe I'll say something over breakfast.

Back in the bedroom I see she is smoking another cigarette. I see, too, that it's nearly four in the morning. I'm starting to worry. When it's four o'clock it'll soon be five o'clock, and then it will be six, then six-thirty, then time to get up for work. I lie back down, close my eyes, and decide I'll count to sixty, slowly, before I say anything else about the light.

"I'm starting to remember," Iris says. "It's coming back to me. You want to hear it, Jack?"

I stop counting, open my eyes, sit up. The bedroom is filled with smoke. I light one up, too. Why not? The hell with it.

She says, "There was a party going on in my dream."

"Where was I when this was going on?" Usually, for whatever reason, I don't figure in her dreams. It irritates me a little, but I don't let on. My feet are uncovered again. I pull them under the covers, raise myself up on my elbow, and use the ashtray. "Is this another dream that I'm not in? It's okay, if that's the case." I pull on the cigarette, hold the smoke, let it out.

"Honey, you weren't in the dream," Iris says. "I'm sorry, but you weren't. You weren't anywhere around. I *missed* you, though. I did miss you, I'm sure of it. It was like I knew you were somewhere nearby, but you weren't there where I needed you. You know how I get into those anxiety states sometimes? If we go someplace together where there's a group of people and we get separated and I can't find you? It was a little like that. You were there, I think, but I couldn't find you."

"Go ahead and tell me about the dream," I say.

She rearranges the covers around her waist and legs and reaches for a cigarette. I hold the lighter for her. Then she goes on to describe this party where all that was being served was beer. "I don't even like beer," she says. But she drank a large quantity anyway, and just when she went to leave—to go home, she says—this little dog took hold of the hem of her dress and made her stay.

She laughs, and I laugh right along with her, even though, when I look at the clock, I see the hands are close to saying four-thirty.

There was some kind of music being played in her dream—a piano, maybe, or else it was an accordion, who knows? Dreams are that way sometimes, she says. Anyway, she vaguely remembers her former husband putting in an appearance. He might have been the one serving the beer. People were drinking beer from a keg, using plastic cups. She thought she might even have danced with him.

"Why are you telling me this?"

She says, "It was a dream, honey."

"I don't think I like it, knowing you're supposed to be here beside me all night but instead you're dreaming about strange dogs, parties, and ex-husbands. I don't like you dancing with him. What the hell is this?

What if I told you I dreamed I danced the night away with Carol? Would you like it?"

"It's just a dream, right?" she says. "Don't get weird on me. I won't say any more. I see I can't. I can see it isn't a good idea." She brings her fingers to her lips slowly, the way she does sometimes when she's thinking. Her face shows how hard she's concentrating; little lines appear on her forehead. "I'm sorry that you weren't in the dream. But if I told you otherwise I'd be lying to you, right?"

I nod. I touch her arm to show her it's okay. I don't really mind. And I don't, I guess. "What happened then, honey? Finish telling the dream," I say. "And maybe we can go to sleep then." I guess I wanted to know the next thing. The last I'd heard, she'd been dancing with Jerry. If there was more, I needed to hear it.

She plumps up the pillow behind her back and says, "That's all I can remember. I can't remember any more about it. That was when the goddamn phone rang."

"Bud," I say. I can see smoke drifting in the light under the lamp, and smoke hangs in the air in the room. "Maybe we should open a window," I say.

"That's a good idea," she says. "Let some of this smoke out. It can't be any good for us."

"Hell no, it isn't," I say.

I get up again and go to the window and raise it a few inches. I can feel the cool air that comes in and from a distance I hear a truck gearing down as it starts up the grade that will take it to the pass and on over into the next state.

"I guess pretty soon we're going to be the last smokers left in America," she says. "Seriously, we should think about quitting." She says this as she puts her cigarette out and reaches for the pack next to the ashtray.

"It's open season on smokers," I say.

I get back in the bed. The covers are turned every which way, and it's five o'clock in the morning. I don't think we're going to sleep any more tonight. But so what if we don't? Is there a law on the books? Is something bad going to happen to us if we don't?

She takes some of her hair between her fingers. Then she pushes it behind her ear, looks at me, and says, "Lately I've been feeling this vein in my forehead. It *pulses* sometimes. It throbs. Do you know what I'm talking about? I don't know if you've ever had anything like that. I hate to think about it, but probably one of these days I'll have a stroke or something. Isn't that how they happen? A vein in your head bursts? That's probably what'll happen to me, eventually. My mother, my grandmother, and one of my aunts died of stroke. There's a history of stroke in my family. It can run in the family, you know. It's hereditary, just like heart disease, or being too fat, or whatever. Anyway," she says, "something's going to happen to me someday, right? So maybe that's what it'll be—a stroke. Maybe that's how I'll go. That's what it feels like it could be the beginning of. First it pulses a little, like it wants my attention, and then it starts to throb. Throb, throb, throb. It scares me silly," she says. "I want us to give up these goddamn cigarettes before it's too late." She looks at what's left of her cigarette, mashes it into the ashtray, and tries to fan the smoke away.

I'm on my back, studying the ceiling, thinking that this is the kind of talk that could only take place at five in the morning. I feel I ought to say something. "I get winded easy," I say. "I found myself out of breath when I ran in there to answer the phone."

"That could have been because of anxiety," Iris says. "Who needs it, anyway! The *idea* of somebody calling at this hour! I could tear that woman limb from limb."

I pull myself up in the bed and lean back against the headboard. I put the pillow behind my back and try to get comfortable, same as Iris. "I'll tell you something I haven't told you," I say. "Once in a while my heart palpitates. It's like it goes crazy." She's watching me closely, listening for whatever it is I'm going to say next. "Sometimes it feels like it's going to jump out of my chest. I don't know what the hell causes it."

"Why didn't you tell me?" she says. She takes my hand and holds it. She squeezes my hand. "You never said anything, honey. Listen, I don't know what I'd *do* if something ever happened to you. I'd fold up. How often does it happen? That's scary, you know." She's still holding my hand. But her fingers slide to my wrist, where my pulse is. She goes on holding my wrist like this.

"I never told you because I didn't want to scare you," I say. "But it happens sometimes. It happened as recently as a week ago. I don't have to be doing anything in particular when it happens, either. I can be sitting in a chair with the paper. Or else driving the car, or pushing a grocery basket. It doesn't matter if I'm exerting myself or not. It just starts—boom, boom,

boom. Like that. I'm surprised people can't hear it. It's that loud, I think. *I* can hear it, anyway, and I don't mind telling you it scares me," I say. "So if emphysema doesn't get me, or lung cancer, or maybe a stroke like what you're talking about, then it's going to be a heart attack probably."

I reach for the cigarettes. I give her one. We're through with sleep for the night. Did we sleep? For a minute, I can't remember.

"Who knows what we'll die of?" Iris says. "It could be anything. If we live long enough, maybe it'll be kidney failure, or something like that. A friend of mine at work, her father just died of kidney failure. That's what can happen to you sometimes if you're lucky enough to get really old. When your kidneys fail, the body starts filling up with uric acid then. You finally turn a whole different color before you die."

"Great. That sounds wonderful," I say. "Maybe we should get off this subject. How'd we get onto this stuff, anyway?"

She doesn't answer. She leans forward, away from her pillow, arms clasping her legs. She closes her eyes and lays her head on her knees. Then she begins to rock back and forth, slowly. It's as if she were listening to music. But there isn't any music. None that I can hear, anyway.

"You know what I'd like?" she says. She stops moving, opens her eyes, and tilts her head at me. Then she grins, so I'll know she's all right.

"What would you like, honey?" I've got my leg hooked over her leg, at the ankle.

She says, "I'd like some coffee, that's what. I could go for a nice strong cup of black coffee. We're awake, aren't we? Who's going back to sleep? Let's have some coffee."

"We drink too much coffee," I say. "All that coffee isn't good for us, either. I'm not saying we shouldn't have any, I'm just saying we drink too much of it. It's just an observation," I add. "Actually, I could drink some coffee myself."

"Good," she says.

But neither of us makes a move.

She shakes out her hair and then lights another cigarette. Smoke drifts slowly in the room. Some of it drifts toward the open window. A little rain begins to fall on the patio outside the window. The alarm comes on, and I reach over and shut it off. Then I take the pillow and put it under my head again. I lie back and stare at the ceiling some more. "What happened to that bright idea we had about a girl who could bring us our coffee in bed?" I say.

"I wish *somebody* would bring us coffee," she says. "A girl or a boy, one or the other. I could really go for some coffee right now."

She moves the ashtray to the nightstand, and I think she's going to get up. Somebody has to get up and start the coffee and put a can of frozen juice in the blender. One of us has to make a move. But what she does instead is slide down in the bed until she's sitting somewhere in the middle. The covers are all over the place. She picks at something on the quilt, and then rubs her palm across whatever it is before she looks up. "Did you see in the paper where that guy took a shotgun into an intensive-care unit and made the nurses take his father off the life-support machine? Did you read about that?" Iris says.

"I saw something about it on the news," I say. "But mostly they were talking about this nurse who unplugged six or eight people from their machines. At this point they don't know exactly how many she unplugged. She started off by unplugging her mother, and then she went on from there. It was like a spree, I guess. She said she thought she was doing everybody a favor. She said she hoped somebody'd do it for *her*, if they cared about her."

Iris decides to move on down to the foot of the bed. She positions herself so that she is facing me. Her legs are still under the covers. She puts her legs between my legs and says, "What about that quadriplegic woman on the news who says she wants to die, wants to starve herself to death? Now she's suing her doctor and the hospital because they insist on force-feeding her to keep her alive. Can you believe it? It's insane. They strap her down three times a day so they can run this tube into her throat. They feed her breakfast, lunch, and dinner that way. And they keep her plugged into this machine, too, because her lungs don't want to work on their own. It said in the paper that she's *begging* them to unplug her, or else to just let her starve to death. She's having to plead with them to let her die, but they won't listen. She said she started out wanting to die with some dignity. Now she's just mad and looking to sue everybody. Isn't that amazing? Isn't that one for the books?" she says. "I have these headaches sometimes," she says. "Maybe it has something to do with the vein. Maybe not. Maybe they're not related. But I don't tell you when my head hurts, because I don't want to worry you."

"What are you talking about?" I say. "Look at me. Iris? I have a right to know. I'm your husband, in case you've forgotten. If something's wrong with you, I should know about it."

"But what could you *do*? You'd just worry." She bumps my leg with her leg, then bumps it again. "Right? You'd tell me to take some aspirin. I know you."

I look toward the window, where it's beginning to get light. I can feel a damp breeze from the window. It's stopped raining now, but it's one of those mornings where it could begin to pour. I look at her again. "To tell you the truth, Iris, I get sharp pains in my side from time to time." But the moment I say the words I'm sorry. She'll be concerned, and want to talk about it. We ought to be thinking of showers; we should be sitting down to breakfast.

"Which side?" she says.

"Right side."

"It could be your appendix," she says. "Something fairly simple like that."

I shrug. "Who knows? I don't know. All I know is it happens. Every so often, for just a minute or two, I feel something sharp down there. Very sharp. At first I thought it might be a pulled muscle. Which side's your gallbladder on, by the way? Is it the left or right side? Maybe it's my gallbladder. Or else maybe a gall*stone*, whatever the hell that is."

"It's not really a stone," she says. "A gallstone is like a little granule, or something like that. It's about as big as the tip of a pencil. No, wait, that might be a *kidney* stone I'm talking about. I guess I don't know anything about it." She shakes her head.

"What's the difference between kidney stone and gallstone?" I say. "Christ, we don't even know which side of the body they're on. You don't know, and I don't know. That's how much we know together. A total of nothing. But I read somewhere that you can pass a kidney stone, if that's what this is, and usually it won't kill you. Painful, yes. I don't know what they say about a gallstone."

"I like that 'usually,'" she says.

"I know," I say. "Listen, we'd better get up. It's getting really late. It's seven o'clock."

"I know," she says. "Okay." But she continues to sit there. Then she says, "My grandma had arthritis so bad toward the end she couldn't get around by herself, or even move her fingers. She had to sit in a chair and wear these mittens all day. Finally, she couldn't even hold a cup of cocoa. That's how bad her arthritis was. Then she had her stroke. And my *grandpa*," she says. "He went into a nursing home not long after Grandma died. It was either that or else somebody had to come in and be with him around the clock, and nobody could do that. Nobody had the money for twenty-four-hour-a-day care, either. So he goes into the nursing home. But he began to deteriorate fast in there. One time, after he'd been in that place for a while, my mom went to visit him and then she came home and said something. I'll never forget what she said." She looks at me as if I'm never going to forget it, either. And I'm not. "She said, 'My dad doesn't recognize me anymore. He doesn't even know who I am. My dad has become a vegetable.' That was my mom who said that."

She leans over and covers her face with her hands and begins to cry. I move down there to the foot of the bed and sit beside her. I take her hand and hold it in my lap. I put my arm around her. We're sitting together looking at the headboard and at the nightstand. The clock's there, too, and beside the clock a few magazines and a paperback. We're sitting on the part of the bed where we keep our feet when we sleep. It looks like whoever was using this bed left in a hurry. I know I won't ever look at this bed again without remembering it like this. We're into something now, but I don't know what, exactly.

"I don't want anything like that to ever happen to me," she says. "Or to you, either." She wipes her face with a corner of the blanket and takes a deep breath, which comes out as a sob. "I'm sorry. I just can't help it," she says.

"It won't happen to us. It won't," I say. "Don't worry about any of it, okay? We're fine, Iris, and we're going to stay fine. In any case, that time's a long time off. Hey, I love you. We love each other, don't we? That's the important thing. That's what counts. Don't worry, honey."

"I want you to promise me something," she says. She takes her hand back. She moves my arm away from her shoulder. "I want you to promise me you'll pull the plug on me, if and when it's ever necessary. If it ever comes to that, I mean. Do you hear what I'm saying? I'm serious about this, Jack. I want you to pull the plug on me if you ever have to. Will you promise?"

I don't say anything right away. What am I supposed to say? They haven't written the book on this one yet. I need a minute to think. I know it won't cost me anything to tell her I'll do whatever she wants. It's just words, right? Words are easy. But there's more to it than this; she wants an honest response from me. And I don't know what I feel about it yet. I shouldn't be hasty. I can't say something without thinking about what I'm saying, about consequences, about what she's going to feel when I say it—whatever it is I say.

I'm still thinking about it when she says, "What about you?"

"What about me what?"

"Do you want to be unplugged if it comes to that? God forbid it ever does, of course," she says. "But I should have some kind of idea, you know—some word from you now—about what you want me to do if worst comes to worst." She's looking at me closely, waiting for me to say. She wants something she can file away to use later, if and when she ever has to. Sure. Okay. Easy enough for me to say, *Unplug me, honey, if you think it's for the best.* But I need to consider this a little more. I haven't even said yet what I will or won't do for *her.* Now I have to think about me and *my* situation. I don't feel I should jump into this. This is nuts. *We're* nuts. But I realize that whatever I say now might come back to me sometime. It's important. This is a life-and-death thing we're talking about here.

She hasn't moved. She's still waiting for her answer. And I can see we're not going anywhere this morning until she has an answer. I think about it some more, and then I say what I mean. "No. Don't unplug me. I don't want to be unplugged. Leave me hooked up just as long as possible. Who's going to object? Are you going to object? Will I be offending anybody? As long as people can stand the sight of me, just so long as they don't start howling, don't unplug anything. Let me keep going, okay? Right to the bitter end. Invite my friends in to say good-bye. Don't do anything rash."

"Be serious," she says. "This is a very serious matter we're discussing."

"I am serious. Don't unplug me. It's as simple as that."

She nods. "Okay, then. I promise you I won't." She hugs me. She holds me tight for a minute. Then she lets me go. She looks at the clock radio and says, "Jesus, we better get moving."

So we get out of bed and start getting dressed. In some ways it's just like any other morning, except we do things faster. We drink coffee and juice and we eat English muffins. We remark on the weather, which is overcast and blustery. We don't talk anymore about plugs, or about sickness and hospitals and stuff like that. I kiss her and leave her on the front porch with her umbrella open, waiting for her ride to work. Then I hurry to my car and get in. In a minute, after I've run the motor, I wave and drive off.

But during the day, at work, I think about some of those things we talked about this morning. I can't help it. For one thing, I'm bone-tired from lack of sleep. I feel vulnerable and prey to any random, gruesome thought. Once, when nobody is around, I put my head on my desk and think I might catch a few minutes' sleep. But when I close my eyes I find myself thinking about it again. In my mind I can see a hospital bed. That's all—just a hospital bed. The bed's in a room, I guess. Then I see an oxygen tent over the bed, and beside the bed some of those screens and some big monitors—the kind they have in movies. I open my eyes and sit up in my chair and light a cigarette. I drink some coffee while I smoke the cigarette. Then I look at the time and get back to work.

At five o'clock, I'm so tired it's all I can do to drive home. It's raining, and I have to be careful driving. Very careful. There's been an accident, too. Someone has rear-ended someone else at a traffic light, but I don't think anyone has been hurt. The cars are still out in the road, and people are standing around in the rain, talking. Still, traffic moves slowly; the police have set out flares.

When I see my wife, I say, "God, what a day. I'm whipped. How are you doing?" We kiss each other. I take off my coat and hang it up. I take the drink Iris gives me. Then, because it's been on my mind, and because I want to clear the deck, so to speak, I say, "All right, if it's what you want to hear, I'll pull the plug for you. If that's what you want me to do, I'll do it. If it will make you happy, here and now, to hear me say so, I'll say it. I'll do it for you. I'll pull the plug, or have it pulled, if I ever think it's necessary. But what I said about my plug still stands. Now I don't want to have to think about this stuff ever again. I don't even want to have to *talk* about it again. I think we've said all there is to say on the subject. We've exhausted every angle. *I'm* exhausted."

Iris grins. "Okay," she says. "At least I know now, anyway. I didn't before. Maybe I'm crazy, but I feel better somehow, if you want to know. I don't want to think about it anymore, either. But I'm glad we talked it over. I'll never bring it up again, either, and that's a promise."

She takes my drink and puts it on the table, next to the phone. She puts her arms around me and holds me and lets her head rest on my shoulder. But here's the thing. What I've just said to her, what I've been thinking about off and on all day, well, I feel as if I've crossed some kind of invisible line. I feel as if I've come to a place I never thought I'd have to come to. And I don't know how I got here. It's a strange place. It's a place where a little harmless dreaming and then some sleepy, early-morning talk has led me into considerations of death and annihilation.

The phone rings. We let go of each other, and I reach to answer it. "Hello," I say.

"Hello, there," the woman says back.

It's the same woman who called this morning, but she isn't drunk now. At least, I don't think she is; she doesn't sound drunk. She is speaking quietly, reasonably, and she is asking me if I can put her in touch with Bud Roberts. She apologizes. She hates to trouble me, she says, but this is an urgent matter. She's sorry for any trouble she might be giving.

While she talks, I fumble with my cigarettes. I put one in my mouth and use the lighter. Then it's my turn to talk. This is what I say to her: "Bud Roberts doesn't live here. He is not at this number, and I don't expect he ever will be. I will never, never lay eyes on this man you're talking about. Please don't ever call here again. Just don't, okay? Do you hear me? If you're not careful, I'll wring your neck for you."

"The *gall* of that woman," Iris says.

My hands are shaking. I think my voice is doing things. But while I'm trying to tell all this to the woman, while I'm trying to make myself understood, my wife moves quickly and bends over, and that's it. The line goes dead, and I can't hear anything.

FOR A LONG TIME THIS WAS GRISELDA'S STORY

ANTHONY DOERR

In 1979 Griselda Drown was a senior volleyballer at Boise High, a terrif-
ically tall girl with trunky thighs, slender arms and a volleyball serve
that won an Idaho State Championship despite T-shirts claiming it was
a team effort. She was a gray-eyed growth spurt, orange-haired, an early
bloomer, and there were rumors about how she took boys two at a time
in the dusty band closet where the dented tubas and ruptured drums
were kept, about how she straddled the physics teacher, about her
escapades during study hall with ice cubes. They were rumors; whether
they were true or not didn't matter. We all knew them. They might as
well have been true.

   Griselda's father was long gone; her mother worked two shifts at Boise
Linen Supply. Her younger sister, Rosemary, too short and plump to play,
was equipment manager for the team. She sat on a fold-up chair and flipped
scoreboard switches, penciled statistics, occasionally pumped air into flat
volleyballs while the coach made the team run windsprints.

   It began on an August afternoon, after practice, with Griselda on the
sidewalk, in the shadow of the bricked gymnasium, a social studies book
slipped under one long arm, listening to the air-brakes of school buses
and the wind rasping in a thin school-front stand of aspens. Her sister,
curly-headed, eyes just clearing the dash, pulled up in the rust-pocked
Toyota the girls shared with their mother. They headed for the Idaho
Fairgrounds, the Great Western Fair, Griselda in the front seat with her
big knees wedged against the glove box, leaning her long face out the

window to catch the wind. Rosemary drove slowly, stopped completely at stop signs, was clumsy with the clutch. They didn't speak.

At the fairgrounds we saw them in the parking lot inhaling the effluvium of carnival, the smells of fried dough, caramel and cinnamon, the flap-flapping of tents, a carousel plinking out music-box songs, voluptuous sounds bouncing down tent ropes and along the trampled dust of the midway. Wind-curled handbills staple-gunned to telephone poles, the hum of gas-powered generators and the gyro truck, the lemonade truck, pretzels and popcorn, baked potatoes, the American flag, the rumblings of rides and the disconnected screams of riders—all of it shimmered before them like a mirage, something not quite real.

Griselda strode to the rope-gate entrance, the ticket seller's cage, where a dwarfish ticket taker stood on a stool, and Rosemary plodded behind, the foothills of Boise lifting beyond the tent peaks, brown and hazed, into a pale sky. Griselda dug a pair of wrinkled singles from her pocket and passed them through.

This is how we told Griselda's story, later, in check-out lanes or in the bleachers during volleyball games: two sisters strolling the midway, single file, Griselda in the lead and Rosemary behind. They bought cotton candy for a quarter, moved about with faces half-wrapped in a pink cumulus of sugar, plodding through the catcalls of game operators: Squirt the gun in the clown's mouth! Break the balloon, now, girls! They paid quarters to sling rings over Coke bottlenecks. Rosemary pulled a rubber ducky from a water trough with a fishing pole and won a small and smudgy panda with plastic button eyes and a scowl made of thread.

The sunlight went long and orange. The sisters drifted among the booths and rides, feeling vaguely sick, cotton candy dissolving in their mouths. Finally, in the purpling dusk, they arrived at the metal eater's tent, at the far corner of the fairgrounds. A crowd had gathered, men mostly, in jeans and boots. Griselda stopped, hipped herself a place between them, easily saw over the capped and hatted heads. There was a card table at the back of the tent, set up from the ground on risers, spotlit yellow. She smelled the rubber tent-smell, saw the lazy lift of insects in the spotlight, heard the men around her discuss the impossibility and strangeness of metal eating.

Rosemary couldn't see. She shifted from foot to foot. She mentioned that they should go—it was getting late. The crowd filled in behind them. Griselda tore off a puff of cotton candy and pressed it into the roof of her mouth with her tongue. She studied her sister, the panda hanging from her fist. I could lift you, she offered. Rosemary blushed, shook her head. It's a metal eater, Griselda whispered. I've never seen one. I don't even know what one is. It'll be fake, Rosemary said. It won't be real. This kind of stuff is never real. Griselda shrugged.

The sisters looked at each other. I want to see it, Griselda insisted. I *can't* see it, Rosemary whined. Now it was Griselda's turn to shake her head. Then don't, she said. Rosemary's face went stern and hurt. She clumped off toward the car, the panda against her chest like a rueful child. Griselda watched the stage.

Soon the metal eater came out, and the men in the tent quieted, and there was only the whispering of the crowd and the slow looping of insects in the yellow spotlight and, far off, the plink-plinking of the carousel. The metal eater was a tidy-looking man in a business suit, trim and small and mannered. Griselda stood transfixed. What a man he was, what glinty spectacles, what shiny shoes, what a neatness to his construction, what pinstripes and cufflinks to wear to eat metal in Boise, Idaho. She had never seen a man like him.

He seated himself at the raised-up table, moving with a delicacy and tidiness that made Griselda want to charge the stage, throw herself upon him and smother him, consume him, flail her body against his. He was madly different, significant, endlessly captivating; she must have discerned something deep beneath his surface, something less acutely evident to the rest of us.

He produced a razor blade from a vest pocket and slit a sheet of paper lengthwise with it. Then he swallowed it. He kept his eyes on hers without blinking. His Adam's apple jerked furiously. He swallowed a half dozen razors, then bowed and disappeared behind the tent. The crowd clapped politely, almost confusedly. Griselda's blood boiled over.

When Rosemary returned to that place after dusk, indignant and frizz-haired, the metal-eating show was long done and Griselda was long gone, leaning over a plate of sausage patties in the Galaxy Diner on Capitol. Her eyes were still on the gray eyes of the metal eater and his were still on hers. By midnight she was gone from Boise altogether, lying across the bench seat of a Ryder truck, the metal eater crossing into Oregon and Griselda's head in his lap, his thin fingers in her hair, his little feet stretching for the pedals.

In the morning Mrs. Drown made Rosemary tell her story to a traffic cop who yawned, thumbs through his belt loops. But you aren't even writing it down, Mrs. Drown stammered. Griselda was eighteen, he told her, what should he be writing down. By law she was a woman. He pronounced woman loudly and carefully. Woman. He said to have hope. He'd heard the same story a thousand times. She'd come home eventually. They always did.

Around school the stories about Griselda took on teeth and venom, even left the school and lived for a while in produce sections and movie queues. She'll be back soon, we told each other, and boy will she be sorry, dashing off with a carnival freak twice her age, a bad seed anyway, you wouldn't believe the things she'd do. Probably knocked up by now. Or worse.

Mrs. Drown went sour immediately. We'd see her in Shaver's Supermarket after work, shrunken, embittered, a basket of celery hung on an arthritic forearm, a handkerchief knotted around her neck. She imagined herself moving at the center of a pocket of formalities—Why, Mrs. Drown, this rain is something, isn't it?—while her daughter's story spun all around her, circulating in the town's whispers, just outside her hearing.

Within a month she refused to leave home. She got fired. Her friends stopped coming by. They talk too much anyhow, is what she told Rosemary, who had dropped out of school to take her job at Boise Linen. Who talks too much, Mom? Everybody. Everybody talks behind your back. You turn your back and off they go, talking at you, telling each other stories they don't know the first thing about.

Of course, it wasn't long before we stopped talking about Griselda. She didn't come back. There was nothing new or interesting about a portly sister who worked fourteen hours a day or a mother made bitter by a lost daughter. There were new bodies in the high school, new fodder for rumors. Griselda's story was scrapped for lack of new material.

Unfortunately for her, Mrs. Drown never stopped believing that the gossip lived just one breath beyond earshot. She shouted at us when we strolled past the bungalow on our way into the hills. Stop blabbing, she'd yell from a window. Rumormongers! She moved into Griselda's room, slept in Griselda's bed. Her skin went sallow, yellow. She didn't go out, even for the mail. Dust mounded up. The yard went brown. The gutters clogged with mulch. The house looked as if it were about to sink into the earth.

All this time Griselda sent letters home. Rosemary found them in the mail, one every month, lying between bills, envelopes addressed with tiny printing beneath a wild series of stamps and postmarks. The letters were short, misspelled things:

Dear Mom and Sis—this city we're in has an acre reserved for dead people. They are kept in tall stacks of things like white cupboards with drawers inside. There are grass aisles to walk between. It is lovely. Our show is going well. The riots are on the other side of the island. Like you, we hardly know they are there.

They never explained, never betrayed a guilty twitch or regretful pause. Rosemary sat on her bed mouthing the names on the stamps and postmarks: Molokai, Belo Horizonte, Kinabalu, Damascus, Samara, Florence. They were names from anywhere and everywhere, each envelope stamped with some euphony like Sicilia, Mazatlán, Nairobi, Fiji or Malta, names that invoked for her imagination the great unknown tracts of land and ocean that lay beyond Boise. She would sit on her bed, holding a letter for hours, imagining the hands that had moved it along its path, all the hands between her sister and Boise, between herself and the cloud-pink alpen-glow of Nepal, the millennial gardens of Kyoto, the black tide of the Caspian Sea. There was a world glimmering beyond Boise Linen, Shaver's Supermarket, outside the cracked and sinking bungalow in the North End. It was another world altogether. Here was the proof. Her sister was out in it.

Rosemary never showed the letters to her mother. She decided it was best for her mother if Griselda was gone permanently, gone for good.

Life for Rosemary yawned around the letters, her mother and work: dull, heavy-footed, tasteless. At Boise Linen she supervised dyed cloth as it rolled onto bobbins, back stinging daylong, sitting behind safety goggles and listening to the grind and groan of spooling machines. She gained weight; her feet wore down the soles of shoes. She took meticulous grocery lists to Shaver's, balanced her checkbook with a nubbed pencil, fed soup to her crumbling mother. She did not bother to clean the house or buy makeup. The curtains went gray; Twinkie wrappers sprouted from couch cushions; ants roved in the metal mouths of soda cans stuck to windowsills.

Eventually she gave her virginity and ring finger to Duck Winters, the timid and overweight butcher at Shaver's who smelled permanently of ground beef. He moved into the sinking bungalow. He helped in a sheepish kind of way, tinkering around the yard, beer can in one hand, flushing out the lopsided gutters, replacing the screen door and the cracked sections of the front walk. He tolerated Mrs. Drown—her inane mutterings about gossipmongers, her insistence on sleeping in Griselda's room and forgetting to flush the toilet—by keeping himself half-drunk on watery beer. He was sincere and big and fell asleep while Rosemary did the Find-A-Word beside him. Occasionally they grappled together at awkward sex. It never took.

And still the letters from Griselda came, each month, missives from all over the world, mishandled prose tucked inside envelopes stamped with heart-pulling names, Katmandu, Auckland, Reykjavík.

Ten years after Griselda ran off with the metal eater, Duck Winters found his mother-in-law dead in the bathroom. Natural causes. Rosemary sprinkled her mother's ashes in the backyard. It was raining and the ashes clumped together undramatically; what was left of Mrs. Drown pooled on the leaves of the pachysandra or ran in mucky trickles under the fence into the neighbor's yard.

When he came home from Shaver's that evening, Duck drudged into the bedroom and found Rosemary splayed on the bed, her thick legs stuck out straight, tears shining on her checks, a tidily tied bundle of envelopes on her knee, a ragged stuffed panda in her lap. Duck lay down beside her and put a hand on her neck. Rosemary looked at him from tear-rimmed eyes. You should know, she blubbered, my sister has been sending letters all this time. I didn't want Mom to find out. I know, whispered Duck. She's been everywhere, all over the world. All these places with the same man. Duck pulled her to him, held her head against his belly and rocked her. She told Duck the story—Griselda's story—while he shushed her and kissed the teardrops sliding over her cheeks. I know, he whispered. Everyone knows.

Rosemary sobbed, buried herself into him. They held on, Duck kissing the top of her head, the smell of her hair in his nose. They began to move together in a salty, careful sweetness, moving patiently and tenderly. He kissed her all over. After, Rosemary lay in Duck's big arms and whispered. Those are my sister's stories. Those are for her. We have our own stories now. Right, Duck? He said nothing. He might have been asleep.

In the morning Duck woke late and when he came into the kitchen Rosemary was burning the last envelope from her carefully preserved bundle. Together they watched it burn black and then flake apart in the sink. Duck took her by the wrist and walked her out under a gleaming sky, the trees and grass greened from rain the day before. They climbed past the neighborhood into a nameless gulch, huffing and wheezing through the sagebrush in their weight-tortured Reeboks, wading through prairie star, peppergrass, sunflower, the gossamery spores of plants kicked free and floating. They stopped on a high ridge, panting, the town stretched out below them, the capitol dome, the arborlined streets, the slim neighborhoods of the North End in rows and, far off, the glittering Owyhee Mountains. Duck took off his flannel shirt, laid it down over the wildflowers, and they made love, among the moaning crickets, the drifting schools of spores, under the sky, in the foothills above the town of Boise.

From then on they lived with a measure of contentment, learning each other finally, imperceptibly. Duck whitewashed the bungalow; Rosemary planted a backyard stone for her mother. They shined up the doors and windows, carted out boxes and bags of old clothes, volleyball trophies, high school notebooks. They tried diets; we'd even see them out walking, hand-holding in a lazy lap around Camel's Back Park. Griselda's monthly letters went into the kitchen trash without so much as a glance at the postmark.

Then, one day, years later, the ad appeared. It was in the funnies section of the Sunday *Idaho Statesman*, an ad for the Metal Eater's World Tour, a kind of cultish extravaganza, selling out all over the globe, coming to the gym at Boise High in January. It was extravagant, a full newspaper page, featuring ludicrous fonts dripping into one another, a barely dressed cartoon girl proclaiming outrageous things, that the metal eater never consumed the same thing twice, that he had eaten a Ford Ranger just two weeks before at his tour stop in Philadelphia.

Rosemary, Duck said over bran cereal and doughnuts, you're not going to believe this.

Everybody wanted tickets. We wouldn't miss it. It sold out in four hours, the telephones blitzed over at the high school, people clamoring for a bigger venue. But Rosemary wouldn't go. She wouldn't hear of it, wouldn't dream of it. Twenty-five dollars a person, she moaned. You've got to be kidding me. Can't we move on, Duck? Can't we forget? A letter from Griselda arrived a week later, a Tampa postmark. Rosemary shredded it and dropped the pieces into the trash.

On the afternoon before the metal eater was to appear in the gym, the management at Shaver's declared that the supermarket would close its doors on the last of the month. It had been losing money for years, they said. Everyone shopped at the Albertson's on State. They would be letting people go immediately.

Duck slogged out to the loading dock in his bloodied apron and sat on a milk crate. It was snowing. Clumps of flakes were melting in the alley. The produce manager tapped Duck on the back and held up a case of beer. They drank and talked a little about where they could find work. They peed in the snow. The produce manager got a call from his wife. She couldn't go to the metal-eating show with him tonight. He offered the ticket to Duck.

My wife, mumbled Duck. She wouldn't let me go. She says it's a waste of money. Duck, groaned the produce manager, we just lost our jobs! You think we don't deserve a night to ourselves? Duck shrugged. Look, the produce manager said, tonight this guy is going to eat *metal*. I heard he might eat a snowmobile.

Besides, he went on, Griselda Drown might be there.

Someone had built a stage in the high school gym, blocked it off with a maroon curtain and surrounded it with fold-up chairs. Twenty-five dollars a head and the place was packed. A half hour late, the curtain groaned upwards and there was the metal eater, seated behind a table. He was little, a well-kept fifty-something in a black suit, white shirt, black necktie. He sat at the table, prim, a halo of gray hair beneath a pink shiny head like a half egg. His eyes were gray, drawn back and too big. He sat complacently, wrists crossed in his lap. Behind him, a sequined blue curtain shifted briefly, then hung still.

We waited, shuffled our snow boots at this plain spectacle, this unimpressive man seated before a bare table in the plain glow of gymnasium lights. We whispered, shifted, sweated. Upon us sat the great steam of a congregated people in parkas.

The snow fell outside, onto minivans and wagons in the school lot, and the air had taken on the smell of slush and impatience. A baby began to howl. The rubber-capped legs of the fold-up chairs creaked on the hardwood. Snow boots squeaked on the three-point line.

We studied our handbills, the drastic fonts, letters bleeding and spilling into one another, claiming impossible and remarkable things: See the Metal Eater who eats scrapped tin, an entire outboard motor, never the same act twice. It was difficult to believe that the little man at the table was going to do anything. Duck came in with the produce manager and found seats near the back, their big thighs sagging over the edges of their chairs.

Then the sequined back curtain floated aside and out came a woman who could only have been Griselda Drown. She was all thighs and calves in a shiny slit-legged dress, heels ridiculously high, tapering down to minuscule points—how did she walk on those shoes, how could she even stand in them?—those long calves scissoring and her dress sparkling madly. A few men whistled. She moved like a giraffe, tall but appropriately graceful, unimpeded by her body. Her hair was yarded back in rows like someone had clamped it in a vise, eyes like whirlpools, long-fingered hands wheeling a cart over the uneven boards of the stage toward the table where the little man sat.

She dwarfed the metal eater, her breasts strapped into that glittering dress, the line between them soft and dark. She took a white napkin from her cart, held it above the metal eater's bald and shining head, snapped it, lowered it, and knotted it behind his neck. In turn she took a butter knife, a fork, and a tin plate from her cart, dinging the knife and fork—to prove they were made of metal—and then dinging them against the plate—that's metal, too. She laid them down, setting the table. Fork, knife, plate.

The metal eater sat, implacable, in front of his table setting. Griselda turned, a flourish of sparkle, and rolled her cart back the way she came. Her thighs flashed under the slit gown; long and thick and suntanned. Her cart rattled, stopped. She disappeared behind the sequined back curtain. The metal eater sat alone at the table under the raw light of humming gym bulbs.

What would he eat? Was Griselda going to wheel out some awful metal repast, a chainsaw or an office chair? The papers claimed that the metal eater had eaten a lawnmower, swallowed down the wing of a Cessna. How could something like that be possible? What would she put on his plate? A nail? A razor blade? A measly thumbtack? We had not paid twenty-five bucks to sit hip to hip and watch a tiny man swallow a thumbtack. The produce manager announced he would ask for his money back if they didn't bring back Duck's sister-in-law in the next ten minutes.

The metal eater sat smugly, napkin around his neck. He took the knife and fork in his little pink fists. He held them against the table, upright, ends down, like a petulant child awaiting supper. Then, with a certainty and casualness that was almost appalling, he took the knife and slid it down his throat and closed his mouth behind it. He sat, natty, unruffled, staring at the crowd, some of whom missed the feat entirely and were only now swinging their heads around as brothers or uncles tugged their sleeves. The metal eater had a fraction of a smile on his lips. His Adam's apple was the only part of him that moved. It jerked freakishly up and down and side to side, like a muscled and angry monkey chained by one ankle.

He followed the knife with the fork, nudging it down. While he swallowed the fork, he folded the plate into quarters, his throat straining wildly, his shoulders perfectly still, and put that into his mouth, and poked it down with one finger. His Adam's apple jerked, seized, thrashed. After a half minute or so, it slowed, then restored itself to its original, sedated state. The little metal eater unknotted the napkin, dabbed at the corners of his mouth, stood up from the table, and bowed. He tossed the napkin into the first rows of the crowd.

Applause started slowly, just the produce manager and some others in the back bringing their hands together, and then others joined in, and it mounted and soon we were beside ourselves, hooting and hollering and pounding the floor with our boot heels. How about that? the produce manager was shouting. How about that?

When the ovation began to subside, three large men in utility belts hustled out, lifted the table and hefted it offstage. The applause faded. The great overhead dome lights in the gym went out, one by one, ticking as they cooled in the growing silence. Over the doors, red exit signs cast the only light.

Finally one blue spotlight switched on, a single shaft of light falling from the ceiling to illuminate the center of the stage where a tall figure had appeared in a suit of plated armor, complete with visored helmet, an ostrich plume canting off the peak. Another spotlight came on, yellow, and shone on the metal eater, stationed like a tiny well-dressed peasant beside the armored figure. He held a stool, which he set down and squatted on, facing the crowd. He withdrew a ball-peen hammer from his suit pocket

and twirled it in his palm. Then he removed the shin legging from one foot
of the armored figure and folded it and banged it flat against the floor of
the stage. He folded it again and banged it flat again. Then he pushed it
down his throat, swallowing contentedly on his stool, his Adam's apple
flailing madly. Beneath the removed armor, in the ray of blue, we could
see one long calf, a bare foot.

It took the metal eater less than a minute to swallow down the legging.
He promptly moved to the other. How about *that*, whispered the produce
manager. Is *that* for real? He was shaking Duck's shoulder. The crowd began
to get into it, clapping as the metal eater removed each subsequent piece of
armor, the thigh pieces next, and when it was clear that the thick, suntanned
legs belonged to Griselda, we stood and pounded the floor and chanted and
cheered and everyone was grinning and enjoying the show. The metal eater
swallowed on, his frenetic Adam's apple riveting each swallow home.

Within twenty minutes the metal eater had done most of his work.
He was standing beside the stool and tenderly sliding off the second
gauntlet. All that remained to eat were the helmet and massive chest piece.
Griselda held her arms out from her body, palms to the sky, had in fact
held them there during the entire spectacle. We stomped the floor to match
the rhythm of the metal eater's swallowing.

When he had choked down the last gauntlet, the metal eater slid his
stool behind Griselda and climbed onto it. The boots pounded the floor. The
metal eater brought his arms above both his head and hers and gently
tugged the ostrich plume free, letting it float to the stage in front of them.
Then, with a flourish of wrists and fingers, he removed her helmet. Her
hair, orange and long, slipped free, and we were rapturous, screaming and
cheering and whistling. The metal eater climbed off his stool, took the
helmet and flattened it under one dazzling wing tip. He folded it and banged
it flat again. Then he lit into it with his teeth. It took him over two minutes
to eat it and we were at frenzy pitch by the time he finished, one great
and frothing roar quaking the rafters of that old gym. The produce manager
was hugging Duck and tears were on his cheeks. If that isn't something,
he shouted. If that isn't something.

The metal eater climbed back on the stool, stretched as widely as he
could and ran his hands along both of Griselda's arms, over her biceps and
onto her shoulders and under the chestpiece. He dislodged it, held it in
front of her for an unbearably long moment, and finally raised it high over

their heads into the trembling blue spotlight, and we beheld Griselda, her broad and flat belly, her navel, her breasts and her outstretched arms— a masterpiece of a woman, a marble column fixed in a blade of light, a golden-blue monument. Amid salvos of ovations, the metal eater folded and flattened the final piece until he could fit his mouth around it. He gulped it down. The big men in utility belts appeared and wrapped Griselda in a red kimono and carried her offstage.

In the aftermath—the pandemonium subsided, bows demanded and demanded again, the gymnasium lights burning once more at full, lacerating power, the men in utility belts already dismantling the stage—Duck sat shaken and sweat-damped. He gathered himself into his big puffy coat, stood, and tottered into the headlight-swept parking lot, shuffling through the new snow, over the slushy curbs.

Rumbling at the back of the parking lot was an eighteen-wheeler, its wipers sliding slowly over the windshield, running lights glowing yellow across the top of the cab and down the lines of the trailer. From bumper to bumper the truck was painted an extravagant green, the metal eater's logo laid lustily across it and before Duck knew what he was doing he walked past his car, to the end of the lot, and rapped on the window of the cab.

Griselda herself answered, leaning through the open door, one foot on the running board, stooped so she could push her head out, orange hair framing her face. She looked like a very tall Rosemary, squinting at him like Rosemary did when she was trying to figure something out. I'm Duck Winters, Duck said. I know all about you. He stammered, he smiled, he asked if she would like to come over the house for tea, or beer, or whatever. I think you should see your sister, he said. It might be good. I lost my job today. He tried for a smile that was more like a shrug. Griselda smiled back. Okay, she said. Once the truck gets loaded.

So that's how it came to be that Duck Winters drove through the snowy and quiet residential streets of Boise's North End, steering slowly and cautiously home, after midnight, with a lurid eighteen-wheeler inches from his rear bumper, its roof knocking snow from overhanging branches.

Rosemary woke to airbrakes sighing in the street. She heard boots on the front walk, low voices, and the refrigerator door unstick as it opened. She pushed herself up in bed. Duck appeared, prancing down the hall, tracking snow along the rug. His hair was slicked down with sweat, his cheeks flushed. He put his mittened hands on her shoulders. Rosie, he hissed, you awake? You're not going to believe it. He was bursting over. You're just not go-ing to be-lieve it.

He took her by the wrists, pulled her out of bed, her hair frizzed, wearing only a tight T-shirt and green sweatpants. He hauled her down the hall, through the melting tracked-in snow, to stand in the kitchen doorway and behold her sister, seated at the kitchen table, towering and radiant and glittering in a red kimono, holding hands with a little man in a black tweed suit with an awkward look on his face. On the table, in front of each of them, stood an unopened can of beer.

Rosemary found it impossible to look at Griselda—her presence was too solar for this kitchen with its cracked countertops and veneered cabinets, a box of stale doughnuts, a wilted amaryllis slumped out of its plastic pot, a porcelain Santa on the windowsill that should have been put away weeks ago. Moonlight fell in parallelograms through the kitchen window. In the basin of the sink sat a bowl half full of sludgy cereal.

Duck squeezed past her, fussing, twitching about with little jumps, his belly quivering under his jacket. This is your sister, he gushed, and her husband, Gene. You should have seen them tonight, Rosie, the *show* they put on. It was incredible! Incredible! You'd never believe it! You guys should talk, Rosie, you and your sister, is what I was thinking, it's her first time home in twenty years! She said she wrote a letter. It was nice of them to come, wasn't it? Their truck's outside. They actually *live* in their truck! We have tea if you guys don't like that beer.

Out the kitchen window Rosemary saw many of us—maybe two dozen neighbors—laboring across the lawn, figures examining the cab of the metal eater's truck, faces peering in the living room window. Griselda asked Rosemary if she'd been getting the letters and Rosemary managed to nod her head. Griselda said something about the new light fixture above the sink, about how it was nice. Rosemary watched a slushy bootprint turning to water on the kitchen floor.

Duck was toddling around the kitchen, rummaging through the fridge. He offered the guests summer sausage, noodle salad, pushed a can of beer into Rosemary's hand and announced that the metal eater had an entire suit of armor inside his stomach, right here, Rosie, in our very own kitchen. Isn't it something?

Rosemary stood rigid and barefoot in the doorway. Her sister, the men, the peeping neighbors and the eighteen-wheeler outside—all this loomed in the outskirts of her vision. She blinked her eyes several times. The beer can in her hand was cold. The bootprint of snow on the kitchen tile was turning to water.

She moved through the kitchen, set the beer on the table and tore a paper towel from the rack under the sink. She swabbed at the bootprint on the floor, watched the paper absorb the gray slush. Duck and me, she said, we've been married fifteen years. You know that, Griselda? Her voice didn't shake and she was glad for it.

She stood and leaned on the table, the damp and crumpled paper towel in her fist. You know Mom would go to sleep with one of your volleyball trophies in her arms? You know that after she died we poured out her ashes in the backyard? Did you know that? At work I dye giant sheets of linen and guide them onto spools all day. That's what Mom used to do; she used to do that while we were at school. Every day.

She took Duck's hand and held it. I used to want to leave, she said. I used to want to get out of Boise so bad. But this—she gestured at the kitchen, the bowl of abandoned cereal, the amaryllis and the porcelain Santa—this is a life at least. This is a place to come home to.

Griselda had begun to cry, quiet sobs like whispers. Rosemary stopped. A moment like this—the four of them around the table under the sad, dusty kitchen lamp—could never accommodate all the things she had to say. She went to the metal eater and took him by the wrist and led him out the door, into the snow. Hey, she yelled, at the eighteen-wheeler, at the foothills standing up white under the moon, at all of us standing there on her lawn. Here he is! I want you all to get a good look. Look at him! She was screaming. You think eating metal is any harder than what I do, than what each of you do? You think this man is amazing? Look at him!

But—and this is what we remembered later—she was the one we looked at: her hair trembling on her head like flames, her shoulders back, her chest quaking—an image of power and fury. She burned, magnificent, in the snow, barefoot, in a T-shirt and green sweatpants, shouting at us. Griselda appeared and took the metal eater by the arm and led him out to their truck. Duck brought Rosemary inside and shut the door and the lights in the house went off and the curtains snapped shut. We watched the big truck labor into gear and rumble past the drive and each of us filed through the snow back to our homes and the sounds of the night finally faded until there was nothing to hear but snow coming down from the hills and pressing against the windows of our houses.

A shouting in the streets. The heart wavers, surges to life, wavers again. Griselda's letters still came once a month and Rosemary and Duck went on living their lives; Duck found work as a grill cook at a steakhouse; Rosemary inherited a beagle from a deceased coworker. This was when Boise was growing like mad and there were always new people around, people building mansions in the hills, people who didn't know there had ever been a Shaver's Supermarket.

Sometimes, in the spring, we'd stroll past the bungalow and see Rosemary on the front step, doing the Find-A-Word in the *Statesman*, Duck dozing in the chair beside her, the beagle watching us from between their feet. Rosemary would be chewing the end of her pencil, thinking hard, and we'd begin to tell whoever was with us the story and we'd hike up into the hills, gesticulating as we talked, up the steep paths to a place where we could see the mountains beyond the hills, jagged and endless, illuminated under the sun, folding back on each other all the way to the horizon.

HOME SWEET HOME

HANNAH TINTI

Pat and Clyde were murdered on pot roast night. The doorbell rang just as Pat was setting the butter and margarine (Clyde was watching his cholesterol) on the table. She was thinking about James Dean. Pat had loved him desperately as a teenager, seen his movies dozens of times, written his name across her notebooks, carefully taped pictures of him to the inside of her locker so that she would have the pleasure of seeing his tortured, sullen face from *East of Eden* as she exchanged her French and English textbooks for science and math. When she graduated from high school, she took down the photos and pasted them to the inside cover of her yearbook, which she perused longingly several times over the summer and brought with her to the University of Massachusetts, where it sat, unopened, alongside her thesaurus and abridged collegiate dictionary until she met Clyde, received her M.R.S. degree, and packed her things to move into their two-bedroom ranch house on Bridge Street.

Before she put the meat in the oven that afternoon, Pat had made herself a cup of tea and turned on the television. Channel 56 was showing *Rebel without a Cause*, and as the light slowly began to rise through the screen of their old Zenith, she saw James Dean on the steps of the planetarium, clutching at the mismatched socks of a dead Sal Mineo and crying. She put down her tea, slid her warm fingertips inside the V neck of her dress, and held her left breast. Her heart was suddenly pounding, her nipple hard and erect against the palm of her hand. It was like seeing an old lover, like remembering a piece of herself that no longer existed. She watched the credits roll and glanced outside to see her husband mowing their lawn. He had a worried expression on his face and his socks pulled up to his knees.

That evening before dinner, as she arranged the butter and margarine side by side on the table—one yellow airy and light, the other hard and dark like the yolk of an egg—she wondered how she could have forgotten the way James Dean's eyebrows curved. *Isn't memory a strange thing*, she thought. *I could forget all of this, how everything feels, what all of these things mean to me.* She was suddenly seized with the desire to grab the sticks of butter and margarine in her hands and squeeze them until her fingers went right through, to somehow imprint their textures and colors on her brain like a stamp, to make them something that she would never lose. And then she heard the bell.

When she opened the door, Pat noticed that it was still daylight. The sky was blue and bright and clear and she had a fleeting, guilty thought that she should not have spent so much time indoors. After that she crumpled backward into the hall as the bullet from a .38-caliber Saturday Night Special pierced her chest, exited below her shoulder blade, and jammed into the wood of the stairs, where it would later be dug out with a pen knife by Lieutenant Sales and dropped gingerly into a transparent plastic baggie.

Pat's husband, Clyde, was found in the kitchen by the back door, a knife in his hand (first considered a defense against his attacker and later determined to be the carver of the roast). He had been shot twice—once in the stomach and once in the head—and then covered with cereal, the boxes lined up on the counter beside him and the crispy golden contents of Cap'n Crunch, cornflakes, and Special K emptied out over what remained of his face.

Nothing had been stolen.

It was a warm spring evening full of summer promises. Pat and Clyde's bodies lay silent and still while the orange sunset crossed the floors of their house and the streetlights clicked on. As darkness came and the skunks waddled through the backyard and the raccoons crawled down from the trees, they were still there, holding their places, suspended in a moment of quiet blue before the sun came up and a new day started and life went on without them.

It was Clyde's mother who called the police. She dialed her son's number every Sunday morning from Rhode Island. These phone calls always somehow perfectly coincided with breakfast, or whenever Pat and Clyde were on the verge of making love.

Thar she blows, Clyde would say, and take his hot coffee with him over to where the phone hung on the wall, or slide out of bed with an apologetic glance at his wife. The coffee and Pat would inevitably cool, and in this way his mother would ruin every Sunday. It had been years now since they had frolicked in the morning, but once, when they were first married and Pat was preparing breakfast, she had heard the phone, walked over to where her husband was reading the paper, dropped to her knees, pulled open his robe, and taken him in her mouth. *Let it ring*, she thought, and he had let it ring. Fifteen minutes later the police were on their front porch with smiles as Clyde, red-faced, bathrobe bulging, answered their questions at the door.

In most areas of her life Clyde's mother was a very nice person. She behaved in such a kind and decorous manner that people would often remark, having met her, *What a lovely woman*. But with Clyde she lost her head. She was suspicious, accusing, and tyrannical. After her husband died, she became even worse. Once she got through her grief, her son became her man. She pushed this sense of responsibility through him like fishhooks, plucking on the line, reeling him back in when she felt her hold slipping, so that the points became embedded in his flesh so deep that it would kill him to take them out.

She dialed the police after trying her son thirty-two times, and because the lieutenant on duty was a soft touch, his own mother having recently passed, a cruiser was dispatched to Pat and Clyde's on Bridge Street, and because one of the policemen was looking to buy in the neighborhood, the officers decided to check out the back of the house after they got no answer, and because there was cereal blowing around in the yard, the men got suspicious, and because it was a windy day and because the hinges had recently been oiled and because the door had been left unlocked and swung open and because one of them had seen a dead body before, a suicide up in Hanover, and knew blood and brain and bits of skull when he saw them, he made the call back to the station, because his partner was quietly vomiting in the rosebushes, and said, *We've got trouble*.

Earlier that morning Mrs. Mitchell had let her dog out with a sad, affectionate pat on his behind. Buster was a Labrador retriever and treated all the yards on Bridge Street as if they were his own, making his way leisurely through flower beds, pausing for a drink from a sprinkler, tearing into garbage bags, and relieving himself among patches of newly planted rutabagas. Before long he was digging a hole in Pat and Clyde's backyard.

There were small golden flakes scattered on the grass. Buster licked one up and crunched. The flakes were food, and the dog followed the promise of more across the lawn, through the back door, and over to Clyde, stiff and covered with flies, the remaining cereal a soggy wet pile of pink plaster across his shoulders. The rug underneath the kitchen table was soaked in blood. Buster left red paw prints as he walked around the body and sniffed at the slippers on the dead man's feet. The dog smelled Clyde's last moment, curled into the arch of his foot.

The doorbell had chimed just as Clyde pierced the roast with the carving fork, releasing two streams of juice, which ran down the sides of the meat until they were captured by the raised edge of the serving plate. He paused then as he lifted the knife, waiting to hear and recognize the voices of his wife and whoever had come to visit. His stomach tightened in the silence. He was hungry. When the shot exploded he felt it all at once and everywhere—in the walls, in his eyes, in his chest, in his arms, in the utensils he was holding, in the piece of meat he was carving, in the slippers that placed him on the floor, in the kitchen, before their evening meal.

Buster pulled off one of the slippers and sank his teeth into it. He worked on removing the stuffing of the inner lining and kept his eye on the dead man, who used to shoo-shoo him away from garbage bags, from munching the daffodils that lined the walk, from humping strays behind the garage. Once, after catching the dog relieving himself in the middle of the driveway, Clyde had dragged him by the collar all the way down Bridge Street. *Listen to me, pooch*, Mr. Mitchell had said after Clyde left, one hand smoothing where the collar had choked and the other hand vigorously scratching the dog's behind. *You shit wherever you feel like shitting.*

When the dog decided to leave the house, he took the slipper with him. He dragged it over to the hole he'd already started and threw it in. Buster walked back and forth over the spot once it was filled, then lifted his leg to mark it.

The Mitchells had brought their dog with them when they moved into the neighborhood. Three years later, a son arrived—not a newborn baby decked out in bonnets but a thin, dark boy of indiscriminate age. His name was Miguel, and it was unclear to the people living on Bridge Street whether he was adopted or a child from a previous marriage. He called the Mitchells his mother and father, enrolled in the public school for their district, and quietly became a part of their everyday lives.

In fact, Miguel was the true son of Mr. Mitchell, sired unknowingly on a business trip with a Venezuelan prostitute some seven years before. The mother had been killed in a bus accident along with 53 other travelers on a road outside of Caracas, and the local police had contacted Mr. Mitchell from a faded company card she had left pressed in her Bible. After a paternity test, the boy arrived at Logan Airport with a worn-out blanket and duffel bag full of chickens (his pets), which were quickly confiscated by customs officials. Mr. Mitchell drove down Route 128 in his station wagon, amazed and panicked at his sudden parenthood, trying to comfort the sobbing boy and wondering how Miguel had managed to keep the birds silent on the plane.

When they pulled into the driveway, Mrs. Mitchell was waiting with a glass of warm milk sweetened with sugar. She was wearing dungarees. She took the boy in her arms and carried him immediately into the bathroom, where she sat him on the counter and washed his face, his hands, his knees, and his feet. Miguel sipped the milk while Mrs. Mitchell gently ran the washcloth behind his ears. When she was finished she tucked him in to their guest bed and read him a stack of Curious George books in Spanish, which she had ordered from their local bookstore. She showed Miguel a picture of the little monkey in the hospital getting a shot from a nurse, and the boy fell asleep, a finger hooked around the belt loop of her jeans. Mrs. Mitchell sat on the bed beside him quietly until he rolled over and let it go.

Mr. Mitchell had met his wife at a gas station in northern California. He had just completed his business degree, and was driving a rented car up the coast to see the Olympic rain forest. She was in a pickup truck with Oregon plates. They both got out and started pumping. Mr. Mitchell finished first, and on his way back to his car after paying, he watched the muscles in her thick arm flexing as she replaced the hose. She glanced up, caught him looking, and smiled. She was not beautiful, but one of her teeth stuck out charmingly sideways. There was a confidence about her, an air of efficiency that made him believe she was the kind of woman who could solve any problem. He started the car, turned out of the station, and glanced into his rearview mirror. He watched the pickup take the opposite road, and as it drove away he felt such a pull that he turned around and followed it for sixty miles.

At the rest stop, he pretended that he was surprised to see her. Later he discovered that many people followed his wife, and that she was used to this, and that it did not seem strange to her. People she had never met came up and began to speak to her in shopping malls, in elevators, in the waiting rooms of doctors, at traffic lights, at concerts, at coffee shops and bistros. An old man took hold of her arm outside of an amusement park and began whispering about his murdered son. A woman carrying three children placed her blanket right on top of theirs at the beach, stretched out next to Mrs. Mitchell, and began to cry. Even their dog, a stray she fed while camping in Tennessee, came scratching outside their door six weeks later. Mr. Mitchell was jealous and frightened by these strangers, and often used himself as a shield between them and his wife. *What do they want from her?* he found himself thinking. But he also felt, *What will they take from me?*

His wife was a quiet woman, in the way that large rocks just beyond the shore are quiet; the waves rush against them and the seaweed hangs on and the birds gather round on top. Mr. Mitchell was amazed that she had married him. He spent the first few years doing what he could to please her and watched for signs that she was leaving.

Sometimes she got depressed and locked herself in the bathroom. It made him furious. When she came out, tender and pink from washing, she would put her arms around him and tell him that he was a good man. Mr. Mitchell was not sure of this, because sometimes he found himself hating her. He wanted her to know what it felt like to be powerless. He began taking risks.

When he got the call from Venezuela telling him about Miguel, he was terrified that he might lose his wife and also secretly happy to have wounded her. But all of the control he felt as they prepared for his son's arrival slipped away as he watched her take the strange dark boy into her arms and tenderly wash his feet. He realized then that she was capable of taking everything from him.

The three of them formed an awkward family. Mr. Mitchell tried to place the boy in a home, but his wife would not let him. He had now been an accidental father for two years. He took the boy to baseball games and bought him comic books and drove him to school in the mornings. Sometimes Mr. Mitchell enjoyed these things; other times they made him angry. One day he walked in on Miguel talking to his wife in Spanish and the boy immediately stopped. He saw that his son was afraid of him, and he was sure that his wife had done this too. Mr. Mitchell began to resent what had initially drawn him to her, and to offset these feelings he began an affair with their neighbor, Pat.

It did not begin innocently. Pat said hello to Mr. Mitchell at the supermarket, then turned and pressed up against him as someone passed in the aisle. Her behind lingered against his hips, her breasts touched his arm. Mr. Mitchell had never had any conversation with Pat that went beyond the weather or the scheduling of trash, but later that week he walked over to her as she was planting bulbs in her garden and slid his hand into the elastic waistband of her Bermuda shorts. He leaned her up against the fence, underneath a birch tree, right there in the middle of a bright, sunny day where everyone could see. Mr. Mitchell didn't say anything, but he could tell by her breath and the way she rocked on his hand that she wasn't afraid.

He did not know it was in him to do something like this. He had been on his way to the library to return some books. Look, there they were, thrown aside on the grass, wrapped in plastic smeared with age and the fingers of readers who were unknown to him. And here was another person he did not know, panting in his ear, streaking his arms with dirt. Someone he had seen bent over in the sunlight, a slight glistening of sweat reflecting in the backs of her knees, and for whom he had suddenly felt a hard sense of lonesomeness and longing. A new kind of warmth spread in the palm of his hand and he tried not to think about his wife.

They had hard, raw sex in public places—movie theaters and parks, elevators and playgrounds. After dark, underneath the jungle gym, his knees pressing into the dirt, Mr. Mitchell began to wonder why they hadn't been caught. Once, sitting on a bench near the reservoir, Pat straddling him in a skirt with no underwear, they had actually waved to an elderly couple passing by. The couple continued on as if they hadn't seen them. The experience left the impression that his meetings with Pat were occurring in some kind of alternative reality, a bubble in time that he knew would eventually pop.

Pat told him that Clyde had been impotent since his father died. The old man had been a mechanic, and was working underneath a bulldozer when the lift slipped, crushing him from the chest down. Clyde held his father's hand as he died, and the coldness that came as life left seemed to spread through Clyde's fingers and into his arms, and he stopped using them to reach for his wife. Since the funeral she'd had two lovers. Mr. Mitchell was number three.

There were rumors, later on, that the lift had been tampered with—that Clyde's father had owed someone money. Pat denied it, but Mr. Mitchell remembered driving by the garage and sensing he'd rather buy his gas somewhere else. It seemed like a shady business.

He started arranging meetings with Pat that were closer to home. Mr. Mitchell's desire increased with the risk of discovery, and in his house he began to fantasize about the dining room table, the dryer in the laundry room, the space on the kitchen counter beside the mixer. He touched these places with his fingertips and trembled, thinking of how he would feel later, watching his wife sip her soup, fold sheets, mix batter for cookies in the same places.

On the day Pat was murdered, before she put the roast in the oven or reminisced about James Dean or thought about the difference between butter and margarine, she was having sex in the vestibule. The coiled inscription of HOME SWEET HOME scratched her behind. Mr. Mitchell had seen Clyde leave for a bowling lesson, and as he waited on the front porch for Pat to open the door, something had made him pick up the welcome mat. Mrs. Mitchell would soon be home with Miguel, and the thought of her so close pricked his ears. When Pat answered he'd thrown the mat down in the hall, then her, then himself, the soles of his shoes knocking over the entry table. Mr. Mitchell brought Pat's knees to his shoulders and listened for the hum of his wife's Reliant.

The following day when Lieutenant Sales climbed the stairs of Pat and Clyde's porch, he did not notice that there was nothing to wipe his feet on. He was an average-looking man: six foot two, 190 pounds, brown hair, brown eyes, brown skin. He had once been a champion deep-sea diver, until a shark attack (which left him with a hole in his side crossed with the pink, puckered scars of new skin) dragged him from the waters with a sense of righteous authority and induced him to join the force. He lived thirty-five minutes away in a basement apartment with a Siamese cat named Frank.

When Sales was a boy he'd had a teacher who smelled like roses. Her name was Mrs. Bosco. She showed him how to blow eggs. Forcing the yolk out of the tiny hole always felt a little disgusting, like blowing a heavy wad of snot from his nose, but when he looked up at Mrs. Bosco's cheeks flushed red with effort, he knew it would be worth it, and it was—the empty shell in his hand like a held breath. Whenever he began an investigation, he'd get the same sensation, and as he stepped into the doorway of Pat and Clyde's house, he felt it rise in his chest and stay.

He interviewed the police who found the bodies first. They were sheepish about their reasons for going into the backyard, but before long they began loudly discussing drywall and Sheetrock and the pros and cons of lancet windows (all of the men, including Lieutenant Sales, carried weekend and part-time jobs in construction). The policeman who had thrown up in the bushes went home early. When Sales spoke to him later, he apologized for contaminating the scene.

Lieutenant Sales found the roast on the counter. He found green beans still on the stove. He found a sour cherry pie nearly burned in the oven. He found the butter and the margarine half-melted on the dining room table. He found that Pat and Clyde used cloth napkins and tiny separate plates for their dinner rolls. The silverware was polished. The edges of the steak knives were turned in.

He found their unpaid bills in a basket by the telephone. He found clean laundry inside the dryer in the basement—towels, sheets, T-shirts, socks, three sets of Fruit of the Loom and one pair of soft pink satin panties, the elastic starting to give, the bottom frayed and thin. He found an unfinished letter Pat had started writing to a friend who had recently moved to Arizona: *What is it like there? How can you stand the heat?* He found Clyde's stamp albums from when he was a boy—tiny spots of brilliant color, etchings of flowers and portraits of kings, painstakingly pasted over the names of countries Lieutenant Sales had never heard of.

He found the bullet that had passed through Pat's body, embedded in the stairs. He found a run in her stocking, starting at the heel and inching its way up the back of her leg. He thought about how Pat had been walking around the day she was going to die not realizing that there was a hole in her panty hose. He found a stain, dark and blooming beneath her shoulders, spreading across the Oriental rug in the foyer and into the hardwood floors, which he noticed, as he got down on his knees for a closer look, still held the scent of Murphy's oil soap. He found a hairpin caught in the carpet fringe. He found a cluster of dandelion seeds, the tiny white filaments coming apart in his fingers. He found a look on Pat's face like a child trying to be brave, lips tightened and thin, forehead just beginning to crease, eyes glazed, dark, and unconvinced. Her body was stiff when they moved her.

There were dog tracks on the back porch. They were the prints of a midsized animal, red and clearly defined as they circled the body in the kitchen, then crisscrossing over themselves and heading out the door, fading down the steps and onto the driveway before disappearing into the yard. Lieutenant Sales sent a man to knock on doors in the neighborhood and find out who let their dogs off the leash. He interviewed Clyde's mother. He went back to the station and checked Pat's and Clyde's records—both clean. When he finally went to sleep that night, the small warmth of his cat tucked next to his shoulder, Lieutenant Sales thought about the feel of satin panties, missing slippers, stolen welcome mats, dandelion seeds from a yard with no dandelions, and the kind of killer who shuts off the oven.

A month before Pat and Clyde were murdered, Mrs. Mitchell was fixing the toilet. Her husband passed by on his way to the kitchen, paused at the door, shook his head, and told her that she was too good for him. The heavy porcelain top was off, her arms elbow deep in rusty water. The man she had married was standing at the entrance to the bathroom and speaking, but Mrs. Mitchell was concentrating on the particular tone in the pipes she was trying to clear, and so she did not respond.

Mr. Mitchell went into the kitchen and began popping popcorn. The kernels cracked against the insides of the kettle as his words settled into her, and when, with a twist of the coat hanger in her hand beneath the water, she stopped the ringing of the pipes, Mrs. Mitchell sensed in the quiet that came next that her husband had done something wrong. She had known in this same way before he told her about Miguel. A breeze came through the window and made the hair on her wet arms rise. She pulled her hands from the toilet and thought, *I fixed it.*

When Miguel came into their home, she had taken all the sorrow she felt at his existence and turned it into a fierce motherly love. Mrs. Mitchell thought her husband would be grateful; instead he seemed to hold it against her. He became dodgy and spiteful. He blamed her for what he'd done, for being a woman too hard to live up to. It was the closest she ever came to leaving. But she hadn't expected the boy.

Miguel spent the first three months of his life in America asking to go home. When the fourth month came he began to sleepwalk. He wandered downstairs to the kitchen, emptied the garbage can onto the floor, and curled up inside. In the morning Mrs. Mitchell would find him asleep, shoulders in the barrel, feet in the coffee grounds and leftovers. He told her he was looking for his mother's head. She had been decapitated in the bus accident, and now she stepped from the corners of Miguel's dreams at night and beckoned him with her arms, his lost chickens resting on her shoulders, pecking at the empty neck.

Mrs. Mitchell suggested that they make her a new one. She bought materials for papier-mâché. The strips of newspaper felt like bandages as she helped Miguel dip them in glue and smooth them over the surface of the inflated balloon. They fashioned a nose and lips out of cardboard. Once it was dry, Miguel described his mother's face and they painted the skin brown, added yarn for hair, cut eyelashes out of construction paper. Mrs. Mitchell took a pair of gold earrings, poked them through where they'd drawn the ears and said, heart sinking, *She's beautiful*. Miguel nodded. He smiled. He put his mother's head on top of the bookcase in his room and stopped sleeping in the garbage.

Sometimes when Mrs. Mitchell checked on the boy at night, she'd feel the head looking at her. It was unnerving. She imagined her husband making love to the papier-mâché face and discovered a hate so strong and hard it made her afraid of herself. She considered swiping the head and destroying it, but she remembered how skinny and pitiful the boy's legs had looked against her kitchen floor. Then Miguel began to love her, and she suddenly felt capable of anything. She thumbed her nose at the face in the corner. She held her heart open.

Mrs. Mitchell had been raised by her aunts in a house near the river where her mother had drowned. The aunts were hunters; birds mostly, which they would clean and cook and eat. As a girl Mrs. Mitchell would retrieve the shots. Even on a clear day, the birds always seemed wet. Sometimes they were still alive when she found them—wings thrashing, pieces of their chests torn away. She learned to take hold of their necks and break them quickly.

Mrs. Mitchell kept a picture of her mother next to the mirror in her room, and whenever she checked her reflection, her eyes would naturally turn from her own face to that of the woman who gave birth to her. The photo was black-and-white and creased near the edges; she was fifteen, her hair plaited, the end of one braid pressed between her lips. It made Mrs. Mitchell think of stories she'd heard of women who spent their lives spinning—years of passing flax through their mouths to make thread would leave them disfigured, lower lips drooping off their faces; a permanent look of being beaten.

The aunts built a shooting range on an area of property behind the house. It was Mrs. Mitchell's job to set up the targets and fetch them iced tea and ammo. She kept a glass jar full of shells in the back of her closet, shiny gold casings from her aunts' collection of .22 calibers and .45s. They made a shooting station out of an old shed, two tables set up with sand-bags to hold the guns, nestling the shape of heavy metal as the pieces were placed down.

When she was twelve years old the aunts gave her a rifle. She already knew the shooting stances, and she practiced them with her new gun every day after school. She could hit a target while kneeling, crouching, lying down, and standing tall, hips parallel to the barrel and her waist turned, the same way the aunts taught her to pose when a picture was being taken. She picked off tin cans and old metal signs and polka-dotted the paper outlines of men.

Mrs. Mitchell remembered this when she pulled into her driveway, glanced over the fence, and saw her husband having sex in the doorway of their neighbors' house. She turned to Miguel in the passenger seat and told him to close his eyes. The boy covered his face with his hands and sat quietly while she got out of the car. Mrs. Mitchell watched her husband moving back and forth and felt her feet give way from the ground. She had the sensation of being caught in a river, the current pulling her body outward, tugging at her ankles, and she wondered why she wasn't being swept away until she realized that she was holding on to the fence. The wood felt smooth and worn, like the handle of her first gun, and she used it to pull herself back down.

Later she thought of the look on Pat's face. It reminded Mrs. Mitchell of the Tin Woodman from the movie *The Wizard of Oz*—disarmingly lovely and greasy with expectation. In the book version she bought for Miguel she'd read that the Woodman had once been real, but his ax kept slipping and he'd dismembered himself, slowly exchanging his flesh piece by piece for hollow metal. Mrs. Mitchell thought Pat's body would rattle with the same kind of emptiness, but it didn't; it fell with the heavy tone of meat. As she waited for the echo, Mrs. Mitchell heard a small cough from the kitchen, the kind a person does in polite society to remind someone else that they are there. She followed it and found Clyde in his slippers, the knife in the roast.

Hello. I just killed your wife. And when she said it, she knew she'd have to shoot Clyde too. The beans were boiling, the water frothing over the sides of the pan and sizzling into the low flame beneath. Mrs. Mitchell turned off the oven and spun all the burners to zero.

The aunts never married. They still lived in the house where they raised their niece. Occasionally they sent her photographs, recipes, information on the NRA, or obituaries of people she had known clipped from the local newspaper. When a reporter called Mrs. Mitchell, asking questions about Pat and Clyde, she thought back to all the notices her aunts had sent over the years, and said: *They were good neighbors and wonderful people. I don't know who would have done something like this. They will be greatly missed.* The truth was that she felt very little for Pat. It was hard to forgive herself for this, so she didn't try. Instead she did her best to forget how Clyde had looked, the surprise on his face, as if he were about to offer her a drink before he crumpled to the floor.

She waited patiently through the following day for someone to come for her. She watched the police cruisers and the news vans come and go. On Monday morning she woke up and let the dog out. She made a sandwich for Miguel and fit it in his lunch box beside a thermos of milk. She poured juice into a glass and cereal into a bowl. Then she locked herself in the bathroom and watched her hands shake. She remembered that she had wanted to cover Clyde with something. Falling out of the box, the cereal had sounded crisp and new like water on rocks, but it quickly turned into a soggy mess that stayed with her as she left him, stepped over Pat, and picked up the welcome mat with her gloves. She could still see her husband moving back and forth on top of it. She wanted to make HOME SWEET HOME disappear, but the longest she could bring herself to touch it was the end of the driveway, and she left it in a garbage can on the street.

She found that she could not say good-bye. Not when her husband pounded on the door to take a shower and not when Miguel asked if he could brush his teeth. She sat on the toilet and listened to them move about the house and leave. Later, she watched through the window as a man wrapped her neighbors' house in police tape. To double it around a tree in the yard, he circled the trunk with his arms. It was a brief embrace and she thought, *That tree felt nothing.*

In the afternoon, when the sun began to slant, Lieutenant Sales crossed the Mitchells' front yard. He was carrying a chewed-up slipper in a bag, jostling the dandelions, and sending seeds of white fluff adrift. Mrs. Mitchell saw him coming. She turned the key in the lock, and once she was beyond the bathroom, she ran her fingers through her hair, smoothing down the rough spots. The bell rang. The dog barked. She opened the door, and offered him coffee.

Miguel turned nine that summer. In the past two years he'd spent with the Mitchells, the boy had grown no more than an inch; but with the warm weather that June, he'd suddenly sprouted—his legs stretching like brown sugar taffy tight over his new knobby bones, as if the genes of his American father had been lying dormant, biding their time until the right combination of spring breezes and processed food kissed them awake. He began to trip over himself. On his way home from baseball practice that Monday, he caught one of his newly distended feet on a trash can just outside the line of police tape that closed in Pat and Clyde's yard. Miguel fell to the sidewalk, smacking his hands against the concrete. The barrel toppled over beside him, and out came a welcome mat. HOME SWEET HOME.

Miguel was not the best student, but he had made friends easily once he hit several home runs in gym class. Norman and Greg Kessler, twins and the most popular kids in school, chose him for their team and for their friend. Norman and Greg helped him with his English, defended him against would-be attackers, and told him when they saw his father naked.

Mr. Mitchell had driven past them on the highway, stripped bare from the waist down. From the window of their mother's minivan, Norman and Greg could see a woman leaning over the gearshift. *It's true*, said the twins. Miguel made them swear on the Bible, on a stack of Red Sox cards, and finally on their grandfather's grave, which they did, bikes thrown aside in the grass and sweaty hands pressed on the polished marble of his years.

At dinner that night the boy watched his father eating. The angle of his jaw clenched and turned.

Miguel felt a memory push past hot dogs, past English, past Hostess cupcakes and his collection of Spiderman comic books. He was five years old and asked his mother where his father was. She was making coffee—squeezing the grounds through a sieve made out of cloth and wire. He'd collected eggs from their chickens for breakfast. He was holding them in his hands and they were still warm. His mother took one from him. *This is the world and we are here*, she said, and pointed to the bottom half of the egg. *Your father is there.* She ran her finger up along the edge and tapped the point with a dark red nail. Then she cracked the yolk in a pan and threw the rest of the egg in the garbage. He retrieved it later and pushed his fingertips back and forth across the slippery inner membrane until the shell came apart into pieces.

Miguel picked up the doormat and shook it to get the dust off. It seemed like something Mrs. Mitchell might be fond of. That morning he had kept watch through the bathroom keyhole. She was out of sight, but he could sense her worry.

In Caracas he had gone through the trash regularly, looking for things to play with and at times for something to eat. Ever since he heard about his father being naked on the highway, he had been remembering more about his life there, and even reverting to some of his old habits, as if the non sequitur of his father's nudity had tenderly shaken him awake. He lay in bed at night and looked into the eyes of the papier-mâché head for guidance. He had two lives now, two countries and two mothers. Soon he would find another life without his father, and another, when he went away to college, and another life, and another, and another, and another, each of them a thin, fragile casing echoing the hum of what had gone before.

The boy walked into the kitchen and found his American mother sitting with a strange man. They both held steaming mugs of coffee. Buster was under the table, waking from his afternoon nap. He saw Miguel and thumped his tail halfheartedly against the floor. The adults turned. *Now, what have you got there?*

Lieutenant Sales took HOME SWEET HOME in his hands. There was something in the look of the boy and the feel of the rope that held possibility, and the twisted pink skin where the shark had bitten him began to itch. It had been tingling all afternoon. Later, in the lab, the welcome mat would reveal tiny spots of Pat's blood, dog saliva, gunpowder, dead ants, mud, fertilizer, and footprints—but not the impression of Mr. Mitchell's knees, or the hesitation of his jealous wife on the doorstep, or the hunger of his son in the garbage. All of this had been shaken off.

Lieutenant Sales would leave the Mitchells' house that afternoon with the same thrill he'd had when the shark passed and he realized his leg was still there. He was exhilarated and then exhausted, as though his life had been drained, and he knew then that he had gone as far as he could go. There would be no scar and no solution to the murder, just the sense that he had missed something, and the familiar taste of things not done. For now, he reached out with a kind of hope and accepted the welcome mat as a gift.

Mrs. Mitchell put her arm around Miguel's shoulders and waited for Lieutenant Sales to arrest her. She would continue to wait in the weeks ahead as suspects were raised and then dismissed and headlines changed and funerals were planned. The possibilities of these moments passed over her like shadows. When they were gone she was left standing chilled.

Clyde's mother arranged for closed caskets. In the pew Mrs. Mitchell sat quietly. Her husband looked nervous and cracked knuckles. After the service they went home and Mr. Mitchell started to pack. His wife listened to the suitcases being dragged down from the attic, the swing of hangers, zipper teeth, the straps of leather buckles. Mr. Mitchell said he was leaving, and his wife felt her throat clutch. She wanted to ask him where he would go; she wanted to ask him what she had done this for; she wanted to ask him why he no longer loved her, but instead she asked for his son.

She had watched Miguel hand the frayed rope to the detective, and as it passed by her, she felt an ache in the back of her mouth as though she hadn't eaten for days. Lieutenant Sales turned HOME SWEET HOME over in his hands. He placed it carefully on the kitchen table and Mrs. Mitchell saw the word *Sweet*. She remembered the milk she had made for the boy when he arrived, and sensed that this would not be the end of her. She could hear the steady breathing of her sleeping dog. She could smell the coffee. She felt the small frame of Miguel steady beneath her hand. These bones, she thought, were everything. *Hey, sport*, Mrs. Mitchell asked, *is that for me?* The boy nodded, and she held him close.

THE JOB

The French have an expression: metro, boulot, dodo. *Translated it means: train, work, sleep. The existential sentiment here is that our lives consist of little more than clocking in and out of a job. Whether we love our jobs or consider them a necessary evil, it's true that the average adult spends a sizable portion of his time* at work. *The ups and downs there sure affect our mood. And we are often defined by our professions. "My daughter Lisa is a doctor." "Jose is a sanitation engineer, but really he's very clean and I'm sure the two of you will get along."*

In Daniel Orozco's "Orientation," you'll become a new employee at one of those offices where the cubicle infrastructure resembles that of anonymous bees in a hive. Personal matters have no place amid the corporate sterility, but, of course, we don't cease to be messy human beings the moment we hit our desk.

Which profession do people view with the most dislike or cynicism? Dentist? Car salesman? Politician? Good guesses, but no profession invites such universal derision as that held by the man in John O'Farrell's "Walking into the Wind." Nevertheless, this fellow is determined to change the world with his life's work, no matter the cost. For a man in his business, he has a lot to say; but how well does he hear the progressively louder sounds of reality?

For some, what must be done to live is unpleasant, even demeaning. The Haitian mother in Edwidge Danticat's "Night Women" labors to protect her child from the reality of her job. And she dreams that her dreaded nights will someday evolve into something better.

Though Ethan Canin's "The Palace Thief" is a very long short story, the pages turn remarkably fast in this tale of a classics teacher at a prestigious boys' school. The teacher views his role as a noble one, to instill in the world's future leaders a sense of the moral fortitude that guided the great leaders of antiquity. Yet we begin to wonder if the future leaders care about such moral niceties, or indeed, whether the leaders of antiquity did either. The teacher must face a disturbing question—is his occupation in life as important as he once believed? The question is all the more challenging when your job is your life.

ORIENTATION
DANIEL OROZCO

Those are the offices and these are the cubicles. That's my cubicle there, and this is your cubicle. This is your phone. Never answer your phone. Let the Voicemail System answer it. This is your Voicemail System Manual. There are no personal phone calls allowed. We do, however, allow for emergencies. If you must make an emergency phone call, ask your supervisor first. If you can't find your supervisor, ask Phillip Spiers, who sits over there. He'll check with Clarissa Nicks, who sits over there. If you make an emergency phone call without asking, you may be let go.

These are your IN and OUT boxes. All the forms in your IN box must be logged in by the date shown in the upper left-hand corner, initialed by you in the upper right-hand corner, and distributed to the Processing Analyst whose name is numerically coded in the lower left-hand corner. The lower right-hand corner is left blank. Here's your Processing Analyst Numerical Code Index. And here's your Forms Processing Procedures Manual.

You must pace your work. What do I mean? I'm glad you asked that. We pace our work according to the eight-hour workday. If you have twelve hours of work in your IN box, for example, you must compress that work into the eight-hour day. If you have one hour of work in your IN box, you must expand that work to fill the eight-hour day. That was a good question. Feel free to ask questions. Ask too many questions, however, and you may be let go.

That is our receptionist. She is a temp. We go through receptionists here. They quit with alarming frequency. Be polite and civil to the temps.

Learn their names, and invite them to lunch occasionally. But don't get close to them, as it only makes it more difficult when they leave. And they always leave. You can be sure of that.

The men's room is over there. The women's room is over there. John LaFountaine, who sits over there, uses the women's room occasionally. He says it is accidental. We know better, but we let it pass. John LaFountaine is harmless, his forays into the forbidden territory of the women's room simply a benign thrill, a faint blip on the dull flat line of his life.

Russell Nash, who sits in the cubicle to your left, is in love with Amanda Pierce, who sits in the cubicle to your right. They ride the same bus together after work. For Amanda Pierce, it is just a tedious bus ride made less tedious by the idle nattering of Russell Nash. But for Russell Nash, it is the highlight of his day. It is the highlight of his life. Russell Nash has put on forty pounds, and grows fatter with each passing month, nibbling on chips and cookies while peeking glumly over the partitions at Amanda Pierce, and gorging himself at home on cold pizza and ice cream while watching adult videos on TV.

Amanda Pierce, in the cubicle to your right, has a six-year-old son named Jamie, who is autistic. Her cubicle is plastered from top to bottom with the boy's crayon artwork—sheet after sheet of precisely drawn concentric circles and ellipses, in black and yellow. She rotates them every other Friday. Be sure to comment on them. Amanda Pierce also has a husband, who is a lawyer. He subjects her to an escalating array of painful and humiliating sex games, to which Amanda Pierce reluctantly submits. She comes to work exhausted and freshly wounded each morning, wincing from the abrasions to her breasts, or the bruises on her abdomen, or the second-degree burns on the backs of her thighs.

But we're not supposed to know any of this. Do not let on. If you let on, you may be let go.

Amanda Pierce, who tolerates Russell Nash, is in love with Albert Bosch, whose office is over there. Albert Bosch, who only dimly registers Amanda Pierce's existence, has eyes only for Ellie Tapper, who sits over there. Ellie Tapper, who hates Albert Bosch, would walk through fire for Curtis Lance. But Curtis Lance hates Ellie Tapper. Isn't the world a funny place? Not in the ha-ha sense, of course.

Anika Bloom sits in that cubicle. Last year, while reviewing quarterly reports in a meeting with Barry Hacker, Anika Bloom's left palm began to bleed. She fell into a trance, stared into her hand, and told Barry Hacker when and how his wife would die. We laughed it off. She was, after all, a new employee. But Barry Hacker's wife is dead. So unless you want to know exactly when and how you'll die, never talk to Anika Bloom.

Colin Heavey sits in that cubicle over there. He was new once, just like you. We warned him about Anika Bloom. But at last year's Christmas Potluck, he felt sorry for her when he saw that no one was talking to her. Colin Heavey brought her a drink. He hasn't been himself since. Colin Heavey is doomed. There's nothing he can do about it, and we are powerless to help him. Stay away from Colin Heavey. Never give any of your work to him. If he asks to do something, tell him you have to check with me. If he asks again, tell him I haven't gotten back to you.

This is the Fire Exit. There are several on this floor, and they are marked accordingly. We have a Floor Evacuation Review every three months, and an Escape Route Quiz once a month. We have our Biannual Fire Drill twice a year, and our Annual Earthquake Drill once a year. These are precautions only. These things never happen.

For your information, we have a comprehensive health plan. Any catastrophic illness, any unforeseen tragedy is completely covered. All dependents are completely covered. Larry Bagdikian, who sits over there, has six daughters. If anything were to happen to any of his girls, or to all of them, if all six were to simultaneously fall victim to illness or injury—stricken with a hideous degenerative muscle disease or some rare toxic blood disorder, sprayed with semiautomatic gunfire while on a class field trip, or attacked in their bunk beds by some prowling nocturnal lunatic—if any of this were to pass, Larry's girls would all be taken care of. Larry Bagdikian would not have to pay one dime. He would have nothing to worry about.

We also have a generous vacation and sick leave policy. We have an excellent disability insurance plan. We have a stable and profitable pension fund. We get group discounts for the symphony, and block seating at the ballpark. We get commuter ticket books for the bridge. We have Direct Deposit. We are all members of Costco.

This is our kitchenette. And this, this is our Mr. Coffee. We have a coffee pool, into which we each pay two dollars a week for coffee, filters, sugar, and CoffeeMate. If you prefer Cremora or half-and-half to CoffeeMate, there is a special pool for three dollars per week. If you prefer Sweet'n Low to sugar, there is a special pool for two-fifty a week. We do not do decaf.

You are allowed to join the coffee pool of your choice, but you are not allowed to touch the Mr. Coffee.

This is the microwave oven. You are allowed to *heat* food in the microwave oven. You are not, however, allowed to cook food in the microwave oven.

We get one hour for lunch. We also get one fifteen-minute break in the morning, and one fifteen-minute break in the afternoon. Always take your breaks. If you skip a break, it is gone forever. For your information, your break is a privilege, not a right. If you abuse the break policy, we are authorized to rescind your breaks. Lunch, however, is a right, not a privilege. If you abuse the lunch policy, our hands will be tied, and we will be forced to look the other way. We will not enjoy that.

This is the refrigerator. You may put your lunch in it. Barry Hacker, who sits over there, steals food from this refrigerator. His petty theft is an outlet for his grief. Last New Year's Eve, while kissing his wife, a blood vessel burst in her brain. Barry Hacker's wife was two months pregnant at the time, and lingered in a coma for half a year before dying. It was a tragic loss for Barry Hacker. He hasn't been himself since. Barry Hacker's wife was a beautiful woman. She was also completely covered. Barry Hacker did not have to pay one dime. But his dead wife haunts him. She haunts all of us. We have seen her, reflected in the monitors of our computers, moving past our cubicles. We have seen the dim shadow of her face in our photocopies. She pencils herself in in the receptionist's appointment book with the notation: To see Barry Hacker. She has left messages in the receptionist's Voicemail box, messages garbled by the electronic chirrups and buzzes in the phone line, her voice echoing from an immense distance within the ambient hum. But the voice is hers. And beneath her voice, beneath the tidal *whoosh* of static and hiss, the gurgling and crying of a baby can be heard.

In any case, if you bring a lunch, put a little something extra in the bag for Barry Hacker. We have four Barrys in this office. Isn't that a coincidence?

This is Matthew Payne's office. He is our Unit Manager, and his door is always closed. We have never seen him, and you will never see him. But he is here. You can be sure of that. He is all around us.

This is the Custodian's Closet. You have no business in the Custodian's Closet.

And this, this is our Supplies Cabinet. If you need supplies see Curtis Lance. He will log you in on the Supplies Cabinet Authorization Log, then give you a Supplies Authorization Slip. Present your pink copy of the supplies Authorization Slip to Ellie Tapper. She will log you in on the Supplies Cabinet Key Log, then give you the key. Because the Supplies Cabinet is located outside the Unit Manager's office, you must be very quiet. Gather your supplies quietly. The Supplies Cabinet is divided into four sections. Section One contains letterhead stationery, blank paper and envelopes, memo and note pads, and so on. Section Two contains pens and pencils and typewriter and printer ribbons, and the like. In Section Three we have erasers, correction fluids, transparent tapes, glue sticks, et cetera. And in Section Four we have paper clips and push pins and scissors and razor blades. And here are the spare blades for the shredder. Do not touch the shredder, which is located over there. The shredder is of no concern to you.

Gwendolyn Stich sits in that office there. She is crazy about penguins, and collects penguin knickknacks: penguin posters and coffee mugs and stationery, penguin stuffed animals, penguin jewelry, penguin sweaters and T-shirts and socks. She has a pair of penguin fuzzy slippers she wears when working late at the office. She has a tape cassette of penguin sounds which she listens to for relaxation. Her favorite colors are black and white. She has personalized license plates that read PEN GWEN. Every morning she passes through all the cubicles to wish each of us a *good* morning. She brings Danish on Wednesdays for Hump Day morning break, and dough-nuts on Fridays for TGIF afternoon break. She organizes the Annual Christmas Potluck, and is in charge of the Birthday List. Gwendolyn Stich's door is always open to all of us. She will always lend an ear, and put in a good word for you; she will always give you a hand, or the shirt off her back, or a shoulder to cry on. Because her door is always open, she hides and cries in a stall in the women's room. And John LaFountaine—who, enthralled when a woman enters, sits quietly in his stall with his knees to his chest—John LaFountaine has heard her vomiting in there. We have come upon Gwendolyn Stich huddled in the stairwell, shivering in the updraft, sipping a Diet Mr. Pibb and hugging her knees. She does not let any of this interfere with her work. If it interfered with her work, she might have to be let go.

Kevin Howard sits in that cubicle over there. He is a serial killer, the one they call the Carpet Cutter, responsible for the mutilations across town.

We're not supposed to know that, so do not let on. Don't worry. His compulsion inflicts itself on strangers only, and the routine established is elaborate and unwavering. The victim must be a white male, a young adult no older than thirty, heavyset, with dark hair and eyes, and the like. The victim must be chosen at random, before sunset, from a public place; the victim is followed home, and must put up a struggle; et cetera. The carnage inflicted is precise: the angle and direction of the incisions; the layering of skin and muscle tissue; the rearrangement of the visceral organs; and so on. Kevin Howard does not let any of this interfere with his work. He is, in fact, our fastest typist. He types as if he were on fire. He has a secret crush on Gwendolyn Stich, and leaves a red-foil-wrapped Hershey's Kiss on her desk every afternoon. But he hates Anika Bloom, and keeps well away from her. In his presence, she has uncontrollable fits of shaking and trembling. Her left palm does not stop bleeding.

In any case, when Kevin Howard gets caught, act surprised. Say that he seemed like a nice person, a bit of a loner, perhaps, but always quiet and polite.

This is the photocopier room. And this, this is our view. It faces southwest. West is down there, toward the water. North is back there. Because we are on the seventeenth floor, we are afforded a magnificent view. Isn't it beautiful? It overlooks the park, where the tops of those trees are. You can see a segment of the bay between those two buildings over there. You can see this building reflected in the glass panels of that building across the way. There. See? That's you, waving. And look there. There's Anika Bloom in the kitchenette, waving back.

Enjoy this view while photocopying. If you have problems with the photocopier, see Russell Nash. If you have any questions, ask your supervisor. If you can't find your supervisor, ask Phillip Spiers. He sits over there. He'll check with Clarissa Nicks. She sits over there. If you can't find them, feel free to ask me. That's my cubicle. I sit in there.

WALKING INTO THE WIND

JOHN O'FARRELL

There's a moment when you're up on stage when you suddenly become aware that everyone is looking at you; that the entire room is totally focused upon what *you* are doing. In that terrifying split second your performance can crash to the ground or it can soar to great new heights; but the fact that you have the power to throw it all away is partly what's so thrilling about being in the spotlight. It happens to every performer—I bet you that in the middle of the Nuremberg rallies Adolf Hitler was tempted just to spoil it all by blowing a raspberry and saying "Actually I'm gay and I'm proud." But of course you never do shatter the magic because for that precious hour or so the audience completely love you and that is why being on stage is the greatest job in the world.

"You have got to be the luckiest bloke I know," said Richard the first time he saw me perform at the Edinburgh Festival. "Twenty-three years old; doing exactly what you want to do, everyone thinks you're great; no office, no boss, no suit and you get paid a bloody fortune to boot. How cool is that!"

"It's cool," agreed Neal.

It was quite cool I have to admit. In fact it was very, very cool, but the thing about being cool is you can't really let on how delighted you are about it. You never see James Bond ringing his mum to tell her how well he's doing.

Fifteen minutes earlier I'd been bowing and wearing my modest "no-you're-embarrassing-me" smile, as two hundred people cheered me and clapped and shouted for more. I'd glanced down and seen Richard and Neal in the front row clapping proudly and then as the rest of the audience got up to leave they rushed up to me slightly too quickly. "Guy, that was brilliant, Guy!" they said and then everyone else knew that they weren't just ordinary members of the audience, they were friends of Guy's.

Now we sat in the pub opposite the theatre and I counted out the two hundred pounds cash that I'd just been paid. I knew it took Richard and Neal a couple of weeks to earn that much money, so I thought I'd better just check it again. A beautiful girl approached our table and asked for my autograph. She blushed and told me that she'd really enjoyed my show and thought I was brilliant. "Well, I can't take all the credit myself," I said, which probably sounded a little insincere after a one-man show that I'd written and produced on my own. My friends looked on openmouthed as I scribbled my name in her programme. It was the first time this had ever happened to me. "You sort of get used to it," I told them.

I think that day was the first time they understood why I'd refused to follow them into the slavery of a normal job. Now that they'd glimpsed this world of fringe festivals and beer tents and circus arts, they couldn't believe that this was my everyday life. Richard watched the girl disappear and then continued his eulogy to my existence.

"You know how people become bone-marrow donors or kidney donors?" he said. "Well how about if you just donate your entire life to me? How about if we have a life transplant?"

And he took another gulp of beer but tipped the glass back too much so that it spilled all over his shirt and his offer looked even less attractive.

"Last week . . ." I confided, "I had a fling with a Marilyn Monroe lookalike."

"And did she kill herself afterwards?" said Neal.

"Funny you should say that, because she does top herself in this play she's in. It alleges that the policeman who found her proceeded to have sex with her dead body. It's called 'Some Like it Cold.'"

They quizzed me about other actresses I'd met, and I told them about the life on the road, the festivals I'd played and the European capitals I'd visited and after a while they just stared silently into their pints. I hadn't meant to depress them. Maybe the sentence "So what's happening in

Dorking?" is always followed by a long silence. But they were impressed, amazed and jealous and I realized why I'd got them up there. I was engineering envy.

And yet they'd thought I was completely mad when I'd first told them what I was going to do when I left school.

"Mime?" they'd said. "That's not a job."

"Mime?" they kept repeating in sardonic disbelief. It was amazing how it was possible to pack so much contempt into one syllable. Everyone's reaction had been the same. I'd grown up in Surrey, not famous for it's theatrical traditions, although I did once take my nephew to see *Adventures in Smurfland* at the Epsom Playhouse. My hometown of Dorking was however home to the national headquarters of Friends Provident Insurance. The job of my school careers advisor seemed to consist of getting sixth formers into his office, establishing in which particular department of Friends Provident they imagined themselves spending the rest of their lives and then setting up the job interview. I don't know why he was called a *"careers adviser"* because there was only ever the one option. In Manchester in the 1850s you went into the cotton mills. In Dorking in the 1970s you got a job at Friends Provident.

"Well, Guy . . ." he said to me, "you're in luck . . . we could be looking at quite a decent starting salary. For an eighteen-year-old trainee claims assessor at Friends Provident."

It wasn't until about halfway through the interview that I finally summoned up the courage to tell him, "I don't want to work at Friends Provident . . ." I said, "I want to be a mime artist."

He paused and looked over his glasses at me. I got the feeling he was not inundated with eighteen-year-olds who wanted to go into the expressive arts. "Mime artist?" he said, flicking through his index box. Management consultant . . . Marketing executive . . . there was no card for mime artist. So a conversation then ensued during which he suggested that a foothold in the world of pensions and life insurance might be the most sensible first step for an aspiring performer. I think he was trying to rack his brains for a department of Friends Provident where an interest in mime might be a bonus. "Sales and marketing? No . . . Personnel? No . . . The Pretending to be Stuck in a Glass Box Department maybe?" If they'd had one of those I'm sure he would have mentioned it.

"I know!" he said, as if he'd just hit upon the perfect solution. "How about if you just do a couple of years at Friends Provident and then once you've got the basic qualifications under your belt you could keep up your interest in performing by specialising in *theatrical* insurance?"

"Theatrical insurance?" I said. "Is there any actual mime involved in that?"

"Well . . ." he said. "I'm sure one or two of the theatres that Friends Provident insure put on mime shows from time to time. . . . But most of the time it would be more office work than actually miming things."

I spent a couple of years living at home and signing on the dole wondering about how one broke into the closed world of corporeal theatre. There was nothing in the local paper. My parents worried about me and I was sullen and withdrawn. "The amount he talks . . ." my dad said, "bloody mime's the only thing he'd be any good for." Dad was not the intellectual type. I told him about the famous Jacques Lecoq school in Paris but he thought this through and then explained why this might not be the theatre school for me. "Jacques Lecoq?" he said. "Well he's obviously a poof with a name like that." In the end it was my mother who secretly encouraged me to apply. "You get your interest in the theatre from me," she said. "I've seen everything Andrew Lloyd Webber's ever done."

I thought my audition piece was fantastic, though looking back there was probably quite a low risk of them thinking "There's nothing left we can teach this young man." It was copied directly from a Charlie Chaplin set piece, and I suppose I was rather hoping that the French might not be aware of the world's greatest ever film star. They said they liked my "interpretation of the Chaplin" and to my astonished delight I was in. I bought the makeup and tights and Dad blamed himself for not having taken me to watch rugby more often. Paris was a revelation. They have a different attitude to artistic pursuits on the Continent. They don't say "Mime artist, eh? Well, I suppose it saves having to learn all those lines!" I studied pantomime, though not the sort that stars Frank Bruno as Widow Twanky. I learned how to use my posture to suggest different facial expressions while wearing a wooden mask.

"Wouldn't it be easier just to take off the mask?" suggested Neal.

"The art of mime . . ." I told my friends, ". . . is like learning to play your body as if it were a musical instrument."

"Well, I think I'd be a wind instrument," said Richard, "then I could just go on stage and fart for an hour."

The three of us carried on drinking in this scruffy Edinburgh pub until we were told that if we wanted to stay there we'd have to pay to watch the comedy that was being put on at eight o'clock. Apparently the saloon bar had been converted into a comedy venue for the duration of the festival, by means of putting a piece of paper on the door saying Comedy Club— Entry £2. Richard and Neal were excited about seeing some stand-up; alternative comedy was quite a new concept back then, so we paid up and the bar gradually filled up around us. There was no P.A., no stage, no lighting, just a space by the dart board where the comic was supposed to perform. It was so intimate that all you could do was adopt a benign smile and hope for the best.

The comedian shuffled out in front of us. He was a bloke about our age who had taken it upon himself to adopt the stage name "Mussolini's Mother-in-law." It has to be said that as a stand-up comic he was only partially successful. The "standing-up" bit, he did excellently. He didn't fall over once during his entire set, his balance was impeccable. But as for the description "comic," well I hadn't been so embarrassed since my parents danced to *Anarchy in the UK* at my eighteenth birthday party.

He stood there for a moment clutching a hand-rolled cigarette which turned out to be far too small to hide behind. Then he hit us with the opening line of his comedy act.

"Have you ever noticed how there are too many words for small oranges?" he said. An awkward silence fell across the room, which was filled slightly too quickly with the next line. "I mean, there's tangerines, mandarins, clementines, satsumas—why can't we just call them all *small oranges*?" Neal, Richard and I were right at the front, only five feet away from him, we had to give some sort of reaction. A strangled noise came out of my throat which wasn't so much a laugh as a nervous grunt to punctuate the awkward silence. It was an attempt to communicate to him that although I wasn't laughing, I was at least aware of the point at which the laughter was supposed to come. I noticed that, like me, everyone had their legs and arms crossed as a sort of improvised "crap-comic barrier."

"Er, because, I mean, the Eskimos have forty words for snow, right . . ." he went on. "Because like snow is really important to Eskimos. So clearly Anglo-Saxon society totally revolved around small oranges." There was a pre-planned pause for laughter and I gave a brave smile because it was easier to fake than convulsive giggles. Even though I am a trained performer, I don't think I could ever again recreate that combination of horror and pity in my eyes with the compassionate smile that was locked upon my mouth. In the Middle Ages when a heretic was being publicly disembowelled, at least the onlookers could acknowledge that the victim was not having a very nice time. They weren't expected to sit there with an artificial cheerful grin that said "Well, this is all going very well for you!" A chair scraped and a couple of people at the back slipped away. Comedy clubs are like plane crashes, you're always safer sitting at the back.

"He was rubbish," said Richard afterwards. "I can't believe it cost the same to see him as it did you." I can't deny I felt a smug sort of personal triumph. Our two genres were at completely opposite ends of the theatrical spectrum. I used no words and so had to work much harder to communicate with my audience. I had to be an actor, a dancer and a gymnast— every second of my performance was carefully choreographed. Whereas "Mussolini's Mother-in-law" communicated in the easiest manner possible and thus the content became as lazy as the form. I explained this to Richard and he said, "Well that, and the fact he was just a crap comic."

The next day I was just waving them off at the station when the Marilyn Monroe lookalike came up and threw her arms around me. I can still see their faces pressed against the window as the train pulled away. I was a free man while they were being transported back to the forced labour camps in Surrey. On the Monday I travelled to Prague and they returned to work at Friends Provident.

The following year, Richard and Neal came and saw me at the Glastonbury Festival and were really positive about the new show. I gave them a fantastic time. We'd never smoked dope at school—there were no drug dealers in Dorking as the careers adviser had not had a card for that job either. Cannabis was a sudden revelation to them and we got out of our heads lying in a field listening to Van Morrison, giggling and singing along to "And It Stoned Me." It was one of those perfect moments that stay with you forever after. I said to them as they left the next day that I think I'd put that sunny afternoon into my lifetime highlights video. This was an imaginary compilation that I was assembling in my head; all my happiest and proudest moments, cut together into a five-minute edited greatest hits of my life.

"What would you have in your lifetime highlights video, Neal?" I asked him.

He thought for a while and said nervously "Getting a B in my geography O' level."

He looked hurt when I burst out laughing.

"Oh come on . . ." I said, "you've got to do better than that. You can't have that on your tombstone—*Here lies Neal Evans. He got a B in his geography O' level.* What have you done that you really loved and will always remember? What are you really proud of?"

He shrugged. "Getting off with Abigail Parsons?"

"That was when you were fourteen." I laughed. "What about recently?"

Richard came to Neal's defence. "Look it's alright for you," he said. "You're a mime artist. You have lifetime highlights every week. We're in an office all day and we go to night school in the evenings. We've got exams to get, promotion to work towards. We can't all be bloody mime artists."

We walked in silence up to the fields where all the cars were parked. They both had company cars by now, Neal had a Ford Sierra and Richard had a Vauxhall Cavalier, and they were neatly parked in between all the beaten-up VW vans and 2CVs. I watched them pull away and then I saw Richard stop at the top of the lane to get his suit out of the boot and hang it up in the back of the car.

I saw them both intermittently throughout the winter and persuaded them to come to Glastonbury the following year. I found the same spot in the field where we could lie and get stoned again, but Neal got cow dung on his trousers and then the end of the spliff fell out and burned Richard on his chest. They said they liked my show though. In fact I think it really bowled them over because it was like they were lost for words. I had that experience in Paris once—when I saw a really moving piece of mime—I just didn't want to talk about it, I simply had to talk about something else. So they talked about their jobs. Richard had got a pay rise so he insisted on buying all the drinks. Neal wasn't working at Friends Provident anymore, he said he needed a new challenge. He'd got a job at Commercial Union.

I continued to tour around the country although it became a little frustrating when one or two of the venues in which I had done really well still didn't want me back the following year. "You're the mime bloke, aren't you?" said the man from North West Arts. "Are you still doing the same sort of thing?"

"No, it's a completely new show," I announced proudly.

"But is it still no words and white makeup and all that?" he said.

"I'm still doing mime if that's what you mean, yes," I said.

"Well, we can't have mime every year, can we? We've got acrobats this year. There's lots of them but they're Chinese so they actually work out cheaper."

Then I secured a booking at the Pontefract Arts and Leisure Centre, but two days before the show the manager phoned me to cancel my performance.

"Listen, we've not sold enough tickets," he said in his gruff Yorkshire accent. "There's folk who want to use sports hall to play badminton. And if no one's coming to see you, then how can I justify cancelling Sunday night badminton?"

I told him that he couldn't pull the show now; that it had taken me ages to persuade my two best friends to come up and see it. And that he had a duty to put on pieces of original theatre—that it was an Arts *and* Leisure centre; that people could play badminton any day of the week, but they only had this one chance to see my performance.

"My, you've got a lot to say for yourself—for a mime artist," he said. Then he proposed a compromise which would involve me reducing the stage size so that half the hall could still be used for badminton. Call me a precious old luvvie, but I did not feel that my powerful mimodrama about the genocide taking place in the Amazon rainforests would be made all the more poignant by having middle-aged couples lumbering around playing badminton on either side of me.

"Don't be ridiculous!" I said. "You can't put on a piece of theatre with people playing badminton all around you."

"Why not?" said the Yorkshireman.

It was hard to know where to start. "Well, what if a shuttlecock is mis-hit and lands on the stage?"

"Well, a shuttlecock's not going to hurt you, is it?" he said. "It's not like a cricket ball."

"But they'll grunt and talk and their plimsoles will squeak."

"Yes, but you do mime. They don't have to listen to any words, do they?"

Did Shakespeare ever have to go through this, I wondered? Negotiating with the manager of the Globe Theatre who wanted to cancel *Hamlet* because Thursday night was the Southwark Over-Sixties Music and Movement class? I was forced to agree to having three courts at the far end of the sports hall kept open for badminton and then he came out with it; "Now what about the rock climbers? Our concrete re-creation of Scaffel Pike is on the wall overhanging your stage and it's very popular on Sunday nights."

It was still a great show though. My most challenging to date, in fact. A two-hour narrative mime tackling issues like the environment and the annihilation of the indigenous people of the Amazon basin by the multinational mining corporations.

"Was it about Jack and the Beanstalk?" said Richard afterwards.

"Jack and the Beanstalk?" I said. "What on earth are you talking about?"

"Well, when you were doing all that chopping—I thought that might be Jack chopping down the beanstalk."

"That was the destruction of the rainforest," I said.

"Oh. Yeah, well I thought it was probably something like that," he said.

Honestly! It did make we wonder if I was being overambitious dealing with serious social issues in my work. But I think I really conveyed the terrible suffering that was happening in Brazil. Because the audience looked quite depressed by the end of the evening.

The following Christmas Eve we went on a pub crawl through Dorking as we'd always done when Richard let slip that he and Neal had already booked to go to Club Mark Warner with their girlfriends at the end of June.

"What about Glastonbury?" I said, "I've got this new army-surplus tent which I thought could sleep all five of us."

"It's a bit of a clash actually," said Richard.

"Well bring the girls up to Edinburgh instead. Or there's the East Midlands mime festival in Leicester in September."

"Erm, to be honest, Guy . . ." he said, "I'm just a bit bored with all that farting about with white makeup on."

What a strange thing to say, I thought. Richard was trying to tell me something and I was determined to find out what it was.

"But you love my stuff," I said. "You said *Return to Hiroshima* was a very brave piece of theatre."

"Did I?" he said "Er, yeah, well it's quite interesting to see someone do it once or twice. But you don't sit down with your missus every night, turn on the telly and flick through the channels till you get to *UK Mime* do you?"

"Is there really a mime channel?" I said excitedly.

"Of course there bloody isn't. That's the whole point," he said.

"So you're not going to see the new show at all?" I asked him, straight out.

"Probably not," he confessed. "Sally doesn't like mime. She likes musicals."

Aha! That was the giveaway, wasn't it, mentioning Sally. Of course, they didn't want to appear all boring and square in front of their other halves, did they? They didn't want their girlfriends to see what they were missing, the magic of corporeal mime, the life on the road, sleeping in the van, the excitement of setting out the chairs in some farflung arts centre. No, don't let your world be challenged by groundbreaking art, just write out a cheque and fly off to the sunshine for a fortnight's windsurfing. It's just so easy, isn't it? I sent them details of the Barcelona Mime Workshop, which was only five hours' drive from their resort, but if they went, they never mentioned it to me.

A couple of years went by and before I knew it their girlfriends had become their wives. Neal was the best man at Richard's wedding and Richard was the best man at Neal's. Obviously they'd seen a lot more of each other down the years, and besides, I don't think either of them felt they could trust me with a best man's speech! I think they were worried I might have mimed it the whole way through. Honestly, I'm not that obsessed. I would have done some talking as well.

But it was at Neal's wedding that I met Carol and the triangle was finally complete. She had that petite elfin quality that reminded me of Mia Farrow, though fortunately she didn't have a house full of adopted Vietnamese kids that I'd have to be father to. We had a modest little wedding at the registry office and then round to the pub for a couple of pints and some miniature vol-au-vents. At closing time her dad took me aside and went all serious on me. He told me that before he was married he'd been in a jazz band; played all the clubs and dreamed of making it big. But he said that when he started a family he realized his priorities had to change. And then he looked at me meaningfully as he struggled to keep his balance.

"Message received loud and clear," I said to him.

"Good man," he replied, looking reassured as he patted me on the back. But really; as if I'd ever be even remotely interested in playing in a jazz band.

Carol worked in the health service, dealing with psychologically disturbed children, which was tough for her because it wasn't always easy to get time off to come to the shows. But in the evening we'd talk about all the problems we'd had at work—trying to hang on to my Arts Council grant, having to find rehearsal space, trying to discover why I'd not been invited to perform at the London Mime festival. "I'm glad to be out of that one actually," I said to her, "because the whole British mime scene is far too London-based already . . ."

"Guy . . ." she said.

"It's all stitched up at the Montreal festival anyway," I told her. "If you can't afford to fly over to Canada then you can forget London."

"Guy," she said, "I think I'm pregnant."

Carol had planned to go back to work after she'd had the baby, but then we had another one and she couldn't bear to leave them. "We can live on what I earn," I said, confident that this suggestion would be contradicted. When she agreed with me I wanted to say, "Are you mad?" The flat was only one bedroom so they had to sleep in our room, but it wasn't too cramped because I was away a lot of the time performing around the country. My pieces worked best in more intimate settings, so I tended to get bookings from smaller venues. But the trouble with these little halls is that a lot of them put out those awful plastic chairs which are very uncomfortable if you're sitting through a two-hour show. It means that some people with bad backs or whatever can't come back for the second half, which is a shame because they miss the real message of the piece. But in a way, I almost prefer a small audience, the exchange is all the more personal. Of course if you're on a door split you don't take so much home, but I never became a mime artist to make my million. I hate the way that everything has become so commercial in our society—the way that money is held up as being more important than mime.

Even Carol isn't immune to this, I regret to say. Things were obviously a bit tight after she gave up work to look after the boys, but sometimes I worried that she was turning into a breadhead like everyone else. I wasn't so insensitive that I didn't get the hint when she started talking about the different types of children's car seat one could buy. She wanted us to get a car. But if all this sudden materialism wasn't bad enough, she started going on about life insurance and a pension and all that other square stuff that keeps Friends Provident in business and pays for Richard's big house in Leatherhead. Like he needs any more money. I told her we couldn't afford to go mad at the moment—things were always tighter in the winter—"mime work is seasonal," I said, "you knew that when you married me. Anyway there's a recession on and mime artists are always the first to feel the pinch." Oh yes, if you're a teacher or a fireman, your job's fine; you're safe enough, but mime artists—well we're suddenly surplus to requirements, aren't we? But then mime has never been a pursuit that is particularly overvalued in British society—it's not like being a doctor or something. You don't get a sudden crisis where a member of the public shouts "Help! Help! It's got very windy outside—is anyone here a mime artist who can show us how to walk against a really strong wind?"

· So Carol and I had our ups and downs like any couple. She did threaten to leave me once, said she'd find a man who might talk to her about things more. She thought it was because of what I did for a living. But her mother said to her, "No, dear, all men are like that, it's not just the mime artists." But she worried about us being in debt and the boys seemed to be costing more and more and they were getting too big to be sharing a room with their parents, and then one day she just suddenly came out with it. "Guy, you're forty-one years old," she said. "I don't think you should be a mime artist anymore."

There comes a point in a man's life when he must face up to his responsibilities; when he has to put his family first and sacrifice the dreams he had when he was young and carefree. This was the theme that I explored in my next one-man mime entitled "Sell out in the Suburbs." For the first time ever I spoke during a performance, I actually re-enacted that moment with Carol, at the very end of the show, I said out loud, "And my wife told me not to be a mime artist anymore!" You should have heard the applause. Something in that piece really connected with people.

I know why she'd said it. All her friends in Dorking had money and husbands with flashy cars and thought that Carol was strange because she didn't have a nanny or a black labrador. They were always going on at her about me, they just couldn't handle that I did what I did, like I was some sort of threat to their comfy suburban existence. That was the trouble with living in Surrey; it was full of people who lived in Surrey. When the pubs shut in Dorking the landlord shouts, "Come on; haven't you all got second homes to go to?"

Why did people always imply I ought to be spending my life doing something else? Teaching mime was the usual suggestion, but that's not being a mime artist, is it, that's being a teacher. People didn't look at the Sistine chapel and say to Michaelangelo, "Hmm, nice ceiling, Mike, why don't you teach interior decor."

I'd go to pick the boys up from school and the mothers would go quiet as I approached as if I was some sort of social leper. I may not have been the richest father at the school gates, but my kids loved the fact that their dad did something a bit more interesting and exciting than all the others. Marcel is nearly six now so he's seen some of my more recent pieces. He's so funny, I was talking to him about my work when he was sitting in the bath a few months back, when he said, "Dad, it would be much less boring if you talked at the same time." The things that kids come out with! So I told him about the sublimated tragedy of the comic performer who's lost the power of speech. About how silent mime evolved out of performing restrictions imposed on the early French theatre and that I used no spoken words because mime is a poem written in the air. And when I finished this explanation I looked down at him in the bath to see if he had taken it in. He was stretching his foreskin into different shapes and he said, "Look, I can make Pokémon faces with my willy."

I'm taking the boys to see their first ever Kabuki theatre on Saturday. They're very excited, bless them; I hope I haven't built it up too much. It's hard to explain to kids that so much of the material stuff that they want won't really make them happy. That they're being tricked by big businesses and advertisers and that it's a never-ending spiral. Someone has to say this to them because the talking Buzz Lightyear (£34.99 from Toys "Я" Us) didn't seem like he was going to mention it. I'm sure Carol knows I'm right but she can't seem to help herself from buying them bits of plastic junk that have been made in some sweat-shop in China. Eventually we got so far into debt that I had to take some drastic action. So I swallowed a few principles and joined the other commuters squashed onto the 9.07 from Dorking to Waterloo. I had heard what Carol had said to me. That something had to change, that I needed to take some serious action. So I started doing a bit of street theatre up at Covent Garden.

You may have seen me there in my cyberman get-up; silver makeup on my face, the bacofoil suit; Kraftwerk blaring out of the tinny beat box. I had a private chuckle about the irony of it all, because there was me dressed as a robot when of course the real robots were all those poor office workers who came out to watch me during their permitted one-hour lunch-break. My act involved standing completely still for a few minutes and then suddenly coming to life. My head would swivel and my arms would mechanically relocate; each joint and muscle was activated with precision control as if individually powered by its own electric motor. This would cause great delight; I could feel the buzz of excitement in the circle of tourists around me but I could not even acknowledge that I knew they were there. I was a machine, you see; a piece of mechanical hardware, and when you're giving a public performance convention demands that you remain in character whatever might be happening around you. However, this long-established principle does not take into account the possibility of being kicked up the arse by a drunken teenager.

It had started with just a bit of heckling. There were three of them, lurching dangerously between the tourists, clutching cans of cheap lager.

"Oi, C-3PO! Where's Obi Wan Kenobi?" shouted the tall one.

I didn't understand how this was supposed to constitute an actual joke, but his friends fell about in hysterics anyway. Professional pride meant that I could not allow myself to even blink as they continued to harangue me.

"Oi, Robot! When you have a piss, how do you stop your knob going all rusty?" he said. Now the crowd were laughing as well and I wondered if he was the theatre critic from the *Sun*. I tried to cling on to some professional dignity but it's hard to conjure up witty put-downs with mime. The best I could do was to swivel round slowly and just stare at him; my face remaining totally deadpan. This didn't intimidate him in the way that I'd hoped. He surveyed me up and down, swayed dangerously and then with no warning whatsoever just kicked me up the bum.

I think some of the crowd imagined that this was part of the show because they laughed and applauded all the more. A Japanese tourist had failed to capture the moment on video and asked him if he'd do it again and he was more than happy to oblige. Finally I breathed a huge internal sigh of relief; a couple of policemen had seen what was going on and were heading towards us. The performance-artist-baiting section of the show would now be over and the yobs would be sent on their way. But no. Instead of coming to my rescue and ordering the delinquents to leave me alone, the policemen stood on the edge of the crowd, folded their arms and chuckled along at the show with everyone else. They adopted one of those benevolent "it's all just a bit of good-natured fun" expressions that they learn at Hendon Police College. I wanted to shout out to them—"No, it's not just a bit of good-natured fun, it's not fun at all; arrest these drunken yobs at once." Agents of the state condoning the kicking of the mime artist; that just about says it all. Because the next day I lost my Arts Council grant as well.

They said they didn't have to give a reason. I went down to their offices and no one was available to talk to me. I'm afraid I lost control a bit actually and I shouted at the bloke on the desk that I couldn't carry on without the grant anymore, that the philistines upstairs had just killed off the only one-man performer in the whole country who was trying to deal with serious social and political issues through the medium of mime. "Is that what you want?" I shouted. "To live in a country where there is not one socially-aware mime artist touring the regions?"

"I think I could live with it," he said.

I walked back through the West End and as I was walking down Shaftesbury Avenue I saw a face on a poster that I recognized. "Johnny Lee—live one-man show!" the theatre boasted. I stared and stared at that familiar face and eventually it came to me. It was "Mussolini's Mother-in-law," the comic from the Edinburgh Festival all those years ago. He'd lost the stupid name but gained a successful career judging by the queue at the box office. "Single tickets only" said a note on the window, so I bought one and took my place in the audience. A solitary microphone stood in a circular pool of light in the middle of the stage, like some sort of statement about the minimalism of one man and his jokes. There was a warm-up act who played seventies glam-rock tunes on different size Marmite jars, and then finally a booming deep voice came over the PA and announced, "Ladies and Gentlemen—Johnny Lee!"

Johnny rushed up the centre aisle, leapt up on stage and confidently grabbed the microphone out of its stand. He waited for the applause and cheering to die down, until he shouted into the mic with amazed and outraged incomprehension, "Have you ever noticed how there are too many words for small oranges?" A huge laugh washed across the room. I looked round at the rest of the audience in disbelief but they genuinely seemed to think that this was hilarious. "I mean, there's tangerines, mandarins, clementines, satsumas—why can't we just call them all *small oranges*?" he went on, as the people on either side of me doubled up with laughter. He hit them with the next line, "Because, I mean, the Eskimos have forty words for snow, right; because, like, snow is really important to Eskimos. So clearly Anglo-Saxon society totally revolved around small fucking oranges." By now the audience were red-faced and weeping with laughter and it was inexplicable. He'd just, well—got better.

Johnny Lee went from strength to strength after that. He got the lager ad, which made him a household name, and soon the networks were falling over each other to give him his own series. He must be a multi-millionaire by now. He presents a show on Carlton called *Celebri-TV*, linking clips taken from closed-circuit TV cameras in which celebrities have been spotted shopping or putting petrol in their cars. There's a picture of him in *OK!* magazine this week. He's at a charity drinks party, chatting with TV gardener Charlie Dimmock and Falklands hero Simon Weston. Richard and Neal tell people that we saw him right at the beginning of his career at the Edinburgh Festival. "He was brilliant back then as well," they say. I suppose it's just the luck of the draw if your particular talent is in vogue during your lifetime. Comedy was the new rock 'n' roll. Then cookery was the new rock 'n' roll. And mime; well, mime was the new mime.

I've re-applied for Arts Council funding every year since, but with no success so far. They're probably frightened that putting on white makeup is racist or something. I'm investigating getting funding from the National Lottery, and I've just written to Channel 4 using Neal's name suggesting that it's about time that their remit for minority interests included a season of mime, and then I mentioned this very good performer called

Guy Jessop who I saw doing a wonderful show at the Harry Secombe Theatre in Sutton. I was spending so much of my time writing letters and submissions that I had a rather good idea. Instead of doing all my office work from the kitchen table with the kids getting under my feet, I've got myself a part-time job, which allows me to do all my admin and get paid at the same time.

So that's why I'm sitting here now. I haven't told them it's only a temporary arrangement, but I'm just doing it to clear a few debts till I get some funding. I work on my own and I don't talk to anyone so that's a bit like what I was doing before. I sit in this little booth from 7 A.M. till 3 P.M. and when the cars come into the car park I press the button and the gate goes up. And then I press another button and the gate goes down. So now I'm stuck inside a real glass box! I said to them, "You don't have to provide me with a glass box, I can do glass boxes, you know, that was day one at mime school." I reckon I could have done a passable electric gate with my arm as well; right arm goes up—a little judder when it stops at the top, hold it up there for a second or two, and then like a piece of well-oiled machinery the arm goes slowly down again. "I'll be the gate if you want," I joked to the head of security. He looked at me as if I was a nutcase.

I wanted to talk to Richard about corporate sponsorship for my next show, but it never seemed the right moment, so this morning I wouldn't let him into the car park until he gave me a straight answer! He said that Friends Provident did put some money into the local community, but they'd already spent this year's budget paying for a flower bed to be put in the middle of that new round-about on the A24. "Anyway," he said, "it might look odd spending the community sponsorship allocation on an employee." I said, "I'm not an employee, I've just got a part-time job here to subsidize my theatre work, that's all."

Because I am a mime artist, that's what I do. Oh, here comes another car! Press the green button, gate goes up, a little nod and a smile, press the red button; gate goes down. "You're the luckiest bloke I know," Richard said to me once. Well, he didn't say that as he drove past this morning— he didn't say anything—he was too busy talking on his mobile. Neal and Richard are renting a converted farmhouse out in the Dordogne this summer, swimming pool for the kids and everything. I think they knew we wouldn't be able to afford it, so they didn't embarrass me by inviting us along. Anyway I can't commit to dates in the summer, I'm going to be touring the new show by then, probably. It's just a question of plugging away for a bit until enough people get what you're on about. But sitting in this box all day, you do sometimes wonder if anybody really cares. Richard and Neal stopped coming years ago. Even Carol didn't come to my last production. Talk about walking into the wind. It seems that more people want to go and see the latest Julia Roberts movie than my mime about the African AIDS crisis—what does that say about our society? Oh they've got money if it's for the pub or the curry house. But ask them to pay £7.50 for an evening of thought-provoking mime and they've already spent it on a chicken tikka massala. Actually, I could murder a chicken tikka massala right now. A couple of onion bhajis, pilau rice, lovely. Except I can't really afford it. Bloody mime. It's freezing inside this little box. I wonder if Richard could get me a job inside the main building.

NIGHT WOMEN

EDWIDGE DANTICAT

I cringe from the heat of the night on my face. I feel as bare as open flesh. Tonight I am much older than the twenty-five years that I have lived. The night is the time I dread most in my life. Yet if I am to live, I must depend on it.

Shadows shrink and spread over the lace curtain as my son slips into bed. I watch as he stretches from a little boy into the broom-size of a man, his height mounting the innocent fabric that splits our one-room house into two spaces, two mats, two worlds.

For a brief second, I almost mistake him for the ghost of his father, an old lover who disappeared with the night's shadows a long time ago. My son's bed stays nestled against the corner, far from the peeking jalousies. I watch as he digs furrows in the pillow with his head. He shifts his small body carefully so as not to crease his Sunday clothes. He wraps my long blood-red scarf around his neck, the one I wear myself during the day to tempt my suitors. I let him have it at night, so that he always has something of mine when my face is out of sight.

I watch his shadow resting still on the curtain. My eyes are drawn to him, like the stars peeking through the small holes in the roof that none of my suitors will fix for me, because they like to watch a scrap of the sky while lying on their naked backs on my mat.

A firefly buzzes around the room, finding him and not me. Perhaps it is a mosquito that has learned the gift of lighting itself. He always slaps the mosquitoes dead on his face without even waking. In the morning, he will have tiny blood spots on his forehead, as though he had spent the whole night kissing a woman with wide-open flesh wounds on her face.

In his sleep he squirms and groans as though he's already discovered that there is pleasure in touching himself. We have never talked about love. What would he need to know? Love is one of those lessons that you grow to learn, the way one learns that one shoe is made to fit a certain foot, lest it cause discomfort.

There are two kinds of women: day women and night women. I am stuck between the day and night in a golden amber bronze. My eyes are the color of dirt, almost copper if I am standing in the sun. I want to wear my matted tresses in braids as soon as I learn to do my whole head without numbing my arms.

Most nights, I hear a slight whisper. My body freezes as I wonder how long it would take for him to cross the curtain and find me.

He says, "Mommy."

I say, "*Darling.*"

Somehow in the night, he always calls me in whispers. I hear the buzz of his transistor radio. It is shaped like a can of cola. One of my suitors gave it to him to plug into his ears so he can stay asleep while Mommy *works*.

There is a place in Ville Rose where ghost women ride the crests of waves while brushing the stars out of their hair. There they woo strollers and leave the stars on the path for them. There are nights that I believe that those ghost women are with me. As much as I know that there are women who sit up through the night and undo patches of cloth that they have spent the whole day weaving. These women, they destroy their toil so that they will always have more to do. And as long as there's work, they will not have to lie next to the lifeless soul of a man whose scent still lingers in another woman's bed.

The way my son reacts to my lips stroking his cheeks decides for me if he's asleep. He is like a butterfly fluttering on a rock that stands out naked in the middle of a stream. Sometimes I see in the folds of his eyes a longing for something that's bigger than myself. We are like faraway lovers, lying to one another, under different moons.

When my smallest finger caresses the narrow cleft beneath his nose, sometimes his tongue slips out of his mouth and he licks my fingernail. He moans and turns away, perhaps thinking that this too is a part of the dream.

I whisper my mountain stories in his ear, stories of the ghost women and the stars in their hair. I tell him of the deadly snakes lying at one end of a rainbow and the hat full of gold lying at the other end. I tell him that if I cross a stream of glass-clear hibiscus, I can make myself a goddess. I blow on his long eyelashes to see if he's truly asleep. My fingers coil themselves into visions of birds on his nose. I want him to forget that we live in a place where nothing lasts.

I know that sometimes he wonders why I take such painstaking care. Why do I draw half-moons on my sweaty forehead and spread crimson powders on the rise of my cheeks. We put on his ruffled Sunday suit and I tell him that we are expecting a sweet angel and where angels tread the hosts must be as beautiful as floating hibiscus.

In his sleep, his fingers tug his shirt ruffles loose. He licks his lips from the last piece of sugar candy stolen from my purse.

No more, no more, or your teeth will turn black. I have forgotten to make him brush the mint leaves against his teeth. He does not know that one day a woman like his mother may judge him by the whiteness of his teeth.

It doesn't take long before he is snoring softly. I listen for the shy laughter of his most pleasant dreams. Dreams of angels skipping over his head and occasionally resting their pink heels on his nose.

I hear him humming a song. One of the madrigals they still teach children on very hot afternoons in public schools. *Kompè Jako, domé vou?* Brother Jacques, are you asleep?

The hibiscus rustle in the night outside. I sing along to help him sink deeper into his sleep. I apply another layer of the Egyptian rouge to my cheeks. There are some sparkles in the powder, which make it easier for my visitor to find me in the dark.

Emmanuel will come tonight. He is a doctor who likes big buttocks on women, but my small ones will do. He comes on Tuesdays and Saturdays. He arrives bearing flowers as though he's come to court me. Tonight he brings me bougainvillea. It is always a surprise.

"How is your wife?" I ask.

"Not as beautiful as you."

On Mondays and Thursdays, it is an accordion player named Alexandre. He likes to make the sound of the accordion with his mouth in my ear. The rest of the night, he spends with his breadfruit head rocking on my belly button.

Should my son wake up, I have prepared my fabrication. One day, he will grow too old to be told that a wandering man is a mirage and that naked flesh is a dream. I will tell him that his father has come, that an angel brought him back from Heaven for a while.

The stars slowly slip away from the hole in the roof as the doctor sinks deeper and deeper beneath my body. He throbs and pants. I cover his mouth to keep him from screaming. I see his wife's face in the beads of sweat marching down his chin. He leaves with his body soaking from the dew of our flesh. He calls me an avalanche, a waterfall, when he is satisfied.

After he leaves at dawn, I sit outside and smoke a dry tobacco leaf. I watch the piece-worker women march one another to the open market half a day's walk from where they live. I thank the stars that at least I have the days to myself.

When I walk back into the house, I hear the rise and fall of my son's breath. Quickly, I lean my face against his lips to feel the calming heat from his mouth.

"Mommy, have I missed the angels again?" he whispers softly while reaching for my neck.

I slip into the bed next to him and rock him back to sleep.

"Darling, the angels have themselves a lifetime to come to us."

THE PALACE THIEF

ETHAN CANIN

I tell this story not for my own honor, for there is little of that here, and not as a warning, for a man of my calling learns quickly that all warnings are in vain. Nor do I tell it in apology for St. Benedict's School, for St. Benedict's School needs no apologies. I tell it only to record certain foretellable incidents in the life of a well-known man, in the event that the brief candle of his days may sometime come under the scrutiny of another student of history. That is all. This is a story without surprises.

There are those, in fact, who say I should have known what would happen between St. Benedict's and me, and I suppose that they are right; but I loved that school. I gave service there to the minds of three generations of boys and always left upon them, if I was successful, the delicate imprint of their culture. I battled their indolence with discipline, their boorishness with philosophy, and the arrogance of their stations with the history of great men before them. I taught the sons of nineteen senators. I taught a boy who, if not for the vengeful recriminations of the tabloids, would today have been president of the United States. That school was my life.

This is why, I suppose, I accepted the invitation sent to me by Mr. Sedgewick Bell at the end of last year, although I should have known better. I suppose I should have recalled what kind of boy he had been at St. Benedict's forty-one years before instead of posting my response so promptly in the mail and beginning that evening to prepare my test. He, of course, was the son of Senator Sedgewick Hyram Bell, the West Virginia demagogue who kept horses at his residence in Washington, D.C., and had swung several southern states for Wendell Wilkie. The younger Sedgewick was a dull boy.

I first met him when I had been teaching history at St. Benedict's for only five years, in the autumn after his father had been delivered to office on the shoulders of southern patricians frightened by the unionization of steel and mine workers. Sedgewick appeared in my classroom in November of 1945, in a short-pants suit. It was midway through the fall term, that term in which I brought the boys forth from the philosophical idealism of the Greeks into the realm of commerce, military might, and the law, which had given Julius Caesar his prerogative from Macedonia to Seville. My students, of course, were agitated. It is a sad distinction of that age group, the exuberance with which the boys abandon the moral endeavor of Plato and embrace the powerful, pragmatic hand of Augustus. The more sensitive ones had grown silent, and for several weeks our class discussions had been dominated by the martial instincts of the coarser boys. Of course I was sorry for this, but I was well aware of the import of what I taught at St. Benedict's. Our headmaster, Mr. Woodbridge, made us continually aware of the role our students would eventually play in the affairs of our country.

My classroom was in fact a tribute to the lofty ideals of man, which I hoped would inspire my boys, and at the same time to the fleeting nature of human accomplishment, which I hoped would temper their ambition with humility. It was a dual tactic, with which Mr. Woodbridge heartily agreed. Above the door frame hung a tablet, made as a term project by Henry L. Stimson when he was a boy here, that I hoped would teach my students of the irony that history bestows upon ambition. In clay relief it said:

> *I am Shutruk-Nahhunte, King of Anshan and Susa,*
> *sovereign of the land of Elam.*
> *By the command of Inshushinak,*
> *I destroyed Sippar, took the stele of Naram-Sin,*
> *and brought it back to Elam,*
> *where I erected it as an offering to my god,*
> *Inshushinak.*

> *—Shutruk-Nahhunte, 1158 B.C.*

I always noted this tablet to the boys on their first day in my classroom, partly to inform them of their predecessors at St. Benedict's and partly to remind them of the great ambition and conquest that had been utterly forgotten centuries before they were born. Afterward I had one of them recite, from the wall where it hung above my desk, Shelley's "Ozymandias." It is critical for any man of import to understand his own insignificance before the sands of time, and this is what my classroom always showed my boys.

As young Sedgewick Bell stood in the doorway of that classroom his first day at St. Benedict's, however, it was apparent that such efforts would be lost on him. I could see that he was not only a dullard but a roustabout. The boys happened to be wearing the togas they had made from sheets and safety pins the day before, spreading their knees like magistrates in the wooden desk chairs, and I was taking them through the recitation of the emperors, when Mr. Woodbridge entered alongside the stout, red-faced Sedgewick, and introduced him to the class.

I had taught for several years already, as I have said, and I knew the look of frightened, desperate bravura on a new boy's face. Sedgewick Bell did not wear this look. Rather, he wore one of disdain. The boys, fifteen in all, were instantly intimidated into sensing the foolishness of their improvised cloaks, and one of them, Fred Masoudi, the leader of the dullards—though far from a dullard himself—said, to mild laughter, "Where's your toga, kid?"

Sedgewick Bell answered, "Your mother must be wearing your pants today."

It took me a moment to regain the attention of the class, and when Sedgewick was seated I had him go to the board and copy out the emperors. Of course, he did not know the names of any of them, and my boys had to call them out, repeatedly correcting his spelling as he wrote out in a sloppy hand:

Augustus
Tiberius
Caligula
Claudius
Nero
Galba
Otho

all the while lifting and resettling the legs of his short pants in mockery of what his new classmates were wearing. "Young man," I said, "this is a serious class, and I expect that you will take it seriously."

"If it's such a serious class, then why're they all wearing dresses?" he responded, again to laughter, although by now Fred Masoudi had loosened the rope belt at his waist and the boys around him were shifting uncomfortably in their togas.

From that first day, Sedgewick Bell was a boor and a bully, a damper to the illumination of the eager minds of my boys and a purveyor of the mean-spirited humor that is like kerosene in a school such as ours. What I asked of my boys that semester was simple—that they learn the facts I presented to them in an "Outline of Ancient Roman History," which I had whittled, through my years of teaching, to exactly four closely typed pages; yet Sedgewick Bell was unwilling to do so. He was a poor student and on his first exam could not even tell me who it was that Mark Antony and Octavian had routed at Philippi, nor who Octavian later became, although an average wood-beetle in the floor of my classroom could have done so with ease.

Furthermore, as soon as he arrived he began a stream of capers using spitballs, wads of gum, and thumbtacks. Of course it was common for a new boy to engage his comrades thusly, but Sedgewick Bell then began to add the dangerous element of natural leadership—which was based on the physical strength of his features—to his otherwise puerile antics. He organized the boys. At exactly fifteen minutes to the hour, they would all drop their pencils at once, or cough, or slap closed their books so that writing at the blackboard my hands would jump in the air.

At a boys' school, of course, punishment is a cultivated art. Whenever one of these antics occurred, I simply made a point of calling on Sedgewick Bell to answer a question. General laughter usually followed his stabs at answers, and although Sedgewick himself usually laughed along with everyone else, it did not require a great deal of insight to know that the tactic would work. The organized events began to occur less frequently.

In retrospect, however, perhaps my strategy was a mistake, for to convince a boy of his own stupidity is to shoot a poisonous arrow indeed. Perhaps Sedgewick Bell's life would have turned out more nobly if I had understood his motivations right away and treated him differently at the start. But such are the pointless speculations of a teacher. What was irrefutably true was that he was performing poorly on his quizzes, even if his behavior had improved somewhat, and therefore I called him to my office.

In those days I lived in small quarters off the rear of the main hall, in what had been a slave's room when the grounds of St. Benedict's had been the estate of the philanthropist and horse breeder Cyrus Beck. Having been at school as long as I had, I no longer lived in the first-form dormitory that stood behind my room, but supervised it, so that I saw most of the boys only in matters of urgency. They came sheepishly before me.

With my bed folded into the wall, the room became my office, and shortly after supper one day that winter of his first-form year, Sedgewick Bell knocked and entered. Immediately he began to inspect the premises, casting his eyes, which had the patrician set of his father's, from the desk to the shelves to the bed folded into the wall.

"Sit down, boy."

"You're not married, are you, sir?"

"No, Sedgewick, I am not. However, we are here to talk about *you*."

"That's why you like puttin' us in togas, right?"

Frankly, I had never encountered a boy like him before, who at the age of thirteen would affront his schoolmaster without other boys in audience. He gazed at me flatly, his chin in his hand.

"Young man," I said, sensing his motivations with sudden clarity, "we are concerned about your performance here, and I have made an appointment to see your father."

In fact, I had made no appointment with Senator Bell, but at that moment I understood that I would have to. "What would you like me to tell the senator?" I said.

His gaze faltered. "I'm going to try harder, sir, from now on."

"Good, Sedgewick. Good."

Indeed, that week the boys reenacted the pivotal scenes from *Julius Caesar*, and Sedgewick read his lines quite passably and contributed little that I could see to the occasional fits of giggles that circulated among the slower boys. The next week, I gave a quiz on the triumvirate of Crassus, Pompey, and Caesar, and he passed for the first time yet, with a C plus.

Nonetheless, I had told him that I was going to speak with his father, and this is what I was determined to do. At the time, Senator

Sedgewick Hyram Bell was appearing regularly in the newspapers and on the radio in his stand against Truman's plan for national health insurance, and I was loath to call upon such a well-known man concerning the behavior of his son. On the radio his voice was a tobacco drawl that had won him populist appeal throughout West Virginia, although his policies alone would certainly not have done so. I was at the time in my late twenties, and although I was armed with scruples and an education, my hands trembled as I dialed his office. To my surprise, I was put through, and the senator, in the drawl I recognized instantly, agreed to meet me one afternoon the following week. The man already enjoyed national stature, of course, and although any other father would no doubt have made the journey to St. Benedict's himself, I admit that the prospect of seeing the man in his own office intrigued me. Thus I journeyed to the capital.

St. Benedict's lies in the bucolic, equine expanse of rural Virginia, nearer in spirit to the Carolinas than to Maryland, although the drive to Washington requires little more than an hour. The bus followed the misty, serpentine course of the Passamic, then entered the marshlands that are now the falsebrick suburbs of Washington, and at last left me downtown in the capital, where I proceeded the rest of the way on foot. I arrived at the Senate office building as the sun moved low against the bare-limbed cherries among the grounds. I was frightened but determined, and I reminded myself that Sedgewick Hyram Bell was a senator but also a father, and I was here on business that concerned his son. The office was as grand as a duke's.

I had not waited long in the anteroom when the man himself appeared, feisty as a game hen, bursting through a side door and clapping me on the shoulder as he urged me before him into his office. Of course I was a novice then in the world of politics and had not yet realized that such men are, above all, likeable. He put me in a leather seat, offered me a cigar, which I refused, and then with real or contrived wonder—perhaps he did something like this with all of his visitors—he proceeded to show me an antique sidearm that had been sent to him that morning by a constituent and that had once belonged, he said, to the coachman of Robert E. Lee. "You're a history buff," he said, "right?"

"Yes, sir."

"Then take it. It's yours."

"No, sir. I couldn't."

"Take the damn thing."

"All right, I will."

"Now, what brings you to this dreary little office?"

"Your son, sir."

"What the devil has he done now?"

"Very little, sir. We're concerned that he isn't learning the material."

"What material is that?"

"We're studying the Romans now, sir. We've left the Republic and entered the Empire."

"Ah," he said. "Be careful with that, by the way. It still fires."

"Your son seems not to be paying attention, sir."

He again offered me the box of cigars across the desk and then bit off the end of his own. "Tell me," he said, puffing the thing until it flamed suddenly, "what's the good of what you're teaching them boys?"

This was a question for which I was well prepared, fortunately, having recently written a short piece in *The St. Benedict's Crier* answering the same challenge put forth there by an anonymous boy. "When they read of the reign of Augustus Caesar," I said without hesitation, "when they learn that his rule was bolstered by commerce, a postal system, and the arts, by the reformation of the senate and by the righting of an inequitable system of taxation, when they see the effect of scientific progress through the census and the enviable network of Roman roads, how these advances led mankind away from the brutish rivalries of potentates into the two centuries of Pax Romana, then they understand the importance of character and high ideals."

He puffed at his cigar. "Now, that's a horse who can talk," he said. "And you're telling me my son Sedgewick has his head in the clouds."

"It's my job, sir, to mold your son's character."

He thought for a moment, idly fingering a match. Then his look turned stern. "I'm sorry, young man," he said slowly, "but you will not mold him. I will mold him. You will merely teach him."

That was the end of my interview, and I was politely shown the door. I was bewildered, naturally, and found myself in the elevator before I could even take account of what had happened. Senator Bell was quite likeable, as I have noted, but he had without doubt cut me, and as I made my way back to the bus station, the gun stowed deep in my briefcase, I considered what it must have been like to have been raised under such a tyrant. My heart warmed somewhat toward young Sedgewick.

Back at St. Benedict's, furthermore, I saw that my words had evidently had some effect on the boy, for in the weeks that followed he continued on his struggling, uphill course. He passed two more quizzes, receiving an A minus on one of them. For his midterm project he produced an adequate papier-mâché rendering of Hadrian's gate, and in class he was less disruptive to the group of do-nothings among whom he sat, if indeed he was not in fact attentive.

Such, of course, are the honeyed morsels of a teacher's existence, those students who come, under one's own direction, from darkness into the light, and I admit that I might have taken a special interest that term in Sedgewick Bell. If I gave him the benefit of the doubt on his quizzes when he straddled two grades, if I began to call on him in class only for those questions I had reason to believe he could answer, then I was merely trying to encourage the nascent curiosity of a boy who, to all appearances, was struggling gamely from beneath the formidable umbra of his father.

The fall term was by then drawing to a close, and the boys had begun the frenzy of preliminary quizzes for the annual "Mr. Julius Caesar" competition. Here again, I suppose I was in my own way rooting for Sedgewick. "Mr. Julius Caesar" is a St. Benedict's tradition, held in reverence among the boys, the kind of mythic ritual that is the currency of a school like ours. It is a contest, held in two phases. The first is a narrowing maneuver, by means of a dozen written quizzes, from which three boys from the first form emerge victorious. The second is a public tournament, in which these three take the stage before the assembled student body and answer questions about ancient Rome until one alone emerges triumphant, as had Caesar himself from among Crassus and Pompey. Parents and graduates fill out the audience. In front of Mr. Woodbridge's office a plaque attests to the "Mr. Julius Caesars" of the previous half-century—a list that begins with John F. Dulles in 1901— and although the ritual might seem quaint to those who have not attended St. Benedict's, I can only say that in a school like ours one cannot overstate the importance of a public joust.

That year I had three obvious contenders: Fred Masoudi, who, as I intimated, was a somewhat gifted boy; Martin Blythe, a studious type;

and Deepak Mehta, the son of a Bombay mathematician, who was dreadfully quiet but clearly my best student. It was Deepak, in fact, who on his own and entirely separate from the class had studied the disparate peoples, from the Carthaginians to the Egyptians, whom the Romans had conquered.

By the end of the narrowing quizzes, however, a surprising configuration had emerged: Sedgewick Bell had pulled himself to within a few points of third place in my class. This was when I made my first mistake. Although I should certainly have known better, I was impressed enough by his efforts that I broke one of the cardinal rules of teaching: I gave him an A on a quiz on which he had earned only a B, and in so doing, I leapfrogged him over Martin Blythe. On the fifteenth of March, when the three finalists took their seats on stage in front of the assembled population of the school, Sedgewick Bell was among them, and his father was among the audience.

The three boys had donned their togas for the event and were arranged around the dais, on which a pewter platter held the green silk garland that, at the end of the morning, I would place upon the brow of the winner. As the interrogator, I stood front row, center, next to Mr. Woodbridge.

"Which language was spoken by the Sabines?"

"Oscan," answered Fred Masoudi without hesitation.

"Who composed the Second Triumvirate?"

"Mark Antony, Octavian, and Marcus Aemilius Lepidus, sir," answered Deepak Mehta.

"Who was routed at Philippi?"

Sedgewick Bell's eyes showed no recognition. He lowered his head in his hands as though pushing himself to the limit of his intellect, and in the front row my heart dropped. Several boys in the audience began to twitter. Sedgewick's leg began to shake inside his toga. When he looked up again, I felt that it was I who had put him in this untenable position, I who had brought a tender bud too soon into the heat, and I wondered if he would ever forgive me; but then, without warning, he smiled slightly, folded his hands, and said, "Brutus and Cassius."

"Good," I said, instinctively. Then I gathered my poise. "Who deposed Romulus Augustulus, the last emperor of the Western Empire?"

"Odoacer," Fred Masoudi answered, then added, "in 476 A.D."

"Who introduced the professional army to Rome?"

"Gaius Marius, sir," answered Deepak Mehta, then himself added, "in 104 B.C."

When I asked Sedgewick his next question—Who was the leading Carthaginian general of the Second Punic War?—I felt some unease because the boys in the audience seemed to sense that I was favoring him with an easier examination. Nonetheless, his head sank into his hands, and he appeared once again to be straining the limits of his memory before he looked up and produced the obvious answer, "Hannibal."

I was delighted. Not only was he proving my gamble worthwhile but he was showing the twittering boys in the audience that, under fire, discipline produces accurate thought. By now they had quieted, and I had the sudden, heartening premonition that Sedgewick Bell was going to surprise us after all, that his tortoiselike deliberation would win him, by morning's end, the garland of laurel.

The next several rounds of questions proceeded much in the same manner as had the previous two. Deepak Mehta and Fred Masoudi answered without hesitation, and Sedgewick Bell did so only after a tedious and deliberate period of thought. What I realized, in fact, was that his style made for excellent theater. The parents, I could see, were impressed, and Mr. Woodbridge next to me, no doubt thinking about the next Annual Fund drive, was smiling broadly.

After a second-form boy had brought a glass of water to each of the contestants, I moved on to the next level of questions. These had been chosen for their difficulty, and on the first round Fred Masoudi fell out, not knowing the names of Augustus's children. He left the stage and moved back among his dim-witted pals in the audience. By the rule of clockwise progression the same question then went to Deepak Mehta, who answered it correctly, followed by the next one, which concerned King Jugurtha of Numidia. Then, because I had no choice, I had to ask Sedgewick Bell something difficult: "Which general had the support of the aristocrats in the civil war of 88 B.C.?"

To the side, I could see several parents pursing their lips and furrowing their brows, but Sedgewick Bell appeared to not even notice the greater difficulty of the query. Again he dropped his head into his hands. By now the audience expected his period of deliberation, and they sat quietly. One could hear the hum of the ventilation system and the dripping of the icicles outside. Sedgewick Bell cast his eyes downward, and it was at this moment that I realized he was cheating.

I had come to this job straight from my degree at Carleton College at the age of twenty-one, having missed enlistment due to myopia, and carrying with me the hope that I could give to my boys the more important vision that my classical studies had given to me. I knew that they responded best to challenge. I knew that a teacher who coddled them at that age would only hold them back, would keep them in the bosoms of their mothers so long that they would remain weak-minded through preparatory school and inevitably then through college. The best of my own teachers had been tyrants. I well remembered this. Yet at that moment I felt an inexplicable pity for the boy. Was it simply the humiliation we had both suffered at the hands of his father? I peered through my glasses at the stage and knew at once that he had attached the "Outline of Ancient Roman History" to the inside of his toga.

I don't know how long I stood there, between the school assembled behind me and the two boys seated in front, but after a period of internal deliberation, during which time I could hear the rising murmurs of the audience, I decided that in the long run it was best for Sedgewick Bell to be caught. Oh, how the battle is lost for want of a horse! I leaned to Mr. Woodbridge next to me and whispered, "I believe Sedgewick Bell is cheating."

"Ignore it," he whispered back.

"What?"

Of course, I have great respect for what Mr. Woodbridge did for St. Benedict's in the years he was among us. A headmaster's world is a far more complex one than a teacher's, and it is historically inopportune to blame a life gone afoul on a single incident in childhood. However, I myself would have stood up for our principles had Mr. Woodbridge not at that point said, "Ignore it, Hundert, or look for another job."

Naturally, my headmaster's words startled me for a moment; but being familiar with the necessities of a boys' school, and having recently entertained my first thoughts about one day becoming a headmaster myself, I simply nodded when Sedgewick Bell produced the correct answer, Lucius Cornelius Sulla. Then I went on to the next question, which concerned Scipio Africanus Major. Deepak Mehta answered it correctly, and I turned once again to Sedgewick Bell.

In a position of moral leadership, of course, compromise begets only more compromise, and although I know this now from my own experience, at the time I did so only from my study of history. Perhaps that is why I again found an untenable compassion muddying my thoughts. What kind of desperation would lead a boy to cheat on a public stage? His father and mother were well back in the crowded theater, but when I glanced behind me, my eye went instantly to them, as though they were indeed my own parents, out from Kansas City. "Who were the first emperors to reign over the divided Empire?" I asked Sedgewick Bell.

When one knows the magician's trick, the only wonder is in its obviousness, and as Sedgewick Bell lowered his head this time, I clearly saw the nervous flutter of his gaze directed into the toga. Indeed I imagined him scanning the entire "Outline," from Augustus to Jovian, pasted inside the twill, before coming to the answer, which pretending to ponder, he then spoke aloud: "Valentinian the First, and Valens."

Suddenly Senator Bell called out, "That's my boy!"

The crowd thundered, and I had the sudden, indefensible urge to steer the contest in young Sedgewick Bell's direction. In a few moments, however, from within the subsiding din, I heard the thin, accented voice of a woman speaking Deepak Mehta's name; and it was the presence of his mother, I suppose, that finally brought me to my senses. Deepak answered the next question, about Diocletian, correctly, and then I turned to Sedgewick Bell and asked him, "Who was Hamilcar Barca?"

Of course, it was only Deepak who knew that this answer was not in the "Outline," because Hamilcar Barca was a Phoenician general eventually routed by the Romans; it was only Deepak, as I have noted, who had bothered to study the conquered peoples. He briefly widened his eyes at me—in recognition? in gratitude? in disapproval?—while beside him Sedgewick Bell again lowered his head into his hands. After a long pause, Sedgewick asked me to repeat the question.

I did so, and after another long pause, he scratched his head. Finally, he said, "Jeez."

The boys in the audience laughed, but I turned and silenced them. Then I put the same question to Deepak Mehta, who answered it correctly, of course, and then received a round of applause that was polite but not sustained.

It was only as I mounted the stage to present Deepak with the garland of Laurel, however, that I glanced at Mr. Woodbridge and realized that he too had wanted me to steer the contest toward Sedgewick

Bell. At the same moment, I saw Senator Bell making his way toward the rear door of the hall. Young Sedgewick stood limply to the side of me, and I believe I had my first inkling then of the mighty forces that would twist the life of that boy. I could only imagine his thoughts as he stood there on stage while his mother, struggling to catch up with the senator, vanished through the fire door at the back. By the next morning, our calligraphers would add Deepak Mehta's name to the plaque outside Mr. Woodbridge's office, and young Sedgewick Bell would begin his life-long pursuit of missed glory.

Yet perhaps because of the disappointment I could see in Mr. Woodbridge's eyes, it somehow seemed that I was the one who had failed the boy, and as soon as the auditorium was empty, I left for his room. There I found him seated on the bed, still in his toga, gazing out the small window to the lacrosse fields. I could see the sheets of my "Outline" pressed against the inside of his garment.

"Well, young man," I said, knocking on the door frame, "that certainly was an interesting performance."

He turned around from the window and looked at me coldly. What he did next I have thought about many times over the years, the labyrinthine wiliness of it, and I can only attribute the precociousness of his maneuvering to the bitter education he must have received at home. As I stood before him in the doorway, Sedgewick Bell reached inside his cloak and one at a time lifted out the pages of my "Outline."

I stepped inside and closed the door. Every teacher knows a score of boys who do their best to be expelled; this is a cliché in a school like ours, but as soon as I closed the door to his room and he acknowledged the act with a feline smile, I knew that this was not Sedgewick Bell's intention at all.

"I knew you saw," he said.

"Yes, you are correct."

"How come you didn't say anything, eh, Mr. Hundert?"

"It's a complicated matter, Sedgewick."

"It's because my pop was there."

"It had nothing to do with your father."

"Sure, Mr. Hundert."

Frankly, I was at my wits' end, first from what Mr. Woodbridge had said to me in the theater and now from the audacity of the boy's accusation.

I myself went to the window then and let my eyes wander over the campus so that they would not have to engage the dark, accusatory gaze of Sedgewick Bell. What transpires in an act of omission like the one I had committed? I do not blame Mr. Woodbridge, of course, any more than a soldier can blame his captain. What had happened was that instead of enforcing my own code of morals, I had allowed Sedgewick Bell to sweep me summarily into his. I did not know at the time what an act of corruption I had committed, although what is especially chilling to me is that I believe that Sedgewick Bell, even at the age of thirteen, did.

He knew also, of course, that I would not pursue the matter, although I spent the ensuing several days contemplating a disciplinary action. Each time I summoned my resolve to submit the boy's name to the honor committee, however, my conviction waned, for at these times I seemed to myself to be nothing more than one criminal turning in another. I fought this battle constantly—in my simple rooms, at the long, chipped table I governed in the dining hall, and at the dusty chalkboard before my classes. I felt like an exhausted swimmer trying to climb a slippery wall out of the sea.

Furthermore, I was alone in my predicament, for among a boarding school faculty, which is as perilous as a medieval court, one does not publicly discuss a boy's misdeeds. This is true even if the boy is not the son of a senator. In fact, the only teacher I decided to trust with my situation was Charles Ellerby, our new Latin instructor and a kindred lover of antiquity. I had liked Charles Ellerby as soon as we had met because he was a moralist of no uncertain terms, and indeed when I confided in him about Sedgewick Bell's behavior and Mr. Woodbridge's response, he suggested that it was my duty to circumvent our headmaster and speak directly to the boy's father. Of course, this made sense to me, even if I knew it would be difficult to do. I decided to speak to Senator Bell again.

Less than a week after I had begun to marshal my resolve, however, the senator himself called *me*. He proffered a few moments of small talk, asked after the gun he had given me, and then said gruffly, "Young man, my son tells me the Hannibal Barca question was not on the list he had to know."

Now, indeed, I was shocked. Even from young Sedgewick Bell I had not expected this audacity. "How deeply the viper is a viper," I said, before I could help myself.

"Excuse me?"

"The Phoenician general was *Hamilcar* Barca, sir, not Hannibal."

The senator paused. "My son tells me you asked him a question that was not on the list, which the Oriental fellow knew the answer to in advance. He feels you've been unfair, is all."

"It's a complex situation, sir," I said. I marshaled my will again by imagining what Charles Ellerby would do in the situation. However, no sooner had I resolved to confront the senator than it became perfectly clear to me that I lacked the character to do so. I believe this had long been clear to Sedgewick Bell.

"I'm sure it is complex," Senator Bell said, "But I assure you, there are situations more complex. Now, I'm not asking you to correct anything this time, you understand. My son has told me a great deal about you, Mr. Hundert. If I were you, I'd remember that."

"Yes, sir," I said, although by then I realized he had hung up.

And thus young Sedgewick Bell and I began an uneasy compact that lasted out his days at St. Benedict's. He was a dismal student from that day forward, scratching at the very bottom of a class that was itself a far cry from the glorious yesteryear classes of John Dulles and Henry Stimson. His quizzes were abominations, and his essays were pathetic digestions of those of the boys sitting next to him. He chatted amiably in study hall, smoked cigarettes in the third-form linen room, and when called upon in class could be counted on to blink and stutter as if called upon from sleep.

But perhaps the glory days of St. Benedict's had already begun their wane, for even then, well before the large problems that beset us, no action was taken against the boy. For Charles Ellerby and me, he became a symbol, evidence of the first tendrils of moral rot that seemed to be twining among the posts and timbers of our school. Although we told nobody else of his secret, the boy's dim-witted recalcitrance soon succeeded in alienating all but the other students. His second- and third-form years passed as ingloriously as his first, and by the outset of his last with us he had grown to mythic infamy among the faculty members who had known the school in its days of glory.

He had grown physically larger as well, and now when I chanced upon him on the campus, he held his ground against my disapproving stare with a dark one of his own. To complicate matters, he had cultivated, despite his boorish character, an impressive popularity among his schoolmates, and it was only through the subtle intervention of several of his teachers that he had failed on two occasions to win the presidency of the student body. His stride had become a strut. His favor among the other boys, of course, had its origin in the strength of his physical features, in the precocious evil of his manner, and in the bellowing timbre of his voice, but unfortunately such crudities are all the more impressive to a group of boys living out of sight of their parents.

That is not to say that the faculty of St. Benedict's had given up hope for Sedgewick Bell. Indeed, a teacher's career is punctuated with difficult students like him, and despite the odds one could not help but root for his eventual rehabilitation. As did all the other teachers, I held out hope for Sedgewick Bell. In his fits of depravity and intellectual feebleness I continued to look for glimpses of discipline and progress.

By his fourth-form year, however, when I had become dean of seniors, it was clear that Sedgewick Bell would not change, at least not while he was at St. Benedict's. Despite his powerful station, he had not even managed to gain admission to the state university. It was with a sense of failure, then, finally, that I handed him his diploma in the spring of 1949, on an erected stage at the north end of the great field, on which he came forward, met my disapproving gaze with his own flat one, and trundled off to sit among his friends.

It came as a surprise, then, when I learned in the Richmond *Gazette*, thirty-seven years later, of Sedgewick Bell's ascension to the chairmanship of EastAmerica Steel, at that time the second-largest corporation in America. I chanced upon the news one morning in the winter of 1987, the year of my great problems with St. Benedict's, while reading the newspaper in the east-lighted breakfast room of the assistant headmaster's house. St. Benedict's, as everyone knows, had fallen upon difficult times by then, and an unseemly aspect of my job was that I had to maintain a lookout for possible donors to the school. Forthwith, I sent a letter to Sedgewick Bell.

Apart from the five or six years in which a classmate had written to *The Benedictine* of his whereabouts, I had heard almost nothing about the boy since the year of his graduation. This was unusual, of course, as St. Benedict's makes a point of keeping abreast of its graduates, and I can only assume that his absence in the yearly alumni notes was due to an act of will on his own part. One wonders how much of the boy remained in the man. It is indeed a rare vantage that a St. Benedict's teacher holds, to have known our statesmen, our policymakers, and our captains of industry in their days of short pants and classroom pranks, and I admit that it was with some nostalgia that I composed the letter.

Since his graduation, of course, my career had proceeded with the steady ascension that the great schools have always afforded their dedicated teachers. Ten years after Sedgewick Bell's departure I had moved from dean of seniors to dean of the upper school, and after a decade there to dean of academics, a post that some would consider a demotion but that I seized with reverence because it afforded me the chance to make inroads on the minds of a generation. At the time, of course, the country was in the throes of a violent, peristaltic rejection of tradition, and I felt a particular urgency to my mission of staying a course that had led a century of boys through the rise and fall of ancient civilizations.

In those days our meetings of the faculty and trustees were rancorous affairs in which great pressure was exerted in attempts to alter the time-tested curriculum of the school. Planning a course was like going into battle, and hiring a new teacher was like crowning a king. Whenever one of our ranks retired or left for another school, the different factions fought tooth and nail to influence the appointment. I was the dean of academics, as I have noted, and these skirmishes naturally were waged around my foxhole. For the lesser appointments I often feinted to gather leverage for the greater ones, whose campaigns I fought with abandon.

At one point especially, midway through that decade in which our country had lost its way, St. Benedict's arrived at a crossroads. The chair of humanities had retired, and a pitched battle over his replacement developed between Charles Ellerby and a candidate from outside. A meeting ensued in which my friend and this other man spoke to the assembled faculty and trustees, and though I will not go into detail, I will say that the outside candidate felt that, because of the advances in our society, history had become little more than a relic.

Oh, what dim-sighted times those were! The two camps sat on opposite sides of the chapel as speakers took the podium one after another to wage war. The controversy quickly became a forum concerning the relevance of the past. Teacher after teacher debated the import of what we in history had taught for generations, and assertion after assertion was met with boos and applause. Tempers blazed. One powerful member of the board had come to the meeting in blue jeans and a tie-dyed shirt, and after we had been arguing for several hours and all of us were exhausted, he took the podium and challenged me personally, right then and there, to debate with him the merits of Roman history.

He was not an ineloquent man, and he chose to speak his plea first, so that by the time he had finished his attack against antiquity, I sensed that my battle on behalf of Charles Ellerby, and of history itself, was near to lost. My heart was gravely burdened, for if we could not win our point here among teachers, then among whom indeed could we win it? The room was silent, and on the other side of the chapel our opponents were gathering nearer to one another in the pews.

When I rose to defend my calling, however, I also sensed that victory was not beyond my reach. I am not a particularly eloquent orator, but as I took my place at the chancel rail in the amber glow of the small rose window above us, I was braced by the sudden conviction that the great men of history had sent me forward to preserve their deeds. Charles Ellerby looked up at me biting his lip, and suddenly I remembered the answer I had written long ago in *The Crier*. Its words flowed as though unbidden from my tongue, and when I had finished, I knew that we had won. It was my proudest moment at St. Benedict's.

Although the resultant split among the faculty was an egregious one, Charles Ellerby secured the appointment, and together we were able to do what I had always dreamed of doing: We redoubled our commitment to classical education. In times of upheaval, of course, adherence to tradition is all the more important, and perhaps this was why St. Benedict's was brought intact through that decade and the one that followed. Our fortunes lifted and dipped with the gentle rhythm to which I had long ago grown accustomed. Our boys won sporting events and prizes, endured minor scandals and occasional tragedies, and then passed on to good colleges. Our endowment rose when the government was in the hands of Republicans, as did the caliber of our boys when it was in the hands of Democrats. Senator Bell declined from prominence, and within a few years I read that he had passed away. In time, I was made assistant headmaster. Indeed it was not until a few years ago that anything out of the ordinary happened at all, for it was then, in the late

1980s, that some ill-advised investments were made and our endowment suffered a decline.

Mr. Woodbridge had by this time reached the age of seventy-four, and although he was a vigorous man, one Sunday morning in May while the school waited for him in chapel he died open-eyed in his bed. Immediately there occurred a Byzantine struggle for succession. There is nothing wrong with admitting that by then I myself coveted the job of headmaster, for one does not remain five decades at a school without becoming deeply attached to its fate; but Mr. Woodbridge's death had come suddenly, and I had not yet begun the preparations for my bid. I was, of course, no longer a young man. I suppose, in fact, that I lost my advantage here by under-estimating my opponents, who indeed were younger, as Caesar had done with Brutus and Cassius.

I should not have been surprised, then, when after several days of maneuvering, my principal rival turned out to be Charles Ellerby. For several years, I discovered, he had been conducting his own internecine campaign for the position, and although I had always counted him as my ally and my friend, in the first meeting of the board he rose and spoke accusations against me. He said that I was too old, that I had failed to change with the times, that my method of pedagogy might have been relevant forty years ago but that it was not today. He stood and said that a headmaster needed vigor and that I did not have it. Although I watched him the entire time he spoke, he did not once look back at me.

I was wounded, of course, both professionally and in the hidden part of my heart in which I had always counted Charles Ellerby as a companion in my lifelong search for the magnificence of the past. When several of the older teachers booed him, I felt cheered. At this point I saw that I was not alone in my bid, merely behind, and so I left the meeting without coming to my own defense. Evening had come, and I walked to the dining commons in the company of allies.

How it is, when fighting for one's life, to eat among children! As the boys in their school blazers passed around the platters of fish sticks and the bowls of sliced bread, my heart was pierced with their guileless grace. How soon, I wondered, would they see the truth of the world? How long before they would understand that it was not dates and names that I had always meant to teach them? Not one of them seemed to notice what had descended like thunderheads above their faculty. Not one of them seemed unable to eat.

After dinner I returned to the assistant headmaster's house in order to plot my course and confer with those I still considered allies, but before I could begin my preparations, there was a knock at the door. Charles Ellerby stood there, red in the cheeks. "May I ask you some questions?" he said breathlessly.

"It is I who ought to ask them of you" was my answer.

He came in without being asked and took a seat at my table. "You've never been married, am I correct, Hundert?"

"Look, Ellerby, I've been at St. Benedict's since you were in prep school yourself."

"Yes, yes," he said, in an exaggeration of boredom. Of course, he knew as well as I that I had never married nor started a family because history itself had always been enough for me. He rubbed his head and appeared to be thinking. To this day I wonder how he knew about what he said next, unless Sedgewick Bell had somehow told him the story of my visit to the senator. "Look," he said. "There's a rumor you keep a pistol in your desk drawer."

"Hogwash."

"Will you open it for me," he said, pointing there.

"No, I will not. I have been a dean here for twenty years."

"Are you telling me there is no pistol in this house?"

He then attempted to stare me down. We had known each other for the good part of both of our lives, however, and the bid withered. At that point, in fact, as his eyes fell in submission to my determined gaze, I believe the headmastership became mine. It is a largely unexplored element of history, of course, and one that has long fascinated me, that a great deal of political power and thus a great deal of the arc of nations arises not from intellectual advancements nor social imperatives but from the simple battle of wills among men at tables, such as had just occurred between Charles Ellerby and me.

Instead of opening the desk and brandishing the weapon, however, which of course meant nothing to me but no doubt would have seized the initiative from Ellerby, I denied to him its existence. Why, I do not know; for I was a teacher of history, and was not the firearm its greatest engine? Ellerby, on the other hand, was simply a gadfly to the passing morals of the time. He gathered his things and left my house.

That evening I took the pistol from my drawer. A margin of rust had appeared along the filigreed handle, and despite the ornate workmanship I saw clearly now that in its essence the weapon was ill-proportioned and blunt, the crude instrument of a violent, historically meager man. I had not even wanted it when the irascible demagogue Bell had foisted it upon me, and I had only taken it out of some vague sentiment that a pistol might eventually prove decisive. I suppose I had always imagined firing it someday in a moment of drama. Yet now here it stood before me in a moment of torpor. I turned it over and cursed it.

That night I took it from the drawer again, hid it in the pocket of my overcoat, and walked to the far end of the campus, where I crossed the marsh a good mile from my house, removed my shoes, and stepped into the babbling shallows of the Passamic. *The die is cast*, I said, and I threw it twenty yards out into the water. The last impediment to my headmastership had been hurdled, and by the time I came ashore, walked back whistling to my front door, and changed for bed, I was ecstatic.

Yet that night I slept poorly, and in the morning when I rose and went to our faculty meeting, I felt that the mantle of my fortitude had slipped somehow from my shoulders. How hushed is demise! In the hall outside the faculty room, most of the teachers filed by without speaking to me, and once inside, I became obsessed with the idea that I had missed this most basic lesson of the past, that conviction is the alpha and the omega of authority. Now I see that I was doomed the moment I threw that pistol in the water, for that is when I lost my conviction. It was as though Sedgewick Bell had risen, all these years later, to drag me down again. Indeed, once the meeting had begun, the older faculty members shrunk back from their previous support of my bid, and the younger ones encircled me as though I were a limping animal. There might as well have been a dagger among the cloaks. By four o'clock that afternoon Charles Ellerby, a fellow antiquarian whose job I had once helped secure, had been named headmaster, and by the end of that month he had asked me to retire.

And so I was preparing to end my days at St. Benedict's when I received Sedgewick Bell's response to my letter. It was well written, which I noted with pleasure, and contained no trace of rancor, which is what every teacher hopes to see in the maturation of his disagreeable students. In closing he asked me to call him at EastAmerica Steel, and I did so that afternoon.

When I gave my name first to one secretary and then to a second, and after that, moments later, heard Sedgewick's artfully guileless greeting, I instantly recalled speaking to his father some forty years before.

After small talk, including my condolences about his father, he told me that the reason he had replied to my letter was that he had often dreamed of holding a rematch of "Mr. Julius Caesar," and that he was now willing to donate a large sum of money to St. Benedict's if I would agree to administer the event. Naturally, I assumed he was joking and passed off the idea with a comment about how funny it was, but Sedgewick Bell repeated the invitation. He wanted very much to be onstage again with Deepak Mehta and Fred Masoudi. I suppose I should not have been surprised, for it is precisely this sort of childhood slight that will drive a great figure. I told him that I was about to retire. He expressed sympathy but then suggested that the arrangement could be ideal, as now I would no doubt have time to prepare. Then he said that at this station in his life he could afford whatever he wanted materially—with all that this implied, of course, concerning his donation to the Annual Fund—but that more than anything else, he desired the chance to reclaim his intellectual honor. I suppose I was flattered.

Of course, he also offered a good sum of money to me personally. Although I had until then led a life in which finances were never more than a distant concern, I was keenly aware that my time in the school's houses and dining halls was coming to an end. On the one hand, it was not my burning aspiration to secure an endowment for the reign of Charles Ellerby; on the other hand, I needed the money, and I felt a deep loyalty to the school regarding the Annual Fund. That evening I began to prepare my test.

As assistant headmaster I had not taught my beloved Roman history in many years, so that poring through my reams of notes was like returning at last to my childhood home. I stopped here and there among the files. I reread the term paper of young Derek Bok entitled "The Search of Diogenes" and the scrawled one of James Watson called "Archimedes' Method." Among the art projects I found John Updike's reproduction of the Obelisk of Cleopatra and a charcoal drawing of the Baths of Caracala by the abstract expressionist Robert Motherwell, unfortunately torn in two and no longer worth anything.

I had always been a diligent note taker, furthermore, and I believe that what I came up with was a surprisingly accurate reproduction of the subjects on which I had once quizzed Fred Masoudi, Deepak Mehta, and Sedgewick Bell, nearly half a century before. It took me only two evenings to gather enough material for the task, although in order not to appear eager, I waited several days before sending off another letter to Sedgewick Bell. He called me soon after.

It is indeed a surprise to one who toils for his own keep to see the formidable strokes with which our captains of industry demolish the tasks before them. The morning after talking to Sedgewick Bell I received calls from two of his secretaries, a social assistant, and a woman at a New York travel agency, who confirmed the arrangements for late July, two months hence. The event was to take place on an island off the Outer Banks of Carolina that belonged to EastAmerica Steel, and I sent along a list from the St. Benedict's archives so that everyone in Sedgewick Bell's class would be invited.

I was not prepared, however, for the days of retirement that intervened. What little remained of that school year passed speedily in my preoccupation, and before I knew it, the boys were taking their final exams. I tried not to think about my future. At the commencement exercises in June a small section of the ceremony was spent in my honor, but it was presided over by Charles Ellerby and gave rise to a taste of copper in my throat. "And thus we bid adieu," he began, "to our beloved Mr. Hundert." He gazed out over the lectern, extended his arm in my direction, and proceeded to give a nostalgic rendering of my years at the school to the audience of jacketed businessmen, parasoled ladies, students in St. Benedict's blazers, and children in church suits, who, like me, were squirming at the meretriciousness of the man.

Yet how quickly it was over! Awards were presented, "Hail, Fair Benedict's" was sung, and as the birches began to lean their narrow shadows against the distant edge of the marsh the seniors came forward to receive their diplomas. The mothers wept, the alumni stood misty-eyed, and the graduates threw their hats into the air. Afterward everyone dispersed for the headmaster's reception.

I wish now that I had made an appearance there, for to have missed it, the very last one of my career, was a far more grievous blow to me than to Charles Ellerby. Furthermore, the handful of senior boys who over their tenure had been pierced by the bee sting of history no doubt missed my presence or at least wondered at its lack. I spent the remainder of the afternoon in my house, and the evening walking out along the marsh, where the smell of woodsmoke from a farmer's bonfire and the distant sounds of the gathered celebrants filled me with the great, sad pride of teaching. My boys were passing once again into the world without me.

The next day, of course, parents began arriving to claim their children; jitney buses ferried students to airports and train stations; the groundsman went around pulling up lacrosse goals and baseball bleachers, hauling the long black sprinkler hoses behind his tractor into the fields. I spent most of that day and the next one sitting at the desk in my study, watching through the window as the school wound down like a clock spring toward the strange, bird-filled calm of that second afternoon of my retirement, when all the boys had left and I was alone, once again, in the eerie quiet of summer. I own few things besides my files and books; I packed them, and the next day the groundsman drove me into Woodmere.

There I found lodging in a splendid Victorian rooming house run by a descendant of Nat Turner who joked, when I told her that I was a newly retired teacher, about how the house had always welcomed escaped slaves. I was surprised at how heartily I laughed at this, which had the benefit of putting me instantly on good terms with the landlady. We negotiated a monthly rent, and I went upstairs to set about charting a new life for myself. I was sixty-eight years old—yes, perhaps, too old to be headmaster—but I could still walk three miles before dinner and did so the first afternoon of my freedom. However, by evening my spirits had taken a beating.

Fortunately, there was the event to prepare for, as I fear that without it, those first days and nights would have been unbearable. I pored again and again over my old notes, extracting devilish questions from the material. But this only occupied a few hours of the day, and by late morning my eyes would grow weary. Objectively speaking, the start of that summer should have been no different from the start of any other; yet it was. Passing my reflection in the hallway mirror on my way down to dinner, I would think to myself, *Is that you?*, and on the way back up to my room, *What now?* I wrote letters to my brothers and sister and to several of my former boys. The days crawled by. I reintroduced myself to the town librarian. I made the acquaintance of a retired railroad man who liked as much as I did to sit on the grand, screened porch of that house. I took the bus into Washington a few times to spend the day in museums.

But as the summer progressed, a certain dread began to form in my mind, which I tried through the diligence of walking, museum-going, and reading, to ignore; that is, I began to fear that Sedgewick Bell had forgotten about the event. The thought would occur to me in the midst of the long path along the outskirts of town; and as I reached the Passamic, took my break, and then started back again toward home, I would battle with my urge to contact the man. Several times I went to the telephone downstairs in the rooming house, and twice I wrote out letters that I did not send. Why would he go through all the trouble just to mock me, I thought; but then I would recall the circumstances of his tenure at St. Benedict's, and a darker gloom would descend upon me. I began to have second thoughts about events that had occurred half a century before: Should I have confronted him in the midst of the original contest? Should I never even have leapfrogged another boy to get him there? Should I have spoken up to the senator?

In early July, however, Sedgewick Bell's secretary finally did call, and I felt that I had been given a reprieve. She apologized for her tardiness, asked me more questions about my taste in food and lodging, and then informed me of the date, three weeks later, when a car would call to take me to the airport in Williamsburg. An EastAmerica jet would fly me from there to Charlotte, from whence I was to be picked up by helicopter.

Helicopter! Less than a month later I stood before the craft, which was painted head to tail in EastAmerica's green and gold insignia, polished to a shine, with a six-man passenger bay and red-white-and-blue sponsons over the wheels. One does not remain at St. Benedict's for five decades without gaining a certain familiarity with privilege, yet as it lifted me off the pad in Charlotte, hovered for a moment, then lowered its nose and turned eastward over the gentle hills and then the chopping slate of the sea channel, I felt a headiness that I had never known before; it was what Augustus Caesar must have felt millennia ago, carried head-high on a litter past the Tiber. I clutched my notes to my chest. Indeed, I wondered what my life might have been like if I had felt this just once in my youth. The rotors buzzed like a swarm of bees above us. On the island I was shown to a suite of rooms in a high corner of the lodge, with windows and balconies overlooking the sea.

For a conference on the future of childhood education or the plight of America's elderly, of course, you could not get one-tenth of these men to attend, but for a privileged romp on a private island it had merely been a matter of making the arrangements. I stood at the window of my room and watched the helicopter ferry back and forth across the channel, disgorging on the island a Who's Who of America's largest corporations, universities, and organs of policy.

Oh, but what it was to see the boys! After a time I made my way back out to the airstrip, and whenever the craft touched down on the landing platform and one or another of my old students ducked out, clutching his suit lapel as he ran clear of the snapping rotors, I was struck anew with how great a privilege my profession had been.

That evening all of us ate together in the lodge, and the boys toasted me and took turns coming to my table, where several times one or another of them had to remind me to continue eating my food. Sedgewick Bell ambled over and with a charming air of modesty showed me the flash cards of Roman history that he'd been keeping in his desk at EastAmerica. Then, shedding his modesty, he went to the podium and produced a long and raucous toast, referring to any number of pranks and misdeeds at St. Benedict's that I had never even heard of but that the chorus of boys greeted with stamps and whistles. At a quarter to nine they all dropped their forks onto the floor, and I fear that tears came to my eyes.

The most poignant part of all, however, was how plainly the faces of the men still showed the eager expressiveness of the first-form boys of forty-one years ago. Martin Blythe had lost half his leg as an officer in Korea, and now, among his classmates, he tried to hide his lurching stride, but he wore the same knitted brow that he used to wear in my classroom; Deepak Mehta, who had become a professor of Asian history, walked with a slight stoop, yet he still turned his eyes downward when spoken to; Fred Masoudi seemed to have fared physically better than his mates, bouncing about in the Italian suit and alligator shoes of the advertising industry, yet he was still drawn immediately to the other do-nothings from his class.

But of course it was Sedgewick Bell who commanded everyone's attention. He had grown stout across the middle and bald over the crown of his head, and I saw in his ear, although it was artfully concealed, the flesh-colored bulb of a hearing aid; yet he walked among the men like a prophet. Their faces grew animated when he approached, and at the tables I could see them competing for his attention. He patted one on the back, whispered in the ear of another, gripped hands and grasped shoulders and kissed the wives on the lips. His walk was firm and imbued not with the seriousness of his post, it seemed to me, but with the ease of it, so that his stride among the tables was jocular. He was the host and clearly in his element. His laugh was voluble.

I went to sleep early that evening so that the boys could enjoy themselves downstairs in the saloon, and as I lay in bed, I listened to their songs and revelry. It had not escaped my attention, of course, that they no doubt spent some time mocking me, but this is what one grows to expect in my post, and indeed it was part of the reason I left them alone. Although I was tempted to walk down and listen from outside the theater, I did not.

The next day was spent walking the island's serpentine spread of coves and beaches, playing tennis on the grass court, and paddling in wooden boats on the small, inland lake behind the lodge. How quickly one grows accustomed to luxury! Men and women lounged on the decks and beaches and patios, sunning like seals, gorging themselves on the largesse of their host.

As for me, I barely had a moment to myself, for the boys took turns at my entertainment. I walked with Deepak Mehta along the beach and succeeded in getting him to tell me the tale of his rise through academia to a post at Columbia University. Evidently his career had taken a toll, for although he looked healthy enough, he told me that he had recently had a small heart attack. It was not the type of thing one talked about with a student, however, so I let his revelation pass without comment. Later Fred Masoudi brought me onto the tennis court and tried to teach me to hit a ball, an activity that drew a crowd of boisterous guests to the stands. They roared at Fred's theatrical antics and cheered and stomped their feet whenever I sent one back across the net. In the afternoon Martin Blythe took me out in a rowboat.

St. Benedict's, of course, has always had a more profound effect than most schools on the lives of its students, yet nonetheless it was strange that once in the center of the pond, where he had rowed us with his lurching stroke, Martin Blythe set down the oars in their locks and told me he had something he'd always meant to ask me.

"Yes," I said.

He brushed back his hair with his hand. "*I* was supposed to be the one up there with Deepak and Fred, wasn't I, sir?"

"Don't tell me you're still thinking about that."

"It's just that I've sometimes wondered what happened."

"Yes, you should have been," I said.

Oh, how little we understand of men if we think that their childhood slights are forgotten! He smiled. He did not press the subject further, and while I myself debated the merits of explaining why I had passed him over for Sedgewick Bell forty-one years before, he pivoted the boat around and brought us back to shore. The confirmation of his suspicions was enough to satisfy him, it seemed, so I said nothing more. He had been an air force major in our country's endeavors on the Korean peninsula, yet as he pulled the boat onto the beach, I had the clear feeling of having saved him from some torment.

Indeed, that evening when the guests had gathered in the lodge's small theater, and Deepak Mehta, Fred Masoudi, and Sedgewick Bell had taken their seats for the reenactment of "Mr. Julius Caesar," I noticed an ease in Martin Blythe's face that I believe I had never seen in it before. His brow was not knit, and he had crossed his legs so that above one sock we could clearly see the painted wooden calf.

It was then that I noticed that the boys who had paid the most attention to me that day were in fact the ones sitting before me on the stage. How dreadful a thought this was—that they had indulged me to gain advantage—but I put it from my mind and stepped to the microphone. I had spent the late afternoon reviewing my notes, and the first rounds of questions were called from memory.

The crowd did not fail to notice the feat. There were whistles and stomps when I named fifteen of the first sixteen emperors in order and asked Fred Masoudi to produce the one I had left out. There was applause when I spoke Caesar's words, *Il Iacta alea esto*, and then, continuing in carefully pronounced Latin, asked Sedgewick Bell to recall the circumstances of their utterance. He had told me that afternoon of the months he had spent preparing, and as I was asking the question, he smiled. The boys had not worn togas, of course—although I personally feel they might have—yet the situation was familiar enough that I felt a rush of unease as Sedgewick Bell's smile then waned and he hesitated several moments before answering. But this time, forty-one years later, he looked straight out into the audience and spoke his answers with the air of a scholar.

It was not long before Fred Masoudi had dropped out, of course, but then, as it had before, the contest proceeded neck and neck between Sedgewick Bell and Deepak Mehta. I asked Sedgewick Bell about Caesar's battles at Pharsalus and Thapsus, about the shift of power to Constantinople, and about the war between the patricians and the plebeians; I asked Deepak Mehta about the Punic wars, the conquest of Italy, and the fall of the Republic. Deepak of course had an advantage, for certainly he had studied this material at university, but I must say that the straightforward determination of Sedgewick Bell had begun to win my heart. I recalled the bashful manner in which he had shown me his flash cards at dinner the night before, and as I stood now before the microphone I seemed to be in the throes of an affection for him that had long been under wraps.

"What year were the Romans routed at Lake Trasimene?" I asked him.

He paused. "Two hundred seventeen B.C., I believe."

"Which general later became Scipio Africanus Major?"

"Publius Cornelius Scipio, sir," Deepak Mehta answered softly.

It does not happen as often as one might think that an unintelligent boy becomes an intelligent man, for in my own experience the love of thought is rooted in an age long before adolescence; yet Sedgewick Bell now seemed to have done just that. His answers were spoken with the composed demeanor of a scholar. There is no one I like more, of course, than the man who is moved by the mere fact of history, and as I contemplated the next question to him I wondered if I had indeed exaggerated the indolence of his boyhood. Was it true, perhaps, that he had simply not come into his element yet while at St. Benedict's? He peered intently at me from the stage, his elbows on his knees. I decided to ask him a difficult question. "Chairman Bell," I said, "which tribes invaded Rome in 102 B.C.?"

His eyes went blank and he curled his shoulders in his suit. Although he was by then one of the most powerful men in America, and although moments before that I had been rejoicing in his discipline, suddenly I saw him on that stage once again as a frightened boy. How powerful is memory! And once again, I feared that it was I who had betrayed him. He brought his hand to his head to think.

"Take your time, sir," I offered.

There were murmurs in the audience. He distractedly touched the side of his head. Man's character is his fate, says Heraclitus, and at that moment, as he brushed his hand down over his temple, I realized that the flesh-colored device in his ear was not a hearing aid but a transmitter through which he was receiving the answers to my questions. Nausea rose in me. Of course I had no proof, but was it not exactly what I should have expected? He touched his head once again and appeared to be deep in thought, and I knew it as certainly as if he had shown me. "The Teutons," he said, haltingly, "and—I'll take a stab here—the Cimbri?"

I looked for a long time at him. Did he know at that point what I was thinking? I cannot say, but after I had paused as long as I could bear to in front of that crowd, I cleared my throat and granted that he was right. Applause erupted. He shook it off with a wave of his hand. I knew that it was my duty to speak up. I knew it was my duty as a teacher to bring him clear of the moral dereliction in which I myself had been his partner, yet at the same time I felt myself adrift in the tide of my own vacillation and failure. The boy had somehow got hold of me again. He tried to quiet the applause with a wave of his hand, but this gesture only caused the clapping to increase, and I am afraid to say that it was merely the sound of a throng of boisterous men that finally prevented me from making my stand. Quite suddenly I was aware that this was not the situation I had known at St. Benedict's School. We were guests now of a significant man on his splendid estate, and to expose him would be a serious act indeed. I turned and quieted the crowd.

From the chair next to Sedgewick Bell, Deepak Mehta merely looked at me, his eyes dark and resigned. Perhaps he too had just realized, or perhaps in fact he had long known, but in any case I simply asked him the next question; after he answered it, I could do nothing but put another before Sedgewick Bell. Then Deepak again, then Sedgewick, and again to Deepak, and it was only then, on the third round after I had discovered the ploy, that an idea came to me. When I returned to Sedgewick Bell, I asked him, "Who was Shutruk-Nahhunte?"

A few boys in the crowd began to laugh, and when Sedgewick Bell took his time thinking about the answer, more in the audience joined in. Whoever was the mercenary professor talking in his ear, it was clear to me that he would not know the answer to this one, for if he had not gone to St. Benedict's School he would never have heard of Shutruk-Nahhunte; and in a few moments, sure enough, I saw Sedgewick Bell begin to grow uncomfortable. He lifted his pant leg and scratched at his sock. The laughter increased, and then I heard the wives, who had obviously never lived in a predatory pack, trying to stifle their husbands. "Come on, Bell!" someone shouted, "Look at the damn door!" Laughter erupted again.

How can it be that for a moment my heart bled for him? He, too, tried to laugh, but only halfheartedly. He shifted in his seat, shook his arms loose in his suit, looked uncomprehendingly out at the snickering crowd, then braced his chin and said, "Well, I guess if Deepak knows the answer to this one, then it's *his* ball game."

Deepak's response was nearly lost in the boisterous stamps and whistles that followed, for I am sure that every boy but Sedgewick recalled Henry Stimson's tablet above the door of my classroom. Yet what was strange was that I felt disappointment. As Deepak Mehta smiled, spoke the answer, and stood from his chair, I watched confusion and then a flicker of panic cross the face of Sedgewick Bell. He stood haltingly. How clear it was to me then that the corruption in his character had always arisen from fear, and I could not help remembering that as his teacher I had once tried to convince him of his stupidity. I cursed that day. But then in a moment he summoned a smile, called me up to the stage, and crossed theatrically to congratulate the victor.

How can I describe the scene that took place next? I suppose I was naïve to think that this was the end of the evening—or even the point of it—for after Sedgewick Bell had brought forth a trophy for Deepak Mehta, and then one for me as well, an entirely different cast came across his features. He strode once again to the podium and asked for the attention of the guests. He tapped sharply on the microphone. Then he leaned his head forward, and in a voice that I recognized from long ago on the radio, a voice in whose deft leaps from boom to whisper I heard the willow-tree drawl of his father, he launched into an address about the problems of our country. He had the orator's gift of dropping his volume at the moment when a less gifted man would have raised it. *We have opened our doors to all the world*, he said, his voice thundering, then pausing, then plunging nearly to a murmur, *and now the world has stripped us bare*. He gestured with his hands. The men in the audience, first laughing, now turned serious. *We have given away too much for too long*, he said. *We have handed our fiscal leadership to men who don't care about the taxpayers of our country, and our moral course to those who no longer understand our role in history.* Although he gestured to me here, I could not return his gaze. *We have abandoned the moral education of our families.* Scattered applause drifted up from his classmates, and here, of course, I almost spoke. *We have left our country adrift on dangerous seas.* Now the applause was more hearty. Then he quieted his voice again, dropped his head as though in supplication, and announced that he was running for the United States Senate.

Why was I surprised? I should not have been, for since childhood the boy had stood so near to the mantle of power that its shadow must have been as familiar to him as his boyhood home. Virtue had no place in the palaces he had known. I was ashamed when I realized he had contrived the entire rematch of "Mr. Julius Caesar" for no reason other than to gather his classmates for donations, yet still I chastened myself for not realizing his ambition before. In his oratory, in his physical presence, in his conviction, he had always possessed the gifts of a leader, and now he was using them. I should have expected this from the first day he stood in his short-pants suit in the doorway of my classroom and silenced my students. He already wielded a potent role in the affairs of our county; he enjoyed the presumption of his family name; he was blindly ignorant of history and therefore did not fear his role in it. Of course it was exactly the culmination I should long ago have seen. The crowd stood cheering.

As soon as the clapping abated, a curtain was lifted behind him and a band struck up "Dixie." Waiters appeared at the side doors, a dance platform was unfolded in the orchestra pit, and Sedgewick Bell jumped down from the stage into the crowd of his friends. They clamored around him. He patted shoulders, kissed wives, whispered and laughed and nodded his head. I saw checkbooks come out. The waiters carried champagne on trays at their shoulders, and at the edge of the dance floor the women set down their purses and stepped into the arms of their husbands. When I saw this I ducked out a side door and returned to the lodge, for the abandon with which the guests were dancing was an unbearable counterpart to the truth I knew. One can imagine my feelings. I heard the din late into the night.

Needless to say, I resolved to avoid Sedgewick Bell for the remainder of my stay. How my mind raced that night through humanity's endless history of injustice, depravity, and betrayal! I could not sleep, and several times I rose and went to the window to listen to the revelry. Standing at the glass, I felt like the spurned sovereign in the castle tower, looking down from his balcony onto the procession of the false potentate.

Yet, sure enough, my conviction soon began to wane. No sooner had I resolved to avoid my host than I began to doubt the veracity of my secret knowledge about him. Other thoughts came to me. How, in fact, had I been so sure of what he'd done? What proof had I at all? Amid the distant celebrations of the night, my conclusion began to seem farfetched, and by the quiet of the morning I was muddled. I did not go to breakfast. As boy after boy stopped by my rooms to wish me well, I assiduously avoided commenting on either Sedgewick Bell's performance or on his announcement for the Senate. On the beach that day I endeavored to walk by myself, for by then I trusted neither my judgment of the incident nor my discretion with the boys. I spent the afternoon alone in a cove across the island.

I did not speak to Sedgewick Bell that entire day. I managed to avoid him, in fact, until the next evening, by which time all but a few of the guests had left, when he came to bid farewell as I stood on the tarmac awaiting the helicopter for the mainland. He walked out and motioned for me to stand back from the platform, but I pretended not to hear him and kept my eyes up to the sky. Suddenly the shining craft swooped in from beyond the wavebreak, churning the channel into a boil, pulled up in a hover and then touched down on its flag-colored sponsons before us. The wind and noise could have thrown a man to the ground, and Sedgewick Bell seemed to pull at me like a magnet, but I did not retreat. It was he, finally, who ran out to me. He gripped his lapels, ducked his head, and offered me his hand. I took it tentatively, the rotors whipping our jacket sleeves. I had been expecting this moment and had decided the night before what I was going to say. I leaned toward him. "How long have you been hard of hearing?" I asked.

His smile dropped. I cannot imagine what I had become in the mind of that boy. "Very good, Hundert," he said. "Very good. I thought you might have known."

My vindication was sweet, although now I see that it meant little. By then I was on the ladder of the helicopter, but he pulled me toward him again and looked darkly into my eyes. "And I see that *you* have not changed either," he said.

Well, had I? As the craft lifted off and turned westward toward the bank of clouds that hid the distant shoreline, I analyzed the situation with some care. The wooden turrets of the lodge grew smaller and then were lost in the trees, and I found it easier to think then, for everything on that island had been imbued with the sheer power of the man. I relaxed a bit in my seat. One could say that in this case I indeed had acted properly, for is it not the glory of our legal system that acquitting a guilty man is less heinous than convicting an innocent one? At the time of the contest, I certainly had no proof of Sedgewick Bell's behavior.

Yet back in Woodmere, as I have intimated, I found myself with a great deal of time on my hands, and it was not long before the incident began to replay itself in my mind. Following the wooded trail toward the river or sitting in the breeze at dusk on the porch, I began to see that a different ending would have better served us all. Conviction had failed me again. I was well aware of the foolish consolation of my thoughts, yet I vividly imagined what I should have done. I heard myself speaking up; I saw my resolute steps to his chair on the stage, then the insidious, flesh-colored device in my palm, held up to the crowd; I heard him stammering.

As if to mock my inaction, however, stories of his electoral effort soon began to appear in the papers. It was a year of spite and rancor in our country's politics, and the race in West Virginia was less a campaign than a brawl between gladiators. The incumbent was as versed in treachery as Sedgewick Bell, and over my morning tea I followed their battles. Sedgewick Bell called him "a liar when he speaks and a crook when he acts," and he called Sedgewick Bell worse. A fistfight erupted when their campaigns crossed at an airport.

I was revolted by the spectacle, but of course I was also intrigued, and I cannot deny that although I was rooting for the incumbent, a part of me was also cheered at each bit of news chronicling Sedgewick Bell's assault on his lead. Oh, why was this so? Are we all, at base, creatures without virtue? Is fervor the only thing we follow?

Needless to say, that fall had been a difficult one in my life, especially those afternoons when the St. Benedict's bus roared by the guest house in Woodmere taking the boys to track meets, and perhaps the Senate race was nothing more than a healthy distraction for me. Indeed, I needed distractions. To witness the turning of the leaves and to smell the apples in their barrels without hearing the sound of a hundred boys in the fields, after all, was almost more than I could bear. My walks had grown longer, and several times I had crossed the river and ventured to the far end of the marsh, from where in the distance I could make out the blurred figures of St. Benedict's. I knew this was not good for me, and perhaps that is why, in late October of that year when I read that Sedgewick Bell would be making a campaign stop at a coal-miners' union hall near the Virginia border, I decided to go hear him speak.

Perhaps by then the boy had become an obsession for me—I will admit this, for I am as aware as anyone that time is but the thinnest bandage for our wounds—but on the other hand, the race had grown quite close and would have been of natural interest to anyone. Sedgewick Bell had drawn himself up from underdog to challenger. Now it was clear that the election hinged on the votes of labor, and Sedgewick Bell, though he was the son of aristocrats and the chairman of a formidable corporation, began to cast himself as a champion of the working man. From newspaper reports I gleaned that he was helped along by the power of his voice and bearing, and I could easily imagine these men turning to him. I well knew the charisma of the boy.

The day arrived, and I packed a lunch and made the trip. As the bus wound west along the river valley, I envisioned the scene ahead and wondered whether Sedgewick Bell would at this point care to see me. Certainly I represented some sort of truth to him about himself, yet at the same time I also seemed to have become a part of the very delusion that he had foisted on those around him. How far my boys would always stride upon the world's stage, yet how dearly I would always hope to change them! The bus arrived early, and I went inside the union hall to wait.

Shortly before noon the miners began to come in. I don't know what I had expected, but I was surprised to see them looking as though they had indeed just come out of the mines. They wore hard hats, their faces were stained with dust, and their gloves and tool belts hung at their waists. For some reason, I had worn my St. Benedict's blazer, which I now removed. Reporters began to filter in as well, and by the time the noon whistle blew, the crowd was overflowing from the hall.

As the whistle subsided I heard the thump-thump of his helicopter, and through the door a moment later I saw the twisters of dust as it hovered into view from above. How clever was the man I had known as a boy! The craft had been repainted the colors of military camouflage, but he had left the sponsons the red, white, and blue of their previous incarnation. He jumped from the side door when the craft was still a foot above the ground, entered the hall at a jog, and was greeted with an explosion of applause. His aides lined the stairs to the high platform on which the microphone stood under a banner and a flag, and as he crossed the crowd toward them the miners jostled to be near him, knocking their knuckles against his hard hat, reaching for his hands and his shoulders, cheering like Romans at a chariot race.

I do not need to report on his eloquence, for I have dwelled enough upon it. When he reached the staircase and ascended to the podium, stopping first at the landing to wave and then at the top to salute the flag above him, jubilation swept among the throng. I knew then that he had succeeded in his efforts, that these miners counted him somehow as their own, so that when he actually spoke and they interrupted him with cheers, it was no more unexpected than the promises he made then to carry their interests with him to the Senate. He was masterful. I found my own arm upraised.

Certainly there were five hundred men in that hall, but there was only one with a St. Benedict's blazer over his shoulder and no hard hat on his head, so of course I should not have been surprised when within a few minutes one of his aides appeared beside me and told me that the candidate had asked for me at the podium. At that moment I saw Sedgewick Bell's glance pause for a moment on my face. There was a flicker of a smile on his lips, but then he looked away.

Is there no battle other than the personal one? Was Sedgewick Bell at that point willing to risk the future of his political ideas for whatever childhood demon I still remained to him? The next time he turned toward me, he gestured down at the floor, and in a moment the aide had pulled my arm and was escorting me toward the platform. The crowd opened as we passed, and the miners in their ignorance and jubilation were reaching to shake my hand. This was indeed a heady feeling. I climbed the steps and stood beside Sedgewick Bell at the smaller microphone. How it was to stand above the mass of men like that! He raised his hand and they cheered; he lowered it and they fell silent.

"There is a man here today who has been immeasurably important in my life," he whispered into his microphone.

There was applause, and a few of the men whistled. "Thank you," I said into my own. I could see the blue underbrims of five hundred hard hats turned up toward me. My heart was nearly bursting.

"My history teacher," he said, as the crowd began to cheer again. Flashbulbs popped and I moved instinctively toward the front of the platform. "Mr. Hundert," he boomed, "from forty-five years ago at Richmond Central High School."

It took me a moment to realize what he had said. By then he too was clapping and at the same time lowering his head in what must have appeared to the men below to be respect for me. The blood engorged my veins. "Just a minute," I said, stepping back to my own microphone. "I taught you at St. Benedict's School in Woodmere, Virginia. Here is the blazer."

Of course, it makes no difference in the course of history that as I tried to hold up the coat Sedgewick Bell moved swiftly across the podium, took it from my grip, and raised my arm high in his own, and that this pose, of all things, sent the miners into jubilation; it makes no difference that by the time I spoke, he had gestured with his hand so that one of his aides had already shut off my microphone. For one does not alter history without conviction. It is enough to know that I *did* speak, and certainly a consolation that Sedgewick Bell realized, finally, that I would.

He won that election not in small part because he managed to convince those miners that he was one of them. They were ignorant people, and I cannot blame them for taking to the shrewdly populist rhetoric of the man. I saved the picture that appeared the following morning in the *Gazette*: Senator Bell radiating all the populist magnetism of his father, holding high the arm of an old man who has on his face the remnants of a proud and foolish smile.

I still live in Woodmere, and I have found a route that I take now and then to the single high hill from which I can see the St. Benedict's steeple across the Passamic. I take two walks every day and have grown used to this life. I have even come to like it. I am reading of the ancient Japanese civilizations now, which I had somehow neglected before, and every so often one of my boys visits me.

One afternoon recently Deepak Mehta did so, and we shared some brandy. This was in the fall of last year. He was still the quiet boy he had always been, and not long after he had taken a seat on my couch, I had to turn on the television to ease for him the burden of conversation. As it happened, the Senate Judiciary Committee was holding its famous hearings then, and the two of us sat there watching, nodding our heads or chuckling whenever the camera showed Sedgewick Bell sitting alongside the chairman. I had poured the brandy liberally, and whenever Sedgewick Bell leaned into the microphone and asked a question of the witness, Deepak would mimic his affected southern drawl. Naturally, I could not exactly encourage this behavior, but I did nothing to stop it. When he finished his drink I poured him another. This, of course, is perhaps the greatest pleasure of a teacher's life, to have a drink one day with a man he has known as a boy.

Nonetheless, I only wish we could have talked more than we actually did. But I am afraid that there must always be a reticence between a teacher and his student. Deepak had had another small heart attack, he told me, but I felt it would have been improper of me to inquire more. I tried to bring myself to broach the subject of Sedgewick Bell's history, but here again I was aware that a teacher does not discuss one boy with another. Certainly Deepak must have known about Sedgewick Bell as well, but probably because of his own set of St. Benedict's morals he did not bring it up with me. We watched Sedgewick Bell question the witness and then whisper into the ear of the chairman. Neither of us was surprised at his ascendence, I believe, because both of us were students of history. Yet we did not discuss this either. Still, I wanted desperately for him to ask me something more, and perhaps this was why I kept refilling his glass. I wanted him to ask, "How is it to be alone, sir, at this age?" or perhaps to say, "You have made a difference in my life, Mr. Hundert." But of course these were not things Deepak Mehta would ever say. A man's character is his character. Nonetheless, it was startling, every now and then when I looked over at the sunlight falling across his bowed head, to see that Deepak Mehta, the quietest of my boys, was now an old man.

STRANGENESS

None of us are total strangers to strangeness. Even the most normal life takes an occasional left turn into something resembling the Twilight Zone. An odd phone call. A mind-boggling coincidence. The sense of an unseen presence. A visit to a land of alien languages and ways. While most of us like experiencing the surreal in fiction or films or sitting by the campfire, in everyday life we flee the unexpected like a runaway train. But if there were no strangeness in our days, how would we know what normal is?

There is no telling what a knock on the door may bring. In Jorge Luis Borges's "The Book of Sand," the door is opened to a Bible salesman. His wares seem innocent enough until he produces a book so fascinating and inexplicable that perhaps it was better left unopened.

Our lives can be altered by something as random as a gust of wind. A scrap of paper bearing an ominous threat is blown toward the bland banker in Charles Baxter's "The Next Building I Plan to Bomb." No one seems to know what is being threatened, or why. Is mass destruction imminent? Or is the greater danger within the banker's own mind?

In Jess Row's "The Secrets of Bats," an American teacher has begun adjusting to the strangeness of teaching in a Hong Kong school when he encounters a student who seems even more foreign than Chinese; this girl appears to have developed the bats' technique of echolocation, the ability to "see" via sound waves. The teacher can't help but follow his student on a search through the darkness that is puzzling, unsettling, and, ultimately, quite dangerous.

In Jhumpa Lahiri's "The Third and Final Continent," a Bengali man travels from India to Great Britain and finally to the United States to make a better life for himself. He finds adjusting to local customs less difficult than adjusting to certain people, specifically the boisterous old woman he rents a room from and the shy young woman who becomes his "arranged" wife. As the years unfold, this immigrant strives to become a citizen of his own strange life.

THE BOOK OF SAND

JORGE LUIS BORGES

... thy rope of sands ...
George Herbert (1593–1623)

The line consists of an infinite number of points; the plane, of an infinite number of lines; the volume, of an infinite number of planes; the hypervolume, of an infinite number of volumes ... No—this, *more geometrico*, is decidedly not the best way to begin my tale. To say that the story is true is by now a convention of every fantastic tale; mine, nevertheless, *is* true.

I live alone, in a fifth-floor apartment on Calle Belgrano. One evening a few months ago, I heard a knock at my door. I opened it, and a stranger stepped in. He was a tall man, with blurred, vague features, or perhaps my nearsightedness made me see him that way. Everything about him spoke of honest poverty: he was dressed in gray, and carried a gray valise. I immediately sensed that he was a foreigner. At first I thought he was old; then I noticed that I had been misled by his sparse hair, which was blond, almost white, like the Scandinavians'. In the course of our conversation, which I doubt lasted more than an hour, I learned that he hailed from the Orkneys.

I pointed the man to a chair. He took some time to begin talking. He gave off an air of melancholy, as I myself do now.

"I sell Bibles," he said at last.

"In this house," I replied, not without a somewhat stiff, pedantic note, "there are several English Bibles, including the first one, Wyclif's. I also have Cipriano de Valera's, Luther's (which is, in literary terms, the worst of the lot), and a Latin copy of the Vulgate. As you see, it isn't exactly Bibles I might be needing."

After a brief silence he replied.

"It's not only Bibles I sell. I can show you a sacred book that might interest a man such as yourself. I came by it in northern India, in Bikaner."

He opened his valise and brought out the book. He laid it on the table. It was a clothbound octavo volume that had clearly passed through many hands. I examined it; the unusual heft of it surprised me. On the spine was printed *Holy Writ*, and then *Bombay*.

"Nineteenth century, I'd say," I observed.

"I don't know," was the reply. "Never did know."

I opened it at random. The characters were unfamiliar to me. The pages, which seemed worn and badly set, were printed in double columns, like a Bible. The text was cramped, and composed into versicles. At the upper corner of each page were Arabic numerals. I was struck by an odd fact: the even-numbered page would carry the number 40,514, let us say, while the odd-numbered page that followed it would be 999. I turned the page; the next page bore an eight-digit number. It also bore a small illustration, like those one sees in dictionaries: an anchor drawn in pen and ink, as though by the unskilled hand of a child.

It was at that point that the stranger spoke again.

"Look at it well. You will never see it again."

There was a threat in the words, but not in the voice.

I took note of the page, and then closed the book. Immediately I opened it again. In vain I searched for the figure of the anchor, page after page. To hide my discomfiture, I tried another tack.

"This is a version of Scripture in some Hindu language, isn't that right?"

"No," he replied.

Then he lowered his voice, as though entrusting me with a secret.

"I came across this book in a village on the plain, and I traded a few rupees and a Bible for it. The man who owned it didn't know how to read. I suspect he saw the Book of Books as an amulet. He was of the lowest caste; people could not so much as step on his shadow without being defiled. He told me his book was called the Book of Sand because neither sand nor this book has a beginning or an end."

He suggested I try to find the first page.

I took the cover in my left hand and opened the book, my thumb and forefinger almost touching. It was impossible: several pages always lay between the cover and my hand. It was as though they grew from the very book.

"Now try to find the end."

I failed there as well.

"This can't be," I stammered, my voice hardly recognizable as my own.

"It can't be, yet it *is*," the Bible peddler said, his voice little more than a whisper. "The number of pages in this book is literally infinite. No page is the first page; no page is the last. I don't know why they're numbered in this arbitrary way, but perhaps it's to give one to understand that the terms of an infinite series can be numbered any way whatever."

Then, as though thinking out loud, he went on.

"If space is infinite, we are anywhere, at any point in space. If time is infinite, we are at any point in time."

His musings irritated me.

"You," I said, "are a religious man, are you not?"

"Yes, I'm Presbyterian. My conscience is clear. I am certain I didn't cheat that native when I gave him the Lord's Word in exchange for his diabolic book."

I assured him he had nothing to reproach himself for, and asked whether he was just passing through the country. He replied that he planned to return to his own country within a few days. It was then that I learned he was a Scot, and that his home was in the Orkneys. I told him I had great personal fondness for Scotland because of my love for Stevenson and Hume.

"And Robbie Burns," he corrected.

As we talked I continued to explore the infinite book.

"Had you intended to offer this curious specimen to the British Museum, then?" I asked with feigned indifference.

"No," he replied, "I am offering it to you," and he mentioned a great sum of money.

I told him, with perfect honesty, that such an amount of money was not within my ability to pay. But my mind was working; in a few moments I had devised my plan.

"I propose a trade," I said. "You purchased the volume with a few rupees and the Holy Scripture; I will offer you the full sum of my pension, which I have just received, and Wyclif's black-letter Bible. It was left to me by my parents."

"A black-letter Wyclif!" he murmured.

I went to my bedroom and brought back the money and the book. With a bibliophile's zeal he turned the pages and studied the binding.

"Done," he said.

I was astonished that he did not haggle. Only later was I to realize that he had entered my house already determined to sell the book. He did not count the money, but merely put the bills into his pocket.

We chatted about India, the Orkneys, and the Norwegian jarls that had once ruled those islands. Night was falling when the man left. I have never seen him since, nor do I know his name.

I thought of putting the Book of Sand in the space left by the Wyclif, but I chose at last to hide it behind some imperfect volumes of the *Thousand and One Nights*.

I went to bed but could not sleep. At three or four in the morning I turned on the light. I took out the impossible book and turned its pages. On one, I saw an engraving of a mask. There was a number in the corner of the page—I don't remember now what it was—raised to the ninth power.

I showed no one my treasure. To the joy of possession was added the fear that it would be stolen from me, and to that, the suspicion that it might not be truly infinite. Those two points of anxiety aggravated my already habitual misanthropy. I had but few friends left, and those, I stopped seeing. A prisoner of the Book, I hardly left my house. I examined the worn binding and the covers with a magnifying glass, and rejected the possibility of some artifice. I found that the small illustrations were spaced at two-thousand-page intervals. I began noting them down in an alphabetized notebook, which was very soon filled. They never repeated themselves. At night, during the rare intervals spared me by insomnia, I dreamed of the book.

Summer was drawing to a close, and I realized that the book was monstrous. It was cold consolation to think that I, who looked upon it with my eyes and fondled it with my ten flesh-and-bone fingers, was no less monstrous than the book. I felt it was a nightmare thing, an obscene thing, and that it defiled and corrupted reality.

I considered fire, but I feared that the burning of an infinite book might be similarly infinite, and suffocate the planet in smoke.

I remembered reading once that the best place to hide a leaf is in the forest. Before my retirement I had worked in the National Library, which contained nine hundred thousand books; I knew that to the right of the lobby a curving staircase descended into the shadows of the basement, where the maps and periodicals are kept. I took advantage of the librarians' distraction to hide the Book of Sand on one of the library's damp shelves; I tried not to notice how high up, or how far from the door.

I now feel a little better, but I refuse even to walk down the street the library's on.

THE NEXT BUILDING
I PLAN TO BOMB

CHARLES BAXTER

In the parking lot next to the bank, Harry Edmonds saw a piece of gray
scrap paper the size of a greeting card. It had blown up next to his leg and
attached itself to him there. Across the top margin was some scrabby writing
in purple ink. He picked it up and examined it. On the upper lefthand
corner someone had scrawled the phrase: THE NEXT BUILDING I PLAN TO BOMB.
Harry unfolded the paper and saw an inked drawing of what appeared to
be a sizable train station or some other public structure, perhaps an airport
terminal. In the drawing were arched windows and front pillars but very
little other supporting detail. The building looked solid, monumental, and
difficult to destroy.

He glanced around the parking lot. There he was in Five Oaks,
Michigan, where there were no such buildings. In the light wind other pieces
of paper floated by in an agitated manner. One yellow flyer was stuck to a
fire hydrant. On the street was the usual crowd of bankers, lawyers, shop-
pers, and students. As usual, no one was watching him or paying much
attention to him. He put the piece of paper into his coat pocket.

All afternoon, while he sat at his desk, his hand traveled down to his
pocket to touch the drawing. Late in the day, half as a joke, he showed the
paper to the office receptionist.

"You've got to take it to the police," she told him. "This is dangerous.
This is the work of a maniac. That's LaGuardia there, the airport? In the
picture? I was there last month. I'm sure it's LaGuardia, Mr. Edmonds. No
kidding. Definitely LaGuardia."

So at the end of the day, before going home, he drove to the main police station on the first floor of the City Hall. Driving into the sun, he felt his eyes squinting against the burrowing glare. He had stepped inside the front door when the waxy bureaucratic smell of the building hit him and gave him an immediate headache. A cop in uniform, wearing an impatient expression, sat behind a desk, shuffling through some papers, and at that moment it occurred to Harry Edmonds that if he showed what was in his pocket to the police he himself would become a prime suspect and an object of intense scrutiny, all privacy gone. He turned on his heel and went home.

At dinner, he said to his girlfriend, "Look what I found in a parking lot today." He handed her the drawing.

Lucia examined the soiled paper, her thumb and finger at its corner, and said, "'The next building I plan to bomb.'" Her tone was light and urbane. She sold computer software and was sensitive to gestures. Then she said, "That's Union Station, in Chicago." She smiled. "Well, Harry, what are you going to do with this? Some nut case did this, right?"

"Actually, I got as far as the foyer in the police station this afternoon," he said. "Then I turned around. I couldn't show it to them. I thought they'd suspect me or something."

"Oh, that's so melodramatic," she said. "You've never committed a crime in your life. You're a banker, for Chrissake. You're in the trust department. You're harmless."

Harry sat back in his chair and looked at her. "I'm not that harmless."

"Yes, you are," she laughed. "You're quite harmless."

"Lucia," he said, "I wish you wouldn't use that word."

"'Harmless?' It's a compliment."

"Not in this country, it isn't," he said.

On the table were the blue plates and matching napkins and the yellow candles that Lucia brought out whenever she was proud of what she or Harry had cooked. Today it was Burmese chicken curry. "Well, if you're worried, take it to the cops," Lucia told him. "That's what the cops are there for. Honey," she said, "no one will suspect you of anything. You're handsome and stable and you're my sweetie, and I love you, and what else happened today? Put that awful creepy paper back into your pocket. How do you like the curry?"

"It's delicious," he said.

* * *

After Harry had gotten up his nerve sufficiently to enter the police station again, he walked in a determined manner toward the front desk. After looking carefully at the drawing and the inked phrase, and writing down Harry Edmonds' name and address, the officer, whose badge identified him as Sergeant Bursk, asked, "Mr. Edmonds, you got any kids?"

"Kids? No, I don't have kids. Why?"

"Kids did this," Sergeant Bursk told him, waving the paper in front of him as if he were drying it off. "My kids could've done this. Kids do this. Boys do this. They draw torture chambers and they make threats and what-have-you. That's what they do. It's the youth. But they're kids. They don't mean it."

"How do you know?"

"Because I have three of them," Sergeant Bursk said. "I'm not saying that you should have kids, I'm just saying that I have them. I'll keep this drawing, though, if you don't mind."

"Actually," Harry said, "I'd like it back."

"Okay," Sergeant Bursk said, handing it to him, "but if we hear of any major bombings, and, you know, large-scale serious death, maybe we'll give you a call."

"Yeah," Harry said. He had been expecting this. "By the way," he asked, "does this look like any place in particular to you?"

The cop examined the picture. "Sure," he said. "That's Grand Central. In New York, on Forty-second Street, I think. I was there once. You can tell by the clock. See this clock here?" He pointed at a vague circle. "That's Grand Central, and this is the big clock that they've got there on the front."

"The fuck it is," the kid said. The kid was in bed with Harry Edmonds in the Motel 6. They had found each other in a bar downtown and then gone to this motel, and after they were finished, Harry drew the drawing out of his pants' pocket on the floor and showed it to him. The kid's long brown hair fell over his eyes and, loosened from its ponytail, spread out on the pillow. "I know this fucking place," the kid said. "I've, like, traveled, you know, all over Europe. This is in Europe, this place, this is fucking Deutschland we're talking about here." The kid got up on his elbows to see better. "Oh, yeah, I remember this place. I was there, two summers ago? Hamburg? This is the Dammtor Bahnhof."

"Never heard of it," Harry Edmonds said.

"You never heard of it 'cause you've never been there, man. You have to fucking be there to know about it." The kid squinched his eyebrows together like a professor making a difficult point. "A *bahnhof*, see, is a train station, and the Dammtor Bahnhof is, like, one of the stations there, and this is the one that the Nazis rounded up the Jews to. And, like, sent them off from. This place, man. Absolutely. It's still standing. This one, it fucking deserves to be bombed. Just blow it totally the fuck away, off the face of the earth. That's just my opinion. It's evil, man."

The kid moved his body around in bed, getting himself comfortable again after stating his opinions. He was slinky and warm, like a cat. The kid even made back-of-the-throat noises, a sort of satisfied purr.

"I thought we were finished with that," Harry's therapist said. "I thought we were finished with the casual sex. I thought, Harry, that we had worked through those fugitive impulses. I must tell you that it troubles me that we haven't. I won't say that we're back to square one, but it is a backwards step. And what I'm wondering now is, why did it happen?"

"Lucia said I was harmless, that's why."

"And did that anger you?"

"You bet it angered me." Harry sat back in his chair and looked directly at his therapist. He wished she would get a new pair of eyeglasses. These eyeglasses made her look like one of those movie victims killed within the first ten minutes, right after the opening credits. One of those innocent bystanders. "Bankers are not harmless, I can assure you."

"Then why did you pick up that boy?" She waited. When he didn't say anything, she said, "I can't think of anything more dangerous to do."

"It was the building," Harry said.

"What building?"

"I showed Lucia the building. On the paper. This paper." He took it out of his pocket and handed it to his therapist. By now the paper was becoming soft and wrinkled. While she studied the picture, Harry watched the second hand of the wall clock turn.

"You found this?" she asked. "You didn't draw this."

"Yes, I found it." He waited. "I found it in a parking lot six blocks from here."

"All right. You showed Lucia this picture. And perhaps she called you harmless. Why did you think it so disturbing to be called harmless?"

"Because," Harry said, "in this country, if you're harmless, you get killed and eaten. That's the way things are going these days. That's the current trend. I thought you had noticed. Perhaps not."

"And why do you say that people get killed and eaten? That's an extravagant metaphor. It's a kind of hysterical irony."

"No, it isn't. I work in a bank and I see it happen every day. I mop up the blood."

"I don't see what this has to do with picking up young men and taking them to motels," she said. "That's back in the country of acting out. And what I'm wondering is, what does this mean about your relationship to Lucia? You're endangering her, you know." As if to emphasize the point, she said, "It's wrong, what you did. And very very dangerous. With all your thinking, did you think about that?"

Harry didn't answer. Then he said, "It's funny. Everybody has a theory about what that building is. You haven't said anything about it. What's your theory?"

"This building?" Harry's therapist examined the paper through her movie-victim glasses. "Oh, it's the Field Museum, in Chicago. And that's not a theory. It is the Field Museum."

On Tuesday night, at 3 A.M., Harry fixed his gaze on the bedroom ceiling. There, as if on a screen, shaped by the light through the curtains luffing in the window, was a public building with front pillars and curved arched windows and perhaps a clock. On the ceiling the projected sun of Harry's mind rose wonderfully, brilliantly gold, one or two mind-wisp cumulus clouds passing from right to left across it, but not so obscured that its light could not penetrate the great public building into which men, women, and children—children in strollers, children hand in hand with their parents—now filed, shadows on the ceiling, lighted shadows, and for a moment Harry saw an explosive flash.

Harry Edmonds lay in his bed without sleeping. Next to him was his girlfriend, whom he had planned to marry, once he ironed out a few items of business in his personal life and got them settled. He had made love to her, to this woman, this Lucia, a few hours earlier, with earnest caresses, but now he seemed to be awake again. He rose from bed and went down to the kitchen. In the harsh fluorescence he ate a cookie and on an impulse turned on the radio. The radio blistered with the economy of call-in hatred and religion revealed to rabid-mouthed men who now gasped and screamed into all available microphones. He adjusted the dial to a call-in station. Speaking from Delaware, a man said, "There's a few places I'd do some trouble to, believe me, starting with the Supreme Court and moving on to a clinic or two." Harry snapped off the radio.

Now he sits in the light of the kitchen. He feels as dazed as it is possible for a sane man to feel at three-thirty in the morning. I am not silly, nor am I trivial, Harry says to himself, as he reaches for a pad of paper and a no. 2 pencil. At the top of the pad, Harry writes, "The next place I plan to bomb," and then very slowly, and with great care, begins to draw his own face, its smooth cleanshaven contours, its courteous half-smile. When he perceives his eyes beginning to water, he rips off the top sheet with his picture on it and throws it in the wastebasket. The refrigerator seems to be humming some tune to him, some tune without a melody, and he flicks off the overhead light before he recognizes that tune.

It is midday in downtown Five Oaks, Michigan, the time for lunch and rest and conversation, and for a remnant, a lucky few, it may be a time for love, but here before us is Harry Edmonds, an officer in the trust department at Southeastern Michigan Bank and Trust, standing on a street corner in a strong spring wind. The wind pulls at his tie and musses his hair. Nearby, a recycling container appears to have overturned, and sheets of paper, hundreds of them, papers covered with drawings and illustrations and words, have scattered. Like a flock of birds, they have achieved flight. All around Harry Edmonds they are gripped in this whirlwind and flap and snap in circles. Some stick to him. There are glossy papers with perfumed inserts, and there are yellowing papers with four-color superheroes, and there are the papers with attractive unclothed airbrushed bodies, and there are the papers with bills and announcements and loans. Here are the personals, swirling past, and there a flyer for home theater big-screen TV. Harry Edmonds, a man uncertain of the value of his own life, who at this moment does not know whether his life has, in fact, any importance at all, or any future, lifts his head in the wind, increasing in volume and intensity, and for a moment he imagines himself being blown away. From across the street, the way he raises his head might appear, to an observer, as a posture of prayer. God, it is said, resides in the whirlwind, and certainly Harry

Edmonds' eyes are closed and now his head is bowed. He does not move forward or backward, and it is unclear from the expression on his face whether he is making any sort of wish. He remains stationary, on this street corner, while all about him the papers fly first toward him, and then away.

A moment later he is gone from the spot where he stood. No doubt he has returned to his job at the bank, and that is where we must leave him.

THE SECRETS OF BATS

JESS ROW

Alice Leung has discovered the secrets of bats: how they see without seeing, how they own darkness, as we own light. She walks the halls with a black headband across her eyes, keening a high C—*cheat cheat cheat cheat cheat cheat*—never once veering off course, as if drawn by an invisible thread. Echolocation, she tells me, it's not as difficult as you might think. Now she sees a light around objects when she looks at them, like halos on her retinas from staring at the sun. In her journal she writes, *I had a dream that was all in blackness. Tell me how to describe.*

It is January: my fifth month in Hong Kong.

In the margin I write, *I wish I knew.*

After six, when the custodians leave, the school becomes a perfect acoustic chamber; she wanders from the basement laboratories to the basketball courts like a trapped bird looking for a window. She finds my door completely blind, she says, not counting flights or paces. Twisting her head from side to side like Stevie Wonder, she announces her progress: another room mapped, a door, a desk, a globe, detected and identified by its aura.

You'll hurt yourself, I tell her. I've had nightmares: her foot missing the edge of a step, the dry crack of a leg breaking. Try it without the blindfold, I say. That way you can check yourself.

Her mouth wrinkles. This not important, she says. This only practice.

Practice for what, I want to ask. All the more reason you have to be careful.

You keep saying, she says, grabbing a piece of chalk. E-x-p-e-r-i-m-e-n-t, she writes on the blackboard, digging it in until it squeals.

That's right. Sometimes experiments fail.

Sometimes, she repeats. She eyes me suspiciously, as if I invented the word.

Go home, I tell her. She turns her pager off and leaves it in her locker; sometimes police appear at the school gate, shouting her name. Somebody, it seems, wants her back.

In the doorway she whirls, flipping her hair out of her eyes. Ten days more, she says. You listen. Maybe then you see why.

The name of the school is Po Sing Uk: a five-story concrete block, cracked and eroded by dirty rain, shoulder-to-shoulder with the tenements and garment factories of Cheung Sha Wan. No air conditioning and no heat; in September I shouted to be heard over a giant fan, and now, in January, I teach in a winter jacket. When it rains, mildew spiderwebs across the ceiling of my classroom. Schoolgirls in white jumpers crowd into the room forty at a time, falling asleep over their textbooks, making furtive calls on mobile phones, scribbling notes to each other on pink Hello Kitty paper. If I call on one who hasn't raised her hand, she folds her arms across her chest and stares at the floor, and the room falls silent, as if by a secret signal. There is nothing more terrifying, I've found, than the echo of your own voice: *Who are you?* it answers. *What are you doing here?*

I've come to see my life as a radiating circle of improbabilities that grow from each other, like ripples in water around a dropped stone. That I became a high school English teacher, that I work in another country, that I live in Hong Kong. That a city can be a mirage, hovering above the ground: skyscrapers built on mountainsides, islands swallowed in fog for days. That a language can have no tenses or articles, with seven different ways of saying the same syllable. That my best student stares at the blackboard only when I erase it.

She stayed behind on the first day of class: a tall girl with a narrow face, pinched around the mouth, her cheeks pitted with acne scars. Like most of my sixteen-year-olds, she looked twelve, in a baggy uniform that hung to her knees like a sack. The others streamed past her without looking up, as if she were a boulder in the current; she stared down at my desk with a fierce vacancy, as if looking itself was an act of will.

How do you think about bats?

Bats?

She joined her hands at the wrist and fluttered them at me.

People are afraid of them, I said. I think they're very interesting.

Why? she said. Why very interesting?

Because they live in the dark, I said. We think of them as being blind, but they aren't blind. They have a way of seeing, with sound waves—just like we see with light.

Yes, she said. I know this. Her body swayed slightly, in an imaginary breeze.

Are you interested in bats?

I am interest, she said. I want to know how—she made a face I'd already come to recognize: *I know how to say it in Chinese*—when one bat sees the other. The feeling.

You mean how one bat recognizes another?

Yes—recognize.

That's a good idea, I said. You can keep a journal about what you find. Write something in it every day.

She nodded vehemently, as if she'd already thought of that.

There are books on bat behavior that will tell you—

Not in books. She covered her eyes with one hand and walked forward until her hip brushed the side of my desk, then turned away, at a right angle. Like this, she said. There is a sound, she said. I want to find the sound.

18 September

First hit tuning fork. Sing one octave higher: A B C. This is best way. Drink water or lips get dry.

I must have eyes totally closed. No light!!! So some kind of black—like cloth—is good.

Start singing. First to the closest wall—sing and listen. Practice ten times, twenty times. IMPORTANT: can not move until I HEAR the

wall. Take step back, one time, two time. Listen again. I have to hear
DIFFERENCE first, then move.

Then take turn, ninety degrees left.

Then turn, one hundred eighty degrees left. Feel position with feet.
Feet very important—they are wings!!!

I don't know what this is, I told her the next day, opening the journal
and pushing it across the desk. Can you help me?

I tell you already, she said. She hunched her shoulders so that her
head seemed to rest on them, spreading her elbows to either side. It is like
a test.

A test?

In the courtyard rain crackled against the asphalt; a warm wind lifted
scraps of paper from the desk, somersaulting them through the air.

The sound, she said impatiently. I told you this.

I covered my mouth to hide a smile.

Alice, I said, humans can't do that. It isn't a learned behavior. It's
something you study.

She pushed up the cover of the composition book and let it fall.

I think I can help you, I said. Can you tell me why you want to write
this?

Why I want? She stared at me wide-eyed.

Why do you want to do this? What is the test for?

Her eyes lifted from my face to the blackboard behind me, moved to
the right, then the left, as if measuring the dimensions of the room.

Why you want come to Hong Kong?

Many reasons, I said. After college I wanted to go to another country,
and there was a special fellowship available here. And maybe someday I
will be a teacher.

You are teacher.

I'm just learning, I said. I am trying to be one.

Then why you have to leave America?

I don't, I said. The two things—I took off my glasses and rubbed my
eyes. All at once I was exhausted; the effort seemed useless, a pointless
evasion. When I looked up she was nodding, slowly, as if I'd just said something profound.

I think I will find the reason for being here only after some time, I said. Do you know what I mean? There could be a purpose I don't know about.

So you don't know for good. Not sure.

You could say that.

Hai yat yeung, she said. This same. Maybe if you read you can tell me why.

This is what's so strange about her, I thought, studying her red rimmed eyes, the tiny veins standing out like wires on a circuit board. She doesn't look down. I am fascinated by her, I thought. Is that fair?

You're different from the others, I said. You're not afraid of me. Why is that?

Maybe I have other things be afraid of.

At first the fifth-floor bathroom was her echo chamber; she sat in one corner, on a stool taken from the physics room, and placed an object directly opposite her: a basketball, a glass, a feather. Sound waves triangulate, she told me, corners are best. Passing by at the end of the day, I stopped, closing my eyes, and listened for the difference. She sang without stopping for five minutes, hardly taking a breath: almost a mechanical sound, as if someone had forgotten their mobile phone. Other teachers walked by in groups, talking loudly. If they noticed me, or the sound, I was never aware of it, but always, instinctively, I looked at my watch and followed them down the stairs. As if I too had to rush home to cook for hungry children or boil medicine for my mother-in-law. I never stayed long enough to see if anything changed.

Document everything, I told her, and she did; now I have two binders of entries, forty-one in all. *Hallway. Chair. Notebook.* As if we were scientists writing a grant proposal, as if there were something actual to show at the end of it.

I don't keep a journal or take photographs, and my letters home are factual and sparse. No one in Larchmont would believe me—not even my parents—if I told them the truth. *It sounds like quite an experience you're having! Don't get run over by a rickshaw.* And yet if I died tomorrow—why should I ever think this way?—these binders would be the record of my days. Those and Alice herself, who looks out of her window and with her eyes closed sees ships passing in the harbor, men walking silently in the streets.

26 January
Sound of light bulb—low like bees hum. So hard to listen!

A week ago I dreamed of bodies breaking apart, arms and legs and torsos, fragments of bone, bits of tissue. I woke up flailing in the sheets, and remembered her immediately; there was too long a moment before I believed I was awake. *It has to stop*, I thought, *you have to say something.* Though I know that I can't.

Perhaps there was a time when I might have told her, *This is ridiculous*, or, *You're sixteen, find some friends. What will people think?* But this is Hong Kong, of course, and I have no friends, no basis to judge. I leave the door open, always, and no one ever comes to check; we walk out of the gates together, late in the afternoon, past the watchman sleeping in his chair. For me she has a kind of professional courtesy, ignoring my whiteness politely, as if I had horns growing from my head. And she returns, at the end of each day, as a bat flies back to its cave at daybreak. All I have is time; who am I to pack my briefcase and turn away?

There was only once when I slipped up.

Pretend I've forgotten, I told her, one Monday in early October. The journal was open in front of us, the pages covered in red; she squinted down at it, as if instead of corrections I'd written hieroglyphics. I'm an English teacher, I thought, this is what I'm here for. We should start again at the beginning, I said. Tell me what it is that you want to do here. You don't have to tell me about the project—just about the writing. Whom are you writing these for? Whom do you want to read them?

She stretched, catlike, curling her fingers like claws.

Because I don't think I understand, I said. I think you might want to find another teacher to help you. There could be something you have in mind in Chinese that doesn't come across.

Not in Chinese, she said, as if I should have known that already. In Chinese cannot say like this.

But it isn't really English, either.

I know this. It is like both.

I can't teach that way, I said. You have to learn the rules before you can—

You are not teaching me.

Then what's the point?

She strode across the room to the window and leaned out, placing her hands on the sill and bending at the waist. Come here, she said, look. I stood up and walked over to her.

She ducked her head down, like a gymnast on a bar, and tilted forward, her feet lifting off the floor.

Alice!

I grabbed her shoulder and jerked her upright. She stumbled, falling back; I caught her wrist, and she pulled it away, steadying herself. We stood there a moment staring at each other, breathing in short huffs that echoed in the hallway.

Maybe I hear something and forget, she said. You catch me then. Okay?

28 January

It is like photo negative, all the colors are the opposite. Black sky, white trees, this way. But they are still shapes—I can see them.

I read standing at the window, in a last sliver of sunlight. Alice stands on my desk, already well in shadow, turning around slowly as if trying to dizzy herself for a party game. Her winter uniform cardigan is three sizes too large; unopened, it falls behind her like a cape.

This is beautiful.

Quiet, she hisses, eyebrows bunched together above her headband. One second. There—there.

What is it?

A man on the stairs.

I go out into the hallway and stand at the top of the stairwell, listening. Five floors below, very faintly, I hear sandals skidding on the concrete, keys jangling on the janitor's ring.

You heard him open the gate, I say. That's cheating.

She shakes her head. I hear heartbeat.

The next Monday, Principal Ho comes to see me during the lunch hour. He stands at the opposite end of the classroom, as always: a tall, slightly chubby man in a tailored shirt, gold-rimmed glasses, and Italian shoes, who blinks as he reads the ESL posters I've tacked up on the wall.

When he asks how my classes are and I tell him that the girls are un-motivated, disengaged, he nods quickly, as if to save me the embarrassment. How lucky he was, he tells me, to go to boarding school in Australia, and then pronounces it with a flattened *a, Australhia,* so I have to laugh.

Principal Ho, I ask, do you know Alice Leung?

He turns his head toward me and blinks more rapidly. Leung Ka Yee, he says. Of course. You have problem with her?

No sir. I need something to hold; my hands dart across the desk behind me and find my red marking pen.

How does she perform?

She's very gifted. One of the best students in the class. Very creative.

He nods, scratches his nose, and turns away.

She likes to work alone, I say. The other girls don't pay much atten-tion to her. I don't think she has many friends.

It is very difficult for her, he says slowly, measuring every word. Her mother is—her mother was a suicide.

In the courtyard, five stories down, someone drops a basketball and lets it bounce against the pavement, little *pings* that trill and fade into the infinite.

In Yau Ma Tei, Ho says. He makes a little gliding motion with his hand. Nowadays this is not so uncommon in Hong Kong. But still there are superstitions.

What kind of superstitions?

He frowns and shakes his head. Difficult to say in English. Maybe just that she is unlucky girl. Chinese people, you understand—some are still afraid of ghosts.

She isn't a ghost.

He gives a high-pitched, nervous laugh. No, no, he says. Not her. He puts his hands into his pockets, searching for something. Difficult to explain. I'm sorry.

Is there someone she can talk to?

He raises his eyebrows. *A counselor,* I am about to say, and explain what it means, when my hand relaxes, and I realize I have been crushing the pen in my palm. For a moment I am water-skiing again at Lake Patchogue: releasing the handle, settling against the surface, enfolded in water. When I look up, Ho glances at his watch.

If you have any problem, you can talk to me.

It's nothing, I say. Just curious, that's all.

She wears the headband all the time now, I've noticed: pulling it over her eyes whenever possible, in the halls between classes, in the courtyard at lunchtime, sitting by herself. No one shoves her or calls her names; she passes through the crowds unseen. If possible, I think, she's grown thinner, her skin translucent, blue veins showing at the wrists. Occasionally I notice the other teachers shadowing her, frowning, their arms crossed, but if our eyes meet they stare through me, disinterested, and look away.

I have to talk to you about something.

She is sitting in a desk at the far end of the room, reading her chemistry textbook, drinking from a can of soymilk with a straw. When the straw gurgles she bangs the can down, and we sit silently, the sound reverberating in the hallway.

I give you another journal soon. Two more days.

Not about that.

She doesn't move: fixed, alert, waiting. I stand up and move down the aisle toward her, sitting two desks away, and as I move her eyes grow slightly rounder and her cheeks puff out slightly, as if she's holding her breath.

Alice, I say, can you tell me about your mother?

Her hands fall down on the desk, and the can clatters to the floor, white drops spinning in the air.

Mother? Who tell you I have mother?

It's all right—

I reach over to touch one hand, and she snatches it back.

Who tell you?

It doesn't matter. You don't have to be angry.

You big mistake, she says, wild-eyed, taking long swallows of air and spitting them out. Why you have to come here and mess everything?

I don't understand, I say. Alice, what did I do?

I trust you, she says, and pushes the heel of one palm against her cheek. I write and you read. I *trust* you.

What did you expect? I ask, my jaw trembling. Did you think I would never know?

Believe me. She looks at me pleadingly. Believe *me*.

* * *

Two days later she leaves her notebook on my desk, with a note stuck to the top. *You keep.*

1 February
Now I am finished
It is out there I hear it

I call out to her after class, and she hesitates in the doorway for a moment before turning, pushing her back against the wall.

Tell me what it was like, I say. Was it a voice? Did you hear someone speaking?

Of course no voice. Not so close to me. It was a feeling.

How did it feel?

She reaches up and slides the headband over her eyes.

It is all finish, she says. You not worry about me anymore.

Too late, I say. I stand up from my chair and take a tentative step toward her: weak-kneed, as if it were a staircase in the dark. You chose me, I say. Remember?

Go back to America. Then you forget all about this crazy girl.

This is my life too. Did you forget about that?

She raises her head and listens, and I know what she hears: a stranger's voice, as surely as if someone else had entered the room. She nods. *Whom do you see?* I wonder. *What will he do next?* I reach out, blindly, and my hand misses the door; on the second try I close it.

I choose this, I say. I'm waiting. Tell me.

Her body sinks into a crouch; she hugs her knees and tilts her head back.

Warm. It was warm. It was—it was a body.

But not close to you?

Not close. Only little feeling, then no more.

Did it know you were there?

No.

How can you be sure?

When I look up to repeat the question, shiny tracks of tears have run out from under the blindfold.

I am sorry, she says. She reaches into her backpack and splits open a packet of tissues without looking down, her fingers nimble, almost autonomous. You are my good friend, she says, and takes off the blindfold, turning her face to the side and dabbing her eyes. Thank you for help me.

It isn't over, I say. How can it be over?

Like you say. Sometimes experiment fails.

No, I say, too loudly, startling us both. It isn't that easy. You have to prove it to me.

Prove it you?

Show me how it works. I take a deep breath. I believe you. Will you catch me?

Her eyes widen, and she does not look away; the world swims around her irises. Tonight, she says, and writes something on a slip of paper, not looking down. I see you then.

In a week it will be the New Year: all along the streets the shop fronts are hung with firecrackers, red-and-gold character scrolls, pictures of grinning cats, and the twin cherubs of good luck. Mothers lead little boys dressed in red silk pajamas, girls with New Year's pigtails. The old woman sitting next to me on the bus is busily stuffing twenty-dollar bills into red *lai see* packets: lucky money for the year to come. When I turn my head from the window, she holds one out to me, and I take it with both hands, automatically, bowing my head. This will make you rich, she says to me in Cantonese. And lots of children.

Thank you, I say. The same to you.

She laughs. Already happened. Jade bangles clink together as she holds up her fingers. Thirteen grandchildren! she says. Six boys. All fat and good-looking. You should say Live long life to me.

I'm sorry. My Chinese is terrible.

No, it's very good, she says. You were born in Hong Kong?

Outside, night is just falling, and Nathan Road has become a canyon of light: blazing neon signs, brilliant shop windows, decorations blinking across the fronts of half-finished tower blocks. I stare at myself a moment in the reflection, three red characters passing across my forehead, and look away. No, I say. In America. I've lived here only since August.

Ah. Then what is America like?

Forgive me, aunt, I say. I forget.

* * *

Prosperous Garden no. 4. Tung Kun Street. Yau Ma Tei.

A scribble of Chinese characters.

Show this to doorman he let you in.

The building is on the far edge of Kowloon, next to the reclamation; a low concrete barrier separates it from an elevated highway that thunders continuously as cars pass. Four identical towers around a courtyard, long poles draped with laundry jutting from every window, like spears hung with old rotted flags.

Gong hei fat choi, I say to the doorman through the gate, and he smiles with crooked teeth, but when I pass the note to him all expression leaves his face; he presses the buzzer and turns away quickly. Twenty-three A-ah, he calls out to the opposite wall. You understand?

Thank you.

When I step out into the hallway I breathe in boiled chicken, oyster sauce, frying oil, the acrid steam of medicine, dried fish, Dettol. Two young boys are crouched at the far end, sending a radio-controlled car zipping past me; someone is arguing loudly over the telephone; a stereo plays loud Cantopop from a balcony somewhere below. All the apartment doors are open, I notice, walking by, and only the heavy sliding gates in front of them are closed. Like a honeycomb, I can't help thinking, or an ant farm. But when I reach 23A the door behind the gate is shut, and no sound comes from behind it. The bell rings several times before the locks begin to snap open.

You are early, Alice says, rubbing her eyes, as if she's been sleeping. Behind her the apartment is dark; there is only a faint blue glow, as if from a TV screen.

I'm sorry. You didn't say when to come. I look at my watch: eight-thirty. I can come back, I say, another time, maybe another night—

She shakes her head and opens the gate.

When she turns on the light I draw a deep breath, involuntarily, and hide it with a cough. The walls are covered with stacks of yellowed paper, file boxes, brown envelopes, and ragged books; on opposite sides of the room are two desks, each holding a computer with a flickering screen. I peer at the one closest to the door. At the top of the screen there is a rotating globe and, below it, a ribbon of letters and numbers, always changing. The other, I see, is just the same: a head staring at its twin.

Come, Alice says. She has disappeared for a moment and reemerged dressed in a long dress, silver running shoes, a hooded sweatshirt.

Are these yours?

No. My father's.

Why does he need two? They're just the same.

Nysee, she says impatiently, pointing. Footsie. New York Stock Exchange. London Stock Exchange.

Sau Yee, a hoarse voice calls from another room. Who is it?

It's my English teacher, she says loudly. Giving me a homework assignment.

Gwailo a?

Yes, she says. The white one.

Then call a taxi for him. He appears in the kitchen doorway: a stooped old man, perhaps five feet tall, in a dirty white T-shirt, shorts, and sandals. His face is covered with liver spots, his eyes shrunken into their sockets. I sorry-ah, he says to me. No speakee English.

It's all right, I say. There is a numbness growing behind my eyes: I want to speak to him, but the words are all jumbled, and Alice's eyes burning on my neck. Goodbye, I say, take care.

See later-ah.

Alice pulls the hood over her head and opens the door.

She leads me to the top of a dark stairwell, in front of a rusting door with light pouring through its cracks. *Tin paang*, she says, reading the characters stenciled on it in white. Roof. She hands me a black headband, identical to her own.

Hold on, I say, gripping the railing with both hands. The numbness behind my eyes is still there, and I feel my knees growing weak, as if there were no building below me, only a framework of girders and air. Can you answer me a question?

Maybe one.

Has he always been like that?

What like?

With the computers, I say. Does he do that all the time?

Always. Never turn them off.

In the darkness I can barely see her face: only the eyes, shining, daring me to speak. *If I were in your place*, I say to myself, and the phrase dissolves, weightless.

Listen, I say. I'm not sure I'm ready.

She laughs. When you be sure?

Her fingers fall across my face, and I feel the elastic brushing over my hair, and then the world is black: I open my eyes and close them, no difference.

We just go for a little walk, she says. You don't worry. Only listen.

I never realized, before, the weight of the air: at every step I feel the great mass of it pressing against my face, saddled on my shoulders. I am breathing huge quantities, as if my lungs were a giant recirculation machine, and sweat is running down from my forehead and soaking the edge of the headband. Alice takes normal-sized steps and grips my hand fiercely, so I can't let go. Don't be afraid, she shouts. We still in the middle. Not near the edge.

What am I supposed to do?

Nothing, she says. Only wait. Maybe you see something.

I stare fiercely into blackness, into my own eyelids. There is the afterglow of the hallway light, and the computer screens, very faint; or am I imagining it? What is there on a roof? I wonder, and try to picture it: television antennas, heating ducts, clotheslines. Are there guardrails? I've never seen any on a Hong Kong building. She turns, and I brush something metal with my hand. Do you know where you're going? I shout.

Here, she says, and stops. I stumble into her, and she catches my shoulder. Careful, she says. We wait here.

Wait for what?

Just listen, she says. I tell to you. Look to left side: there's a big building there. Very tall white building, higher than us. Small windows.

All right. I can see that.

Right side is highway. Very bright. Many cars and trucks passing.

If I strain to listen I can hear a steady whooshing sound, and then the high whine of a motorcycle, like a mosquito passing my ear. Okay, I say. Got that.

In the middle is very dark. Small buildings. Only few lights on.

Not enough, I say.

One window close to us, she says. Two little children there. You see them?

No.

Lift your arm, she says, and I do. Put your hand up. See? They wave to you.

My God, I say. How do you do that?

She squeezes my hand.

You promise me something.

Of course. What is it?

You don't take it off, she says. No matter nothing. You promise me?

I do. I promise.

She lets go of my hand, and I hear running steps, soles skidding on concrete.

Alice! I shout, rooted to the spot; I crouch down, and balance myself with my hands. Alice! You don't—

Mama, she screams, ten feet away, and the sound carries, echoes; I can see it slanting with the wind, bright as daylight, as if a roman candle had exploded in my face. *Mama mama mama mama mama mama mama*, she sings, and I am crawling toward her on hands and knees, feeling in front of me for the edge.

She is there, Alice shouts. You see? She is in the air.

I see her. Stay where you are.

You watch, she says. I follow her.

She doesn't want you, I shout. She doesn't want you there. Let her go.

There is a long silence, and I stay where I am, the damp concrete soaking through to my knees. My ears are ringing, and the numbness has blossomed through my head; I feel faintly seasick.

Alice?

You can stand up, she says in a small voice, and I do.

You are shaking, she says. She puts her arms around me from behind and clasps my chest, pressing her head against my back. I thank you, she says.

She unties the headband.

6 February

Man waves white hands at black sky

He says arent you happy be alive

arent you

He kneels and kisses floor

THE THIRD AND FINAL CONTINENT

JHUMPA LAHIRI

I left India in 1964 with a certificate in commerce and the equivalent, in those days, of ten dollars to my name. For three weeks I sailed on the *SS Roma*, an Italian cargo vessel, in a third-class cabin next to the ship's engine, across the Arabian Sea, the Red Sea, the Mediterranean, and finally to England. I lived in north London, in Finsbury Park, in a house occupied entirely by penniless Bengali bachelors like myself, at least a dozen and sometimes more, all struggling to educate and establish ourselves abroad.

I attended lectures at LSE and worked at the university library to get by. We lived three or four to a room, shared a single, icy toilet, and took turns cooking pots of egg curry, which we ate with our hands on a table covered with newspapers. Apart from our jobs we had few responsibilities. On weekends we lounged barefoot in drawstring pajamas, drinking tea and smoking Rothmans, or set out to watch cricket at Lord's. Some weekends the house was crammed with still more Bengalis, to whom we had introduced ourselves at the greengrocer, or on the Tube, and we made yet more egg curry, and played Mukhesh on a Grundig reel-to-reel, and soaked our dirty dishes in the bathtub. Every now and then someone in the house moved out, to live with a woman whom his family back in Calcutta had determined he was to wed. In 1969, when I was thirty-six years old, my own marriage was arranged. Around the same time I was offered a full-time job in America, in the processing department of a library at MIT. The salary was generous enough to support a wife, and I was honored to be hired by a world-famous university, and so I obtained a sixth-preference green card, and prepared to travel farther still.

By now I had enough money to go by plane. I flew first to Calcutta, to attend my wedding, and a week later I flew to Boston, to begin my new job. During the flight I read *The Student Guide to North America*, a paperback volume that I'd bought before leaving London, for seven shillings six pence on Tottenham Court Road, for although I was no longer a student I was on a budget all the same. I learned that Americans drove on the right side of the road, not the left, and that they called a lift an elevator and an engaged phone busy. "The pace of life in North America is different from Britain as you will soon discover," the guidebook informed me. "Everybody feels he must get to the top. Don't expect an English cup of tea." As the plane began its descent over Boston Harbor, the pilot announced the weather and time, and that President Nixon had declared a national holiday: two American men had landed on the moon. Several passengers cheered. "God bless America!" one of them hollered. Across the aisle, I saw a woman praying.

I spent my first night at the YMCA in Central Square, Cambridge, an inexpensive accommodation recommended by my guidebook. It was walking distance from MIT, and steps from the post office and a supermarket called Purity Supreme. The room contained a cot, a desk, and a small wooden cross on one wall. A sign on the door said cooking was strictly forbidden. A bare window overlooked Massachusetts Avenue, a major thoroughfare with traffic in both directions. Car horns, shrill and prolonged, blared one after another. Flashing sirens heralded endless emergencies, and a fleet of buses rumbled past, their doors opening and closing with a powerful hiss, throughout the night. The noise was constantly distracting, at times suffocating. I felt it deep in my ribs, just as I had felt the furious drone of the engine on the SS *Roma*. But there was no ship's deck to escape to, no glittering ocean to thrill my soul, no breeze to cool my face, no one to talk to. I was too tired to pace the gloomy corridors of the YMCA in my drawstring pajamas. Instead I sat at the desk and stared out the window, at the city hall of Cambridge and a row of small shops. In the morning I reported to my job at the Dewey Library, a beige fortlike building by Memorial Drive. I also opened a bank account, rented a post office box, and bought a plastic bowl and a spoon at Woolworth's, a store whose name I recognized from London. I went to

Purity Supreme, wandering up and down the aisles, converting ounces to grams and comparing prices to things in England. In the end I bought a small carton of milk and a box of cornflakes. This was my first meal in America. I ate it at my desk. I preferred it to hamburgers or hot dogs, the only alternative I could afford in the coffee shops on Massachusetts Avenue, and, besides, at the time I had yet to consume any beef. Even the simple chore of buying milk was new to me; in London we'd had bottles delivered each morning to our door.

In a week I had adjusted, more or less. I ate cornflakes and milk, morning and night, and bought some bananas for variety, slicing them into the bowl with the edge of my spoon. In addition I bought tea bags and a flask, which the salesman in Woolworth's referred to as a thermos (a flask, he informed me, was used to store whiskey, another thing I had never consumed). For the price of one cup of tea at a coffee shop, I filled the flask with boiling water on my way to work each morning, and brewed the four cups I drank in the course of a day. I bought a larger carton of milk, and learned to leave it on the shaded part of the windowsill, as I had seen another resident at the YMCA do. To pass the time in the evenings I read the *Boston Globe* downstairs, in a spacious room with stained-glass windows. I read every article and advertisement, so that I would grow familiar with things, and when my eyes grew tired I slept. Only I did not sleep well. Each night I had to keep the window wide open; it was the only source of air in the stifling room, and the noise was intolerable. I would lie on the cot with my fingers pressed into my ears, but when I drifted off to sleep my hands fell away, and the noise of the traffic would wake me up again. Pigeon feathers drifted onto the windowsill, and one evening, when I poured milk over my cornflakes, I saw that it had soured. Nevertheless I resolved to stay at the YMCA for six weeks, until my wife's passport and green card were ready. Once she arrived I would have to rent a proper apartment, and from time to time I studied the classified section of the newspaper, or stopped in at the housing office at MIT during my lunch break, to see what was available in my price range. It was in this manner that I discovered a room for immediate occupancy, in a house on a quiet street, the listing said, for eight dollars per week. I copied the number into my guidebook and dialed from a pay telephone, sorting through the coins with which

I was still unfamiliar, smaller and lighter than shillings, heavier and brighter than *paisas*.

"Who is speaking?" a woman demanded. Her voice was bold and clamorous.

"Yes, good afternoon, madame. I am calling about the room for rent."

"Harvard or Tech?"

"I beg your pardon?"

"Are you from Harvard or Tech?"

Gathering that Tech referred to the Massachusetts Institute of Technology, I replied, "I work at Dewey Library," adding tentatively, "at Tech."

"I only rent rooms to boys from Harvard or Tech!"

"Yes, madame."

I was given an address and an appointment for seven o'clock that evening. Thirty minutes before the hour I set out, my guidebook in my pocket, my breath fresh with Listerine. I turned down a street shaded with trees, perpendicular to Massachusetts Avenue. Stray blades of grass poked between the cracks of the footpath. In spite of the heat I wore a coat and a tie, regarding the event as I would any other interview; I had never lived in the home of a person who was not Indian. The house, surrounded by a chain-link fence, was off-white with dark brown trim. Unlike the stucco row house I'd lived in in London, this house, fully detached, was covered with wooden shingles, with a tangle of forsythia bushes plastered against the front and sides. When I pressed the calling bell, the woman with whom I had spoken on the phone hollered from what seemed to be just the other side of the door, "One minute, please!"

Several minutes later the door was opened by a tiny, extremely old woman. A mass of snowy hair was arranged like a small sack on top of her head. As I stepped into the house she sat down on a wooden bench positioned at the bottom of a narrow carpeted staircase. Once she was settled on the bench, in a small pool of light, she peered up at me with undivided attention. She wore a long black skirt that spread like a stiff tent to the floor, and a starched white shirt edged with ruffles at the throat and cuffs. Her hands, folded together in her lap, had long pallid fingers, with swollen knuckles and tough yellow nails. Age had battered her features so that she almost resembled a man, with sharp, shrunken eyes and prominent creases on either side of her nose. Her lips, chapped and faded, had nearly disappeared, and her eyebrows were missing altogether. Nevertheless she looked fierce.

"Lock up!" she commanded. She shouted even though I stood only a few feet away. "Fasten the chain and firmly press that button on the knob! This is the first thing you shall do when you enter, is that clear?"

I locked the door as directed and examined the house. Next to the bench on which the woman sat was a small round table, its legs fully concealed, much like the woman's, by a skirt of lace. The table held a lamp, a transistor radio, a leather change purse with a silver clasp, and a telephone. A thick wooden cane coated with a layer of dust was propped against one side. There was a parlor to my right, lined with bookcases and filled with shabby claw-footed furniture. In the corner of the parlor I saw a grand piano with its top down, piled with papers. The piano's bench was missing; it seemed to be the one on which the woman was sitting. Somewhere in the house a clock chimed seven times.

"You're punctual!" the woman proclaimed. "I expect you shall be so with the rent!"

"I have a letter, madame." In my jacket pocket was a letter confirming my employment from MIT, which I had brought along to prove that I was indeed from Tech.

She stared at the letter, then handed it back to me carefully, gripping it with her fingers as if it were a dinner plate heaped with food instead of a sheet of paper. She did not wear glasses, and I wondered if she'd read a word of it. "The last boy was always late! Still owes me eight dollars! Harvard boys aren't what they used to be! Only Harvard and Tech in this house! How's Tech, boy?"

"It is very well."

"You checked the lock?"

"Yes, madame."

She slapped the space beside her on the bench with one hand, and told me to sit down. For a moment she was silent. Then she intoned, as if she alone possessed this knowledge:

"There is an American flag on the moon!"

"Yes, madame." Until then I had not thought very much about the moon shot. It was in the newspaper, of course, article upon article. The astronauts had landed on the shores of the Sea of Tranquillity, I had read, traveling farther than anyone in the history of civilization. For a few hours they explored the moon's surface. They gathered rocks in their pockets, described their surroundings (a magnificent desolation, according to one astronaut), spoke by phone to the president, and planted a flag in lunar soil. The voyage was hailed as man's most awesome achievement. I had seen full-page photographs in the *Globe*, of the astronauts in their inflated costumes, and read about what certain people in Boston had been doing at the exact moment the astronauts landed, on a Sunday afternoon. A man said that he was operating a swan boat with a radio pressed to his ear; a woman had been baking rolls for her grandchildren.

The woman bellowed, "A flag on the moon, boy! I heard it on the radio! Isn't that splendid?"

"Yes, madame."

But she was not satisfied with my reply. Instead she commanded, "Say 'splendid'!"

I was both baffled and somewhat insulted by the request. It reminded me of the way I was taught multiplication tables as a child, repeating after the master, sitting cross-legged, without shoes or pencils, on the floor of my one-room Tollygunge school. It also reminded me of my wedding, when I had repeated endless Sanskrit verses after the priest, verses I barely understood, which joined me to my wife. I said nothing.

"Say 'splendid'!" the woman bellowed once again.

"Splendid," I murmured. I had to repeat the word a second time at the top of my lungs, so she could hear. I am soft-spoken by nature and was especially reluctant to raise my voice to an elderly woman whom I had met only moments ago, but she did not appear to be offended. If anything the reply pleased her because her next command was:

"Go see the room!"

I rose from the bench and mounted the narrow carpeted staircase. There were five doors, two on either side of an equally narrow hallway, and one at the opposite end. Only one door was partly open. The room contained a twin bed under a sloping ceiling, a brown oval rug, a basin with an exposed pipe, and a chest of drawers. One door, painted white, led to a closet, another to a toilet and a tub. The walls were covered with gray and ivory striped paper. The window was open; net curtains stirred in the breeze. I lifted them away and inspected the view: a small back yard, with a few fruit trees and an empty clothesline. I was satisfied. From the bottom of the stairs I heard the woman demand, "What is your decision?"

When I returned to the foyer and told her, she picked up the leather change purse on the table, opened the clasp, fished about with her fingers, and produced a key on a thin wire hoop. She informed me that there was a kitchen at the back of the house, accessible through the parlor. I was welcome to use the stove as long as I left it as I found it. Sheets and towels were provided, but keeping them clean was my own responsibility. The rent was due Friday mornings on the ledge above the piano keys. "And no lady visitors!"

"I am a married man, madame." It was the first time I had announced this fact to anyone.

But she had not heard. "No lady visitors!" she insisted. She introduced herself as Mrs. Croft.

My wife's name was Mala. The marriage had been arranged by my older brother and his wife. I regarded the proposition with neither objection nor enthusiasm. It was a duty expected of me, as it was expected of every man. She was the daughter of a schoolteacher in Beleghata. I was told that she could cook, knit, embroider, sketch landscapes, and recite poems by Tagore, but these talents could not make up for the fact that she did not possess a fair complexion, and so a string of men had rejected her to her face. She was twenty-seven, an age when her parents had begun to fear that she would never marry, and so they were willing to ship their only child halfway across the world in order to save her from spinsterhood.

For five nights we shared a bed. Each of those nights, after applying cold cream and braiding her hair, which she tied up at the end with a black cotton string, she turned from me and wept; she missed her parents. Although I would be leaving the country in a few days, custom dictated that she was now a part of my household, and for the next six weeks she was to live with my brother and his wife, cooking, cleaning, serving tea and sweets to guests. I did nothing to console her. I lay on my own side of the bed, reading my guidebook by flashlight and anticipating my journey. At times I thought of the tiny room on the other side of the wall which had belonged to my mother. Now the room was practically empty; the wooden pallet on which she'd once slept was piled with trunks and old bedding. Nearly six years ago, before leaving for London, I had watched her die on that bed, had found her playing with her excrement in her final days. Before we cremated her I had cleaned each of her fingernails with a hairpin, and then, because my brother could not bear it, I had assumed the role of eldest son, and had touched the flame to her temple, to release her tormented soul to heaven.

The next morning I moved into the room in Mrs. Croft's house. When I unlocked the door I saw that she was sitting on the piano bench, on the same side as the previous evening. She wore the same black skirt, the same starched white blouse, and had her hands folded together the same way in her lap. She looked so much the same that I wondered if she'd spent the whole night on the bench. I put my suitcase upstairs, filled my flask with boiling water in the kitchen, and headed off to work. That evening when I came home from the university, she was still there.

"Sit down, boy!" She slapped the space beside her.

I perched beside her on the bench. I had a bag of groceries with me— more milk, more cornflakes, and more bananas, for my inspection of the kitchen earlier in the day had revealed no spare pots, pans, or cooking utensils. There were only two saucepans in the refrigerator, both containing some orange broth, and a copper kettle on the stove.

"Good evening, madame."

She asked me if I had checked the lock. I told her I had.

For a moment she was silent. Then suddenly she declared, with the equal measures of disbelief and delight as the night before, "There's an American flag on the moon, boy!"

"Yes, madame."

"A flag on the moon! Isn't that splendid?"

I nodded, dreading what I knew was coming. "Yes, madame."

"Say 'splendid'!"

This time I paused, looking to either side in case anyone were there to overhear me, though I knew perfectly well that the house was empty. I felt like an idiot. But it was a small enough thing to ask. "Splendid!" I cried out.

Within days it became our routine. In the mornings when I left for the library Mrs. Croft was either hidden away in her bedroom, on the other side of the staircase, or she was sitting on the bench, oblivious to my presence, listening to the news or classical music on the radio. But each evening when I returned the same thing happened: she slapped the bench, ordered me to sit down, declared that there was a flag on the moon, and declared that it was splendid. I said it was splendid, too, and then we sat in silence. As awkward as it was, and as endless as it felt to me then, the nightly encounter lasted only about ten minutes; inevitably she would drift off to sleep, her head falling abruptly toward her chest, leaving me free to retire to my room. By then, of course, there was no flag on the moon. The astronauts, I had read in the paper, had taken it down before flying back to Earth. But I did not have the heart to tell her.

Friday morning, when my first week's rent was due, I went to the piano in the parlor to place my money on the ledge. The piano keys were dull and discolored. When I pressed one, it made no sound at all. I had put eight one-dollar bills in an envelope and written Mrs. Croft's name on the front of it. I was not in the habit of leaving money unmarked and unattended. From where I stood I could see the profile of her tent-shaped skirt. She was sitting on the bench, listening to the radio. It seemed unnecessary to make her get up and walk all the way to the piano. I never saw her walking about, and assumed, from the cane always propped against the round table at her side, that she did so with difficulty. When I approached the bench she peered up at me and demanded:

"What is your business?"

"The rent, madame."

"On the ledge above the piano keys!"

"I have it here." I extended the envelope toward her, but her fingers, folded together in her lap, did not budge. I bowed slightly and lowered the envelope, so that it hovered just above her hands. After a moment she accepted, and nodded her head.

That night when I came home, she did not slap the bench, but out of habit I sat beside her as usual. She asked me if I had checked the lock, but she mentioned nothing about the flag on the moon. Instead she said:

"It was very kind of you!"

"I beg your pardon, madame?"

"Very kind of you!"

She was still holding the envelope in her hands.

On Sunday there was a knock on my door. An elderly woman introduced herself: she was Mrs. Croft's daughter, Helen. She walked into the room and looked at each of the walls as if for signs of change, glancing at the shirts that hung in the closet, the neckties draped over the doorknob, the box of cornflakes on the chest of drawers, the dirty bowl and spoon in the basin. She was short and thick-waisted, with cropped silver hair and bright pink lipstick. She wore a sleeveless summer dress, a row of white plastic beads, and spectacles on a chain that hung like a swing against her chest. The backs of her legs were mapped with dark blue veins, and her upper arms sagged like the flesh of a roasted eggplant. She told me she lived in Arlington, a town farther up Massachusetts Avenue. "I come once a week to bring Mother groceries. Has she sent you packing yet?"

"It is very well, madame."

"Some of the boys run screaming. But I think she likes you. You're the first boarder she's ever referred to as a gentleman."

"Not at all, madame."

She looked at me, noticing my bare feet (I still felt strange wearing shoes indoors, and always removed them before entering my room). "Are you new to Boston?"

"New to America, madame."

"From?" She raised her eyebrows.

"I am from Calcutta, India."

"Is that right? We had a Brazilian fellow, about a year ago. You'll find Cambridge a very international city."

I nodded, and began to wonder how long our conversation would last. But at that moment we heard Mrs. Croft's electrifying voice rising up the stairs. When we stepped into the hallway we heard her hollering:

"You are to come downstairs immediately!"

"What is it?" Helen hollered back.

"Immediately!"

I put on my shoes at once. Helen sighed.

We walked down the staircase. It was too narrow for us to descend side by side, so I followed Helen, who seemed to be in no hurry, and complained at one point that she had a bad knee. "Have you been walking without your cane?" Helen called out. "You know you're not supposed to walk without that cane." She paused, resting her hand on the banister, and looked back at me. "She slips sometimes."

For the first time Mrs. Croft seemed vulnerable. I pictured her on the floor in front of the bench, flat on her back, staring at the ceiling, her feet pointing in opposite directions. But when we reached the bottom of the staircase she was sitting there as usual, her hands folded together in her lap. Two grocery bags were at her feet. When we stood before her she did not slap the bench, or ask us to sit down. She glared.

"What is it, Mother?"

"It's improper!"

"What's improper?"

"It is improper for a lady and gentleman who are not married to one another to hold a private conversation without a chaperone!"

Helen said she was sixty-eight years old, old enough to be my mother, but Mrs. Croft insisted that Helen and I speak to each other downstairs, in the parlor. She added that it was also improper for a lady of Helen's station to reveal her age, and to wear a dress so high above the ankle.

"For your information, Mother, it's 1969. What would you do if you actually left the house one day and saw a girl in a miniskirt?"

Mrs. Croft sniffed. "I'd have her arrested."

Helen shook her head and picked up one of the grocery bags. I picked up the other one, and followed her through the parlor and into the kitchen. The bags were filled with cans of soup, which Helen opened up one by one with a few cranks of a can opener. She tossed the old soup in the saucepans into the sink, rinsed the pans under the tap, filled them with soup from the newly opened cans, and put them back in the refrigerator. "A few years ago she could still open the cans herself," Helen said. "She hates that I do it for her now. But the piano killed her hands." She put on her spectacles, glanced at the cupboards, and spotted my tea bags. "Shall we have a cup?"

I filled the kettle on the stove. "I beg your pardon, madame. The piano?"

"She used to give lessons. For forty years. It was how she raised us after my father died." Helen put her hands on her hips, staring at the open refrigerator. She reached into the back, pulled out a wrapped stick of butter, frowned, and tossed it into the garbage. "That ought to do it," she said, and put the unopened cans of soup in the cupboard. I sat at the table and watched as Helen washed the dirty dishes, tied up the garbage bag, watered a spider plant over the sink, and poured boiling water into two cups. She handed one to me without milk, the string of the tea bag trailing over the side, and sat down at the table.

"Excuse me, madame, but is it enough?"

Helen took a sip of her tea. Her lipstick left a smiling pink stain on the inside rim of the cup. "Is what enough?"

"The soup in the pans. Is it enough food for Mrs. Croft?"

"She won't eat anything else. She stopped eating solids after she turned one hundred. That was, let's see, three years ago."

I was mortified. I had assumed Mrs. Croft was in her eighties, perhaps as old as ninety. I had never known a person who had lived for over a century. That this person was a widow who lived alone mortified me further still. It was widowhood that had driven my own mother insane. My father, who worked as a clerk at the General Post Office of Calcutta, died of encephalitis when I was sixteen. My mother refused to adjust to life without him; instead she sank deeper into a world of darkness from which neither I, nor my brother, nor concerned relatives, nor psychiatric clinics on Rashbihari Avenue could save her. What pained me most was to see her so unguarded, to hear her burp after meals or expel gas in front of company without the slightest embarrassment. After my father's death my brother abandoned his schooling and began to work in the jute mill he would eventually manage, in order to keep the household running. And so it was my job to sit by my mother's feet and study for my exams as she counted and recounted the bracelets on her arm as if they were the beads of an abacus. We tried to keep an eye on her. Once she had wandered half naked to the tram depot before we were able to bring her inside again.

"I am happy to warm Mrs. Croft's soup in the evenings," I suggested, removing the tea bag from my cup and squeezing out the liquor. "It is no trouble."

Helen looked at her watch, stood up, and poured the rest of her tea into the sink. "I wouldn't if I were you. That's the sort of thing that would kill her altogether."

That evening, when Helen had gone back to Arlington and Mrs. Croft and I were alone again, I began to worry. Now that I knew how very old she was, I worried that something would happen to her in the middle of the night, or when I was out during the day. As vigorous as her voice was, and imperious as she seemed, I knew that even a scratch or a cough could kill a person that old; each day she lived, I knew, was something of a miracle.

Although Helen had seemed friendly enough, a small part of me worried that she might accuse me of negligence if anything were to happen. Helen didn't seem worried. She came and went, bringing soup for Mrs. Croft, one Sunday after the next.

In this manner the six weeks of that summer passed. I came home each evening, after my hours at the library, and spent a few minutes on the piano bench with Mrs. Croft. I gave her a bit of my company, and assured her that I had checked the lock, and told her that the flag on the moon was splendid. Some evenings I sat beside her long after she had drifted off to sleep, still in awe of how many years she had spent on this earth. At times I tried to picture the world she had been born into, in 1866—a world, I imagined, filled with women in long black skirts, and chaste conversations in the parlor. Now, when I looked at her hands with their swollen knuckles folded together in her lap, I imagined them smooth and slim, striking the piano keys. At times I came downstairs before going to sleep, to make sure she was sitting upright on the bench, or was safe in her bedroom. On Fridays I made sure to put the rent in her hands. There was nothing I could do for her beyond these simple gestures. I was not her son, and apart from those eight dollars, I owed her nothing.

At the end of August, Mala's passport and green card were ready. I received a telegram with her flight information; my brother's house in Calcutta had no telephone. Around that time I also received a letter from her, written only a few days after we had parted. There was no salutation; addressing me by name would have assumed an intimacy we had not yet discovered. It contained only a few lines. "I write in English in preparation for the journey. Here I am very much lonely. Is it very cold there. Is there snow. Yours, Mala."

I was not touched by her words. We had spent only a handful of days in each other's company. And yet we were bound together; for six weeks she had worn an iron bangle on her wrist, and applied vermilion powder to the part in her hair, to signify to the world that she was a bride. In those six weeks I regarded her arrival as I would the arrival of a coming month, or season—something inevitable, but meaningless at the time. So little did I know her that, while details of her face sometimes rose to my memory, I could not conjure up the whole of it.

A few days after receiving the letter, as I was walking to work in the morning, I saw an Indian woman on the other side of Massachusetts Avenue, wearing a sari with its free end nearly dragging on the footpath, and pushing a child in a stroller. An American woman with a small black dog on a leash was walking to one side of her. Suddenly the dog began barking. From the other side of the street I watched as the Indian woman, startled, stopped in her path, at which point the dog leapt up and seized the end of the sari between its teeth. The American woman scolded the dog, appeared to apologize, and walked quickly away, leaving the Indian woman to fix her sari in the middle of the footpath, and quiet her crying child. She did not see me standing there, and eventually she continued on her way. Such a mishap, I realized that morning, would soon be my concern. It was my duty to take care of Mala, to welcome her and protect her. I would have to buy her her first pair of snow boots, her first winter coat. I would have to tell her which streets to avoid, which way the traffic came, tell her to wear her sari so that the free end did not drag on the footpath. A five-mile separation from her parents, I recalled with some irritation, had caused her to weep.

Unlike Mala, I was used to it all by then: used to cornflakes and milk, used to Helen's visits, used to sitting on the bench with Mrs. Croft. The only thing I was not used to was Mala. Nevertheless I did what I had to do. I went to the housing office at MIT and found a furnished apartment a few blocks away, with a double bed and a private kitchen and bath, for forty dollars a week. One last Friday I handed Mrs. Croft eight one-dollar bills in an envelope, brought my suitcase downstairs, and informed her that I was moving. She put my key into her change purse. The last thing she asked me to do was hand her the cane propped against the table, so that she could walk to the door and lock it behind me. "Good-bye, then," she said, and retreated back into the house. I did not expect any display of emotion, but I was disappointed all the same. I was only a boarder, a man who paid her a bit of money and passed in and out of her home for six weeks. Compared to a century, it was no time at all.

At the airport I recognized Mala immediately. The free end of her sari did not drag on the floor, but was draped in a sign of bridal modesty over her head, just as it had draped my mother until the day my father died.

Her thin brown arms were stacked with gold bracelets, a small red circle was painted on her forehead, and the edges of her feet were tinted with a decorative red dye. I did not embrace her, or kiss her, or take her hand. Instead I asked her, speaking Bengali for the first time in America, if she was hungry.

She hesitated, then nodded yes.

I told her I had prepared some egg curry at home. "What did they give you to eat on the plane?"

"I didn't eat."

"All the way from Calcutta?"

"The menu said oxtail soup."

"But surely there were other items."

"The thought of eating an ox's tail made me lose my appetite."

When we arrived home, Mala opened up one of her suitcases, and presented me with two pullover sweaters, both made with bright blue wool, which she had knitted in the course of our separation, one with a V neck, the other covered with cables. I tried them on; both were tight under the arms. She had also brought me two new pairs of drawstring pajamas, a letter from my brother, and a packet of loose Darjeeling tea. I had no present for her apart from the egg curry. We sat at a bare table, each of us staring at our plates. We ate with our hands, another thing I had not yet done in America.

"The house is nice," she said. "Also the egg curry." With her left hand she held the end of her sari to her chest, so it would not slip off her head.

"I don't know many recipes."

She nodded, peeling the skin off each of her potatoes before eating them. At one point the sari slipped to her shoulders. She readjusted it at once.

"There is no need to cover your head," I said. "I don't mind. It doesn't matter here."

She kept it covered anyway.

I waited to get used to her, to her presence at my side, at my table and in my bed, but a week later we were still strangers. I still was not used to coming home to an apartment that smelled of steamed rice, and finding that the basin in the bathroom was always wiped clean, our two toothbrushes lying side by side, a cake of Pears soap from India resting in the soap dish. I was not used to the fragrance of the coconut oil she rubbed every other night into her scalp, or the delicate sound her bracelets made as she moved about the apartment. In the mornings she was always awake before I was. The first morning when I came into the kitchen she had heated up the left-overs and set a plate with a spoonful of salt on its edge on the table, assuming I would eat rice for breakfast, as most Bengali husbands did. I told her cereal would do, and the next morning when I came into the kitchen she had already poured the cornflakes into my bowl. One morning she walked with me down Massachusetts Avenue to MIT, where I gave her a short tour of the campus. On the way we stopped at a hardware store and I made a copy of the key, so that she could let herself into the apartment. The next morning before I left for work she asked me for a few dollars. I parted with them reluctantly, but I knew that this, too, was now normal. When I came home from work there was a potato peeler in the kitchen drawer, and a tablecloth on the table, and chicken curry made with fresh garlic and ginger on the stove. We did not have a television in those days. After dinner I read the newspaper, while Mala sat at the kitchen table, working on a cardigan for herself with more of the bright blue wool, or writing letters home.

At the end of our first week, on Friday, I suggested going out. Mala set down her knitting and disappeared into the bathroom. When she emerged I regretted the suggestion; she had put on a clean silk sari and extra bracelets, and coiled her hair with a flattering side part on top of her head. She was prepared as if for a party, or at the very least for the cinema, but I had no such destination in mind. The evening air was balmy. We walked several blocks down Massachusetts Avenue, looking into the windows of restaurants and shops. Then, without thinking, I led her down the quiet street where for so many nights I had walked alone.

"This is where I lived before you came," I said, stopping at Mrs. Croft's chain-link fence.

"In such a big house?"

"I had a small room upstairs. At the back."

"Who else lives there?"

"A very old woman."

"With her family?"

"Alone."

"But who takes care of her?"

I opened the gate. "For the most part she takes care of herself."

I wondered if Mrs. Croft would remember me; I wondered if she had a new boarder to sit with her on the bench each evening. When I pressed the bell I expected the same long wait as that day of our first meeting, when I did not have a key. But this time the door was opened almost immediately, by Helen. Mrs. Croft was not sitting on the bench. The bench was gone.

"Hello there," Helen said, smiling with her bright pink lips at Mala. "Mother's in the parlor. Will you be visiting awhile?"

"As you wish, madame."

"Then I think I'll run to the store, if you don't mind. She had a little accident. We can't leave her alone these days, not even for a minute."

I locked the door after Helen and walked into the parlor. Mrs. Croft was lying flat on her back, her head on a peach-colored cushion, a thin white quilt spread over her body. Her hands were folded together on top of her chest. When she saw me she pointed at the sofa, and told me to sit down. I took my place as directed, but Mala wandered over to the piano and sat on the bench, which was now positioned where it belonged.

"I broke my hip!" Mrs. Croft announced, as if no time had passed.

"Oh dear, madame."

"I fell off the bench!"

"I am so sorry, madame."

"It was the middle of the night! Do you know what I did, boy?"

I shook my head.

"I called the police!"

She stared up at the ceiling and grinned sedately, exposing a crowded row of long gray teeth. Not one was missing. "What do you say to that, boy?"

As stunned as I was, I knew what I had to say. With no hesitation at all, I cried out, "Splendid!"

Mala laughed then. Her voice was full of kindness, her eyes bright with amusement. I had never heard her laugh before, and it was loud enough so that Mrs. Croft had heard, too. She turned to Mala and glared.

"Who is she, boy?"

"She is my wife, madame."

Mrs. Croft pressed her head at an angle against the cushion to get a better look. "Can you play the piano?"

"No, madame," Mala replied.

"Then stand up!"

Mala rose to her feet, adjusting the end of her sari over her head and holding it to her chest, and, for the first time since her arrival, I felt sympathy. I remembered my first days in London, learning how to take the Tube to Russell Square, riding an escalator for the first time, being unable to understand that when the man cried "piper" it meant "paper," being unable to decipher, for a whole year, that the conductor said "mind the gap" as the train pulled away from each station. Like me, Mala had traveled far from home, not knowing where she was going, or what she would find, for no reason other than to be my wife. As strange as it seemed, I knew in my heart that one day her death would affect me, and stranger still, that mine would affect her. I wanted somehow to explain this to Mrs. Croft, who was still scrutinizing Mala from top to toe with what seemed to be placid disdain. I wondered if Mrs. Croft had ever seen a woman in a sari, with a dot painted on her forehead and bracelets stacked on her wrists. I wondered what she would object to. I wondered if she could see the red dye still vivid on Mala's feet, all but obscured by the bottom edge of her sari. At last Mrs. Croft declared, with the equal measures of disbelief and delight I knew well:

"She is a perfect lady!"

Now it was I who laughed. I did so quietly, and Mrs. Croft did not hear me. But Mala had heard, and, for the first time, we looked at each other and smiled.

I like to think of that moment in Mrs. Croft's parlor as the moment when the distance between Mala and me began to lessen. Although we were not yet fully in love, I like to think of the months that followed as a honeymoon of sorts. Together we explored the city and met other Bengalis, some of whom are still friends today. We discovered that a man named Bill sold fresh fish on Prospect Street, and that a shop in Harvard Square called Cardullo's sold bay leaves and cloves. In the evenings we walked to the Charles River to watch sailboats drift across the water, or had ice cream cones in Harvard Yard. We bought an Instamatic camera with which to document our life together, and I took pictures of her posing in front of the Prudential building, so that she could send them to her parents. At night we kissed, shy at first but quickly bold, and discovered pleasure and solace in each other's arms. I told her about my voyage on the SS *Roma*, and about Finsbury Park and the YMCA, and my evenings on the bench with Mrs. Croft. When I told her stories about my mother, she wept. It was Mala who consoled me when, reading the *Globe* one evening, I came across Mrs. Croft's obituary. I had not thought of her in several months—by then those six weeks of the summer were already a remote interlude in my past—but when I learned of her death I was stricken, so much so that when Mala looked up from her knitting she found me staring at the wall, the newspaper neglected in my lap, unable to speak. Mrs. Croft's was the first death I mourned in America, for hers was the first life I had admired; she had left this world at last, ancient and alone, never to return.

As for me, I have not strayed much farther. Mala and I live in a town about twenty miles from Boston, on a tree-lined street much like Mrs. Croft's, in a house we own, with a garden that saves us from buying tomatoes in summer, and room for guests. We are American citizens now, so that we can collect social security when it is time. Though we visit Calcutta every few years, and bring back more drawstring pajamas and Darjeeling tea, we have decided to grow old here. I work in a small college library. We have a son who attends Harvard University. Mala no longer drapes the end of her sari over her head, or weeps at night for her parents, but occasionally she weeps for our son. So we drive to Cambridge to visit him, or bring him home for a weekend, so that he can eat rice with us with his hands, and speak in Bengali, things we sometimes worry he will no longer do after we die.

Whenever we make that drive, I always make it a point to take Massachusetts Avenue, in spite of the traffic. I barely recognize the buildings now, but each time I am there I return instantly to those six weeks as if they were only the other day, and I slow down and point to Mrs. Croft's street, saying to my son, here was my first home in America, where I lived with a woman who was 103. "Remember?" Mala says, and smiles, amazed, as I am, that there was ever a time that we were strangers. My son always expresses his astonishment, not at Mrs. Croft's age, but at how little I paid in rent, a fact nearly as inconceivable to him as a flag on the moon was to a woman born in 1866. In my son's eyes I see the ambition that had first hurled me across the world. In a few years he will graduate and pave his way, alone and unprotected. But I remind myself that he has a father who is still living, a mother who is happy and strong. Whenever he is discouraged, I tell him that if I can survive on three continents, then there is no obstacle he cannot conquer. While the astronauts, heroes forever, spent mere hours on the moon, I have remained in this new world for nearly thirty years. I know that my achievement is quite ordinary. I am not the only man to seek his fortune far from home, and certainly I am not the first. Still, there are times I am bewildered by each mile I have traveled, each meal I have eaten, each person I have known, each room in which I have slept. As ordinary as it all appears, there are times when it is beyond my imagination.

SUNSET

Perhaps the most frightening concept we face is that we will grow older—with all the requisite wrinkles, weakness, and forgetfulness—and eventually die. The only way out is the even less appealing alternative of a premature death. On the bright side, no one is exempt, not even the rich. In our early years, most of us don't really believe our days will wane, but whether it creeps up on us gradually or startles us with a look in the mirror, the truth will come. And, whether we accept it gracefully or rage against the dying light, our time will arrive.

John Cheever's "The Swimmer" presents us with a man in the middle of life about to cross over to the older side. At the story's outset, he believes he's in the full bloom of youth, immortal as a Greek god, but he can't flee, or swim away, from the truth forever. In a single day, time seems to pass from cheerful summer to the chill of autumn and a man's life is laid bare as tree branches in winter.

When a loved one dies, the mourners often experience a kaleidoscope of emotions. The young woman in Kate Chopin's "The Story of an Hour" is shocked to learn of her husband's sudden death. Her subsequent feelings, however, are even more alarming.

In Thom Jones's "I Want to Live!" a woman slugs it out with cancer, enduring round after round of treatment and physical deterioration. This story tells it like it is, no punches pulled, taking you right inside the woman's battle-racked body and delirious thoughts. Though the woman's no saint, she's a good-hearted fighter with a wicked sense of humor and you won't be able to tear away from her side or resist rooting for her until . . . whatever happens.

If you could drink a potion that would transform you into your younger self, would you do it? And if you did, would you truly do anything better or wiser? These are the questions posed in Nathaniel Hawthorne's "Dr. Heidegger's Experiment," in which four old folks are offered water from the Fountain of Youth by their mysterious doctor friend. This story also takes us back in literary time to the birth of the short story; it is one of the very first.

THE SWIMMER

JOHN CHEEVER

It was one of those midsummer Sundays when everyone sits around saying, "I *drank* too much last night." You might have heard it whispered by the parishioners leaving church, heard it from the lips of the priest himself, struggling with his cassock in the *vestiarium*, heard it from the golf links and the tennis courts, heard it from the wildlife preserve where the leader of the Audubon group was suffering from a terrible hangover. "I *drank* too much," said Donald Westerhazy. "We all *drank* too much," said Lucinda Merrill. "It must have been the wine," said Helen Westerhazy. "I *drank* too much of that claret."

This was at the edge of the Westerhazys' pool. The pool, fed by an artesian well with a high iron content, was a pale shade of green. It was a fine day. In the west there was a massive stand of cumulus cloud so like a city seen from a distance—from the bow of an approaching ship—that it might have had a name. Lisbon. Hackensack. The sun was hot. Neddy Merrill sat by the green water, one hand in it, one around a glass of gin. He was a slender man—he seemed to have the especial slenderness of youth—and while he was far from young he had slid down his banister that morning and given the bronze backside of Aphrodite on the hall table a smack, as he jogged toward the smell of coffee in his dining room. He might have been compared to a summer's day, particularly the last hours of one, and while he lacked a tennis racket or a sail bag the impression was definitely one of youth, sport, and clement weather. He had been swimming and now he was breathing deeply, stertorously as if he could gulp into his lungs the components of that moment, the heat of the sun, the intenseness of his pleasure. It all seemed to flow into his chest. His own house stood in Bullet Park, eight miles to the south, where his four beautiful daughters would have had their lunch and might be playing tennis. Then it occurred to him that by taking a dogleg to the southwest he could reach his home by water.

His life was not confining and the delight he took in this observation could not be explained by its suggestion of escape. He seemed to see, with a cartographer's eye, that string of swimming pools, that quasi-subterranean stream that curved across the county. He had made a discovery, a contribution to modern geography; he would name the stream Lucinda after his wife. He was not a practical joker nor was he a fool but he was determinedly original and had a vague and modest idea of himself as a legendary figure. The day was beautiful and it seemed to him that a long swim might enlarge and celebrate its beauty.

He took off a sweater that was hung over his shoulders and dove in. He had an inexplicable contempt for men who did not hurl themselves into pools. He swam a choppy crawl, breathing either with every stroke or every fourth stroke and counting somewhere well in the back of his mind the one-two one-two of a flutter kick. It was not a serviceable stroke for long distances but the domestication of swimming had saddled the sport with some customs and in his part of the world a crawl was customary. To be embraced and sustained by the light green water was less a pleasure, it seemed, than the resumption of a natural condition, and he would have liked to swim without trunks, but this was not possible, considering his project. He hoisted himself up on the far curb—he never used the ladder—and started across the lawn. When Lucinda asked where he was going he said he was going to swim home.

The only maps and charts he had to go by were remembered or imaginary but these were clear enough. First there were the Grahams, the Hammers, the Lears, the Howlands, and the Crosscups. He would cross Ditmar Street to the Bunkers and come, after a short portage, to the Levys, the Welchers, and the public pool in Lancaster. Then there were the Hallorans, the Sachses, the Biswangers, Shirley Adams, the Gilmartins, and the Clydes. The day was lovely, and that he lived in a world so generously supplied with water seemed like a clemency, a beneficence. His heart was high and he ran across the grass. Making his way home by an uncommon route gave him the feeling that he was a pilgrim, an explorer, a man with a destiny, and he knew that he would find friends all along the way; friends would line the banks of the Lucinda River.

He went through a hedge that separated the Westerhazys' land from the Grahams', walked under some flowering apple trees, passed the shed that housed their pump and filter, and came out at the Grahams' pool. "Why, Neddy," Mrs. Graham said, "what a marvelous surprise. I've been trying to get you on the phone all morning. Here, let me get you a drink." He saw then, like any explorer, that the hospitable customs and traditions of the natives would have to be handled with diplomacy if he was ever going to reach his destination. He did not want to mystify or seem rude to the Grahams nor did he have the time to linger there. He swam the length of their pool and joined them in the sun and was rescued, a few minutes later, by the arrival of two carloads of friends from Connecticut. During the uproarious reunions he was able to slip away. He went down by the front of the Grahams' house, stepped over a thorny hedge, and crossed a vacant lot to the Hammers'. Mrs. Hammer, looking up from her roses, saw him swim by although she wasn't quite sure who it was. The Lears heard him splashing past the open windows of their living room. The Howlands and the Crosscups were away. After leaving the Howlands' he crossed Ditmar Street and started for the Bunkers', where he could hear, even at that distance, the noise of a party.

The water refracted the sound of voices and laughter and seemed to suspend it in midair. The Bunkers' pool was on a rise and he climbed some stairs to a terrace where twenty-five or thirty men and women were drinking. The only person in the water was Rusty Towers, who floated there on a rubber raft. Oh, how bonny and lush were the banks of the Lucinda River! Prosperous men and women gathered by the sapphire-colored waters while caterer's men in white coats passed them cold gin. Overhead a red de Haviland trainer was circling around and around and around in the sky with something like the glee of a child in a swing. Ned felt a passing affection for the scene, a tenderness for the gathering, as if it was something he might touch. In the distance he heard thunder. As soon as Enid Bunker saw him she began to scream: "Oh, look who's here! What a marvelous surprise! When Lucinda said that you couldn't come I thought I'd *die*." She made her way to him through the crowd, and when they had finished kissing she led him to the bar, a progress that was slowed by the fact that he stopped to kiss eight or ten other women and shake the hands of as many men. A smiling bartender he had seen at a hundred parties gave him a gin and tonic and he stood by the bar for a moment, anxious not to get stuck in any conversation that would delay his voyage. When he seemed about to be surrounded he dove in and swam close to the side to avoid colliding with Rusty's raft. At the far end of the pool he bypassed the Tomlinsons with a broad smile and jogged up the garden path. The gravel cut his feet but this was the only unpleasantness. The party was confined to the pool, and as he went toward the house he heard the brilliant, watery sound of voices fade, heard the noise of a radio from the Bunkers' kitchen, where someone was listening to a ball game. Sunday afternoon. He made his way through the parked cars and down the grassy border of their driveway to Alewives Lane. He did not want to be seen on the road in his bathing trunks but there was no traffic and he made the short distance to the Levys' driveway, marked with a PRIVATE PROPERTY sign and a green tube for *The New York Times*. All the doors and windows of the big house were open but there were no signs of life; not even a dog barked. He went around the side of the house to the pool and saw that the Levys had only recently left. Glasses and bottles and dishes of nuts were on a table at the deep end, where there was a bathhouse or gazebo, hung with Japanese lanterns. After swimming the pool he got himself a glass and poured a drink. It was his fourth or fifth drink and he had swum nearly half the length of the Lucinda River. He felt tired, clean, and pleased at that moment to be alone; pleased with everything.

It would storm. The stand of cumulus cloud—that city—had risen and darkened, and while he sat there he heard the percussiveness of thunder again. The de Haviland trainer was still circling overhead and it seemed to Ned that he could almost hear the pilot laugh with pleasure in the afternoon; but when there was another peal of thunder he took off for home. A train whistle blew and he wondered what time it had gotten to be. Four? Five? He thought of the provincial station at that hour, where a waiter, his tuxedo concealed by a raincoat, a dwarf with some flowers wrapped in newspaper, and a woman who had been crying would be waiting for the local. It was suddenly growing dark; it was that moment when the pin-headed birds seem to organize their song into some acute and knowledgeable recognition of the storm's approach. Then there was a fine noise of rushing water from the crown of an oak at his back, as if a spigot there had been turned. Then the noise of fountains came from the crowns of all the tall trees. Why did he love storms, what was the meaning of his excitement when the door sprang open and the rain wind fled rudely up the stairs, why had the simple task of shutting the windows of an old house seemed fitting and urgent, why did the first watery notes of a storm wind have for him the unmistakable sound of good news, cheer, glad tidings? Then there was an explosion, a smell of cordite, and rain lashed the Japanese lanterns that Mrs. Levy had bought in Kyoto the year before last, or was it the year before that?

He stayed in the Levys' gazebo until the storm had passed. The rain had cooled the air and he shivered. The force of the wind had stripped a maple of its red and yellow leaves and scattered them over the grass and the water. Since it was midsummer the tree must be blighted, and yet he felt a peculiar sadness at this sign of autumn. He braced his shoulders, emptied his glass, and started for the Welchers' pool. This meant crossing the Lindley's riding ring and he was surprised to find it overgrown with grass and all the jumps dismantled. He wondered if the Lindleys had sold their horses or gone away for the summer and put them out to board. He seemed to remember having heard something about the Lindleys and their horses but the memory was unclear. On he went, barefoot through the wet grass, to the Welchers', where he found their pool was dry.

This breach in his chain of water disappointed him absurdly, and he felt like some explorer who seeks a torrential headwater and finds a dead stream. He was disappointed and mystified. It was common enough to go away for the summer but no one ever drained his pool. The Welchers had definitely gone away. The pool furniture was folded, stacked, and covered with a tarpaulin. The bathhouse was locked. All the windows of the house were shut, and when he went around to the driveway in front he saw a FOR SALE sign nailed to a tree. When had he last heard from the Welchers— when, that is, had he and Lucinda last regretted an invitation to dine with them? It seemed only a week or so ago. Was his memory failing or had he so disciplined it in the repression of unpleasant facts that he had damaged his sense of the truth? Then in the distance he heard the sound of a tennis game. This cheered him, cleared away all his apprehensions and let him regard the overcast sky and the cold air with indifference. This was the day that Neddy Merrill swam across the county. That was the day! He started off then for his most difficult portage.

Had you gone for a Sunday afternoon ride that day you might have seen him, close to naked, standing on the shoulders of Route 424, waiting for a chance to cross. You might have wondered if he was the victim of foul play, had his car broken down, or was he merely a fool. Standing barefoot in the deposits of the highway—beer cans, rags, and blowout patches—exposed to all kinds of ridicule, he seemed pitiful. He had known when he started that this was a part of his journey—it had been on his maps—but confronted with the lines of traffic, worming through the summery light, he found himself unprepared. He was laughed at, jeered at, a beer can was thrown at him, and he had no dignity or humor to bring to the situation. He could have gone back, back to the Westerhazys', where Lucinda would still be sitting in the sun. He had signed nothing, vowed nothing, pledged nothing, not even to himself. Why, believing as he did, that all human obduracy was susceptible to common sense, was he unable to turn back? Why was he determined to complete his journey even if it meant putting his life in danger? At what point had this prank, this joke, this piece of horseplay become serious? He could not go back, he could not even recall with any clearness the green water at the Westerhazys', the sense of inhaling the day's components, the friendly and relaxed voices saying that they had *drunk* too much. In the space of an hour, more or less, he had covered a distance that made his return impossible.

An old man, tooling down the highway at fifteen miles an hour, let him get to the middle of the road, where there was a grass divider. Here he was exposed to the ridicule of the northbound traffic, but after ten or fifteen minutes he was able to cross. From here he had only a short walk to the Recreation Center at the edge of the village of Lancaster, where there were some handball courts and a public pool.

The effect of the water on voices, the illusion of brilliance and suspense, was the same here as it had been at the Bunkers' but the sounds here were louder, harsher, and more shrill, and as soon as he entered the crowded enclosure he was confronted with regimentation. "ALL SWIMMERS MUST TAKE A SHOWER BEFORE USING THE POOL. ALL SWIMMERS MUST USE THE FOOTBATH. ALL SWIMMERS MUST WEAR THEIR IDENTIFICATION DISKS." He took a shower, washed his feet in a cloudy and bitter solution, and made his way to the edge of the water. It stank of chlorine and looked to him like a sink. A pair of lifeguards in a pair of towers blew police whistles at what seemed to be regular intervals and abused the swimmers through a public address system. Neddy remembered the sapphire water at the Bunkers' with longing and thought that he might contaminate himself—damage his own prosperousness and charm—by swimming in this murk, but he reminded himself that he was an explorer, a pilgrim, and that this was merely a stagnant bend in the Lucinda River. He dove, scowling with distaste, into the chlorine and had to swim with his head above water to avoid collisions, but even so he was bumped into, splashed, and jostled. When he got to the shallow end both lifeguards were shouting at him: "Hey, you, you without the identification disk, get outa the water." He did, but they had no way of pursuing him and he went through the reek of suntan oil and chlorine out through the hurricane fence and passed the handball courts. By crossing the road he entered the wooded part of the Halloran estate. The woods were not cleared and the footing was treacherous and difficult until he reached the lawn and the clipped beech hedge that encircled their pool.

The Hallorans were friends, an elderly couple of enormous wealth who seemed to bask in the suspicion that they might be Communists. They were zealous reformers but they were not Communists, and yet when they were accused, as they sometimes were, of subversion, it seemed to gratify and excite them. Their beech hedge was yellow and he guessed this had been blighted like the Levys' maple. He called hullo, hullo, to warn the Hallorans of his approach, to palliate his invasion of their privacy. The Hallorans, for reasons that had never been explained to him, did not wear bathing suits. No explanations were in order, really. Their nakedness was a detail in their uncompromising zeal for reform and he stepped politely out of his trunks before he went through the opening in the hedge.

Mrs. Halloran, a stout woman with white hair and a serene face, was reading the *Times*. Mr. Halloran was taking beech leaves out of the water with a scoop. They seemed not surprised or displeased to see him. Their pool was perhaps the oldest in the country, a fieldstone rectangle, fed by a brook. It had no filter or pump and its waters were the opaque gold of the stream.

"I'm swimming across the county," Ned said.

"Why, I didn't know one could," exclaimed Mrs. Halloran.

"Well, I've made it from the Westerhazys'," Ned said. "That must be about four miles."

He left his trunks at the deep end, walked to the shallow end, and swam this stretch. As he was pulling himself out of the water he heard Mrs. Halloran say, "We've been *terribly* sorry to hear about all your misfortunes, Neddy."

"My misfortunes?" Ned asked. "I don't know what you mean."

"Why, we heard that you'd sold the house and that your poor children . . ."

"I don't recall having sold the house," Ned said, "and the girls are at home."

"Yes," Mrs. Halloran sighed. "Yes . . ." Her voice filled the air with an unseasonable melancholy and Ned spoke briskly. "Thank you for the swim."

"Well, have a nice trip," said Mrs. Halloran.

Beyond the hedge he pulled on his trunks and fastened them. They were loose and he wondered if, during the space of an afternoon, he could have lost some weight. He was cold and he was tired and the naked Hallorans and their dark water had depressed him. The swim was too much for his strength but how could he have guessed this, sliding down the banister that morning and sitting in the Westerhazys' sun? His arms were lame. His legs felt rubbery and ached at the joints. The worst of it was the cold in his bones and the feeling that he might never be warm again. Leaves were falling down around him and he smelled wood smoke on the wind. Who would be burning wood at this time of year?

He needed a drink. Whiskey would warm him, pick him up, carry him through the last of his journey, refresh his feeling that it was original and valorous to swim across the county. Channel swimmers took brandy. He needed a stimulant. He crossed the lawn in front of the Hallorans' house and went down a little path to where they had built a house for their only daughter, Helen, and her husband, Eric Sachs. The Sachses' pool was small and he found Helen and her husband there.

"Oh, *Neddy*," Helen said. "Did you lunch at Mother's?"

"Not *really*," Ned said. "I *did* stop to see your parents." This seemed to be explanation enough. "I'm terribly sorry to break in on you like this but I've taken a chill and I wonder if you'd give me a drink."

"Why, I'd *love* to," Helen said, "but there hasn't been anything in this house to drink since Eric's operation. That was three years ago."

Was he losing his memory, had his gift for concealing painful facts let him forget that he had sold his house, that his children were in trouble, and that his friend had been ill? His eyes slipped from Eric's face to his abdomen, where he saw three pale, sutured scars, two of them at least a foot long. Gone was his navel, and what, Neddy thought, would the roving hand, bed-checking one's gifts at 3 A.M., make of a belly with no navel, no link to birth, this breach in the succession?

"I'm sure you can get a drink at the Biswangers'," Helen said. "They're having an enormous do. You can hear it from here. Listen!"

She raised her head and from across the road, the lawns, the gardens, the woods, the fields, he heard again the brilliant noise of voices over water. "Well, I'll get wet," he said, still feeling that he had no freedom of choice about his means of travel. He dove into the Sachses' cold water and, gasping, close to drowning, made his way from one end of the pool to the other. "Lucinda and I want *terribly* to see you," he said over his shoulder, his face set toward the Biswangers'. "We're sorry it's been so long and we'll call you *very* soon."

He crossed some fields to the Biswangers' and the sounds of revelry there. They would be honored to give him a drink, they would be happy to give him a drink. The Biswangers invited him and Lucinda for dinner four times a year, six weeks in advance. They were always rebuffed and yet they continued to send out their invitations, unwilling to comprehend the rigid and undemocratic realities of their society. They were the sort of people who discussed the price of things at cocktails, exchanged market tips during dinner, and after dinner told dirty stories to mixed company. They did not belong to Neddy's set—they were not even on Lucinda's Christmas-card list. He went toward their pool with feelings of indifference, charity, and some unease, since it seemed to be getting dark and these were the longest days of the year. The party when he joined it was noisy and large. Grace Biswanger was the kind of hostess who asked the optometrist, the veterinarian, the real-estate dealer, and the dentist. No one was swimming and the twilight, reflected on the water of the pool, had a wintry gleam. There was a bar and he started for this. When Grace Biswanger saw him she came toward him, not affectionately as he had every right to expect, but bellicosely.

"Why, this party has everything," she said loudly, "including a gate crasher."

She could not deal him a social blow—there was no question about this and he did not flinch. "As a gate crasher," he asked politely, "do I rate a drink?"

"Suit yourself," she said. "You don't seem to pay much attention to invitations."

She turned her back on him and joined some guests, and he went to the bar and ordered a whiskey. The bartender served him but he served him rudely. His was a world in which the caterer's men kept the social score, and to be rebuffed by a part-time barkeep meant that he had suffered some loss of social esteem. Or perhaps the man was new and uninformed. Then he heard Grace at his back say: "They went for broke overnight— nothing but income—and he showed up drunk one Sunday and asked us to loan him five thousand dollars. . . ." She was always talking about money. It was worse than eating your peas off a knife. He dove into the pool, swam its length and went away.

The next pool on his list, the last but two, belonged to his old mistress, Shirley Adams. If he had suffered any injuries at the Biswangers' they would be cured here. Love—sexual roughhouse in fact—was the supreme elixir, the pain killer, the brightly colored pill that would put the spring back into his step, the joy of life in his heart. They had had an affair last week, last month, last year. He couldn't remember. It was he who had broken it off, his was the upper hand, and he stepped through the gate of the wall that surrounded her pool with nothing so considered as self-confidence. It seemed in a way to be his pool, as the lover, particularly the illicit lover, enjoys the possessions of his mistress with an authority unknown to holy matrimony. She was there, her hair the color of brass, but her figure, at the edge of the lighted, cerulean water, excited in him no profound memories. It had been, he thought, a lighthearted affair, although she had wept when he broke it off. She seemed confused to see him and he wondered if she was still wounded. Would she, God forbid, weep again?

"What do you want?" she asked.

"I'm swimming across the county."

"Good Christ. Will you ever grow up?"

"What's the matter?"

"If you've come here for money," she said, "I won't give you another cent."

"You could give me a drink."

"I could but I won't. I'm not alone."

"Well, I'm on my way."

He dove in and swam the pool, but when he tried to haul himself up onto the curb he found that the strength in his arms and shoulders had gone, and he paddled to the ladder and climbed out. Looking over his shoulder he saw, in the lighted bathhouse, a young man. Going out onto the dark lawn he smelled chrysanthemums or marigolds—some stubborn autumnal fragrance—on the night air, strong as gas. Looking overhead he saw that the stars had come out, but why should he seem to see Andromeda, Cepheus, and Cassiopeia? What had become of the constellations of midsummer? He began to cry.

It was probably the first time in his adult life that he had ever cried, certainly the first time in his life that he had ever felt so miserable, cold, tired, and bewildered. He could not understand the rudeness of the caterer's barkeep or the rudeness of a mistress who had come to him on her knees and showered his trousers with tears. He had swum too long, he had been immersed too long, and his nose and his throat were sore from the water. What he needed then was a drink, some company, and some clean, dry clothes, and while he could have cut directly across the road to his home he went on to the Gilmartins' pool. Here, for the first time in his life, he did not dive but went down the steps into the icy water and swam a hobbled sidestroke that he might have learned as a youth. He staggered with fatigue on his way to the Clydes' and paddled the length of their pool, stopping again and again with his hand on the curb to rest. He climbed up the ladder and wondered if he had the strength to get home. He had done what he wanted, he had swum the county, but he was so stupefied with exhaustion that his triumph seemed vague. Stooped, holding on to the gateposts for support, he turned up the driveway of his own house.

The place was dark. Was it so late that they had all gone to bed? Had Lucinda stayed at the Westerhazys' for supper? Had the girls joined her there or gone someplace else? Hadn't they agreed, as they usually did on Sunday, to regret all their invitations and stay at home? He tried the garage doors to see what cars were in but the doors were locked and rust came off the handles onto his hands. Going toward the house, he saw that the force of the thunderstorm had knocked one of the rain gutters loose. It hung down over the front door like an umbrella rib, but it could be fixed in the morning. The house was locked, and he thought that the stupid cook or the stupid maid must have locked the place up until he remembered that it had been some time since they had employed a maid or a cook. He shouted, pounded on the door, tried to force it with his shoulder, and then, looking in at the windows, saw that the place was empty.

THE STORY OF AN HOUR

KATE CHOPIN

Knowing that Mrs. Mallard was afflicted with a heart trouble, great care was taken to break to her as gently as possible the news of her husband's death.

It was her sister Josephine who told her, in broken sentences; veiled hints that revealed in half concealing. Her husband's friend Richards was there, too, near her. It was he who had been in the newspaper office when intelligence of the railroad disaster was received, with Brently Mallard's name leading the list of "killed." He had only taken the time to assure himself of its truth by a second telegram, and had hastened to forestall any less careful, less tender friend in bearing the sad message.

She did not hear the story as many women have heard the same, with a paralyzed inability to accept its significance. She wept at once, with sudden, wild abandonment, in her sister's arms. When the storm of grief had spent itself she went away to her room alone. She would have no one follow her.

There stood, facing the open window, a comfortable, roomy armchair. Into this she sank, pressed down by a physical exhaustion that haunted her body and seemed to reach into her soul.

She could see in the open square before her house the tops of trees that were all aquiver with the new spring life. The delicious breath of rain was in the air. In the street below a peddler was crying his wares. The notes of a distant song which some one was singing reached her faintly, and countless sparrows were twittering in the eaves.

There were patches of blue sky showing here and there through the clouds that had met and piled one above the other in the west facing her window.

She sat with her head thrown back upon the cushion of the chair, quite motionless, except when a sob came up into her throat and shook her, as a child who has cried itself to sleep continues to sob in its dreams.

She was young, with a fair, calm face, whose lines bespoke repression and even a certain strength. But now there was a dull stare in her eyes, whose gaze was fixed away off yonder on one of those patches of blue sky. It was not a glance of reflection, but rather indicated a suspension of intelligent thought.

There was something coming to her and she was waiting for it, fearfully. What was it? She did not know; it was too subtle and elusive to name. But she felt it, creeping out of the sky, reaching toward her through the sounds, the scents, the color that filled the air.

Now her bosom rose and fell tumultuously. She was beginning to recognize this thing that was approaching to possess her, and she was striving to beat it back with her will—as powerless as her two white slender hands would have been.

When she abandoned herself a little whispered word escaped her slightly parted lips. She said it over and over under her breath: "free, free, free!" The vacant stare and the look of terror that had followed it went from her eyes. They stayed keen and bright. Her pulses beat fast, and the coursing blood warmed and relaxed every inch of her body.

She did not stop to ask if it were or were not a monstrous joy that held her. A clear and exalted perception enabled her to dismiss the suggestion as trivial.

She knew that she would weep again when she saw the kind, tender hands folded in death; the face that had never looked save with love upon her, fixed and gray and dead. But she saw beyond that bitter moment a long procession of years to come that would belong to her absolutely. And she opened and spread her arms out to them in welcome.

There would be no one to live for during those coming years; she would live for herself. There would be no powerful will bending hers in that blind persistence with which men and women believe they have a right to impose a private will upon a fellow-creature. A kind intention or a cruel intention made the act seem no less a crime as she looked upon it in that brief moment of illumination.

And yet she had loved him—sometimes. Often she had not. What did it matter! What could love, the unsolved mystery, count for in face of this possession of self-assertion which she suddenly recognized as the strongest impulse of her being!

"Free! Body and soul free!" she kept whispering.

Josephine was kneeling before the closed door with her lips to the keyhole, imploring for admission. "Louise, open the door! I beg, open the door—you will make yourself ill. What are you doing Louise? For heaven's sake open the door."

"Go away. I am not making myself ill." No; she was drinking in a very elixir of life through that open window.

Her fancy was running riot along those days ahead of her. Spring days, and summer days, and all sorts of days that would be her own. She breathed a quick prayer that life might be long. It was only yesterday she had thought with a shudder that life might be long.

She arose at length and opened the door to her sister's importunities. There was a feverish triumph in her eyes, and she carried herself unwittingly like a goddess of Victory. She clasped her sister's waist, and together they descended the stairs. Richards stood waiting for them at the bottom.

Some one was opening the front door with a latchkey. It was Brently Mallard who entered, a little travel-stained, composedly carrying his gripsack and umbrella. He had been far from the scene of accident, and did not even know there had been one. He stood amazed at Josephine's piercing cry; at Richards' quick motion to screen him from the view of his wife.

But Richards was too late.

When the doctors came they said she had died of heart disease—of joy that kills.

I WANT TO LIVE!

THOM JONES

She wondered how many times a week he had to do this. Plenty, no doubt. At least every day. Maybe twice . . . three times. Maybe, on a big day, five times. It was the ultimate bad news, and he delivered it dryly, like Sergeant Joe Friday. He was a young man, but his was a tough business and he had gone freeze-dried already. Hey, the bad news wasn't really a surprise! She . . . *knew*. Of course, you always hope for the best. She heard but she didn't hear.

"What?" she offered timidly. She had hoped . . . for better. Geez! Give me a break! What was he saying? Breast and uterus? Double trouble! She *knew* it would be the uterus. There had been the discharge. The bloating, the cramps. The fatigue. But it was common and easily curable provided you got it at stage one. Eighty percent cure. But the breast— that one came out of the blue and that could be really tricky—that was fifty-fifty. Strip out the lymph nodes down your arm and guaranteed chemo. God! Chemo. The worst thing in the world. Goodbye hair—there'd be scarves, wigs, a prosthetic breast, crying your heart out in "support" groups. Et cetera.

"Mrs. Wilson?" The voice seemed to come out of a can. Now the truth was revealed and all was out in the open. Yet how—tell me this—how would it ever be possible to have a life again? The voice from the can had chilled her. To the core.

"Mrs. Wilson, your last CA 125 hit the ceiling," he said. "I suspect that this could be an irregular kind of can . . . cer."

Some off-the-wall kind of can . . . cer? A kind of wildfire cancer! Not the easygoing, 80-percent-cure, tortoise, as-slow-as-molasses-in-January cancer!

January. She looked past the thin oncologist, wire-rimmed glasses, white coat, inscrutable. Outside, snowflakes tumbled from the sky, kissing the pavement—each unique, wonderful, worth an hour of study, a microcosm of the Whole: awe-inspiring, absolutely fascinating, a gift of divinity gratis. Yet how abhorrent they seemed. They were white, but the whole world had lost its color for her now that she'd heard those words. The shine was gone from the world. Had she been Queen of the Universe for a million years and witnessed glory after glory, what would it have mattered now that she had come to this?

She . . . came to . . . went out, came back again . . . went out. There was this . . . wonderful show. Cartoons. It was the best show. This wasn't so bad. True, she had cancer but . . . these wonderful cartoons. Dilaudid. On Dilaudid, well, you live, you die—that's how it is . . . life in the Big City. It happens to everyone. It's part of the plan. Who was she to question the plan?

The only bad part was her throat. Her throat was on fire. "Intubation." The nurse said she'd phone the doctor and maybe he'd authorize more dope.

"Oh, God, please. Anything."

"Okay, let's just fudge a little bit, no one needs to know," the nurse said, twisting the knob on Tube Control Central. Dilaudid. Cartoons. Oh, God, thank God, Dilaudid! Who invented that drug? Write him a letter. Knight him. Award the Nobel Prize to Dilaudid Man. Where was that knob? A handy thing to know. Whew! Whammo! Swirling, throbbing ecstasy! And who was that nurse? Florence Nightingale, Mother Teresa would be proud . . . oh, boy! It wasn't just relief from the surgery; she suddenly realized how much psychic pain she had been carrying and now it was gone with one swoop of a magic wand. The cartoons. Bliss . . .

His voice wasn't in a can, never had been. It was a normal voice, maybe a little high for a man. Not that he was effeminate. The whole problem with him was that he didn't seem real. He wasn't a flesh-and-blood kinda guy. Where was the *empathy*? Why did he get into this field if he couldn't empathize? In this field, empathy should be your stock-in-trade.

"The breast is fine, just a benign lump. We brought a specialist in to get it, and I just reviewed the pathology report. It's nothing to worry about.

The other part is not . . . so good. I'm afraid your abdomen . . . it's spread throughout your abdomen . . . it looks like little Grape-Nuts, actually. It's exceedingly rare and it's . . . it's a rapid form of . . . can . . . cer. We couldn't really take any of it out. I spent most of my time in there untangling adhesions. We're going to have to give you cisplatin . . . if it weren't for the adhesions, we could pump it into your abdomen directly—you wouldn't get so sick that way—but those adhesions are a problem and may cause problems further along." Her room was freezing, but the thin oncologist was beginning to perspire. "It's a shame," he said, looking down at her chart. "You're in such perfect health . . . otherwise."

She knew this was going to happen yet she heard herself say, "Doctor, do you mean . . . I've got to take—"

"Chemo? Yeah. But don't worry about that yet. Let's just let you heal up for a while." He slammed her chart shut and . . . whiz, bang, he was outta there.

Goodbye, see ya.

The guessing game was over and now it was time for the ordeal. She didn't want to hear any more details—he's said something about a 20 percent five-year survival rate. Might as well bag it. She wasn't a fighter, and she'd seen what chemo had done to her husband, John. This was it. Finis!

She had to laugh. Got giddy. It was like in that song—*Freedom's just another word for nothing left to lose* . . . When you're totally screwed, nothing can get worse, so what's to worry? Of course she could get lucky . . . it would be a thousand-to-one, but maybe . . .

The ovaries and uterus were gone. The root of it all was out. Thank God for that. Those befouled organs were gone. Where? Disposed of. Burned. In a dumpster? Who cares? The source was destroyed. Maybe it wouldn't be so bad. How could it be that bad? After all, the talk about pain from major abdominal surgery was overdone. She was walking with her little cart and tubes by the third day—a daily constitutional through the ward.

Okay, the Dilaudid was permanently off the menu, but morphine sulfate wasn't half bad. No more cartoons but rather a mellow glow. Left, right, left, right. Hup, two, three, four! Even a journey of a thousand miles begins with the first step. On the morphine she was walking a quarter of an inch off the ground and everything was . . . softer, mercifully so. Maybe she could hack it for a thousand miles.

But those people in the hospital rooms, gray and dying, that was her. Could such a thing be possible? To die? Really? Yes, at some point she guessed you did die. But her? Now? So soon? With so little time to get used to the idea?

No, this was all a bad dream! She'd wake up. She'd wake up back in her little girl room on the farm near Battle Lake, Minnesota. There was a depression, things were a little rough, but big deal. What could beat a sun-kissed morning on Battle Lake and a robin's song? There was an abundance of jays, larks, bluebirds, cardinals, hummingbirds, red-winged blackbirds in those days before acid rain and heavy-metal poisoning, and they came to her yard to eat from the cherry, apple, plum, and pear trees. What they really went for were the mulberries.

Ah, youth! Good looks, a clean complexion, muscle tone, a full head of lustrous hair—her best feature, although her legs were pretty good, too. Strength. Vitality. A happy kid with a bright future. Cheerleader her senior year. Pharmacy scholarship at the college in Fergus Falls. Geez, if her dad hadn't died, she could have been a pharmacist. Her grades were good, but hard-luck stories were the order of the day. It was a Great Depression. She would have to take her chances. Gosh! It had been a great, wide, wonderful world in those days, and no matter what, an adventure lay ahead, something marvelous—a handsome prince and a life happily ever after. Luck was with her. Where had all the time gone? How had all the dreams . . . fallen away? Now she was in the Valley of the Shadow. The morphine sulfate was like a warm and friendly hearth in Gloom City, her one and only consolation.

He was supposed to be a good doctor, one of the best in the field, but he had absolutely no bedside manner. She really began to hate him when he took away the morphine and put her on Tylenol 3. Then it began to sink in that things might presently go downhill in a hurry.

They worked out a routine. If her brother was busy, her daughter drove her up to the clinic and then back down to the office, and the thin oncologist is . . . called away, or he's . . . running behind, or he's . . . *something*. Couldn't they run a business, get their shit together? Why couldn't they anticipate? It was one thing to wait in line at a bank when you're well, but when you've got cancer and you're this cancer patient and you wait an hour, two hours, or they tell you to come back next week . . . come back for something that's worse than anything, the very worst thing in the world! Hard to get up for that. You really had to brace yourself. Cisplatin, God! Metal mouth, restlessness, pacing. Flop on the couch, but that's no good; get up and pace, but you can't handle that, so you flop on the couch again. Get up and pace. Is this really happening to me? *I can't believe this is really happening to me!* How can such a thing be possible?

Then there were the episodes of simultaneous diarrhea and vomiting that sprayed the bathroom from floor to ceiling! Dry heaves and then dry heaves with bile and then dry heaves with blood. You could drink a quart of tequila and then a quart of rum and have some sloe gin too and eat pink birthday cakes and five pounds of licorice, Epsom salts, a pint of kerosene, some Southern Comfort—and you're on a Sunday picnic compared to cisplatin. Only an archfiend could devise a dilemma where to maybe *get well* you first had to poison yourself within a whisker of death, and in fact if you didn't die, you wished that you had.

There were visitors in droves. Flowers. Various intrusions at all hours. Go away. Leave me alone . . . please, God, leave me . . . alone.

Oh, hi, thanks for coming. Oh, what a lovely—such beautiful flowers . . .

There were moments when she felt that if she had one more episode of diarrhea, she'd jump out of the window. Five stories. Would that be high enough? Or would you lie there for a time and die slowly? Maybe if you took a header right onto the concrete. Maybe then you wouldn't feel a thing. Cisplatin: she had to pace. But she had to lie down, but she was squirrelly as hell and she couldn't lie down. TV was no good—she had double vision, and it was all just a bunch of stupid shit, anyhow. Soap operas—good grief! What absolute crap. Even her old favorites. You only live once, and to think of all the time she pissed away watching soap operas.

If only she could sleep. God, couldn't they give her Dilaudid? No! Wait! Hold that! Somehow Dilaudid would make it even worse. Ether then. Put her out. Wake me up in five days. Just let me sleep. She *had* to get up to pace. She *had* to lie down. She *had* to vomit. *Oh, hi, thanks for coming. Oh, what a lovely—such beautiful flowers.*

The second treatment made the first treatment seem like a month in the country. The third treatment—oh, damn! The whole scenario had been underplayed. Those movie stars who got it and wrote books about it were stoics, valiant warriors compared to her. She had no idea anything could be so horrible. Starving in Bangladesh? No problem, I'll trade. Here's my MasterCard and the keys to the Buick—I'll pull a rickshaw, anything!

Anything but this. HIV-positive? Why just sign right here on the dotted line and you've got a deal! I'll trade with anybody! Anybody.

The thin oncologist with the Bugs Bunny voice said the CA 125 number was still up in the stratosphere. He said it was up to her if she wanted to go on with this. What was holding her up? She didn't know, and her own voice came from a can now. She heard herself say, "Doctor, what would you do . . . if you were me?"

He thought it over for a long time. He pulled off his wire rims and pinched his nose, world-weary. "I'd take the next treatment."

It was the worst by far—square root to infinity. Five days: no sleep, pacing, lying down, pacing. Puke and diarrhea. The phone. She wanted to tear it off the wall. After all these years, couldn't they make a quiet bell?—did they have shit for brains or what? *Oh, hi, well . . . just fine. Just dandy. Coming by on Sunday? With the kids? Well . . . no, I feel great. No. No. No. I'd love to see you . . .*

And then one day the thin-timbre voice delivered good news. "Your CA 125 is almost within normal limits. It's working!"

Hallelujah! Oh my God, let it be so! A miracle. Hurrah!

"It is a miracle," he said. He was almost human, Dr. Kildare, Dr. Ben Casey, Marcus Welby, M.D.—take your pick. "Your CA is down to rock bottom. I think we should do one, possibly two more treatments and then go back inside for a look. If we do too few, we may not kill it all but if we do too much—you see, it's toxic to your healthy cells as well. You can get cardiomyopathy in one session of cisplatin and you can die."

"One more is all I can handle."

"Gotcha, Mrs. Wilson. One more and in for a look."

"I hate to tell you this," he said. Was he making the cartoons go away? "I'll be up front about it, Mrs. Wilson, we've still got a problem. The little Grape-Nuts—fewer than in the beginning, but the remaining cells will be resistant to cisplatin, so our options are running thin. We could try a month of an experimental form of hard chemotherapy right here in the hospital—very, very risky stuff. Or we could resume the cisplatin, not so much aiming for a cure but rather as a holding action. Or we could not do anything at all . . ."

Her voice was flat. She said, "What if I don't do anything?"

"Dead in three months, maybe six."

She said, "Dead how?"

"Lungs, liver, or bowel. Don't worry, Mrs. Wilson, there won't be a lot of pain. I'll see to that."

Bingo! He flipped the chart shut and . . . whiz, bang, he was outta there!

She realized that when she got right down to it, she wanted to live, more than anything, on almost any terms, so she took more cisplatin. But the oncologist was right, it couldn't touch those resistant rogue cells; they were like roaches that could live through atomic warfare, grow and thrive. Well then, screw it! At least there wouldn't be pain. What more can you do? She shouldn't have let him open her up again. That had been the worst sort of folly. She'd let him steamroll her with Doctor Knows Best. Air had hit it. No wonder it was a wildfire. A conflagration.

Her friends came by. It was an effort to make small talk. How could they know? How could they *know* what it was like? They loved her, they said, with liquor on their breath. They had to get juiced before they could stand to come by! They came with casseroles and cleaned for her, but she had to sweat out her nights alone. Dark nights of the soul on Tylenol 3 and Xanax. A lot of good that was. But then when she was in her loose, giddy *freedom's just another word for nothing left to lose* mood, about ten days after a treatment, she realized her friends weren't so dumb. They knew that they couldn't really *know*. Bugs Bunny told her there was no point in going on with the cisplatin. He told her she was a very brave lady. He said he was sorry.

A month after she was off that poison, cisplatin, there was a little side benefit. She could see the colors of the earth again and taste food and smell flowers—it was a bittersweet pleasure, to be sure. But her friends took her to Hawaii, where they had this great friend ("You gotta meet him!") and he . . . he made a play for her and brought her flowers every day, expensive roses, et cetera. She had never considered another man since John had died from can . . . cer ten years before. How wonderful to forget it all for a moment here and there. A moment? Qualify that—make that ten, fifteen seconds. How can you forget it? Ever since she got the news she could . . . not . . . forget . . . it.

Now there were stabbing pains, twinges, flutterings—maybe it was normal everyday stuff amplified by the imagination or maybe it was real. How fast would it move, this wildfire brand? Better not to ask.

Suddenly she was horrible again. Those nights alone—killers. Finally one night she broke down and called her daughter. Hated to do it, throw in the towel, but this was the fifteenth round and she didn't have a prayer.

"Oh, hi. I'm just fine"—*blah blah blah*—"but I was thinking maybe I could come down and stay, just a while. I'd like to see Janey and—"

"We'll drive up in the morning."

At least she was with blood. And her darling granddaughter. What a delight. Playing with the little girl, she could forget. It was even better than Hawaii. After a year of sheer hell, in which all of the good stuff added up to less than an hour and four minutes total, there was a way to forget. She helped with the dishes. A little light cleaning. Watched the game shows, worked the *Times* crossword, but the pains grew worse. Goddammit, it felt like nasty little yellow-tooth rodents or a horde of translucent termites—thousands of them, chewing her guts out! Tylenol 3 couldn't touch it. The new doctor she had been passed to gave her Dilaudid. She was enormously relieved. But what she got was a vial of little pink tablets and after the first dose she realized it wasn't much good in the pill form; you could squeeze by on it but they'd *promised*—no pain! She was losing steam. Grinding down.

They spent a couple of days on the Oregon coast. The son-in-law—somehow it was easy to be with him. He didn't pretend that things were other than they were. He could be a pain in the bun, like everyone, bitching over trivialities, smoking Kool cigarettes, strong ones—jolters! A pack a day easy, although he was considerate enough to go outside and do it. She wanted to tell him, "Fool! Your health is your greatest fortune!" But she was the one who'd let six months pass after that first discharge.

The Oregon coast was lovely, although the surf was too cold for actual swimming. She sat in the hotel whirlpool and watched her granddaughter swim a whole length of the pool all on her own, a kind of dog-paddle thing but not bad for a kid going on seven. They saw a show of shooting stars one night but it was exhausting to keep up a good front and not to be morbid, losing weight big time. After a shower, standing at the mirror, scars zigzagging all over the joint like the Bride of Frankenstein, it was just awful. She was bald, scrawny, ashen, yet with a bloated belly. She couldn't look. Sometimes she would sink to the floor and just lie there, too sick to even cry, too weak to even get dressed, yet somehow she did get dressed, slapped on that hot, goddamn wig, and showed up for dinner. It was easier to do that if you pretended that it wasn't real, if you pretended it was all on TV.

She felt like a naughty little girl sitting before the table looking at meals her daughter was killing herself to make—old favorites that now tasted like a combination of forty-weight Texaco oil and sawdust. It was a relief to get back to the couch and work crossword puzzles. It was hell imposing on her daughter but she was frightened. Terrified! They were her blood. They *had* to take her. Oh, to come to this!

The son-in-law worked swing shift and he cheered her in the morning when he got up and made coffee. He was full of life. He was real. He was authentic. He even interjected little pockets of hope. Not that he pushed macrobiotics or any of that foolishness, but it was a fact—if you were happy, if you had something to live for, if you loved life, you lived. It had been a mistake for her to hole up there in the mountains after John died. The Will to Live was more important than doctors and medicines. You had to reinvigorate the Will to Live. The granddaughter was good for that. She just couldn't go the meditation-tape route, imagining microscopic, ravenous, good-guy little sharks eating the bad cancer cells, et cetera. At least the son-in-law didn't suggest that or come on strong with a theology trip. She noticed he read the King James Bible, though.

She couldn't eat. There was a milk-shake diet she choked down. Vanilla, chocolate fudge, strawberry—your choice. Would Madame like a bottle of wine with dinner? Ha, ha, ha.

Dilaudid. It wasn't working, there was serious pain, especially in her chest, dagger thrusts—*Et tu, Brute?* She watched the clock like a hawk and had her pills out and ready every four hours—and that last hour was getting to be murder, a morbid sweat began popping out of her in the last fifteen minutes. One morning she caved in and timidly asked the son-in-law, "Can I take three?"

He said, "Hell, take four. It's a safe drug. If you have bad pain, take four." Her eyes were popping out of her head. "Here, drink it with coffee and it will kick in faster."

He was right. He knew more than the doctor. You just can't do everything by the book. Maybe that had been her trouble all along—she was too compliant, one of those "cancer" personalities. She believed in the rules. She was one of those kind who wanted to leave the world a better place than she found it. She had been a good person, had always done the right thing—this just wasn't right. It wasn't fair. She was so . . . angry!

The next day, over the phone, her son-in-law bullied a prescription of methadone from the cancer doctor. She heard one side of a lengthy heated exchange while the son-in-law made a persuasive case for methadone. He came on like Clarence Darrow or F. Lee Bailey. It was a commanding performance. She'd never heard of anyone giving a doctor hell before. God bless him for not backing down! On methadone tablets a warm orange glow sprang forth and bloomed like a glorious, time-lapse rose in her abdomen and then rolled through her body in orgasmic waves. The sense of relief shattered all fear and doubt though the pain was still there to some extent. It was still there but—so what? And the methadone tablets lasted a very long time—no more of that *every four hours* bullshit.

Purple blotches all over her skin, swollen ankles. Pain in her hips and joints. An ambulance trip to the emergency room. "Oh," they said, "it's nothing . . . vascular purpura. Take aspirin. Who's next?"

Who's next? Why hadn't she taken John's old .38 revolver the very day she heard that voice in the can? Stuck it in the back of her mouth and pulled the trigger? She had no fear of hellfire. She was a decent, moral person but she did not believe. Neither was she the Hamlet type— what lies on the other side? It was probably the same thing that occurred before you were born—zilch. And zilch wasn't that bad. What was wrong with zilch?

One morning she waited overlong for the son-in-law to get up, almost smashed a candy dish to get him out of bed. Was he going to sleep forever? Actually, he got up at his usual time.

"I can't. Get. My breath," she told him.

"You probably have water in your lungs," the son-in-law said. He knew she didn't want to go to the clinic. "We've got some diuretic. They were Boxer's when she had congestive heart failure—dog medicine, but it's the same thing they give humans. Boxer weighed fifty-five pounds. Let me see . . . take four, no, take three. To be cautious. Do you feel like you have to cough?"

"Yes." *Kaff, kaff, kaff.*

"This might draw the water out of your lungs. It's pretty safe. Try to eat a banana or a potato skin to keep your potassium up. If it doesn't work, we can go over to the clinic."

How would he know something like that? But he was right. It worked like magic. She had to pee like crazy but she could breathe. The panic to end all panics was over. If she could only go . . . number two. Well, the methadone slows you down. "Try some Metamucil," the son-in-law said.

It worked. Kind of, but it sure wasn't anything to write home about.

"I can't breathe. The diuretics aren't working."

The son-in-law said they could tap her lung. It would mean another drive to the clinic, but the procedure was almost painless and provided instantaneous relief. It worked but it was three days of exhaustion after that one. The waiting room. Why so long? Why couldn't they anticipate? You didn't have to be a genius to know which way the wildfire was spreading. Would the methadone keep that internal orange glow going or would they run out of ammo? Was methadone the ultimate or were there bigger guns? Street heroin? She'd have to put on her wig and go out and score China White.

The little girl began to tune out. Gramma wasn't so much fun anymore; she just lay there and gave off this smell. There was no more dressing up; it was just the bathrobe. In fact, she felt the best in her old red-and-black tartan pattern, flannel, ratty-ass bathrobe, not the good one. The crosswords—forget it, too depressing. You could live the life of Cleopatra but if it came down to this, what was the point?

The son-in-law understood. Of all the people to come through. It's bad and it gets worse and so on until the worst of all. "I don't know how you can handle this," he'd say. "What does it feel like? Does it feel like a hangover? Worse than a hangover? Not like a hangover. Then what? Like drinking ten pots of boiled coffee? Like that? Really? Jittery! Oh, God, that must be awful. How can you stand it? Is it just like drinking too much coffee or is there some other aspect? Your fingers are numb? Blurred vision? It takes eight years to watch the second hand sweep from twelve to one? Well, if it's like that, how did you handle *five days?* I couldn't—I'd take a bottle of pills, shoot myself. Something. What about the second week? Drained? Washed out? Oh, brother! I had a three-day hangover once—I'd rather die than do that again. I couldn't ride out that hangover again for money. I know I couldn't handle chemo . . ."

One afternoon after he left for work, she found a passage circled in his well-worn copy of Schopenhauer: *In early youth, as we contemplate our coming life, we are like children in a theater before the curtain is raised, sitting there in high spirits and eagerly waiting for the play to begin. It is a blessing that we do not know what is really going to happen.* Yeah! She gave up the crosswords and delved into *The World As Will and Idea.* This Schopenhauer was a genius! Why hadn't anyone told her? She was a reader, she had waded through some philosophy in her time—you just couldn't make any sense out of it. The problem was the terminology! She was a crossword ace, but words like *eschatology*—hey! Yet Schopenhauer got right into the heart of all the important things. The things that really mattered. With Schopenhauer she could take long excursions from the grim specter of impending death. In Schopenhauer, particularly in his aphorisms and reflections, she found an absolute satisfaction, for Schopenhauer spoke the truth and the rest of the world was disseminating lies!

Her son-in-law helped her with unfinished business: will, mortgage, insurance, how shall we do this, that, and the other? Cremation, burial plot, et cetera. He told her the stuff that her daughter couldn't tell her. He waited for the right moment and then got it all in—for instance, he told her that her daughter loved her very much but that it was hard for her to say so. She knew she cringed at this revelation, for it was ditto with her, and she knew that he could see it. Why couldn't she say to her own daughter three simple words, "I love you"? She just couldn't. Somehow it wasn't possible. The son-in-law didn't judge her. He had to be under pressure, too. Was she bringing everyone in the house down? Is that why he was reading Schopenhauer? No, Schopenhauer was his favorite. "Someone had to come out and tell it like it is," he would say of the dour old man with muttonchops whose picture he had pasted on the refrigerator. From what she picked up from the son-in-law, Schopenhauer wrote his major work by his twenty-sixth birthday—a philosophy that was ignored almost entirely in his lifetime and even now, in this day and age, it was thought to be more of a work of art than philosophy in the truest sense. A work of art? Why, it seemed irrefutable! According to the son-in-law, Schopenhauer spent the majority of his life in shabby rooms in the old genteel section of Frankfurt, Germany, that he shared with successions of poodles to keep him company while he read, reflected, and wrote about life at his leisure. He had some kind of small inheritance, just enough to get by, take in the concerts, do a little traveling now and then. He was well versed in several languages. He read virtually everything written from the Greeks on, including the Eastern writers, a classical scholar, and had the mind to chew things over and make something of the puzzle of life. The son-in-law, eager to discourse, said Freud called Schopenhauer one of the six greatest men who ever lived. Nietzsche, Thomas Mann, and Richard Wagner all paid tribute to this genius who had been written off with one word—pessimist. The son-in-law lamented that his works were going out of print, becoming increasingly harder to find. He was planning a trip to Frankfurt, where he hoped to find a little bust of his hero. He had written to officials in Germany making inquiries. They had given him the brush-off. He'd have to fly over himself. And she, too, began to worry that the works of this writer would no longer be available . . . she, who would be worms' meat any day.

Why? Because the *truth* was worthwhile. It was more important than anything, really. She'd had ten years of peaceful retirement, time to think, wonder, contemplate, and had come up with nothing. But new vistas of thought had been opened by the curiously ignored genius with the white mutton-chops, whose books were harder and harder to get and whom the world would consider a mere footnote from the nineteenth century—a crank, a guy with an ax to grind, a hypochondriac, a misogynist, an alarmist who slept with pistols under his pillow, a man with many faults. Well, check anyone out and what do you find?

For God's sake, how were you supposed to make any sense out of this crazy-ass shit called life? If only she could simply push a button and never have been born.

The son-in-law took antidepressants and claimed to be a melancho-liac, yet he always seemed upbeat, comical, ready with a laugh. He had a sense of the absurd that she had found annoying back in the old days when she liked to pretend that life was a stroll down Primrose Lane. If she wasn't walking down the "sunny side of the street" at least she was "singin' in the rain." Those were the days.

What a fool!

She encouraged the son-in-law to clown and philosophize, and he flour-ished when she voiced a small dose of appreciation or barked out a laugh. There was more and more pain and discomfort, but she was laughing more, too. Schopenhauer: *No rose without a thorn. But many a thorn and no rose.* The son-in-law finessed all of the ugly details that were impossible for her. Of all the people to come through!

With her lungs temporarily clear and mineral oil enemas to regulate her, she asked her daughter one last favor. Could they take her home just once more?

They made an occasion of it and drove her up into the mountains for her granddaughter's seventh birthday party. Almost everyone in the picturesque resort town was there, and if they were appalled by her deterioration they did not show it. She couldn't go out on the sun porch, had to semi-recline on the couch, but everyone came in to say hello and all of the bad stuff fell away for . . . an entire afternoon! She was deeply touched by the warm affection of her friends. There were . . . so many of them. My God! They loved her, truly they did. She could see it. You couldn't bullshit her anymore; she could see deep into the human heart; she knew what people were. What wonderful friends. What a perfect afternoon. It was the last . . . good thing.

When she got back to her daughter's she began to die in earnest. It was in the lungs and the bowel, much as the doctor said it would be. Hell, it was probably in the liver even. She was getting yellow, not just the skin but even the whites of her eyes. There was a week in the hospital, where they tormented her with tests. That wiped out the last of her physical and emotional stamina.

She fouled her bed after a barium lower G.I. practically turned to cement and they had to give her a powerful enema. Diarrhea in the bed. The worst humiliation. "Happens all the time, don't worry," the orderly said.

She was suffocating. She couldn't get the least bit of air. All the main players were in the room. She knew this was it! Just like that. Bingo! There were whispered conferences outside her room. Suddenly the nurses, those heretofore angels of mercy, began acting mechanically. They could look you over and peg you, down to the last five minutes. She could see them give her that *anytime now* look. A minister dropped in. There! That was the tip-off—the fat lady was singing.

When the son-in-law showed up instead of going to work she looked to him with panic. She'd been fighting it back but now . . . he was there, he would know what to do without being asked, and in a moment he was back with a nurse. They cranked up the morphine sulfate, flipped it on full-bore. Still her back hurt like hell. All that morphine and a backache . . . just give it a minute . . . ahhh! Cartoons.

Someone went out to get hamburgers at McDonald's. Her daughter sat next to her holding her hand. She felt sorry for them. They were the ones who were going to have to stay behind and play out their appointed roles. Like Schopenhauer said, the best they would be able to do for themselves was to secure a little room as far away from the fire as possible, for Hell was surely in the here-and-now, not in the hereafter. Or was it?

She began to nod. She was holding onto a carton of milk. It would spill. Like diarrhea-in-the-bed all over again. Another mess. The daughter tried to take the carton of milk away. She . . . held on defiantly. Forget the Schopenhauer—what a lot of crap that was! She did not want to cross over. She wanted to live! She wanted to live!

The daughter wrenched the milk away. The nurse came back and cranked up the morphine again. They were going for "comfort." Finally the backache . . . the cartoons . . . all of that was gone.

(She was back on the farm in Battle Lake, Minnesota. She was nine years old and she could hear her little red rooster, Mr. Barnes, crowing at first light. Then came her brother's heavy work boots clomping downstairs and the vacuum swoosh as he opened up the storm door, and then his boots crunch-crunching through the frozen snow. Yes, she was back on the farm all right. Her brother was making for the outhouse and presently Barnes would go after him, make a dive-bomb attack. You couldn't discourage Mr. Barnes. She heard her brother curse him and the *thwap* of the tin feed pan hitting the bird. Mr. Barnes's frontal assaults were predictable. From the sound of it, Fred walloped him good. As far as Mr. Barnes was concerned, it was his barnyard. In a moment she heard the outhouse door slam shut and another tin *thwap*. That Barnes—he was something. She should have taken a lesson. Puffed out her chest and walked through life—"I want the biggest and the best and the most of whatever you've got!" There were people who pulled it off. You really could do it if you had the attitude.

Her little red rooster was a mean little scoundrel, but he had a soft spot for her in his heart of steel and he looked out for her, cooed for her and her alone. Later, when young men came to see her, they soon arranged to meet her thereafter at the drugstore soda fountain uptown. One confrontation with Barnes, even for experienced farm boys, was one too many. He was some kind of rooster all right, an eccentric. Yeah, she was back on the farm. She . . . could feel her sister shifting awake in the lower bunk. It was time to get up and milk the cows. Her sister always awoke in good humor. Not her. She was cozy under a feather comforter and milking the cows was the last thing she wanted to do. Downstairs she could hear her mother speaking cheerfully to her brother as he came back inside, cursing the damn rooster, threatening to kill it. Her mother laughed it off; she didn't have a mean bone in her body.

She . . . could smell bacon in the pan, the coffeepot was percolating, and her grandmother was up heating milk for her Ovaltine. She hated Ovaltine, particularly when her grandmother overheated the milk—burned it—but she pretended to like it, insisted that she needed it for her bones, and forced it down so she could save up enough labels to get a free decoder ring to get special messages from Captain Cody, that intrepid hero of the airwaves. She really wanted to have that ring, but there was a Great Depression and money was very dear, so she never got the decoder or the secret messages or the degree in pharmacology. Had she been more like that little banty rooster, had she been a real go-getter . . . Well—it was all but over now.)

The main players were assembled in the room. She . . . was nodding in and out but she could hear. There she was, in this apparent stupor, but she was more aware than anyone could know. She heard someone say somebody at McDonald's put "everything" on her hamburger instead of "cheese and ketchup only." They were making an issue out of it. One day, when they were in her shoes, they would learn to ignore this kind of petty stuff, but you couldn't blame them. That was how things were, that's all. Life. That was it. That was what it was. And here she lay . . . dying.

Suddenly she realized that the hard part was all over now. All she had to do was . . . let go. It really wasn't so bad. It wasn't . . . anything special. It just was. She was trying to bring back Barnes one last time— that little memory of him had been fun, why not go out with a little fun? She tried to remember his coloring—orange would be too bright, rust too drab, scarlet too vivid. His head was a combination of green, yellow, and gold, all blended, and his breast and wings a kind of carmine red? No, not carmine. He was just a little red rooster, overly pugnacious, an ingrate. He could have been a beautiful bird if he hadn't gotten into so many fights. He got his comb ripped off by a raccoon he'd caught stealing eggs in the henhouse, a big bull raccoon that Barnes had fought tooth and nail until Fred ran into the henhouse with his .410 and killed the thieving intruder. Those eggs were precious. They were income. Mr. Barnes was a hero that day. She remembered how he used to strut around the barnyard. He always had his eye on all of the hens; they were his main priority, some thirty to forty of them, depending. They were his harem and he was the sheikh. Boy, was he ever. She remembered jotting down marks on a pad of paper one day when she was home sick with chickenpox. Each mark represented an act of rooster fornication. In less than a day, Mr. Barnes had committed the sexual act forty-seven times that she could see—and she didn't have the whole lay of the land from her window by any means. Why, he often went out roving and carousing with hens on other farms. There were bitter complaints from the neighbors. Barnes really could stir things up. She had to go out on her bicycle and round him up. Mr. Barnes was a legend in the country. Mr. Barnes thought the whole world belonged to him and beyond that—the suns, the stars, and the Milky Way—all of it! Did it feel good or was it torment? It must have been a glorious feeling, she decided. Maybe that was what Arthur Schopenhauer was driving at in his theory about the Will to Live. Mr. Barnes was the very personification of it.

Of course it was hard work being a rooster, but Barnes seemed the happiest creature she had ever known. Probably because when you're doing what you really want to do, it isn't work. No matter how dull things got on the farm, she could watch Barnes by the hour. Barnes could even redeem a hot, dog-day afternoon in August. He wasn't afraid of anything or anybody. Did he ever entertain a doubt? Some kind of rooster worry? Never! She tried to conjure up one last picture of him. He was just a little banty, couldn't have weighed three pounds. Maybe Mr. Barnes would be waiting for her on the other side and would greet her there and be her friend again.

She nodded in and out. In and out. The morphine was getting to be too much. Oh, please God. She hoped she wouldn't puke . . . So much left unsaid, undone. Well, that was all part of it. If only she could see Barnes strut his stuff one last time. "Come on, Barnes. Strut your stuff for me." Her brother, Fred, sitting there so sad with his hamburger. After a couple of beers, he could do a pretty good imitation of Mr. Barnes. Could he . . . would he . . . for old time's sake? Her voice was too weak, she couldn't speak. Nowhere near. Not even close. Was she dead already? Fading to black? It was hard to tell. "Don't feel bad, my darling brother. Don't mourn for me. I'm okay" . . . and . . . one last thing—"Sarah, I do love you, darling! Love you! Didn't you know that? Didn't it show? If not, I'm so, so very sorry. . . ." But the words wouldn't come—couldn't come. She . . . was so sick. You can only get so sick and then there was all that dope. Love! She should have shown it to her daughter instead of . . . assuming. She should have been more demonstrative, more forthcoming. . . . That's what it was all about. *Love your brother as yourself* and *love the Lord God almighty with all your heart and mind and soul.* You were sent here to love your brother. Do your best. Be kind to animals, obey the Ten Commandments, stuff like that. Was that it? Huh? Or was that all a lot of horseshit?

She . . . nodded in and out. Back and forth. In and out. She went back and forth. In and out. Back and forth . . . in and out. There wasn't any tunnel or white light or any of that. She just . . . died.

DR. HEIDEGGER'S EXPERIMENT

NATHANIEL HAWTHORNE

That very singular man, old Dr. Heidegger, once invited four venerable friends to meet him in his study. There were three white-bearded gentlemen, Mr. Medbourne, Colonel Killigrew, and Mr. Gascoigne, and a withered gentlewoman, whose name was the Widow Wycherly. They were all melancholy old creatures, who had been unfortunate in life, and whose greatest misfortune it was, that they were not long ago in their graves. Mr. Medbourne, in the vigor of his age, had been a prosperous merchant, but had lost his all by a frantic speculation, and was now little better than a mendicant. Colonel Killigrew had wasted his best years, and his health and substance, in the pursuit of sinful pleasures, which had given birth to a brood of pains, such as the gout, and divers other torments of soul and body. Mr. Gascoigne was a ruined politician, a man of evil fame, or at least had been so till time had buried him from the knowledge of the present generation, and made him obscure instead of infamous. As for the Widow Wycherly, tradition tells us that she was a great beauty in her day; but, for a long while past, she had lived in deep seclusion, on account of certain scandalous stories, which had prejudiced the gentry of the town against her. It is a circumstance worth mentioning, that each of these three old gentlemen, Mr. Medbourne, Colonel Killigrew, and Mr. Gascoigne, were early lovers of the Widow Wycherly, and had once been on the point of cutting each other's throats for her sake. And, before proceeding farther, I will merely hint, that Dr. Heidegger and all his four guests were sometimes thought to be a little beside themselves; as is not unfrequently the case with old people, when worried either by present troubles or woful recollections.

"My dear old friends," said Dr. Heidegger, motioning them to be seated, "I am desirous of your assistance in one of those little experiments with which I amuse myself here in my study."

If all stories were true, Dr. Heidegger's study must have been a very curious place. It was a dim, old-fashioned chamber, festooned with cobwebs, and besprinkled with antique dust. Around the walls stood several oaken book-cases, the lower shelves of which were filled with rows of gigantic folios, and black-letter quartos, and the upper with little parchment covered duodecimos. Over the central book-case was a bronze bust of Hippocrates, with which, according to some authorities, Dr. Heidegger was accustomed to hold consultations, in all difficult cases of his practice. In the obscurest corner of the room stood a tall and narrow oaken closet, with its door ajar, within which doubtfully appeared a skeleton. Between two of the book-cases hung a looking-glass, presenting its high and dusty plate within a tarnished gilt frame. Among many wonderful stories related of this mirror, it was fabled that the spirits of all the doctor's deceased patients dwelt within its verge, and would stare him in the face whenever he looked thitherward. The opposite side of the chamber was ornamented with the full length portrait of a young lady, arrayed in the faded magnificence of silk, satin, and brocade, and with a visage as faded as her dress. Above half a century ago, Dr. Heidegger had been on the point of marriage with this young lady; but, being affected with some slight disorder, she had swallowed one of her lover's prescriptions, and died on the bridal evening. The greatest curiosity of the study remains to be mentioned: it was a ponderous folio volume, bound in black leather, with massive silver clasps. There were no letters on the back, and nobody could tell the title of the book. But it was well known to be a book of magic; and once, when a chambermaid had lifted it, merely to brush away the dust, the skeleton had rattled in its closet, the picture of the young lady had stepped one foot upon the floor, and several ghastly faces had peeped forth from the mirror; while the brazen head of Hippocrates frowned, and said—"Forbear!"

Such was Dr. Heidegger's study. On the summer afternoon of our tale, a small round table, as black as ebony, stood in the centre of the room, sustaining a cut-glass vase, of beautiful form and elaborate workmanship. The sunshine came through the window, between the heavy festoons of two faded damask curtains, and fell directly across this vase; so that a mild splendor was reflected from it on the ashen visages of the five old people who sat around. Four champaigne glasses were also on the table.

"My dear old friends," repeated Dr. Heidegger, "may I reckon on your aid in performing an exceedingly curious experiment?"

Now Dr. Heidegger was a very strange old gentleman, whose eccentricity had become the nucleus for a thousand fantastic stories. Some of these fables, to my shame be it spoken, might possibly be traced back to mine own veracious self; and if any passages of the present tale should startle the reader's faith, I must be content to bear the stigma of a fiction-monger.

When the doctor's four guests heard him talk of his proposed experiment, they anticipated nothing more wonderful than the murder of a mouse in an air-pump, or the examination of a cobweb by the microscope, or some similar nonsense, with which he was constantly in the habit of pestering his intimates. But without waiting for a reply, Dr. Heidegger hobbled across the chamber, and returned with the same ponderous folio, bound in black leather, which common report affirmed to be a book of magic. Undoing the silver clasps, he opened the volume, and took from among its black-letter pages a rose, or what was once a rose, though now the green leaves and crimson petals had assumed one brownish hue, and the ancient flower seemed ready to crumble to dust in the doctor's hands.

"This rose," said Dr. Heidegger, with a sigh, "this same withered and crumbling flower, blossomed five-and-fifty years ago. It was given me by Sylvia Ward, whose portrait hangs yonder; and I meant to wear it in my bosom at our wedding. Five-and-fifty years it has been treasured between the leaves of this old volume. Now, would you deem it possible that this rose of half a century could ever bloom again?"

"Nonsense!" said the Widow Wycherly, with a peevish toss of her head. "You might as well ask whether an old woman's wrinkled face could ever bloom again."

"See!" answered Dr. Heidegger.

He uncovered the vase, and threw the faded rose into the water which it contained. At first, it lay lightly on the surface of the fluid, appearing to imbibe none of its moisture. Soon, however, a singular change began to be visible. The crushed and dried petals stirred, and assumed a deepening tinge of crimson, as if the flower were reviving from a death-like slumber;

the slender stalk and twigs of foliage became green; and there was the rose of half a century, looking as fresh as when Sylvia Ward had first given it to her lover. It was scarcely full-blown; for some of its delicate red leaves curled modestly around its moist bosom, within which two or three dewdrops were sparkling.

"That is certainly a very pretty deception," said the doctor's friends; carelessly, however, for they had witnessed greater miracles at a conjurer's show: "pray how was it effected?"

"Did you never hear of the 'Fountain of Youth,'" asked Dr. Heidegger, "which Ponce De Leon, the Spanish adventurer, went in search of, two or three centuries ago?"

"But did Ponce De Leon ever find it?" said the Widow Wycherly.

"No," answered Dr. Heidegger, "for he never sought it in the right place. The famous Fountain of Youth, if I am rightly informed, is situated in the southern part of the Floridian peninsula, not far from Lake Macaco. Its source is overshadowed by several gigantic magnolias, which, though numberless centuries old, have been kept as fresh as violets, by the virtues of this wonderful water. An acquaintance of mine, knowing my curiosity in such matters, has sent me what you see in the vase."

"Ahem!" said Colonel Killigrew, who believed not a word of the doctor's story: "and what may be the effect of this fluid on the human frame?"

"You shall judge for yourself, my dear colonel," replied Dr. Heidegger; "and all of you, my respected friends, are welcome to so much of this admirable fluid, as may restore to you the bloom of youth. For my own part, having had much trouble in growing old, I am in no hurry to grow young again. With your permission, therefore, I will merely watch the progress of the experiment."

While he spoke, Dr. Heidegger had been filling the four champaigne glasses with the water of the Fountain of Youth. It was apparently impregnated with an effervescent gas, for little bubbles were continually ascending from the depths of the glasses, and bursting in silvery spray at the surface. As the liquor diffused a pleasant perfume, the old people doubted not that it possessed cordial and comfortable properties; and though utter skeptics as to its rejuvenescent power, they were inclined to swallow it at once. But Dr. Heidegger besought them to stay a moment.

"Before you drink, my respectable old friends," said he, "it would be well that, with the experience of a life-time to direct you, you should draw up a few general rules for your guidance, in passing a second time through the perils of youth. Think what a sin and shame it would be, if, with your peculiar advantages, you should not become patterns of virtue and wisdom to all the young people of the age!"

The doctor's four venerable friends made him no answer, except by a feeble and tremulous laugh; so very ridiculous was the idea, that, knowing how closely repentance treads behind the steps of error, they should ever go astray again.

"Drink, then," said the doctor, bowing: "I rejoice that I have so well selected the subjects of my experiment."

With palsied hands, they raised the glasses to their lips. The liquor, if it really possessed such virtues as Dr. Heidegger imputed to it, could not have been bestowed on four human beings who needed it more wofully. They looked as if they had never known what youth or pleasure was, but had been the offspring of Nature's dotage, and always the gray, decrepit, sapless, miserable creatures, who now sat stooping round the doctor's table, without life enough in their souls or bodies to be animated even by the prospect of growing young again. They drank off the water, and replaced their glasses on the table.

Assuredly there was an almost immediate improvement in the aspect of the party, not unlike what might have been produced by a glass of generous wine, together with a sudden glow of cheerful sunshine, brightening over all their visages at once. There was a healthful suffusion on their cheeks, instead of the ashen hue that had made them look so corpselike. They gazed at one another, and fancied that some magic power had really begun to smooth away the deep and sad inscriptions which Father Time had been so long engraving on their brows. The Widow Wycherly adjusted her cap, for she felt almost like a woman again.

"Give us more of this wondrous water!" cried they, eagerly. "We are younger—but we are still too old! Quick!—give us more!"

"Patience, patience!" quoth Dr. Heidegger, who sat watching the experiment, with philosophic coolness. "You have been a long time growing old. Surely, you might be content to grow young in half an hour! But the water is at your service."

Again he filled their glasses with the liquor of youth, enough of which still remained in the vase to turn half the old people in the city to the age of their own grand-children. While the bubbles were yet sparkling on the brim, the doctor's four guests snatched their glasses from the table, and swallowed the contents at a single gulp. Was it delusion! Even while the draught was passing down their throats, it seemed to have wrought a change on their whole systems. Their eyes grew clear and bright; a dark shade deepened among their silvery locks; they sat around the table, three gentlemen of middle age, and a woman, hardly beyond her buxom prime.

"My dear widow, you are charming!" cried Colonel Killigrew, whose eyes had been fixed upon her face, while the shadows of age were flitting from it like darkness from the crimson day-break.

The fair widow knew, of old, that Colonel Killigrew's compliments were not always measured by sober truth; so she started up and ran to the mirror, still dreading that the ugly visage of an old woman would meet her gaze. Meanwhile, the three gentlemen behaved in such a manner, as proved that the water of the Fountain of Youth possessed some intoxicating qual-ities; unless, indeed, their exhilaration of spirits were merely a lightsome dizziness, caused by the sudden removal of the weight of years. Mr. Gascoigne's mind seemed to run on political topics, but whether relating to the past, present, or future, could not easily be determined, since the same ideas and phrases have been in vogue these fifty years. Now he rattled forth full-throated sentences about patriotism, national glory, and the people's right; now he muttered some perilous stuff or other, in a sly and doubtful whisper, so cautiously that even his own conscience could scarcely catch the secret; and now, again, he spoke in measured accents, and a deeply deferential tone, as if a royal ear were listening to his well-turned periods. Colonel Killigrew all this time had been trolling forth a jolly bottle-song, and ringing his glass in symphony with the chorus, while his eyes wandered towards the buxom figure of the Widow Wycherly. On the other side of the table, Mr. Medbourne was involved in a calculation of dollars and cents, with which was strangely intermingled a project for supplying the East Indies with ice, by harnessing a team of whales to the polar icebergs.

As for the Widow Wycherly, she stood before the mirror, curtseying and simpering to her own image, and greeting it as the friend whom she loved better than all the world beside. She thrust her face close to the glass, to see whether some long-remembered wrinkle or crow's-foot had indeed vanished. She examined whether the snow had so entirely melted from her hair, that the venerable cap could be safely thrown aside. At last, turning briskly away, she came with a sort of dancing step to the table.

"My dear old doctor," cried she, "pray favor me with another glass!"

"Certainly, my dear madam, certainly!" replied the complaisant doctor; "see! I have already filled the glasses."

There, in fact, stood the four glasses, brim full of this wonderful water, the delicate spray of which, as it effervesced from the surface, resembled the tremulous glitter of diamonds. It was now so nearly sunset, that the chamber had grown duskier than ever; but a mild and moon-like splendor gleamed from within the vase, and rested alike on the four guests, and on the doctor's venerable figure. He sat in a high-backed, elaborately-carved, oaken arm-chair, with a gray dignity of aspect that might have well befitted that very Father Time, whose power had never been disputed, save by this fortunate company. Even while quaffing the third draught of the Fountain of Youth, they were almost awed by the expression of his mysterious visage.

But, the next moment, the exhilarating gush of young life shot through their veins. They were now in the happy prime of youth. Age, with its miserable train of cares, and sorrows, and diseases, was remembered only as the trouble of a dream, from which they had joyously awoke. The fresh gloss of the soul, so early lost, and without which the world's successive scenes had been but a gallery of faded pictures, again threw its enchantment over all their prospects. They felt like new-created beings, in a new-created universe.

"We are young! We are young!" they cried, exultingly.

Youth, like the extremity of age, had effaced the strongly marked characteristics of middle life, and mutually assimilated them all. They were a group of merry youngsters, almost maddened with the exuberant frolicksomeness of their years. The most singular effect of their gayety was an impulse to mock the infirmity and decrepitude of which they had so lately been the victims. They laughed loudly at their old-fashioned attire, the wide-skirted coats and flapped waistcoats of the young men, and the ancient cap and gown of the blooming girl. One limped across the floor, like a gouty grandfather; one set a pair of spectacles astride of his nose, and pretended to pore over the black-letter pages of the book of magic; a third seated himself in an arm-chair, and strove to imitate the venerable dignity of Dr. Heidegger. Then all shouted mirthfully, and leaped about the room. The Widow Wycherly—if so fresh a damsel could be called a widow—tripped up to the doctor's chair, with a mischievous merriment in her rosy face.

"Doctor, you dear old soul," cried she, "get up and dance with me!" And then the four young people laughed louder than ever, to think what a queer figure the poor old doctor would cut.

"Pray excuse me," answered the doctor, quietly. "I am old and rheumatic, and my dancing days were over long ago. But either of these gay young gentlemen will be glad of so pretty a partner."

"Dance with me, Clara!" cried Colonel Killigrew.

"No, no, I will be her partner!" shouted Mr. Gascoigne.

"She promised me her hand, fifty years ago!" exclaimed Mr. Medbourne.

They all gathered round her. One caught both her hands in his passionate grasp—another threw his arm about her waist—the third buried his hand among the glossy curls that clustered beneath the widow's cap. Blushing, panting, struggling, chiding, laughing, her warm breath fanning each of their faces by turns, she strove to disengage herself, yet still remained in their triple embrace. Never was there a livelier picture of youthful rivalship, with bewitching beauty for the prize. Yet, by a strange deception, owing to the duskiness of the chamber, and the antique dresses which they still wore, the tall mirror is said to have reflected the figures of the three old, gray, withered grand-sires, ridiculously contending for the skinny ugliness of a shrivelled grand-dam.

But they were young: their burning passions proved them so. Inflamed to madness by the coquetry of the girl-widow, who neither granted nor quite withheld her favors, the three rivals began to interchange threatening glances. Still keeping hold of the fair prize, they grappled fiercely at one another's throats. As they struggled to and fro, the table was overturned, and the vase dashed into a thousand fragments. The precious Water of Youth flowed in a bright stream across the floor, moistening the wings of a butterfly, which, grown old in the decline of summer, had alighted there to die. The insect fluttered lightly through the chamber, and settled on the snowy head of Dr. Heidegger.

"Come, come, gentlemen!—come, Madam Wycherly," exclaimed the doctor, "I really must protest against this riot."

They stood still, and shivered; for it seemed as if gray Time were calling them back from their sunny youth, far down into the chill and darksome vale of years. They looked at old Dr. Heidegger, who sat in his carved arm-chair, holding the rose of half a century, which he had rescued from among the fragments of the shattered vase. At the motion of his hand, the four rioters resumed their seats; the more readily, because their violent exertions had wearied them, youthful though they were.

"My poor Sylvia's rose!" ejaculated Dr. Heidegger, holding it in the light of the sunset clouds: "it appears to be fading again."

And so it was. Even while the party were looking at it, the flower continued to shrivel up, till it became as dry and fragile as when the doctor had first thrown it into the vase. He shook off the few drops of moisture which clung to its petals.

"I love it as well thus, as in its dewy freshness," observed he, pressing the withered rose to his withered lips. While he spoke, the butterfly fluttered down from the doctor's snowy head, and fell upon the floor.

His guests shivered again. A strange chillness, whether of the body or spirit they could not tell, was creeping gradually over them all. They gazed at one another, and fancied that each fleeting moment snatched away a charm, and left a deepening furrow where none had been before. Was it an illusion? Had the changes of a life-time been crowded into so brief a space, and were they now four aged people, sitting with their old friend, Dr. Heidegger?

"Are we grown old again, so soon!" cried they, dolefully.

In truth, they had. The Water of Youth possessed merely a virtue more transient than that of wine. The delirium which it created had effervesced away. Yes! they were old again. With a shuddering impulse, that showed her a woman still, the widow clasped her skinny hands before her face, and wished that the coffin-lid were over it, since it could be no longer beautiful.

"Yes, friends, ye are old again," said Dr. Heidegger; "and lo! the Water of Youth is all lavished on the ground. Well—I bemoan it not; for if the fountain gushed at my very doorstep, I would not stoop to bathe my lips in it—no, though its delirium were for years instead of moments. Such is the lesson ye have taught me!"

But the doctor's four friends had taught no such lesson to themselves. They resolved forthwith to make a pilgrimage to Florida, and quaff at morning, noon, and night, from the Fountain of Youth.

INTERVIEWS

INTERVIEW WITH
T. C. BOYLE

You might call T. C. Boyle the rock star of the literary world. His work is hip and rebellious, he favors funky shirts and stud earrings, and he has mobs of fans clamoring for his newest work or lining up to see him give one of his legendary readings. Like Springsteen or Jagger, he's stayed in top form for a long time, showing no sign of losing his inimitable spark.

T. C. grew up in the Hudson Valley of New York. After stints in college, a garage band, and teaching at his old high school, he headed west to the famed Iowa Writers' Workshop, where he picked up an M.F.A. and Ph.D. Finally he headed further west to teach at USC and launch his pyrotechnical writing career.

He burst onto the publishing world in 1979 with the short-story collection *Descent of Man* and he's since turned out the story collections *Greasy Lake, If the River Was Whiskey, Without a Hero, After the Plague* (which includes the story "After the Plague"), and the massive *T. C. Boyle Stories*. And then there's his novels—*Water Music, Budding Prospects, World's End, East Is East, The Road to Wellville, The Tortilla Curtain, Riven Rock, A Friend of the Earth,* and *Drop City*. He writes seven days a week and he still manages to hang on to his day job at USC. And if you're wondering, the T. C. stands for Thomas Coraghessan (Cor-AG-hessan). But his friends call him Tom.

GWW: *One of the many refreshing things about your work is that you're, well, funny. Your humor is savage and satirical, but people laugh when they're reading your stories. Do you think humor gets too little respect in* *the contemporary fiction scene? More importantly, do you laugh when composing your stories?*

BOYLE: Fiction can move you in many ways, and I suppose that sometimes people (critics, reviewers and the rest of the self-anointed) may tend to feel that humor is too easy or too slight in contrast to drama. To my mind, that ain't necessarily so. I feel that a story is an exercise of the imagination, and that exercise can take me anywhere, from the whimsical humor of "We Are Norsemen" to the drop-dead drama of "The Love of My Life," and all the terrain in between. Do I laugh when writing funny scenes? You better believe it. And I get mighty peckish while writing the food scenes, and, well, is this the place to talk about raw sexuality?

GWW: *In your vast fiction oeuvre, you've found an incredibly diverse and bizarre assortment of story ideas—a Viking poet writing about plunder, an affair between Eisenhower and Khrushchev's wife, bumbling marijuana growers trying to get rich, dating in a postapocalpytic world, etc. Do you write ideas down as they pop into your head? Can you think of an idea that you just couldn't make work?*

BOYLE: Yes, I do write down story ideas as they occur to me—but in brief, a few words at most—and I also clip articles from newspapers and magazines that might bear looking into. Since I only work on one thing at a time, these ideas, inscribed in their very own little book, must sit and wait for me to contemplate them. I wonder if there is an idea that would not work for me if I pursued it. Certainly there are concepts that appeal to me because of my peculiar nature and the nature of my themes and obsessions, but I do believe that for a challenge I could construct a satisfying story from practically anything.

GWW: *There is definitely a T. C. Boyle voice. Your fans would be able to spot one of your tales a mile away, even if your name were not on it (with a few sly exceptions). Did this voice emerge through calculation or instinct? What do you advise your writing students in regard to cultivating their voice?*

BOYLE: The writer's voice is as much a personal signature as one's speaking or singing voice, and it has to do with the individual's personality as that personality is invested with the literature of the world. I am pleased to think that people will know that a given work is mine even if

I were to publish anonymously. How that is or how it came to be, I can't say. It just is. Incidentally, when my story "Zapatos" first appeared in *Harper's*, I was represented as the translator—the author, of course, was Filencio Salmon. This is known as an inside joke, one of those "sly exceptions" that stirs the heart of the passionate fan (who knows full well that Mr. Salmon is an invention of mine, appearing first in *Budding Prospects*, yea, these many long years ago).

GWW: *We placed your story "After the Plague" in the section of our book that includes stories about romance. It appears that even if there are only a handful of people left in the world, finding the right mate is still a challenge. Were you having thoughts on this theme while writing the story? Are you conscious of theme while constructing your stories, or do they mostly just surface on their own?*

BOYLE: Nice, very nice. As you may know, when I published volume I of my collected stories back in the last century ('98), I chose to divide the book into three sections: (a) Love: (b) Death; (c) And Everything in Between. Just for the fun of it. In volume II, due out I would expect in 2012 or so, I think I'll divide them into two categories only: Comedy and Tragedy (though part of the joke, point, exercise, is to indicate how slippery those boundaries are). As for theme: theme emerges just as plot does, just as image and symbol do, as part of the evolutionary process of writing.

GWW: *In "After the Plague," you're obviously writing about something outside your real-life experience—a world where the vast majority of the population has been decimated by disease. Yet you portray this setting, and your protagonist's reaction to it, quite convincingly. Did you do any research to get the physical details right? Did you draw on anything in particular to summon the right emotional state for this surreal situation?*

BOYLE: I had been reading a lot of our environmentalists, all of whom are depressing to the point of suicide. (My reading here later gave rise to my environmental novel, *A Friend of the Earth*.) Laurie Garrett's *The Coming Plague* was particularly instructive. After mulling over the imminent death of humanity, I jammed up the story. And, by the way, I continue to work with this material. My latest piece, hot from the computer, is called "Chicxulub," and it deals with our chances of being obliterated by a comet/asteroid and what that means for the hopes and aspirations of our species (the story will appear in *The New Yorker* some-time this year).

GWW: *The protagonist in "After the Plague" whiles away the time with a book of John Cheever short stories. In an earlier time, Cheever was one of the hottest short-story writers, just as you are now, and you studied with Cheever in graduate school. Were you influenced by Cheever, the man or his work?*

BOYLE: I had read some of John's stories when I was an undergrad, but by the time I knew him I found the work rather old-fashioned, as I was now on to the experimental and bizarre, revering instead Coover, Barth, Pynchon, García Márquez, Gass, et al. John let me know that fashions change and that you shouldn't let fashion dictate your response to literature. He was right, of course. A few years later, when he came out with his collected stories, I was staggered by their breadth and brilliance. Every five years or so, I like to reread them.

GWW: *Readers of literary fiction have become something of an endangered species, especially when it comes to short stories. But, craving a big audience, you really reach out to your readers. You spend lots of time on the road giving readings, you check in with your fans on your Web site. Most significantly, you write stories that people genuinely enjoy. Do you think fiction writers need to work harder to pull readers back into the fold? Any advice on how they can do this in their work?*

BOYLE: Prescriptions never work, and I would be hesitant to say that writers should do one thing or another—we are all cranky tireless individuals with our own perilously cranky agendas. This writer, however, does like to connect with the audience, and the cornerstone of my aesthetic has always been to remember that fiction is entertainment at root, not a cabalistic code to be interpreted only by the high priests of the land. The artist must speak directly to the audience, which is not to say that art can be calculating—the highest art speaks to the complete audience, on every level. Advice? I can barely manage my own life, every thought and moment blacker than the preceding. Art gives me life. It is the deepest expression of the human soul. I make it because I have no other choice.

INTERVIEW WITH
JHUMPA LAHIRI

Pulitzer Prizes for fiction are typically awarded to novels by authors of long-standing reputation. Thus, it came as something of a shock when the 2000 Pulitzer for fiction went to the thirty-two-year-old Jhumpa Lahiri for her short-story collection *Interpreter of Maladies*. It's hard to argue the choice, however, once you begin sampling the book's breathtaking artistry and depth.

The daughter of Bengali parents, Jhumpa was born in London and emigrated to the U.S. as a child. Though she wrote stories as a young girl in Rhode Island, her original career plan was to be an academic, which explains why she studied her way through a B.A, three M.A.s, and a Ph.D. But Jhumpa kept writing fiction (one of those master's degrees was in creative writing at Boston University), and, after her fair share of rejections, magazines began publishing the stories that would eventually make up *Interpreter of Maladies* (which includes "The Third and Final Continent").

For her second book, Jhumpa published a novel, *The Namesake*, which received enough reader and critical acclaim to prove she was no one-hit wonder. Her stories usually contain Indian characters, and some of them are actually set in India (which she has often visited), but her tales are tapestries of life that transcend color lines, attracting readers of all types from all over the globe. Indeed, Jhumpa Lahiri seems poised to become one of the major literary talents of our time.

GWW: *You seem to have an almost mystical power to create stories so compelling and rich that, even in these times when few people read literary fiction, legions of readers fall under your spell. Do you have some little secret that draws readers to your stories? Do you give any thought to pleasing your readers when you write?*

LAHIRI: Putting the reader under a spell is the job of every writer. I am only trying to do what others have done, and continue to do. But I don't really think about that as I'm writing. I'm aware at the back of my mind that any story has to grab the reader by the neck, as Tolstoy famously said. But I don't think about readers as I write. The process is slow and confounding and entirely internal. As I write a story, I feel totally alone with it. It's an intense experience, and there is certainly an element of battle involved, wrestling with all the components—the characters, the actions, the emotions—and trying to put everything into words. Only I can't always see the opponent.

GWW: *Though you are a highly visible figure in the literary world, you are somewhat invisible in your stories. Your narrative voice never screams for attention. The focus in your work seems to be on telling the story simply and clearly, in almost a detached way. Do you make a conscious attempt to "get out of the way" of the story? Similarly, do you make an attempt to let the emotion of a story speak for itself?*

LAHIRI: I tend to read and admire a lot of authors who lurk imperceptibly behind the scenes of their work. William Trevor is a wonderful example. With few exceptions, I've always been drawn to straightforward narrative. That sensibility is what speaks most strongly to me when I read, and it is what I try to do in my own work. I think if an emotion is successfully rendered in a work of fiction, then it must and ought to speak for itself, without the writer pointing to it in an overt way.

GWW: *You have an uncanny ability to get inside a diverse collection of characters, regardless of age, gender, nationality, or personality. How do you zero in on your characters? Do you make detailed dossiers or look for some specific physical or emotional "key" or do you simply intuit these people as you write? In particular, how did Mrs. Croft in "The Third and Final Continent" come about?*

LAHIRI: My characters are generally always composites of people I know, people I've heard of, people I imagine, and a little drop of myself. Again, this is, I feel, every writer's job. Mainly it's a matter of intuition, of putting yourself in the body and mind of another person. It's almost like acting, only instead of performing, you portray the person in language. Mrs. Croft was based on an actual person. When my father first came to America, he lived for a few months in the home of a 103-year-old woman. He told me a few things about her—she insisted that my father sit with her for a while every evening, and she talked endlessly about the man on the moon. He also mentioned that she was a piano teacher. I worked these details into Mrs. Croft's character and imagined the rest.

GWW: *You are sparing with dialogue, but every word of it resonates with characterization and meaning. As an example, in "The Third and Final Continent," it's hard to forget Mrs. Croft's exhortations to "Say 'splendid!'" Do you write lengthy dialogue exchanges then whittle them down to their essence? And how do you know which moments are ripe for dialogue?*

LAHIRI: That's another thing my father told me: that his landlady insisted that he "Say 'splendid!'" whenever they spoke of the moon landing. It's a brilliant detail and I'm glad it works in the world of the story, that it's credible. So often there are details from life that seem perfect for a story but don't ring true on the page. Generally, I'm sparing with dialogue. I sometimes have to make a concerted effort to make people talk to each other. But other stories are much more based in dialogue. I always try to remember one principle, that dialogue must move the story forward in some way.

GWW: *Most of your stories have something of a classical structure—a protagonist pursuing a goal against rising conflict. But "The Third and Final Continent" seems to be more meandering, more like a true-life reminiscence. And, indeed, it seems that at least parts of this story were based on actual experiences of your father. Were you aware this story was less overtly plot-driven than some of your others? Did that present any special challenges?*

LAHIRI: "The Third and Final Continent" presented several unique challenges. First and foremost, I was writing a story based in large part on an experience and a period of time in my father's life. In the beginning I felt hesitant to do this—I'd never written anything based to such a degree on real-life events. I had only the basic facts: the year, the place, the house, the landlady, the flag on the moon. But the only part of the story my father passed down to me was the nightly exchange he had with his landlady on the bench. So I had to fill in quite a bit. In real life my father was already married for three years at the time, and I had already been born. So the bit about Mala arriving and she and the narrator getting to know each other for the first time is all invented. Another challenge was writing in the first person in the voice of a man and, more specifically, trying to "be" my father as I wrote the story. What inspired me to write the story was the juxtaposition of the moon landing, a spectacular landmark in history, and the story of an immigrant's arrival to a new country. The story is very much reminiscence. I don't think I could have written it any other way.

GWW: *It's clear that you craft your stories with great care. Your work feels polished, with every story element in perfect balance. Do you revise mercilessly? Do you seek the advice of others during the process? And however do you know when a story is done?*

LAHIRI: I go through more drafts than I could possibly care to remember. So much of the apprehension of a story, for me, occurs in the act of repeated, rigorous, ruthless revision. The early drafts are really just road maps. The true journey, the discovery, happens much farther along. I also like to set things aside as much as possible and let time pass. I have a few wonderful writer friends with whom I share my work. And in the past few years I've relied on my husband as well. Usually I seek advice when I'm stuck and can't solve the rest of the puzzle. Sometimes there is a whole story, with a beginning and end, but crucial elements missing. I just sent a friend a long story I didn't know how to end. Although I believe anything I've written, and even published, can always be improved, one must stop in order to write the next thing. (That's why I try to avoid reading what I've written as much as possible.) I usually let go when I grow bored with something, when I've said what I wanted to say as best as I can, and when my mind strays to something else.

GWW: *It must be a bit overwhelming to receive so much acclaim so early in your career. Do you ever think to yourself: "I don't know that I'm really as great as everyone says?"*

LAHIRI: I try to shut myself off from the attention as much as possible. Yes, it has been overwhelming at times and it doesn't correspond to my reality as a writer. I still have an enormous amount to learn. I'm very grateful for the kind things people say about my work, but the promise of a compliment or a prize or even of publication has never been the thing that's inspired me to write. To me the act of writing is profoundly separate from the aftermath: publication, reviews, acclaim, attacks, whatever. Certainly those things are an inevitable part of a writer's life, but they have nothing to do with the creative process. I will always doubt my work, question it on some level. That's what keeps pushing me to the next project. I hope never to get to a point where I'm totally satisfied with what I'm doing.

INTERVIEW WITH
HANNAH TINTI

Hannah Tinti is a writer on the verge. She has recently published her first book, a collection of dazzling short stories entitled *Animal Crackers* (which includes "Home Sweet Home"), and she's laboring away at a novel, slated to be published in the near future. In literary circles right now, there is much buzz around the name Hannah Tinti. Will that buzz subside into silence or swell to a roar of enthusiasm? In the perilous world of fiction, one never knows.

Hannah followed a path familiar to many of today's aspiring fiction writers. After acquiring an M.F.A. in fiction (from NYU) she held a parade of odd jobs—waiting, bartending, temping—while collecting enough rejection slips to paper the walls of her small New York City apartment. Eventually magazines began publishing some of her stories. And, unlike most aspiring writers, Hannah wrote her way to the end of the rainbow—a two-book deal with a major publishing house.

Writing isn't her only talent. Hannah has taught at Gotham Writers' Workshop, where she wowed students with her endlessly inventive teaching techniques. And, along with Maribeth Batcha, she founded *One Story*, a unique literary magazine in which each issue features only a single short story. Against all odds, the magazine has found a rapidly growing audience. One thing is certain: Hannah Tinti embraces all her artistic pursuits with a skydiver's sense of adventure.

GWW: *"Writer of literary fiction" is one of the scarier career paths out there. It always was, and now it's probably more difficult than ever. But you've* *managed to make the right moves and launch a promising career. Can you speculate on what you did right?*

TINTI: The most important thing I did was keep writing as the focus of my life. Weekends, evenings after work, whenever I could spare the time I would be writing. I also concentrated on being open to criticism. I think writers fall into two categories—they take the "long way"—figuring their writing problems out on their own and rejecting other people's criticism, or the "shortcut"—listening to other writers, deciding which advice seems true, and learning how to properly implement it in their work. I took the shortcut—found two other writers that I trusted and formed a workshop. Each of us has now published a book.

Persistence is key. Being a writer, you have to deal with a lot of rejection. An important thing to learn is not to take it personally, not to get discouraged, and to keep on trying. I sent one story of mine out to fifty magazines before it was finally accepted and published.

I also found out whatever I could about the industry. I started by taking nonpaying intern jobs at various magazines, worked in bookstores and eventually got a position as an assistant at a literary agency. Learning the "other side" of publishing helped me to make the right decisions with my own work, when the time was right.

GWW: *In "Home Sweet Home," you use the omniscient point of view, where the narrator plays God, entering the minds of numerous characters. Though common in the days of Tolstoy and Dickens, this point of view is seldom used in contemporary fiction. Why did you choose it? Did you find it more challenging than the more conventional types of point of view?*

TINTI: Choosing this point of view was actually one of the starting points for me. I wanted to challenge myself—to tell a story that broke away from the conventional first person and instead moved from character to character, never going back, each section revealing more information to the reader. In the editing process, I ended up going back a little bit at the very end, to clear up some unanswered questions about Lieutenant Sales and Mr. Mitchell. I also realized that I had to return to Mrs. Mitchell, because the story was really about her. The most difficult part of using this point of view was making sure that each of the characters was fully developed. They all have to be equally interesting, but at the same time, you don't want any one character outshining the others. It's a group piece.

GWW: *"Home Sweet Home" has a rather complex plot. Not only do you enter the minds of many characters but you also slide back and forth in time, creating a story that works something like a jigsaw puzzle. Even all the little background details on the characters, like the detective's past encounter with the shark, contribute to the characters' motivations. Did this story require you to do any outlining? And what came first on this story— plot or character?*

TINTI: I started with describing the murder, so in a way the plot came first, but I had no idea who had killed Pat and Clyde until I went into each of the characters. I followed the characters closely when they arrived on the scene. I did everything I could to give them something special— their own little story within the story that would make them come alive and be interesting to read about. These details explained the characters' motivations, giving me a better idea what the action might be. Once I solved the crime and realized who the murderer was, I added some finer points to make it more believable, but since the characters had led me there, I didn't have to alter the plot.

I've never been much of an outliner. Instead I write very, very slowly. I spend a great deal of time on every sentence, then making a paragraph work together as a whole. I also read the story over and over, especially right before I'm about to work on it. This makes certain details stick, and come back in other sections to tie it together. In "Home Sweet Home" this happened with the eggs, and the question of hollowness.

GWW: *"Home Sweet Home" never slows down for descriptive passages and yet you sneak in some real zingers. For example: "She pushed this sense of responsibility through him like fishhooks, plucking on the line, reeling him back in when she felt her hold slipping, so that the points became embedded in his flesh so deep that it would kill him to take them out." Where do you get these images? And, when it comes to description, how do you know when enough is enough?*

TINTI: I get most of my images through a combination of personal experience and listening to other people talk. The fishhooks came from hearing about a man who had a very intense relationship with his grandmother—

she kept a controlling hand over his entire life. I was writing "Home Sweet Home" at the time, and I stared to imagine the grandmother as a fisherman. You can't pull a fish in as soon as it bites—you have to let the fish think it's still free for the hook to work its way in enough for you to catch it—and then, even if the fish is strong enough to break the line, the hook will stay with him until he dies. I tell my students that it is better to use one strong image than three weak ones, so once you've written your description, cut it down, hone it, and punch it up.

GWW: *As a teacher of fiction writing and as an editor of a literary magazine, you've had occasion to read a multitude of stories, both by aspiring and established writers. What do you find to be the most common failing in the stories you read? What most turns you on, making a story leap out of the pack?*

TINTI: I read many, many stories that are well written, that follow all of the rules of plot and structure, but don't have any heart. By "heart" I mean that the author focuses too much on following the story and not enough on engaging the reader's emotions. Another problem is predictable endings. What I look for as an editor is a story that is pushing the boundaries somehow—taking a risk or trying something new in plot or setting or point of view or writing style—while at the same time giving me characters that I can care about.

GWW: *Obviously you're a passionate advocate of the short story. Not only have you written a collection of short fiction but you cofounded a magazine that gives short stories the kind of attention usually reserved for a novel. Do you think short stories can offer as much emotional punch as novels? If so, can you think of any good examples?*

TINTI: I think that short stories are a specific art, falling somewhere just outside of poetry. They can actually be much more difficult to pull off than novels, because in a short story, there isn't room to spend thirty or forty pages digressing on the battle of Waterloo. You've got to bang it in there in a paragraph. By packing so much into a small space, short stories can be extremely powerful, and even have a longer-lasting effect on a reader than a novel. I can't think of a better example of an emotional punch than "I Want to Live!" by Thom Jones. He takes a familiar story of someone dying of cancer, and completely turns it on its head. The voice is incredible—it grabs hold of the reader and makes them experience the roller coaster of death right alongside the main character. I remember the first time I read it, on a train from New York to Boston, and as soon as I came to the bit about the doctor saying "can . . . cer" I knew that I was in the hands of a great writer.

GWW: *When you contemplate your future career as a writer, what do you find most terrifying? What do you find most exhilarating?*

TINTI: There are always the secret fears about writer's block, or whether or not I'll be able to sell another book, or being nervous about reviews, but those things aren't really terrifying. This is going to sound corny, but what I find exhilarating, and what I look forward to, is a good writing day. When I step away from the computer and know that I've nailed a description, or figured out some plot twist, I feel alive, connected to the world, and, I'm not ashamed to admit, blissfully happy. I guess that means I'm in the right business.

CREDITS

THE EDITORS

Thom Didato has published numerous short stories in literary magazines. He teaches at Gotham Writers' Workshop, and is editor and founder of the literary magazine *failbetter*.

Alexander Steele serves as Dean of Faculty of Gotham Writers' Workshop. He has written numerous plays, screenplays, nonfiction pieces, and books for children. He also edited Gotham Writers' Workshop's *Writing Fiction*.

ACKNOWLEDGMENTS

Many people assisted with the assembling of *Fiction Gallery*. In fact, it's surprising how much work goes into the creation of an anthology of short stories, even though most of the material has already been written!

We thank those who set the stage for this book: Jeff Fligelman and David Grae, the founders of Gotham Writers' Workshop; Faith Hamlin of Sanford J. Greenburger Associates; and Colin Dickerman, Sabrina Farber, Peter Janssen, Sara Mercurio, and Greg Villepique at Bloomsbury USA.

We thank Andre Becker, the President of Gotham Writers' Workshop, who always finds a way to make the big dreams come true.

We thank the third editor on our team, Danny Goodman, who worked incredibly hard to make this book what it is.

We thank all those who read stories for us, helping us determine which stories were appropriate and superlative enough for this book. This list includes the miracle-working members of the Gotham staff—Joel Mellin, Dana Miller, Linda Novak, Betsey Odell, Stacey Panousopoulos, Lindsay Ryan, and Charlie Shehadi.

We thank the stellar authors whose work is included in our gallery, with a special thanks to T. C. Boyle, Jhumpa Lahiri, and Hannah Tinti for granting us the privilege of interviewing them. And we are grateful to the publishers and agents who helped us get the work of these writers into our pages.

Finally, we thank the teachers and students at Gotham Writers' Workshop, all of whom do more than they know to keep the love of the written word alive and well in the world.

If you're an aspiring or experienced writer . . . *Writing Fiction* is the perfect companion to *Fiction Gallery*.

Gotham Writers' Workshop has mastered the art of teaching the craft of writing in a way that is practical, accessible, and entertaining. Now, the techniques of this renowned school are available in a book—***Writing Fiction: The Practical Guide from New York's Acclaimed Creative Writing School***.

This book includes:

- The fundamental elements of fiction craft—character, plot, point of view, etc.—explained clearly and completely.
- Key concepts illustrated with passages from great works of fiction.
- The complete text of "Cathedral" by Raymond Carver—a masterpiece of contemporary short fiction that is analyzed throughout the book.
- Exercises that let you immediately apply what you learn to your own writing.

Written by Gotham Writers' Workshop expert instructors and edited by Dean of Faculty Alexander Steele, *Writing Fiction* offers many of the same methods and exercises that have earned the school international acclaim.

Once you've read—and written—your way through this book, you'll have a command of craft that will enable you to turn your ideas into effective short stories and novels.

"*Writing Fiction* is an incredible book, not just for the aspiring writer but for the ardent reader as well."
—Michael Ray, Senior Editor, *Zoetrope: All-Story*

"Here is an honest, engaging guide with lessons every writer, at any stage, will benefit from."
—Jhumpa Lahiri, Pulitzer Prize–winning author of *Interpreter of Maladies*

"This book has a vividness that somehow captures the excitement and fellowship in good writers' workshops. I've clearly found a new book to use in my own writing classes. This is a fine guide."
—Chuck Kinder, Writing Program Director, University of Pittsburgh

"This is an excellent starting place for someone exploring the art and craft of writing fiction."
—*Publishers Weekly*

"A valuable book for aspiring writers *and* aspiring teachers. The Gotham approach to fiction-writing is smart, first-rate, and practical—I highly recommend this text."
—Jonathan Ames, author of *The Extra Man*

ISBN: 1-58234-330-6

Gotham Writers' Workshop®

If you're inspired to write your own short stories . . .

Study Online with Gotham Writers' Workshop

Since 1997, thousands of students have discovered how simple and effective it is to study online with Gotham Writers' Workshop at www.WritingClasses.com. The school's online workshops feature everything you would find in a live workshop—lectures, discussions, writing exercises, teacher feedback, and in-depth critiques of your work. Every class is taught in an easy-to-understand manner by a member of the school's renowned faculty. Class size is limited so the focus remains on you and your writing. All of which may explain why *Forbes* selected these classes as the "Best of the Web."

Save $40.00 on Tuition

Now, for a limited time, you can save $40 off the regular tuition for the ten-week GWW workshop of your choice, either in New York City or online. For a class schedule, to learn more, or to register, call toll-free 877-WRITERS (974–8377) or visit www.WritingClasses.com.

ML   1/05